BLOOD FLIGHT

This Book is dedicated to Billy Stewart Late Secretary, Trimdon Colliery H.S. For his dedication to the Sport.

Graham McArthur

Graham McArthur

BLOOD FLIGHT

Graham McArthur

Graham McArthur

First Published 2005
Ardbeg Publishing
18 Ardmory Road
Rothesay
Isle of Bute
Scotland
PA20 0PG
Tel. 01700 504761
E-mail: ardbegpublishing@hotmail.com

A catalogue record for this book is available from
The British Library

I.S.B.N. 0-9549379-0-2

Printing - Print Point, 15 Watergate, Rothesay, Isle of Bute
Cover Photography - Brian Linfield
Cover Design - Cranium Brother

To my parents, Lewis and Mary
For their parts in the story

BLOOD FLIGHT

CHAPTER 1

"Perfect, bloody perfect." Tam Murdoch exclaimed, under his breath, as he strode confidently down the wide stone steps of the Tradesman's Club's otherwise unimposing entrance.

Aye, he decided. *There's more to it than three drams and a blether with the lads.* It was just what he'd planned and even prayed for. *We were bloody close last year, 3rd Federation, Sartilly, no' bad against Fife's best, bloody close. But tomorrow we'll be first. Jamie and me, we'll top the bloody Fed.*

The one part of the equation he couldn't directly influence had been prayed for, the weather, and more importantly, the wind direction. The forecast for the Channel, England and Central Scotland, tomorrow, Saturday 9th July, had been announced after the late evening news. It suited others in the Rosyth Racing Pigeon Club, but it more than suited Tam Murdoch.

The wind was to be just right, a light south-easterly. He knew the Mealy Hen was right, this, he and Jamie could and had influenced, without the need of divine assistance. She had a years more experience and, as planned weeks before, was sent to the race sitting eggs twelve days, always her best racing condition.

On behalf of T. Murdoch and Son, their official title in the Scottish Homing Union, Tam, with the other top racing men in Fife had presented the partnerships selected candidates for race basketing four days before.

He recalled the occasion with a smile. With his best mate and part-time chauffeur, Maxi Clark; they'd travelled the fifteen miles through to the Raith Community Centre, Kirkcaldy, a venue chosen for its central location rather than its less than salubrious ambience.

Positioned carefully on a rug covering the Renault 5's back seat, the Mealy Hen and Old Pied Cock, both comfortably resting in a small wicker basket, lined with a carpet of soft wood shavings. "Too precious a cargo for the boot, Maxi, aye too precious for the boot".

The Old Pied, now in its eighth season, would make it home okay, Tam decided, with justified confidence, but it was a plodder, fine in a slow race, with the wind against it, but too slow when the wind's up their tails and they're doing thirteen hundred plus. "Aye the Pied would home but the wee Mealy would win."

She had the pace and that something special needed for the distance. She also always performed with the wind behind her. 3rd Federation last year in a south-westerly and a steady build-up this year. Three shorter races, then 1st Rosyth Club, from Cheltenham, 302 miles. Rested for three weeks, down on eggs and then trained from thirty miles on each of the three days up to race basketing. "Perfect, bloody perfect."

This re-statement of his confidence, expressed freely, now that he was far enough from the Social Club to ensure no one was within earshot.

Pigeon fanciers from all parts of the County had gathered at Kirkcaldy, each carrying similar wicker baskets containing their potential champions.

During the race marking process details from the Pied and Mealy's permanent metal rings were recorded and an individually coded rubber race ring placed on their other leg. This code number duly and confidentially noted on the race entry form the candidates then deposited carefully with their fellow competitors into larger wicker panniers, awaiting transportation to the race point.

Although not the most natural socialite, Tam loved the atmosphere of these occasions, particularly as much of the conversation at this one centred around himself, with Maxi as always, taking delight in regularly returning to his side to pass on interesting snippets gleaned from the hall. "You were spot-on, Tam," whispered Maxi with devilment. "When I told that wee weasel Thomson, in confidence of-course, how much you placed on the Mealy; it was round the room in five minutes flat."

Maxi had under-estimated the circulation time, but only slightly. As soon as he thought him out of earshot, the weasel, as predicted, had broken his promise of strict confidentiality. "Murdoch's put fifty notes on his Mealy Hen, aye, fifty notes and that's a man who doesnae spend for the sake o' it. The old bugger must be reckoning on a south-easterly."

Tam wasn't reckoning, he was praying.

The race would be fast and the leading birds, pushed over to the west of the Country, barring disaster, dropping into Fife, early evening. First stop - Rosyth, one of the most westerly villages in the Federation of Fife Racing Pigeon Clubs. "Maxi, my lad, we've got them worried, and so they should be, that wee shite Thomson would kill to win this race, we picked the right one to tell."

Tuesday was great fun, but tonight was perfect.

It wasn't always a pleasant two-mile walk, especially during a Fife Winter. Although he was strong and fit for a pensioner, forty years getting soaked through on a multitude of building sites had their inevitable effects. Tam tried to ignore it. However, the dull but persistent pain often caused him grief and made the trek a struggle, on a now increasing number of occasions. Tonight however the warmth of July, combined with the light south-easterly breeze made this particular journey a pleasure.

Even the solid weight of the Timing Clock, held securely in his right hand, was no burden. Although his knees weren't as sound as they used to be his arms were still strong. Muscle and sinew built up as a shuttering joiner don't disappear overnight, even at sixty-five and officially past-it.

He had now reached the neat privet hedge, which acted as a boundary to the small garden between Maxwell Clark's mid-terraced house and the pavement of Kings Road. The lights were still on and he noticed Maxi's slight frame relaxing in his favourite armchair, which faced the front window and his second best companion, the T.V.

Tam wouldn't call in tonight.

Although he knew Maxi would make him welcome, probably with another dram, Isabel would not be overjoyed. *She doesn't give the poor bugger much lee-way,* he thought, *and she would, no doubt, wind me up about the price of petrol. The old bitch shouldn't worry; I'll see Maxi all right when the wee Mealy does the business tomorrow.*

Maxi did see him pass but was too slow off his armchair to attract his attention. *Maybe just as well* he'd decided, Isabel had been biting his ear all evening about the "price of petrol".

Maxi, of-course, didn't worry about these things, Tam had been a good friend for many years. He would not risk that over a few gallons. *And you never know, the Mealy might just win, wouldn't that be something. My God I hope she does, even for young Jamie's sake.*

Maxi also saw the next passer-by.

"Isabel." - No response

"Isabel." - Now directing his repeated and more urgent whisper towards the open partition door to his right.

Isabel's large frame appeared, instantly restricting much of the light normally borrowed from the adjoining kitchen.

Maxi continued. "That young thug McLagan has just passed the window; I wonder what badness he's up to. Well at least Tam's well down the road - they shouldn't meet up tonight, thank God."

Annoyed at being even momentarily distracted from her culinary duties, she couldn't resist a sarcastic response. "If your best mate Murdoch would mind his own business and stop winding-up the likes of McLagan you wouldn't have to fret. Aye, and by the way, he should be able to afford his own car, now that he's saved so much with not paying for your petrol. - You soft bugger."

Her first opinion, at least, he concurred with. Evil bastards like McLagan should be avoided at all costs. To Maxi's despair however, his friend did not agree with his repeated advices. It was only two weeks ago yesterday, he recalled, that Tam had crossed the road, squared-up to McLagan and threatened to shut his mouth with his fist. Thankfully, to Maxi's relief, McLagan had backed-off, continuing the verbal insults as he walked on, but backed-off just the same.

McLagan, although obviously younger and fitter was not the 'square-go' fighter that Tam Murdoch had been. Even now the old man might severely embarrass him if it came to more than verbals.

Square-go's were not McLagan's style. He preferred a dark alley and the results achieved with the Stanley Knife, tucked away in his right-hand pocket.

Tam was now almost at the halfway stage. Kings Road, which leads directly north and downhill from the Tradesman's Club, would soon be reaching its junction with Park Crescent.

He took his regular Summer short cut through the garages.

Mary would have the kettle on the boil and Jamie would soon be in bed so the few minutes saved would give them time for a longer blether. *He's more excited than I am,* thought Tam. *And so he should be, he's done all the hard work. Aye, the wee Mealy will do it for Jamie."*

Either the recollection of the Mealy Hen or the light from the approaching street lamp sparked his need to check the timing clock. A quick lift into both hands, raising its face to the light revealed what Tam already knew, but had to confirm. It was still going. Carefully set and then security sealed by the Clock Committee, who were probably only now enjoying their first refreshment of the evening.

In the view of the pigeon fraternity, Tam included, setting a pigeon clock while consuming alcohol was a greater offence than drink driving.

This mechanical timing device had never let him down. Old as it was, regular servicing and loving care ensured that the Benzing Imperial never lost or gained a second. 11.05 it said, 11.05 it was.

Tam, of-course, was acutely aware of the critical role this 1933 edition, German manufactured, racing pigeon clock, had to play. It may look like a wooden piece-box but its reliability tomorrow was as important as the Mealy Hen completing her long and hazardous journey home, a distance of 515 miles, 778 yards from Sartilly, France to 211 Park Crescent, Rosyth.

He imagined the pigeon arriving, early evening, exhausted from its efforts, his hand picking her up, gently removing the race-rubber from her leg. Quickly placing it in a small metal thimble, the thimble then immediately into the clock. A split-second later the clock key turned and the proof of the Mealy's return safely secured inside. Her achievement later to be revealed to all by the Clock Checking Committee: -

FIFE RACING PIGEON FEDERATION - SARTILLY
PRIZE MONEY - £1,850
WINNER - Mealy Hen - SU/85/F5866 - Velocity 1339.6 yards per minute
OWNER - T. MURDOCH AND SON, ROSYTH RACING PIGEON CLUB

To the often-vented annoyance of the £50 per annum tenants of the vehicle lock-ups, the Council's Budget and Allocation Committee - "Were not, at this moment in time, in a position to allocate the necessary funding for illumination purposes."

"Too busy allocating funding for trips to New-fucking-York." responded one particularly vociferous tenant at a recent public meeting. This remark, although succinctly put and instantly memorable, had unfortunately yet to achieve its purpose and the garages remained an area "unilluminated". Tonight, visibility was even further impaired by the late evening mist.

Tam was not unduly concerned; he knew the way blindfold and the chestnut boundary fence separating Kings Road from the garages, installed by the Council to prevent would-be short-cutters, was once again conveniently holed, creating just enough space for easy access. *Very good,* he thought. *Saves me tearing the arse off my trousers.*

Through the fence, down a gentle grass banking, a few yards of earth track, then the rest of the way on tarmac. Right through to the official vehicle entrance off Park Crescent. Tam could see the Crescent's streetlights welcoming him in the distance. *Five minutes saved - no problem.*

The problem arose at the gap between Joe McCall's and Fletchers.

At first he thought it was a cat, disturbed by his oncoming footsteps, clambering over and dislodging some obstacle barring its escape. Tam knew from past experience however that cats were quieter in flight, he should know, having put the severe frighteners up several of the would-be pigeon killers. No, he re-considered, trying to reassure himself. Probably a young courting couple up to no good in one of the gaps. Nice and dark and a fine night for it. His confidence now dissipating with each step.

Suddenly, hearing it again, this time heavier, closer he automatically spun left, towards its hidden source. This instinctive reaction however was too late. - Too late to prevent the first blow. It fell against his cheekbone, like a hammer.

This one didn't knock him down nor did the next, which followed on immediately, but from behind.

Tam's strength and fighting instincts provided his best response. His left arm, deflecting a third blow allowed the power of his right to reach its target. The force of this effort combined with the weight of the Benzing crashed into a hooded face.

Although in a state of confusion he knew the blows were coming from different directions - but at least he'd stopped one of them.

Tam, however, had no time to benefit from his achievement. Held for a moment they again rained in relentlessly.

It wasn't a fist or a boot that put him on his knees. The telling blow was much harder, somehow less painful than the others. It struck with a jolting crack against the side of his head.

His lumbering but determined efforts to get back on his feet took three similar strikes before they were confident his unexpected resistance was over.

They stooped over him, two dark creatures, breathing heavily from their exhausting execution. The tallest, removing his black woollen mask snapped an instruction to his partner. "You see to Terry. The old bastard's done him no good, broke his nose a'll wager."

Terry did have a broken nose and by the sound of his moans would need assistance to get to his feet.

Tam Murdoch, however, would not get up again, this fact having now been assessed by the unmasked spokesman. Confident in the knowledge that no one could survive the four strikes, personally delivered, he pronounced. "It's done, he's on his last, now let's get to fuck out o' here."

Before they left him, one final task, almost forgotten. A combined effort was needed to drag Tam into the gap. Not combined by all, Terry could not, as yet, help himself.

The job done - a steady walk, arms linked through Terry's, to the discreetly parked estate car.

"Perfect - bloody perfect!"

Tam lay motionless, he would have moaned or wept if he could, but there was no movement from his broken body. Only the steady flow of blood cascading down his head and face indicated an animate being. He rested quietly, not in pain, that positive sensation having slowly been replaced by the cold chill now meandering through him.

His thoughts as his eyelids slowly closed were not of the Mealy Hen, Mary, or even young Jamie. One face drifted in and out of his blurring vision, shadow-like then clear. He repeated the name, again and again, until it too finally disappeared.

" Michael…. Forgive me, Michael…….forgive me!"

CHAPTER 2

The Air-Canada, Boeing 747, Toronto to Prestwick had at last reached cruising altitude.

He could now begin to relax, his one major fear fast becoming a declining memory. Fortunately, he didn't need to encounter it on many occasions, usually avoiding plane flights, preferring transport he could personally control.

These silent thoughts were interrupted by a soft, unassuming voice directed from the next seat. "You don't like take-off's?" she said. And, although already knowing the answer, was nervously anticipating the tone of his response.

He turned his head replying with a smile. "What makes you think that?"

Now more visibly relaxed, she continued. "Well, I think it was either the fifteen minutes silence, perhaps your unblinking stare, but probably, and correct me if I'm wrong, your vice-grip on my arm-rest."

I'm going to enjoy her company, he decided.

She was around ten years younger than himself, red hair, pretty, freckled face, such a friendly smile and from the accent, definitely Scottish.

"Yes, I give-up," he said. "It's, not my favourite hobby." He then continued to explain that although he had never been totally at ease in an aeroplane, this minor anxiety had increased dramatically following a chance discussion with a drunken, off-duty pilot. This acquaintance, who he presumed, stayed sober during working hours, mentioned the little known fact that certain colleagues of the Catholic persuasion repeat continuous "Hail-Mary's" during a Jumbo's take -off. One having unfortunately repeated them with the passenger intercom still on.

The pilot had added that this was due to the take-off being acknowledged as the riskiest part of the journey. It was seemingly all related to the thrust needed to get the "bloody heap" off the tarmac and into a steep ascent. He had also assured him however that the "Hail-Mary's" ceased around thirty thousand feet. For the rest of the voyage, they usually tried to catch-up with some sleep.

"So, that's why I don't particularly enjoy take-offs."

His young companion, although not having believed his explanation, indicated by her chuckles that she at least enjoyed its method of delivery.

She'd been rather unsure of him when offered a terse "excuse me" while edging past her to his seat. However, his now more relaxed manner and easy sense of humour were now revising her opinions. She could now relax in her re-assessment that combined with being quite pleasant; he was also good looking, despite the stubble and the scar.

He was also happy. Selfish as he knew it was her company for the next few hours may hopefully prevent him from thinking too far ahead. .

Their conversation had now been interrupted. "Complimentary refreshments, sir?"

"Yes, a Canadian Club and American Dry with ice".

"You obviously like it on the rocks, sir?" The steward responded with a lingering smile.　　　　　"Refreshments, madam?" The smile now obligatory.

She nodded, attempting to suppress another chuckle. "But I don't want anything alcoholic, maybe a soda water and lime. Oh. And by the way, I don't like it on the rocks."

"Each to her own." He retorted now dispensing their respective drinks.

Waiting until he was cheerfully carrying out his duties further down the aisle she broke into free laughter. "I bet you get another complimentary refreshment."

"I think I'll need one."

As their laughter subsided she continued, "I see you must have acquired a taste for Canadian Whisky during your holiday?"

"Well, yes and no, I'm actually a Canadian Citizen, have been for almost fifteen years. But you're right, I like Canadian Club."

"I take it you're going back to Scotland for a holiday then?"

His delayed response was expressed with a tenseness she'd half expected at the outset of their conversation. "No," he replied slowly, "I'm going to a funeral."

"I'm really sorry," she responded automatically. "It was obviously someone close?"

He was conscious of only partially answering her question. "My father, he died three days ago."

Although still pleasant, his tone didn't encourage her to enquire further. Her glass now empty, she turned to him explaining that the previous evening's partying was now beginning to catch up with her and she might try to get some sleep.

"That's probably a good idea," he agreed sympathetically, hoping she was genuinely tired and not now uncomfortable in his company.

His fears were soon allayed, between yawns, she gently enquired, "You know, I haven't even asked your name, I'm Shirley Stevenson".

"Well I'm really pleased to make your acquaintance Shirley Stevenson," he replied, "My name's Michael - Michael Murdoch."

Within a few minutes she was asleep, leaving him now with his previously predicted second complimentary Canadian Club, and a decision.

He closed his eyes, but only for a moment. Unlike his pretty companion he could not sleep, instead he reflected on each sparse word in the telegram received only two days earlier.

Michael Murdoch, The Cascade, Banff, Alberta
Thomas Murdoch - (Father) - Deceased
July 8th - Rosyth - Please Return

"It was obviously someone close?"   She'd innocently enquired.

In truth he knew he should have replied, "No, my father."

His decision was now made. Although soon unavoidable, he was not yet prepared to tackle the inevitable.

Aware that almost five hours of probable solitude were now unfortunately available to him he directed his mind to memories of a more acceptable nature.

I'm actually a Canadian Citizen, have been for almost fifteen years.

CHAPTER 3

He had just turned eighteen, his young life in Scotland now behind him, and an uncertain future ahead.

He re-called the desperate relief on boarding the flight at Prestwick and an equally desperate feeling of isolation on his arrival at Toronto International Airport. His worldly possessions neatly folded and packed by his mother only a few hours earlier in the brown canvas rucksack below him.

Sitting on it seemed more sensible than standing beside it, particularly as his flight had arrived early and the wait for his Canadian family to arrive might be prolonged.

He had found the pre-arranged meeting place with relative ease. Despite the vast size of the Airport Terminal and the moving mass around him, the revolving Maple Leaf in front of the Hertz Car Rental Office, Terminal 2 couldn't be missed.

To his relief his isolation was short-lived, the Sutherlands had arrived early. Not because of undue concern, they always arrived everywhere early.

Despite never having met him, Aunt Betty had no difficulty spotting her nephew. "Hi - you must be Michael?"

"Yes that's me," he answered nervously. "Thanks very much for picking me up."

"Well, hello Mike," Bert drawled in his best attempt at a Scottish accent. "How's the weether in the Old Country?"

Michael was tempted to reply, "Cauld enough tae freeze yer baw's aff," but he thought better of it. "Chilly for October, but it's nice here, so the pilot said."

His first impressions of his aunt and uncle were not as he'd expected.

This was partially reciprocated; Bert did not instantly take to him. Perhaps it was his reason for leaving Scotland, also the rucksack; he would have preferred a suitcase owner. Probably the main reason however was the dark shoulder-length hair, which didn't exactly fit his perception of a "Scots Laddie".

Betty was much more positive. Despite being in her mid-sixties her mothering instincts had not depleted and the opportunity to help her wee sister's boy would hopefully brighten her comfortable but recently rather mundane existence.

She was nothing like his mother, blood sisters they may be but completely different in appearance and character. She was tall - thin to the extent of near emaciation and to Michael's great relief, turned out to be one of the most easy-going people he'd ever met.

This was not a criticism of his mother. Both sisters had obviously chosen different paths in life. Mary Murdoch had chosen one that had not benefited from the comforts of a Canadian lifestyle. She had however, often under severe financial restraints, struggled to support the family and her strength over the previous few weeks he would never forget.

As Canadian real-estate went 276A Bell Avenue, Toronto wasn't a large house, however it was detached with tree sheltered front and rear grassed yards and his basement room was excellent, providing just the right degree of privacy, especially from Uncle Bert. It had been vacated a year previously by their only child Louise, now married and happily ensconced in a luxurious condominium in Vancouver.

Bert, despite his initial reservations steadily became more comfortable with his nephew.

He was polite, quiet and although he didn't like the hair, was no "sissy boy." His strength and fitness halved the yard chores and his obvious skills with a hammer and saw resulted in the deck replacement he had promised Betty but failed to deliver.

His uncle, however, did have some attributes. Although recently retired he still had some clout with Toronto Waste Incorporated.

Within a month Bert had set him up in a "find his feet" job as a garbage operative.

"A fucking bin-man." Michael silently exclaimed, when the news of his career prospects was announced. However he couldn't and wouldn't refuse. He needed to become financially independent and even if his aunt would not take money, he wanted to show his appreciation by at least buying the odd gift or beer for Bert. He was also determined to eventually be in a position via his aunt to discretely send money home.

As his uncle had explained, Toronto Waste Inc. always hired temporary labour over the Winter period due to the added burden and delays associated with garbage removal in the snow. "You won't get the same rate as the permanents." Bert had stated knowingly, "But it's better you getting the cash than some wop or blackman."

This prejudice, which encompassed all races except white Canadians, the Irish and, of course, the Scots, although abhorrent to his nephew, was not questioned. *No point in biting the hand that feeds you*, he decided. However it did persuade him that his long-term future did not rest at Bell Avenue.

Michael enjoyed his new profession. It kept him fit, speedily increased his knowledge of Toronto, gave him the opportunity to mix with other young Canadians and, more importantly, quickly accumulate hard earned dollars.

His closest friends at Toronto Waste Inc. did not, however, include the 'permanents' as Bert had hoped. He was more relaxed with his fellow Winter hires, and on each pay day toured the Toronto nightspots with them. Four in total, a Canadian Indian, a Negro, a Jew and, of -course, a Scot.

An Uncle Bert nightmare. Michael thought with some pleasure.
Apart from their youth and hopefully temporary careers they had little in common except the pleasure of Friday night's down-town.

The others were happy in Michael's company; although the quietest of the group, he had a keen sense of humour and to their added benefit, could take care of himself. This particular attribute first surfaced in á late-night pizza parlour off Yonge Street.

Dino appreciated his now regular Friday night customers, however, on this particular evening a group of loud, inebriated all Canadian Boys didn't.

Within minutes of the three Canadians entering the parlour, Michael and his companions knew there would be trouble. Bored with insulting Dino's ancestry they turned their attention to the seated four-some. The drunkest of the three leaned over their table. "Hope you're not sharing your pizza with the nigger - eh?"

Michael slowly turned his head, smiled and replied. "I'm afraid not, you see I lost the bet tonight so my good friend here will be eating a Dino's Special."

"What was the bet Scotty?"

Michael's response was delivered in a deliberately quiet and relaxed tone. "Well I bet that you couldn't be as thick as a Dino's Special and, of-course, you've just proved me wrong."

In the fraction of time it took for the enraged Canadian to attempt his move his face was colliding with the tabletop. The split second taken for Michael to spring upwards, grab him by the neck and smash his head against the solid pine gave him the added momentum to crash his right fist square on the chin of the second attacker.

One punch was enough. Both were now incapable of retaliation. The third realising the situation his friends were in quickly considered his options and, following one glance at Michael's stare and obvious state of readiness, decided to immediately cease hostilities.

Apologising on behalf of his confused and injured colleagues he helped them to their feet and through the door. The end result, four complimentary specials from a glee-full Dino and a quickly spread reputation within Toronto Waste Inc. that Mike Murdoch, as well as being a hard worker, could handle himself.

The welcoming warmth of Spring and resulting snowmelt steadily increased the efficiency of garbage removal and inevitably the Winter hires were paid off.

Michael, partially due to his uncle's influence and his own work-rate was offered a permanent post.

Although he had some regrets in refusing this career opportunity he had now accrued over three thousand dollars and his future plans did not include continuing to live with the Sutherlands or in Toronto.

The genuine fear that his decision to leave Bell Avenue would cause offence, especially to his aunt, was fortunately unfounded. Fortunate for Michael, however, not so for Louise, who was now coming home to Bell Avenue pending her divorce.

The timing of his announcement couldn't have been better. The mutual relief was clearly evident as they sat in the late afternoon sunshine on the re-built and freshly painted deck. Both Bert and Michael, for once in a state of total harmony, fully relaxed in each other's company and, at his uncle's insistence, shared the pleasures of a ten-year-old, special reserve bottle of Canadian Club Rye Whisky.

Within two weeks he was heading west.

CHAPTER 4

The Trailways Coach, Toronto to Vancouver was an experience in itself.

Although he was not going all the way, the two and a half days taken to reach his destination in the foothills of the Rocky Mountains showed him enough of Canada to appreciate its vastness and potential.

The Lakes, Thunder Bay, Winnipeg, The Plains, Regina, Medicine Hat, Calgary, then towards Banff, Alberta; a variety of landscapes each awe-inspiring. The best, as Luke Jackson, his Jewish friend had readily stated, was waiting at the end of his journey.

Luke hadn't exaggerated, The Canadian Rockies were spectacular.

As previously arranged with Pete, the driver on the Calgary - Banff section of the run, an announcement was made over the coach intercom approximately one mile east of Banff Town. "We are now approaching the Scotsman's stop," he stated, to Michael's embarrassment but great convenience. "Just follow that track for about five hundred metres," he added helpfully. "You can't miss it Scottish," at the same time operating the door opening mechanism from his seat. "And remember - take care now."

Michael thanked him for the favour and advice, although the signpost, reading Banff National Park - Youth Hostel, ensured that Pete's directions were not required. The track also led nowhere else.

As he was already aware, from his conversations with Luke, this Youth Hostel was not the traditional stone or timber building sub-divided into male and female quarters. It was set within the edge of a large mature forest with only two permanent structures, a timber office and toilet block. Located under a canopy of pine, in a rough horseshoe circling these buildings, were ten marquee tents each capable of accommodating around fifteen bed spaces.

Michael wasn't disappointed, he had been told what to expect and this was even better. The setting was beautiful, each tent blending in comfortably with the trees, and within the horseshoe several large pines broke the landscape providing welcome shade.

He walked nervously towards the office rehearsing his lines, at the same time noticing the camp's cooking facilities, located directly at the horseshoe's centre.

This cooking range comprised a circle of large stones containing a log fire with metal grill cover; the pine trees surrounding it having been cut to two-foot stumps and shaped like armchairs. *Clever*, he thought. *Very clever.*

Other large trunks had obviously been pulled to the circle and placed on their sides providing ample seating accommodation for around fifty.

Although the fire had recently been lit the kitchen was still awaiting the arrival of its first guests of the now late afternoon.

Michael successfully registered his arrival, stating that he was a student on vacation but had unfortunately mislaid his Youth Hostel Card; however, he would only be staying for five days to explore the wonders of this celebrated National Park. He then, with a justified sense of relief, followed the hostel secretary's directions to his new home.

Tent number seven it was - luxury it wasn't. Canvas apex roof and walls, double-ply, sown-in ground sheet and a log between each bed space. All spaces, except the one closest to the entrance, occupied by rolled out empty sleeping bags. *Obviously first come, first served,* he thought. *Wonder why they don't want the space near the door? Must be the draught.*

He then unstrapped his own sleeping bag from his rucksack rolled it out and positioned the sack at the top, for use as a pillow. Securing his wallet into the back pocket of his jeans he then decided to do a nosey and hopefully find something to eat.

On leaving the tent, he couldn't fail to notice the first arrivals at the cooking range. Both were blonde and beautiful, and as he walked nearer, the succulent aroma of barbecuing steaks added to his anticipation.

He sat down on an adjacent tree trunk. "Any chance of selling me your steaks girls? I'll pay extra now that you've cooked them."

The tallest, disturbed during the process of grilling her now sizzling meal, turned towards him, flicking back her long hair as she examined the prospective purchaser. "Well shit. You from Scotland"? She drawled. "Kate, I've met my very first Scotchman," now chuckling to her equally beautiful companion.

Michael smiled. "How do you know I'm Scots, if I'm the first you've met?"

"Shit," she responded confidently. "That's easy; you sound like Sean Connery, except he's so handsome."

"Thanks for the compliment," he replied, quickly realising that uprooting himself from the security of Toronto, was probably the best decision he had made in his life so far.

Becky Harris was gorgeous, just what he'd imagined for a daughter of California. The hair, the tanned face, blue eyes and a body to match. She was also generous with her steak; Michael shared half of it, at no charge.

Kate, having eaten her whole steak and also noticing potentially more interesting company now entering the camp decided to make herself scarce.

More fellow hostellers were arriving steadily, all laden with food and when the seating around the fire became fully occupied Becky suggested an evening stroll into Banff.

To Michael's surprise she was three years older than him and a trainee nurse. Both she and Kate, on two weeks study leave prior to their final exams, had decided to head north as an alternative to last minute cramming *Laid-back to the point of horizontal.* He thought admiringly, at the same time wondering if he would eventually accompany her in that position.

Following a pleasant stroll around Banff Town, picking up necessary provisions, including a six-pack of Labbats Blue Beer, they returned to the hostel hand in hand having stopped against the occasional pine for a kiss and sip of Blue. It was almost midnight and apart from a small group sitting close to the fire enjoying the fourth verse of 'Blowin' in the Wind', most campers had retired for the night.

They chose a tree trunk slightly back from the fire. Just close enough to enjoy the atmosphere and the warmth from the glowing embers.

During their last shared bottle of Blue, Becky enquired about Michael's sleeping accommodation.

"It's okay," he replied. "I'm in number seven, right at the door."

"Shit." She retorted. "You can't sleep there. Twice this week a bear's visited the camp, two nights ago he stole food from number seven. Put his big claws right through the door flap, grabbed a pack of ham, stopped for a crap and then just ambled away."

Michael, almost choking on the last of the beer, spluttered, "That's why the bastards left me with the space at the door!"

Before he could make any further comment, Becky quietly and almost shyly suggested how the rest of the night might be spent. "Do you know about the couple's tent?" "No," he replied, regaining his composure. "What would that be?"

She pointed through the fire-glow to the outline of a tent at the furthest corner of the camp. "It's not official hostelling policy, but Mabel the Secretary, she's pretty easy going. We can use it if you like, as long as you're not easily embarrassed."

"Okay," Michael agreed, trying to conceal his growing excitement. "That'd be nice, embarrassed by what?"

"Lets get our gear and I'll show you," she replied, kissing him before turning towards her own tent.

After a few minutes they met up again at the fire, each carrying their rucksacks. Although late, the glow from the cooking range illuminated a well-worn path to tent number ten. On arrival Michael pulled back the entrance flap and, on noticing the faint but obvious contours of five pairs of occupied sleeping bags, immediately closed it again.

Indicating by his reaction and nervous whisper that he was, in fact, very easily embarrassed, he turned to Becky. "Do you think they're all asleep in there, will they not hear us?"

"Don't worry," she said reassuringly. "We won't be doing anything that they haven't already done and maybe still are."

Becky confidently entered, found them a space, away from the door, and proceeded expertly to rollout and zip both their sleeping bags together.

His embarrassment now replaced by the anticipation of what was to follow; Michael quickly undressed and slipped into the now double bag.

Becky followed his example, giggling quietly as she prised her naked body close to his, the warmth and softness of her skin instantly negating the cool breeze whisping through a small tear in the tent's wall.

She kissed him gently and whispered, "Mike, do you mind if tonight I call you Sean?"

Despite their best intentions, as passions increased, so did the volume of their lovemaking, resulting at a rather critical stage, in a mild rebuke from a neighbouring sleeping bag. "Hate to interrupt you enjoying your first Scotchman Becky," Kate whispered loudly. "But I've just had a French Canadian and we're both trying to get some sleep, so turn it down a mite, please!"

Michael disturbed by her movement and the early morning sunlight now filtering through the canvas, witnessed the unforgettable vision of her tanned nakedness as Becky stood over him casually locating her clothes. It was only when her jeans and lambs wool jumper were securely in place he remembered what she had confirmed during their evening stroll. Becky was now leaving him.

Following her friend's example Kate slowly released herself from the neighbouring sleeping bag, stretched, yawned and muttered some obscenities about having a shitty sleep.

As Becky had explained, their study break was nearing completion and if they were to make the first exam session at San Clemente, General Hospital, they had to catch the early morning coach to Calgary, which connected with their flight home.

Michael also decided to get dressed and by the time he was fully clothed the girls had unzipped their bags and were fully packed for the road.

Kate's companion was too tired to accompany them and although he managed sleepily to re-zip his now single bag, could only wish her an "Au-revoir, babe," before regaining unconsciousness.

Following the short walk to the main road the threesome were now saying their farewells. There were no tears. Following their last lingering kiss, Becky whispered, "Now I know why I've always wanted to meet a Scotchman."

When the coach came to a halt beside them and as the door opened Michael noticed that Pete was once again in the driver's seat on his return run to Calgary. "Well Scottish," he exclaimed with genuine surprise. "You look as if you've found your way about. How did you manage it?"

"Charm Pete, lots of charm," he replied with a blushing smile. "And, of-course the accent helps."

CHAPTER 5

"Mike, I'm afraid we have a problem," Mabel, the Hostel Secretary, stated with some sympathy. "Your five nights "intended" residence is now twenty-five; I can't allow it to go on any longer. Rules are rules, you know."

"Okay, Mabel, I give in," he replied sheepishly. "Will you give me till the end of next week? I'll find something by then, just another ten days."

Mabel would, of-course, relent. Mike Murdoch, in her experienced view, despite having foxed his way into the camp, was okay. "Ten days it is then, but no more. I'm expecting an audit inspection from the Association anytime, and you know no-one should stay here for more than two weeks."

Michael did know, she'd told him last week.

He was also well aware that Mabel's registration and receipt books would have been creatively accounted to ensure that the fifty six dollars he had paid for his official fourteen day maximum residence period were safely in the coffers of the Canadian Youth Hostel Association. The remainder, safely in Mabel's pocket.

In his opinion, Mabel, although only in her late forties was a bit like his Aunt Betty.

Similar easy-going character, similar maternal instincts, completely dis-similar though when it came to honesty.

Up to now their mutual understanding had benefited both, and he, in addition, had helped her out by taking care of the fire and toilet cleaning chores.

The auditors, though, were in fact "due", not that they had caught her out before, her skills in accounting and the discreet telephone calls from her cousin at Association H.Q. had always, in the past, given her the "edge". However, now repeating her often-used expression; "There was always a first time!"

Although knowing each other for only a short time their confidences were now shared. Michael, on his part, had revealed that he was, in fact, no tourist and his true intentions were to settle in the Banff area, he loved the place. Instead, however, of taking in the National Park's many attractions he'd spent most of his efforts attempting to find employment in the local timber yards. The rest of his attentions taken up with the camp chores and attracting companions to the couples' tent.

Unfortunately, his employment prospects were not going as planned and although still in reasonable funds, he was beginning to feel distinctly uneasy. He was desperately keen to work in timber, the pay was good, four hundred dollars a week average and he was confident he could adapt his basic joinery skills to this raw wood process.

Six out of the six yard foremen he'd approached thought differently. Canadian Timber was almost exclusively in the domain of "Real" Canadians and not, in their opinion, "Some Scot's immigrant kid who could hardly find his way around Banff."

Realising his predicament he attempted to find work in town. Although early in the season, he hoped jobs would be available in the numerous hotels, bars and restaurants which gave Banff its Tourist Trap reputation.

Michael tried most of them. But "Come back in a month," seemed to be the only words he heard during this now despairing search.

In a state of increasing anxiety he paid his second visit to the Banff Park Museum, Banff Avenue, Banff.

Banff Avenue, the town's main street, was not the only thoroughfare with a less than original title. Every other street was named after an indigenous animal. The predictability of which, during this second trudge round them, was now adding to his state of deepening depression.

Bear Street - Beaver Street - Muskrat Street - Otter Street - Grizzly Street - Buffalo Street - Squirrel Street - Wolf Street - Wolverine Street - Lynx Street - Deer Street - Cougar Street - Rabbit Street - Antelope Street - Caribou Street - Elk Street and finally Gopher Street!

Michael imagined the consternation of the Town's Founding Fathers when they ran out of animals and their dilemma as they met to decide the naming of their main street. "Let's think of something different; something unique; something truly original."

So Banff Avenue, Banff, it was and as a restaurant proprietor had just informed him, after telling him to "Come back in a month," the Museum was looking for a guide.

Michael had visited it during his second day in the Rockies, following his farewell to Becky and his only day as a tourist. He hadn't been impressed. In his view it was like a mortuary. "Floor to ceiling dead animals." Every street name of the town, except a "Banff" stared down at him, through piercing glass eyes. "You name it - they stuffed it!" he had decided in disgust before leaving to get some fresh air.

He was now, however, entering its walls again as a prospective official guide.

He passed beyond the two grotesque grizzly bears guarding the Curator's Office and politely announced his arrival. "Excuse me," he said to the stooped and balding officer in charge. "I understand you might have a job going?"

The Curator, sitting at a large oak desk, which took up most of his tiny office, was, unbeknown to Michael, carrying out his regular examination of the Visitors Book. "Name please?" he eventually responded, without the courtesy of an upward glance.

"Michael Murdoch, I'm from Scotland but I want to settle in the Banff Area". He felt he had to explain his accent and honest desire to seek gainful employment.

"Mmm - Murdoch? Michael Murdoch? That name sounds familiar." The Curator stated now pointing his piercing eyes towards his now uncomfortable visitor. "Have you visited us before?"

"Yes," he replied nervously, now slowly recalling a slight error of judgement he may have made during his previous visit. "Yes, beautiful place you have, really st-stimulating." He was now beginning to stutter.

"Yes of-course, here we are!" The Curator, to Michael's horror, was now pointing out a signature in the Visitors Book and reading aloud the offending line.

"Date: - Eleventh April"
"Name: - Michael Murdoch"
"Address: - 'Fae Fife"

"I presume that means from Fife, Scotland?" His long nose now visibly twitching and not waiting for a response quickly completing the delivery of his coup-de-grace.

"Comments on the Exhibits: - 'Pity they're all fucking dead!'"

"No, Mr. Murdoch, I do not think you will be taking up the post of Official Guide in this establishment!"

"Fine," Michael responded before turning to exit the Museum for the second and final time. "You're basically telling me to get stuffed then?"

The curator silently pointed to the door.

As he left the Museum and turned east off Banff Avenue into Caribou Street, Michael felt at his lowest ebb. The feeling of isolation he had experienced during his first few minutes in Canada had now returned and in addition, deeper, more desperate memories were beginning to creep back into his mind. Stopping to physically block the seeds of these thoughts he found himself standing at the door of Jake's Bar.

Although, having frequented most of the local pubs with a variety of young companions, Michael had heeded several warnings and stayed clear of Jake's. It was most definitely lumberjack domain, and even want-to-be timber-hands were apparently not welcome, especially those with long hair and non-Canadian accents. Michael, however, in his present state of mind, decided he had nothing to lose.

A considerable effort was required to push open the ill-fitting, varnish flaking, barrier to the premises. Although it took a little time to acclimatise his vision from the bright sunshine outside to the dingy gloom inside, he soon accurately assessed that Jake's Bar was no Tourist Trap.

It was small for a Canadian pub and the confined space appeared even more restricted due to the low wood panelled ceiling and brown smoke-stained walls.

He nervously made his way across the bare stone floor to the bar counter, noticing the state of near dereliction around him and the equally derelict condition of Jake Mathews perched on a stool behind the bar, in the process of blowing more brown stain towards the ceiling.

Apart from Jake and himself, two others presently occupied the establishment. Unfortunately for Michael he recognised one of them, the foreman from Alberta Timber Ltd., and the bearer of his sixth refusal during his interview for lumberjack period. Both he and a colleague were propped against the bar in deep conversation about the current price of cut spruce.

Before he could make his decision to continue or retreat Jake gave his standard gravel toned welcome to young strangers. "You lost son?" Then following a short pause to stub out his cigarette in the overflowing ash -tray at his side, continued, "McDonald's is three blocks north, Wolf Street."

Michael nervously responded with an abbreviated version of his now well-rehearsed job seekers line, "I'm looking for work, anything going?" He didn't attempt to elaborate, now convinced he was wasting his time.

Jake, to Michael's despair, did elaborate and recognising the Scots accent replied, "You've come all the way from Bonnie Scotland to get a job in Jake's Bar - eh? I'm truly honoured but no thanks; I'm fully staffed at present."

The laughter from the now attentive lumberjacks added to Michael's sense of foolishness. However, attempting to regain a little of his dignity he responded. "Well, thanks anyway, I probably couldn't have kept up the high standards your Canadian staff are obviously maintaining."

The foreman, now recognising Michael, entered the conversation on his behalf. "Jake, what about that little job we were just talking about, the one you keep putting off?" Grinning as he continued. "The boy looks strong enough, probably wrap it up in a week."

Returning an acknowledging grin to the foreman, Jake having pondered his friend's suggestion spoke.

"Well son, following careful consideration, if you come back here in one hour with your hair cut, you'll get a week's work."

"Fine." Michael responded immediately, and to their surprise, "See you in an hour!" He then turned and quickly left the premises, which now resounded with the combined laughter of the three remaining occupants.

Although hesitating for a moment outside, attempting but failing to think of any practical alternatives, his decision was now made. To Jake's genuine surprise, on the hour, Michael was again standing in front of the bar counter with his new look hairstyle, a lumberjack crew-cut.

Fortunately, the bar was now empty, giving time for Jake to ease himself off his stool, hobble slowly to the entrance door and turn the key. He then led Michael to a second similarly varnished door located to the right of the counter. He'd noticed it during his first visit and presumed it led to the toilets or beer cellar.

Although he was correct the narrow corridor now revealed to him went further and as they passed the entrance to the toilets Michael saw a larger padlocked door facing him at the corridor's end. He also couldn't have failed to notice Jake's distinct limp. Michael reckoned he was around seventy, small for a Canadian, but apart from the dishevelled appearance and the calliper supporting his right leg, he still looked in reasonably good shape, for an old bastard.

When Jake eventually managed to unlock the large rusted padlock and slowly prised open the door, it revealed nothing except complete darkness and a strange sense of undisturbed space. He then turned on the lights and Michael almost fell backwards in disbelief. In the dull glow of five hanging bulbs, the remaining twenty or so having been removed from their cut glass shades, he was now staring in amazement at the biggest dance hall he'd ever seen!

"What do you think, son?" Jake said quietly, "Big, eh?" His whisper echoing eerily around the vast building.

Still in a state of shock, at the sight of this man-made cavern, Michael stuttered, "It's unbelievable, is it yours?"

"'Fraid so, all of it." Jake responded casually, at the same time noticing the awed expression on the youngster's face.

Although only five bulbs were emitting light, Michael's widely opened eyes compensated quickly, taking in every detail of this incredible structure. They were standing at its centre edge, facing them over thirty metres away was another large double door, secured with rough timber planks. At both sides of this obviously once main entrance, a slightly raised platform skirted the hall, providing the seating area. The wooden tables and chairs which years ago would have provided a welcome respite for the dancers were now piled haphazardly, in some places up to almost ceiling height.

To their right, around fifty metres from where they stood the dance floor led to the foot of a large wooden stage its two imposing columns draped in now faded red velvet curtains, commemorating the grandeur of a some-what earlier era. Although Michael knew there was a floor he couldn't actually see it due to the varied accumulations of debris littering its surface.

The ceiling however, was in plain view despite the gloom. Varnished timber joists spanned its width, the spaces between filled with damp-stained lath and plaster. Each joist supporting the hanging weight of six circular light shades, the central joist supporting the "Piece de Resistance" a gigantic cut-glass orb.

Michael imagined this revolving globe illuminating every frantic, movement of the old Jivers and early Rock-n-Rollers who must have once filled the place. He had seen similar dance halls on television documentaries depicting the forties and fifties, with bands like Bill Haley and The Comets strutting their stuff on stage and the audience strutting theirs below.

At the moment, however, the scene of chaos and devastation before him looked like the after effects of one of the Comets exploding.

To further answer Michael's query about ownership, Jake confirmed that he had bought it with the bar some twenty-two years earlier. "It used to be called the Cascade - busy in its hey-day, but I never got round to using it for much."

For much except a rubbish dump. Michael agreed silently, now realising the extent of the task ahead.

Before he could make this point to the owner, Jake continued sharply, "I want all the junk cleared out and burnt, and then the joint goes on the market."

"You're joking!" Michael exclaimed in disbelief, "It'll take me a week to get to the far door."

"You can't handle it then?" Jake replied almost sympathetically, "Okay, back to the bar, I'll give you a beer for the road, make up for the hair-cut, eh!"

Michael quickly re-considered. "Right then, how about ten days and four hundred dollars, and I'm your man?"

"Deal!" Jake instantly replied, shaking his new employees hand to conclude the bargain, "You should have asked for more, I would have gone to five hundred and a fortnight."

On his way back to the camp, Michael reflected on his current position. He now at least had a job, temporary as it was, ten days were better than nothing. Also the four hundred dollars added to what he still had in his wallet would ensure his financial security for a while yet. He still, however, had nowhere permanent to stay, and he knew this major problem would have to be tackled before Mabel's impending deadline.

Within the week it was. He had at last reached the stage frontage and to his surprise, hidden by the wide red curtain, he found a narrow wooden stairway. Slowly climbing its creaking steps he then opened a small-unlocked door, to find what could loosely be described as a kitchen and specifically described as his new home. It was tiny, but it did benefit from daylight. A broken window overlooked the yard below. It also had a cooker and sink and just enough space, when cleared, for his sleeping bag.

What surprised him more Jake agreed to his nervous suggestion. Free accommodation until his ten days were up, and five dollars a night after that, maximum three months. "And definitely no visitors!"

Jake, who normally didn't take to many people, except of-course Lumberjacks, was comfortable with his temporary hire. He had quickly recognised that Mike was a good worker, started at seven a.m. finished at eight p.m. and, more importantly, rarely bothered him in between.

He also realised, even during the first week that the task, which he thought was impossible in the time-scale allocated, might now surprisingly be completed on schedule. Allowing, hopefully, this major burden to be removed from his ownership, at a nice profit, of-course.

Michael's first real conversation with his employer took place after he had cleared out the under-stage area. During this extremely awkward operation he came across two large wooden trunks, full of inscribed silver trophies, medals and old team photographs. "Jesus, he's been an ice-hockey player, big league too!"

When approached about these obviously, personal memento's, the old man's annoyance was made clear. "I said burn everything, do you understand? Everything!"

"But." Michael pleaded. "They're your trophies, you were famous, Top Scorer for the Edmonton Oilers, you can't destroy them."

His perseverance paid off; Jake relented. "Do what you like with them then, they're no use to me now."

Michael's genuine interest couldn't be stemmed so easily; he had to know more. "It's a hard game, I bet?"

Jake's response was delivered with a passion which shocked its recipient, "Obviously too hard for me, eh. I take it you've noticed my bloody leg!"

Michael immediately apologised for his innocent indiscretion, which to his relief was now accepted calmly by the old man. Jake, having regained his composure and recognising Michael's discomfort, continued. "What's your sport son?"

Michael wasn't sure if it was the memory of the trophies or a sub-conscious desire to tell Jake he was a similar team-type player that prompted his answer. "Football."

"Do you mean football or soccer?" Jake queried

"Oh. Yes, soccer, we call it football in Scotland." Why had he mentioned Jamie's sport and not admit to his own? His guilt now increasing with this fleeting memory of his older brother.

"Well, whatever you do, don't take up ice-hockey, or you could turn out like me!"

It was now getting late and as Michael retired to his tiny home behind the stage, he reflected on the past few minutes. There was definitely more to Jake than he'd previously thought. Memories of a slightly similar but more important influence in his life were now creeping uncomfortably into his mind. Before however they took hold he pushed them backwards.

His father was now part of his hopefully forgotten past and he would do his best to keep him there.

The mammoth clearing operation was going well. In Michael's opinion another day of burning the contents of the now empty hall would complete his contract with Jake, a full two days ahead of schedule. He then, although not particularly looking forward to it, would seek gainful employment elsewhere.

Unknown to his present employer, however, he'd discovered a large tarpaulin and a discreet corner of the yard to temporarily store potentially re-saleable items he'd come across during the last eight days. The rest of the dance hall's contents were now being burnt.

Apart from Jake's personal memorabilia, which was now safely deposited between Michael's cooker and sink, a variety of less damaged articles from the hall, including tables, chairs, plates and cutlery, were now awaiting the old man's inspection and hopeful agreement to sell. Michael hoped that this arrangement would also include him receiving a cut of the profits.

The yard, which he soon realised, must have once been the Cascades car park, led to padlocked wrought iron gates which presently barred vehicles and sightseers from the hall's main entrance off Elk Street. Elk Street ran parallel to Caribou Street. On Jake's agreement, Michael intended to open the gates during the following Saturday and invite, for the first time in twenty two years, the residents of Banff Town to view the interior of the Cascade and, more importantly, choose a bargain from under the tarpaulin.

Before, however, the contents of the dance hall could be sold off; prospects had changed dramatically for both of them.

Wednesday nights was never busy in Jake's Bar; in fact Michael had noticed that apart from pay-Friday's at the timber yards, the pub was usually always customer disadvantaged.

He was at last at the sweeping up stage of his contract and enjoying the satisfaction of a job well done. "The old bugger's dropped another full bottle!" He exclaimed under his breath, following the unmistakable crash of glass from the vicinity of the bar.

Jake had also forgotten to close the doors serving the connecting corridor, following the most recent of his now regular inspection visits to the hall.

On the second crash of glass Michael dropped his brush and ran through to the bar. Covered with shattered fragments of whisky bottle Jake was sitting on the saturated floor behind the counter.

Michael, although realising that his employer was obviously in a state of extreme discomfort, his hair and shirt also soaked in whisky, he was fully conscious and seemed not to be badly hurt.

He didn't recognise Jake's two customers; they were dressed and built like lumberjacks, one of them in Michael's view, built like two.

Jake, now noticing his presence, shouted an urgent instruction to his young employee. "This ain't your business, Mike, get back in the hall!"

Michael ignored his request and walked slowly towards Jake's other unwelcome guests. "What's the problem lads?" He asked quietly, moving closer. "No children out on the streets tonight to interfere with, so you've opted for an old man?"

The slightly shorter, red-haired, lumberjack, somewhat surprised by Michael's presence and calmly delivered insult replied, "Butt-out, Mike, take old Jake's advice go home or you'll get hurt, real bad!"

Michael now within range, continued with a smile, "You're wrong I'm afraid, this is my home - and this is a Scotch kiss." The explosion of blood, caused by the blunt force of Michael's fore-head colliding with his nose immediately sprayed the pine ceiling and sent the red-haired and now blood-red faced, lumberjack sprawling to the floor.

The agonising cry delayed for a moment the response from his larger colleague. It, however, came with a thundering first against the side of Michael's head. To his relief it was a fraction too slow, allowing Michael to instinctively avoid its full effect. Although knocking him sideways against the bar counter he quickly regained his stance and replied with a barrage of punches to the head, face and body of his bigger but now startled foe.

Unlike the Toronto drunks, however, this one was no pushover and it took Michael to the limits of his determination and fighting skills to eventually put him down. The combined accuracy, speed and quality of the blows had at last gained their desired effect and, despite receiving several in return, the exhausting effort resulted in him now stooping over the slumped giant assessing his chances of re-entering the fight.

Before he could relax in the certainty of it, the bottle struck his temple.

"Michael, son! You okay?   Michael, wake-up, son!" Jake's anxious voice was now filtering through and despite his blurred vision he could make out the hazy presence of the old man leaning over him.

He could also taste the warm blood trickling from its painful source, flowing down his right cheekbone and now through his lips. "What happened, Jake?"

His murmur, although barely audible, providing instant relief to its recipient. "I'm so sorry Mike. Let's get you to the hospital. You'll be fine, just lay still."

His senses now slowly recovering, the casual mention of a hospital seemed slightly disconcerting.

Banff General Hospital, Rabbit Street, had an unusually busy evening. Three and a bit patients admitted to the casualty ward.

Frank "Ginger" McQuire, Big Joe Lindey, Mike Murdoch and Jake Mathews' calliper.

This, unfortunately for the leg-brace but pleasing to Jake, was the only part of his anatomy damaged. Unbuckled and re-united with its owner the calliper and Jake were now positioned at the side of Michael's bed. "You okay son, you look terrible?"

"I'm fine, Jake," Michael replied, not yet knowing whether his answer was in fact totally accurate. "Just a bit sore. What happened?"

Now more relaxed about his young friend's condition, Jake cheerfully described the endplay of the little customer-proprietor misunderstanding back at the bar. "You were doing pretty good son, Big Joe was out cold, but you forgot about Ginger and, of-course, I was too slow, busted calliper and all!" Following a short pause for added effect he continued. "He hit you with a Bottle of Jack Daniel's smashed you right on the head with it before I could nail him."

"You what?" Michael exclaimed in amazement.

Jake concluded his commentary with a satisfied grin, "There's more than one bottle in the bar son, more than one".

Agreeing to return the following Thursday, to have his stitches removed, Michael was finally discharged from Banff General.

Despite his young patient's best attempts, the consultant-in-charge had not been persuaded to reduce his sentence.   Overnight observation was normal practice and this particular head wound had not been easy to deal with due to the nasty bruising and depth of the cut. "Probably leave a scar," he had stated to the nurse, on completion of his hectic evening's work.

Happily though for both Jake and Michael the remaining two casualty patients at Banff General had faired much worse. Ginger McQuire now had a permanently disfigured nose and semi-permanent concussion. Big Joe, although not seriously damaged, jaw fractures required fairly simple operations, would never regain his previously extremely bad reputation around the Alberta yards and soon left for the timber fields of Saskatchewan.

Michael now had a permanent home and a temporary career as minder, barman and substitute son for Jake Mathews Only temporary, within a year he was to become Jake's junior partner and shared owner of the 'Cascade, Restaurant Bar and Grill', Elk Street.

Future tourists directed to it by the Museum Curator and others were told "You can't miss it, from the outside it looks like an old dance-hall."

CHAPTER 6

In the few seconds, emerging from sleep to consciousness, Shirley Stevenson was extremely confused.

The anxious check with her wrist watch didn't help, obviously having not re-set it to compensate for the time difference between Toronto and Scotland. Three-thirty-five a.m.; didn't tie in with the bright sunshine now streaming through the Jumbo's porthole window. "How long have I been asleep?" She worriedly questioned her now smiling companion.

Michael replied reassuringly, "Its eight thirty five a.m. Monday morning in Scotland, and we'll be there in around twenty five minutes."

"You're joking!" she responded, now fully awake.

"Must have been quite a farewell party, you even missed the movie," his smile now a grin, "Endless Flight, It was pretty good, apart from the crash scene of-course."

Although aware she was being misled about the choice of in-flight entertainment, he'd accurately confirmed the stage of the journey, so she had better get organised quickly. Following a frantic search for her make-up she joined the twenty minutes to touch-down queue at the toilet and as a result Michael did not see her again until just before the announcement to "re-fasten seat-belts" in preparation for landing.

When a freshened-up, extremely pretty and now smiling Shirley Stevenson returned to his side, Michael soon realised that her thoughts were now almost totally directed to the anticipation of being happily re-united with her boyfriend at Prestwick.

In contrast he had the less pleasant prospect of soon becoming re-united with the traumas of his earlier life. Its consequences, he now accepted, could no longer be avoided.

These fears, however, were now changing to a resigned determination. He wouldn't run this time. His mother and Jamie were all he'd left in Scotland and they would need his support, at least until the funeral was over. After that he would return to Banff to face, and hopefully resolve, another situation needing overdue attention.

They wished each other well before the "747" finally came to a standstill, and although only a few yards apart, soon lost contact in the mass exodus of over five hundred passengers now flowing through Customs, Luggage Collection and finally the Arrivals Exit.

Michael had fully intended to hire a car, use it for a few days before returning it prior to his, yet to be arranged, homeward flight. Mrs. Andrews had decided differently.

He hadn't argued with his mother's neighbour at No.217, she had sounded so upset on the phone. In his desire to terminate their brief but strained conversation, he had reluctantly agreed to young Peter acting as chauffeur.

Within minutes of receiving the telegram he'd asked Mabel to organise flight arrangements and then trace Mrs. Andrew's phone number, in the certain knowledge that she had one, and presuming correctly that his mother still did not. He now hoped, between sobs, she had accurately taken in the details of his flight and intended arrival time.

These concerns were now abruptly put to rest. He heard the Pie before he saw him.

"Waiting for Michael Murdoch. - Waiting for Michael Murdoch."

Peter Andrews, to the amusement of his intended passenger but to the consternation of family members, friends and other would-be chauffeurs, who were not "Waiting for Michael Murdoch", had not opted for a hand-held notice. Now in full view, standing solidly in front of the rest of the arrivals' audience, Michael recognised him immediately; The Pie was definitely still The Pie.

He had changed little from the ten-year-old who used to be constantly at his and Jamie's side on race days, waiting patiently in the back garden for the first pigeon to arrive. Sharing their pleasures and disappointments and, of course, their mother's tea and digestive biscuits.

Michael couldn't recall whether it was himself or Jamie who invented the youngster's nickname. He did, however, remember that it had started as pie-face and was subsequently finely tuned to The Pie, accurate then and unfortunately still accurate now.

Although he had obviously grown, his proportions remained the same, short and extremely chubby, with the roundest, flattest pie-face imaginable in a human being.

"How you doing P......P... Peter? Thanks a lot for coming through for me, I really appreciate it."

"No problem Michael," Peter Andrews replied with a surprised expression. "How did you know it was me? I wouldn't have known you; you're so bloody tall now, built like a bloody lumberjack!"

He responded with a smile. "Your Fife accent Peter, couldn't miss it, and of-course your mother kindly said she would ask you to pick me up."

"The old witch didnae ask, she tell't me." He responded with a wry grin. "She hasn't changed that much since you left."

They were now accompanying each other to the airport's short-stay car park.

"Well, what do you think Michael, no bad, eh?"

He replied dishonestly. "Very nice, what make is it?"

"Escort XR3I, fuel injection, 1600cc, fucking flying machine! 0 - 60 in 7.3 seconds, resprayed it last month; like the shade of red? Ford war dance! Goes with the black stripes, eh?"

"Oh yes, definitely." Michael, however, now justifiably concerned for his well-being over the next two hours, continued, "I hope you don't mind, Peter, I'd really like to relax and enjoy the scenery, maybe you could keep it nice and steady, say, sixty?"

Although obviously disappointed, the young chauffeur agreed, suggesting for Michael's benefit of course, the scenic route home from Ayrshire via the A80 and Kincardine Bridge, rather than the M8 to the Forth Road Bridge.

The compromise suited them both; Michael recalled that this route would approach Rosyth from the High Road, giving him the opportunity to see the parts of the village he used to know so well.

The Pie was also now happy, sticking to sixty on the M8 motorway with a flying machine like his would be severely embarrassing, however, sixty on the bends between Kincardine and Rosyth would make the drive much more interesting.

With around one third of the ninety five mile journey completed, Michael relaxing in the knowledge that his driver was holding to their speed limit arrangement enquired about the situation in Rosyth.

Peter's response was sadly as expected. "Your mum's really upset, hardly spoken since it happened, Jamie seems okay though, but I don't think he really knows what's going on."

It was the Pie's innocent afterthought that initiated Michael's senses to the dreadful truth.

"But he does get a bit excited when the polis come to the house, they've hardly been away from your mother's since Saturday morning."

"What do the police have to do with it?"

"Oh Christ! Michael do you not know...? Your dad was murdered!"

Michael didn't know, and for a few seconds couldn't believe what he'd just heard. This realisation, now having been accepted by his brain, took a fraction longer to reach his responsive senses and for a moment he could do or say nothing but stare at the driver in disbelief.

Peter Andrews was now regretting allowing his mother to persuade him to be a chauffeur for the day. Why did he not have the sense to say nothing or even lied. Why should he have to be the one to take the brunt of what was now coming his way?

To his relief Michael didn't react as his stare had predicted. Slowly, quietly and with an unexpected calmness, he asked Peter to stop the car at the next lay-by.

Fortunately, for the now, extremely nervous driver, he didn't have to travel much further to oblige. As he switched off the engine, turning quickly towards his passenger, he stammered, "You all right Michael? I had no idea you didn't know, I didn't..."

"That's okay Peter, it's not your fault, now I want you to relax, take your time and tell me exactly what happened to my father, do you understand?" The Pie could not relax but he did understand. The cold determination of Michael's request had not failed to make its mark. This, combined with his physical appearance, particularly the previously noticed but now unmistakable scar, would ensure he would receive all the information desired. Peter, slowly and precisely relayed exactly every personally known fact of the recent tragic events in the Murdoch family's life.

Michael listened in silence, considering every word, every sentence, every traumatic detail.

He questioned Peter only once, requiring more information about Francis McLagan. Who, in the Pie's and seemingly everyone else's opinion, was as "Guilty as Sin."

"Okay Peter, I appreciate what you've just told me and I'm sorry you had to be the one to give me the news. Let's get home now, my mother and Jamie will be waiting."

The remainder of the journey, until they reached the outskirts of Rosyth, passed in almost total silence apart from the occasional curse from the Pie directed to other, less able motorists sharing their chosen route. Michael, to his chauffeur's relief, didn't utter a word, just sat with a tightly clenched fist supporting his chin and stared out of the passenger window.

Now clearly evident, around half a mile away, they looked down on the Park Housing Estate, an integral part of Michael's youth and the Pie's whole existence. Although the Park itself didn't appear to have changed much, a new estate now extended from it, encompassing at least four of the rich clay potato fields that once formed the pleasant, undulating landscape bounding his home.

He broke his silence. "The new scheme's some size Peter, must be three times as big as the Park."

"Aye, your dad forgot to stop." His chauffeur responded with a smile, now more relaxed in the knowledge that Michael seemed okay.

Michael did recall of-course that the construction of the new council estate had in fact started a few months before he'd left home, his father being appointed as charge hand of the No-Fine concrete shuttering squad. The rows of identical two storey terraced houses were obviously more modern in design than the pre-war brick-built scheme, but their white rendered concrete walls and red tiled roofs did not in any way compliment the grey rendered, blue slated colours of the more traditional Park Estate.

Peter obviously now happier in his company continued. "Aye, you'll no' believe it. Four years, six days a week your dad grafted on that job and no' a mention when it was done. The fucking Councillors, though, who didna'e lift a hammer, were in at the finish, queuing up to get the street names sorted out. Every bloody one of them called after themselves, Forbes Avenue, Dixon Way, Bryce Walk, Turner Road, McGonigle Place, every one of the lazy bastards' got his name on a street sign."

"I know what you mean, Peter, something similar once happened where I live."

They were now approaching the High Road's junction with Kings Road and as they got closer a second unexpected change came into view. "Peter what's happened to the Tradesman's Club, it looks as if it's been re-built?"

"Aye, it has. The old club was burnt to the ground five years ago; nothing left but the front steps. The rumour was that Tommy Robertson the Treasurer was cooking the books at the time and the fire got out of control. No' much of a building they put in its place, eh?"

The modern pre-fabricated, flat roofed structure they were now reaching was clearly nothing like the imposing stone building which for many years welcomed generations of Tradesmen, Pigeon Club Members and of-course their occasional signed in guests.

Noticing the flicker of a smile the Pie continued. "You know, Michael, for the six months it took to build the new club there were two thousand homeless men in Rosyth, Shelter was inundated!"

Michael did, as his smile suggested appreciate the humour of these comments, mainly as there probably was more than a grain of truth in them. He, however, now noticed another building which had formed a more important part of his development from boy to man.

Sitting uncomfortably on the waste-ground site to the rear of the Social Club was a large dilapidated wooden shed which, in his view, would have more benefited from a fire and subsequent re-build. "Surely, Bobby McClay's not still running the gym, Peter?"

Recalling his companion's past involvement with the shed, he replied instantly, "Aye Michael, the old bastard is, and you know, he still knocks hell out of the new boys."

Bobby McClay and the Kings Road Amateur Boxing Club had played a critical role in Michael's youth and the Pie's last comment brought back a long forgotten memory. Bobby's weeding out tactics for new boys, which once included himself, didn't follow the normally accepted appraisal techniques of slowly building up fitness, working on skills and then light sparring.

As a sixteen year old, turning up at the gym and nervously asking the flat-nosed, middle aged, ex professional to join the boxing club, his response had come as a shock. "Right son, gloves on, if you can last three minutes with me, you can come back to-morrow night."

Michael recalled with satisfaction that, although taking a pounding, he did survive the audition round and within two years reached the finals of the Scottish Amateur Championships. Unfortunately, although fighting his way to them, he was sitting on a rucksack at Toronto International Airport on the day they were held.

Peter, observing that his passenger now seemed to be engrossed in memories slowed the Escort as they travelled down Kings Road. "Maxi Clark still lives at Number 44, what the poor bugger's going to do now, without your dad, God knows. They were so close." His silent reaction to this casual but completely factual statement was a combined feeling of anger and guilt. Maxi was close to his father and so once was he.

Tam Murdoch's affections for both himself and Jamie were shared equally until, of-course, he refused to follow his older brother's footsteps through Rosyth Dockyard's gates. His father wanted him also to benefit from the security of a technician's apprenticeship. He, however, desperately wanted to follow Tam Murdoch's footsteps as a joiner, taking his chances on the construction sites and utilising the skills he had taught him.

During the erection of the new pigeon loft, Tam Murdoch teaching, Michael Murdoch eagerly learning and Jamie Murdoch playing football, the seeds of his career aspirations had been sown, he was his father's son.

Michael's anger now increased at the recollection of his desperate disappointment when his teacher refused to even consider this inherent desire. His feelings of guilt, however, were also increasing; it was not Maxi, Jamie, or his father who caused their once close family bond to shatter.

They had now turned into Park Crescent and it was the chauffeur's intention to drop his passenger outside Number 211, and then return to the lock-ups to garage the car. Michael decided differently, "Peter, I'd like to come with you, I want to see exactly where it happened. Then we'll walk home together, it's not far and I'm only carrying the hold-all, so it should be no problem."

Uncomfortable in his presumption that their visit to the garages was not likely to be the pleasantest part of their trip, Peter wanted to suggest an alternative proposal, which wouldn't involve him. Before, however, he could express his views they were abruptly interrupted. "Christ Michael, its McLagan!" He exclaimed in a shocked and now trembling voice. "The bastard was in jail yesterday, surely the polis didn't let him go?"

Although he didn't know McLagan, the Pie's earlier graphic description perfectly fitted the appearance of the tall, leather jacketed and extremely scruffy figure walking quickly into Park Crescent from the garages.

Michael, to his companion's surprise, did not react with the same degree of shocked indignation. He did, however, study every visible feature of the young man walking towards and now passing the Escort.

Francis McLagan did notice the car, but took little interest in its occupants. The events of the past four days now encompassed all his thoughts. The Pie, his clapped-out motor and some friend of his in the passenger seat were therefore of no consequence.

He was the centre of attention in Rosyth, and the recent re-establishment of this hard-man image now needed to be further enhanced, "as the bitch at home'll soon find out." His one real concern over the weekend had now been resolved; his search of the grass banking had been successful. "Stanley" was back where he belonged, safely tucked in his right hand pocket.

"Just keep driving, Peter." Michael insisted quietly, and then casually added, "By the way, where does McLagan live?"

Peter replied in a tone of disgust. "Number 11, stays with some wee hoor from Burnside. Knocks her about something terrible, but she'll no' leave him."

Michael didn't need all the information volunteered, just the address.

Having now left The Pie to garage the car, Michael slowly walked over to McCalls and Fletchers. He didn't stay long, there wasn't much to see, just two ordinary lock-ups with a gap in-between. He did notice, however, the thin layer of sawdust covering a small area of tarmac in front of Fletchers. To unsuspecting eyes a sensible precaution for an oil spill, to Michael's stare much more significant. Apart from that, no police, no flashing lights, no barrier tape. He turned away quickly, the evidence of his father's vain struggle for life, just a sprinkle of sawdust on the tarmac.

What had now become clear, however, in these few seconds, was Michael Murdoch's determination to conclude this matter to Tam Murdoch's satisfaction. He re-joined his waiting companion.

Although the Crescent now seemed narrower and the terraced houses even more compact than he recalled from his youth, it comforted him slightly that this part of his old neighbourhood had not really changed. Neat privet hedges securing, in most cases, equally neat front gardens.

The Pie said his good-byes at No. 217. He had not enjoyed his drive as much as anticipated. However, he could now return to the security of his home and inform his mother of the day's traumatic events. Hopefully, after hearing them, she would agree that there was no-way he was taking the big Canadian back to Prestwick!

Michael instinctively gazed skywards when he heard the distinctive wing beat of the team of racing pigeons circling his home. He quickly calculated approximately twenty, Reds, Blues, Mealys and the odd White-splashed Pied. *My God*, he thought, *Jamie's kept them fit.* Knowing of-course that although these particular birds were not the originals from years ago, they would probably still be related in someway to the team that Murdoch Brothers once raced.

Slipping the bolt on the wooden slatted gate, Michael entered the garden of his old home. He didn't knock, just slowly turned the doorknob and walked in. As he entered the tidy narrow lounge he called softly "Mum it's me.... Michael."

Mary Murdoch hurried through from the adjoining kitchen, apron tied around her waist, dish-towel tightly gripped in both hands and tears flowing freely down her cheeks. She hesitated for a moment, as if having to confirm the reality of his presence, before moving slowly towards him, freeing a hand from her dishtowel and clasping his arm gently.

Despite having attempted to prepare his emotions for their re-union he now felt as helpless as a child and for an instant relied solely on his mother's grasp to keep him steady.

Her soft voice, however, immediately refocused his strength. "Yes, you're home, Michael, we've been waiting so long for you, but you're here now, and that's all that matters." She didn't need to say more - her tears were enough.

The passing years since she packed his rucksack for Canada had taken their toll. His mother seemed smaller, frailer and her once dark hair now a shock of white. The anxieties he had caused by his absence had obviously contributed to this ageing process. Michael, now acutely aware of this quietly confirmed his intentions. "Don't worry mum, I know what's happened and I know what I've put you through, I'm going to stay for as long as it takes to get us through this, we're still a family. You, Jamie and me."

Noticing his words had encouraged the trace of a smile he continued, "Now what about a cup of tea and a digestive biscuit?" To his relief this brought out a full smile and a stop to her tears. "You haven't changed, Michael, you young rascal, you still know how to cheer me up." Wiping her eyes with the towel she continued. "Have a seat at the window son and after your tea you can go out to see Jamie, he'll be so pleased you're back."

His lack of sleep over the past three days, the Pie's traumatic news and now the re-union with his mother, were beginning to have their inevitable effects. Michael accepted, however, that he must face this final task. Sitting in the pigeon loft at the bottom of the back garden, Jamie would be waiting for him. He had left his brother there, fifteen years ago, unable to cope then with the consequences of his actions. Could he now deal with the awful reality?

Aware of her son's obvious discomfort, Mary brought the tea and biscuits through from the kitchen without further mention of Jamie.

The view from his chair at the rear lounge window had not altered from his youth. The pigeon loft looked as if he and his father had built it only yesterday, every part of it carefully assembled from the spare wood retrieved at nightfall from the new scheme.

Following precise instructions from their father, he and Jamie, knowing the exact location of the materials required, had happily transferred them from the building site to their back garden. They also, of-course, knew the exact location of the night watchman between nine and eleven p.m. in the Tradesman's Club, signed in by Tam Murdoch. In Michael's view, building a pigeon loft for his sons, for the price of a few pints, would have given his father more satisfaction than seeing his name on any street sign.

He left the digestive biscuits untouched and, although welcomed, the tea had not removed the dryness from his throat. As he got up to leave the lounge he saw, still sitting proudly in its corner, the old mahogany display cabinet, its polished surface shining. Taking pride of place on the top shelf, Jamie's football trophies, team photographs and medals.

Five years ago, with great effort, he had re-united Jake Matthew's with his sporting glories and ten years before that, without any effort, he'd separated Jamie from his.

As he walked towards the loft, forcing his eyes from the concrete path, he heard his brother whistling gently to the birds inside, innocent witnesses to the partnership's imminent re-union. He slid open the door and spoke quietly to Jamie sitting on his bench in the corridor opposite the old bird compartment. "Hello... Jamie it's me... Michael... how are you?"

His brother turned towards him slowly, and replied with a wide grin. "Michael! Guess what? The Old Pieds back! Will it win a medal, Michael? Will it win a medal?"

Michael sat down beside him and grasped his hand. They were now back together sharing their bench in the pigeon loft.

Jamie Murdoch, the eldest, with a comforting arm wrapped around his young brother's shoulder, wondering why Michael was crying.

CHAPTER 7

There was something comforting in placing three plates on the dining table. It seemed to indicate a return to routine, a return to normality. Mary Murdoch, however, would never forget Detective Inspector Miller's visit to the house during the early hours of Saturday morning. In a way she was glad it had been Ian Miller who delivered the devastating news, he had grown up in the neighbourhood with her sons, and despite having severely disappointed her with his choice of wife, had remained a good friend to Jamie.

The nervous tone and genuine emotion in his voice relayed all the information she'd expected. Tam would not be coming home. "Mrs. Murdoch - Mary, I'm afraid you'll have to prepare yourself for the worst. We've found Tam's body in the garages!"

The reality of it didn't fully set-in until breakfast, when she realised that one of the three plates automatically taken from the cupboard had to be returned.

Now, only a few days later, preparing a meal for three again seemed right, she accepted that her husband wouldn't be sitting at the table, however, both her sons would. The worst was over and she knew her strength would return now that Michael was home, his first few words had confirmed what she needed to hear. They were still a family and would get through this together.

Mary looked out to the loft and recalled how both boys used to annoy her so intensely if they were late for their meals. Inevitably it was due to the pigeons, particularly on race days, unwilling to leave the garden until their first bird was safely home and its rubber race ring in the clock. They would then relax and come indoors, Michael would attempt to sweeten her with apologies and compliments about her vegetable soup, Jamie would annoy her further by springing up from the table every time another bird landed.

True to form, she was once again waiting for them, but this time she was far from annoyed. Although deliberately encouraging him to visit the pigeon loft so soon after he had arrived, she had shared Michael's anxiety as she watched him slowly walking to meet his older brother. She knew Jamie would take their re-union in his stride, but could Michael at last cope with the situation? Tam hadn't, and his bitterness, although silent, had pervaded their existence since. It couldn't continue now he was gone.

In a way, she had prepared for this moment since packing her son's rucksack fifteen years before. She had accepted even then that, sadly, it would not occur while her husband influenced their lives.

This bitterness had first revealed itself during Doctor Young's visit two months after the accident. He had called to update them on Jamie's condition and his news, although delivered in a more experienced, calmer manner, had the same dreadful effect as Ian Millers did three days ago. "Well, Mrs. Murdoch - Tam, I'm afraid it's as we expected. Although Jamie's physical recovery, since he came out of coma, is progressing satisfactorily, the extent of internal haemorrhage has impaired a substantial degree of brain function, which, unfortunately, we must now accept, is permanent."

Mary recalled how her husband had received the information in silence; head in hands, unable or unwilling to utter a response. She, although visibly more upset had to enquire further, desperate for at least some glimmer of hope.

The Doctor's response only increased their torment. "I'm afraid Mrs. Murdoch; the psychological examinations carried out have confirmed that Jamie's intellectual capacity is now reduced to that of a six-year- old. This may of-course improve slightly with time. However, we must accept that this is not hopeful."

It was his next contribution, added as an attempt to lessen their burden of grief that stirred Tam into replying. "Take your time to think about it, but I can assure you both, that if required, arrangements can be made to accommodate Jamie at Springwells, even on a short-stay basis."

Rising from his chair, his large frame physically shaking, he spoke slowly. "Doctor Young, we appreciate you coming here, not many would nowadays, and telling us straight, but my son will not be going near Springwells, or anywhere else like it! Do you understand Doctor? Jamie will stay here with me and Mary for as long as we're fit to look after him."

Having been their family doctor for many years, he understood perfectly. "Fine, Mr. Murdoch, but remember we're here to assist in any way possible. Jamie should be ready to return home in around ten days, and I sincerely wish you and Mary all the best. Bye-the-way, how is young Michael coping? It's extremely important that he is encouraged to come to terms with what has occurred."

It was then that her husband, immediately and without further comment, left the room.

Mary accurately predicted two facts from their conversation with the Doctor and Tam's reaction. Jamie would not experience life again, beyond the capacity of a child and her husband would never allow Michael to come to terms with it.

The three-quarters of an hour he'd now spent with his older brother in the pigeon loft however, was very encouraging. Although desperately keen to know all about his life in Canada, she appreciated that this would have to wait until later. She had also noticed the tiredness in her son's eyes as he had sat staring out to the loft. She would therefore call them in before the potatoes boiled dry give them their dinner and afterwards encourage Michael to get some rest.

She had been patiently awaiting his information for so long, another few hours delay was now of no great consequence, especially as, apart from the tiredness and that nasty scar on his temple, he looked so well and strong.   This, added to the positive indicators she had received from Betty in Toronto, convinced Mary that her son, encouraged, of-course, by herself, had made the correct decision to leave 211 Park Crescent, a home at that time which didn't fully welcome him.

Mary Murdoch's desire for her youngest son to reconcile himself would, however, never be totally achieved.   To his despair Michael had realised this as soon as Jamie spoke.   Although physically sound, built much like himself, it was clearly evident that, in every other respect, he would remain as he had left him.

After a few minutes, however, in each others company his brother succeeded with child-like understanding and genuine affection to at least allow Michael to partially accept the inevitable.   He would now, at last, have to take the responsibilities for his actions. His mother, he knew, had the strength to continue, but how could she alone, look after Jamie?

In his present state of fatigue the task seemed daunting but he was determined to somehow succeed.   His family's future well being would be secured and whoever murdered his father would not escape justice. Michael Murdoch's justice, if possible

In their short time together Jamie revealed clearly the one essential factor which had filled the yawning gap between his child-like mind and adult being. His racing pigeons. Although Michael and his father had failed to come to terms with the situation Jamie, through his pigeons, had succeeded.

Despite his severe disability, his management of the loft and control of the occupants could not be surpassed.   His affinity for the birds was fully reciprocated. They loved their master and with no hesitation, at his request, flew confidently from their wooden perches to his side, pecking gently at his fingers until he released one of his handful of peanuts.

From where they sat on their bench in the middle of the narrow corridor, each of the two compartments making up the interior of the loft were in full view. Jamie didn't need to leave the bench to proudly present each pigeon to his brother, he just whistled softly, and they dutifully flew to his side, unperturbed even by a stranger's presence. Then, without effort or fuss, he picked them up in turn and gently handed one after another to his brother for closer inspection, introducing each one by name and to Michael's amazement, without looking, also by ring number.

It was now clear to Michael that the present family of birds still originated from the first racing pigeons Jamie and he started the sport with years before.   He could recognise, from their shape and colour, great grand children from the ten original racing pigeons brought home by their father nineteen years earlier.

Their interest had been initiated by accident, following the rescue of a white fantailed dove, from the clutches of a neighbour's cat. Where this pigeon came from they never confirmed. Not of-course that they made many enquiries, it was beautiful and it was now theirs.

Tam, thinking that the boys would soon lose the dove and therefore interest in their new hobby, didn't mind the temporary alterations to his tool shed. The window could easily be replaced and the wire mesh cage now protruding precariously from its gable would take approximately three hammer blows to remove, when their passing phase had finally passed.

The dove, to his surprise and to the boys' delight, did not disappear when they nervously opened the cage and gave it its freedom. After a week's captivity and the contents of two packets of split peas and barley borrowed from their mother's now depleting stock of vegetable soup ingredients, it had obviously decided that staying in a tool shed with two such attentive owners was better than being eaten by a cat. Added to this was the fact that its experience with the now coincidentally missing feline had resulted in its main flight feathers being lost and until these re-grew it couldn't fly, even to the house roof.

Within two weeks it shared its cage with a new companion, the smallest, ugliest runt of a feral pigeon imaginable. This fellow founding member of the Murdoch brother's colony having been captured at some considerable effort and risk from the ruins of a nearby farm building. To their father's further surprise it also happily took up residence in the caged extension to the tool shed, too young to fly-off and also having been immediately adopted by the white dove.

Within three months the boys had converted half the shed into a pigeon loft and eight birds of extremely doubtful pedigree graced its interior.

Jamie and Michael thought they were superb until the loft was visited by a racing pigeon. Lost on its journey home from a race, exhausted and starving it landed on the shed roof with their own birds and soon entered its temporary refuge. Even in its obvious state of distress it stood out from their own. Blue colouring with two distinctive black bars on each wing, two rings, one metal, one rubber and the most intelligent eyes and proud head they had seen in any bird.

Although only staying for a few days until regaining enough strength to fly home, its almost regal-like presence, compared to even the dove, convinced Tam Murdoch's sons that racing pigeons were their future.

Their father, eventually accepting this as fact, also observing with some pleasure that this interest was creating a close bond between both boys, relented. Racing pigeons it would be, and he knew where to get the best.

He was presently working on the final phase of a housing development on the outskirts of Dundee and one of the local lads he had taken into his squad talked of nothing else except he and his father's prowess with their team of long distance birds. They had apparently won every top prize going, particularly in races from France, including the Scottish Nationals from Rennes and Nantes.

Tam, although only having a very limited knowledge of the sport, quickly realised from their conversations that this level of achievement was extremely good. Pigeons flying to Dundee that could win at National level, in races from France, against competition from all over Scotland, including the Borders, had what it takes.

As soon as he'd mentioned his sons' interest in Pigeon keeping and described the somewhat less than quality occupants of his now converted tool shed, young Jim McMurchie enthusiastically concurred with the boys desires. "They'll need to get rid of every bloody one of them! Keep the fan-tail if they like, as a pet, but tell them no' to breed off it --they want racing pigeons, Tam, no' bloody street vermin!"

Within the week a deal was struck, ten youngsters from McMurchie and Sons best breeding stock. In return unlimited overtime for Jim McMurchie until the job was wrapped up, weekends at double-time, even if he didn't turn out on race Saturdays.

Around two months later the Murdoch brothers were sitting on the front door step impatiently awaiting their father's arrival home with their future racing stock. When the works van eventually dropped him off at the gate, to their disappointment he got out of the passenger's seat with only his piece box. To their delight, however, he then immediately stepped to the rear of the Transit, opened the back door, removed the cardboard box and shouted farewell to the driver. "Six -o'clock. tomorrow, no' quarter past, you lazy bugger!"

The driver smiled, nodded his acceptance of the foreman's instruction and drove off.

Michael vividly recalled the pleasure he and Jamie experienced in placing the box in the tool shed and nervously opening the lid just wide enough to peer inside and remove each young pigeon one by one.

Tam didn't join them. He'd been given a preview of each bird in the site hut a few hours earlier and he knew his sons wouldn't be disappointed. Although he would never admit it openly, even to Mary, sitting at the table with his soup that Summer's evening, watching the boys through the window, the delight on their faces clearly visible as they carried the box carefully to the tool shed, was one of the proudest moments he could remember.

If it was possible their pleasure increased as each of the ten birds were revealed and carefully examined firstly by Jamie, then passed to Michael before being allowed to accompany the loft's only other occupant, the white dove. The other former inhabitants having been transported to Dundee in the same cardboard box at 6.15a.m. that morning. As expected, on release at the building site, they hadn't attempted to tackle the forty miles home and were last seen by Tam and his colleagues heading north towards Dundee City Centre.

The loft, however, was now happily occupied once again and the quality of these young racing pigeons amazed both of them. Their father had been true to his word. These were the best, four Blues, just like the stray racer, two Reds, one with a single white feather on each wing, a Mealy, a beautiful Pied Checker and two plain Checkers, similar to the Pied but without the distinctive white head and wings.

Although the Checkers were similar in colour to ordinary Street pigeons these were in a completely different league. Yes, these birds were quality, their potential obvious; the racing partnership of Murdoch Brothers had arrived. Now they just needed to persuade their father to build them a bigger and better pigeon loft!

Almost nineteen years later, examining each of the present occupants of the new loft, it was obvious to Michael that the basic family of pigeons obtained by his father had changed very little.

The quality if anything had been even further enhanced by the selective introduction of a few new birds over the years. Not so many as would dilute the original stock's influence but just enough to ensure the progression of their strain, which would have otherwise been depleted due to continuous in-breeding.

Michael now realised that although Jamie had looked after these birds extremely well, he couldn't, alone have co-ordinated and controlled the demanding stock management required to achieve this end. He also was obviously not capable of the organisational skills required for racing the birds, arranging for training and all the paperwork and money etc. essential for club fees and race entries. Although Jamie had played an extremely important role, Tam Murdoch's influence was self-evident.

Accepting rather reluctantly that his father's involvement in their sport had been necessary to allow Jamie to continue, Michael now took some pleasure in observing that the pigeon loft he had shared in erecting had faired as well as its occupants, once again with the minimum of change.

The two compartments, which faced the corridor where they sat, were secured in front by wood slatted sliding doors. The left-most compartment was still provided with the bank of nesting boxes he had carefully assembled and secured to the rear wall. Each of the dozen boxes having removable doweled fronts with a small hinged door which, when opened, lay horizontal providing access to the box and a perch for one of the happily mated pairs. In the corner of every box a clay straw-filled nest bowl each occupied at present by the cock birds taking their dutiful and paternal obligation to brood and protect both eggs.

The compartment to their right had no nest boxes. Instead, rows of smaller square wooden perches each just large enough for one bird to roost in comfort. Again Michael noticed that this compartment had also not changed since he helped build these perches so many years before. It was presently empty, awaiting the return of the young-bird team, which were still enjoying the freedom of the sky above Park Crescent.

In time Jamie would also proudly introduce these youngsters to his brother. However, at the moment the last and best of the old birds were patiently awaiting their turn to pass inspection and receive a peanut. "Red Hen SU/86/F2365, Good one. Michael - good one! - Won two big prizes, good one, eh - Michael?"

Michael had to agree, they were all bloody good ones, and there was no doubt it was Jamie's love and caring that had brought out the best in them. They handled perfectly, apple bodies exuding fitness, tight feathers, bright eyes and beautiful bold intelligent heads. The last two, although not in such peak condition were sheer class. The Old Pied Cock, which had only arrived home from France two hours before, although clearly showing signs of its three day sojourn, with Jamie's care, would soon regain its strength and match the condition of the rest. Body weight radically reduced, feathers loose and feet covered in dirt, when released from Michael's hands, the old plodder proudly strutted across the loft floor reasserting its status as boss of the Murdoch team.

"SU/80/F3500 - Old Pied Cock" Jamie confirmed with justified pride, "always comes home, he'll win a big prize next time, won't he Michael?"

"I hope so Jamie," he replied sympathetically, hoping that he could maybe later persuade his brother to retire the old stager from the perils of long distance racing.

"SU/85/F5866 - good one Michael, best one we've got, - dad's wee Mealy Hen!"

For the first time since they were re-united, Michael noticed that his brother's grin had disappeared. "It's okay, Jamie, dad's gone, but I'm home now and we'll be fine, you me and mum."

"A bad man killed dad and broke the clock, Michael. A bad man, and that Ian Miller, he wouldn't give me it back! The wee Mealy won Sartilly and I couldn't time her in. Ian Miller wouldn't give me the clock back. - Will you get it Michael? Will you get it?"

"Okay, Jamie, don't worry, I'll get it back," he replied, gently grasping his brothers shaking hand.

Michael was now extremely confused. He was not yet aware of the Mealy Hen's return from France on Saturday evening, a full thirty minutes before any bird in Fife. Nor did he know of the combined despair Jamie had to contend with, his father's murder and the Mealy Hen returning with no pigeon clock to time her in.

The confusion was further increased with the mention of Ian Miller. He'd been Jamie's best friend for many years, what was his involvement in all this?

Michael placed his father's favourite pigeon back on the loft floor, not having the time or inclination to admire it fully due to his brother's obvious distress. He must quickly change the subject; get back to something more comfortable for both of them. "Jamie, do you remember, just after we started keeping the pigeons, that beautiful Blue Racer that strayed into the tool shed, wasn't it special? Got us hooked on the Racers."

Whether it was Jamie's present state of anxiety or genuine memory loss, to Michael's disappointment, he could not remember this all so significant event of their youth. Following, however, some seconds of strained concentration he gave an excited response, "Aye, Michael, Champion Blue Boy! EHU/85/X2220, best racer in the whole world, worth two million pounds!" To his brother's now increasing distress he continued, "It was my fault Michael, dad told me to keep him in, but I forgot, silly bugger! And let him out with the young birds. Buggered off home, Michael, he buggered off home!"

His mother's call for their dinner couldn't have been better timed.

Mary Murdoch quickly resolved her youngest son's confusion during the short time it took Jamie to wash his hands in the bathroom upstairs. The pigeon clock had been found with Tam and was therefore taken by Ian Miller, now Detective Inspector Miller, as evidence. Seemingly, it had stopped during the attack and was of crucial importance to the police investigation. Although it was of no significance to the current Murdoch family traumas, Mary further explained, with an unusually bitter tone, how this was the second time Ian had taken something precious from her eldest boy. "I don't blame Ian, though, but she didn't wait around long after the accident, four months and then off she went with him, and poor Jamie and her were getting engaged."

The last thing Michael needed was this additional information. Linda hadn't caused the chaos in their young lives, he had, and at least she'd lasted four months, he, his only brother, had fled long before that.

Regretting instantly what she'd said, his mother retreated to the kitchen realising, from Michael's look of despair, that he still carried his burden so heavily and any words of comfort now would be to no avail. Fortunately, for both of them, Jamie entered the room his grin fully retrieved. "I remembered the Blue stray, Michael and the fantail. Good ones Michael! Good ones! But not as good as Champion Blue Boy, he's the best in the world!"

CHAPTER 8

"Peter. I'll not tell you again, its ten past nine and if you're not down here in two minutes, Fluff gets your kipper!"

The Pie now had no choice, the old witch meant what she said, and he was convinced his mother would prefer to give it to the cat anyway. "I'll no' give her the pleasure," he mumbled as he reluctantly left the comforts of his bed. "And why does she call every cat she's had fucking Fluff?"

Peter Andrews had always detested his mother's cats. In his view the lazy buggers, particularly this one, received much more attention than he did.

A smile came to his face however as he recalled the disappearance of her first cat all those years ago. Four months of bliss until she gave up waiting and bought another. Maybe now that Michael was back, the place would become Fluffless again for a while until, of-course, the next edition arrived.

Ina Andrews' morning routine was progressing satisfactorily, up at seven, washing out, vacuuming completed, breakfast made and that idle boy of hers at last moving himself. Now just Fluff to be fed. "Poor wee soul you'd have loved that kipper."

To their mutual annoyance, before the cat's tin could be opened, the bell rang. She opened the door abruptly; intending to ensure that whoever was disturbing her at this time of day would soon realise their folly.

For an instant she was startled into silence. "Hello, Mrs. Andrews, it's Michael, Michael Murdoch, I hope I haven't called too early? I just came to thank you and Peter for everything."

Quickly regaining her composure she replied, "Not at all Michael, in you come, you know you're always welcome here, no matter how early in the day."

Mary Murdoch's boy was no longer the young rascal who gave her son that terrible nickname and was suspected of being involved with the disappearance of her first cat. *If this is what Canada does for them,* she decided, *young Peter had better get on the next plane!.* Have a seat, Michael, my... you've changed, such a handsome man now. How's your poor mother and Jamie?"

"They're okay Mrs. Andrews. Mum hasn't had the chance to thank you personally, so I called on her behalf. Is Peter at home?"

Peter was home; he'd however recognised the voice of his mother's visitor on his way downstairs and immediately returned quietly to the security of his bedroom. "If that big bastard thinks I'm driving him around again all day for nothing, he's got no chance!"

When, eventually, he reluctantly emerged, following another, "I'll not tell you again", from his mother, he was to receive a pleasant surprise. "Peter, I've told Michael you don't want a thing for yesterday, and it's far too much anyway, but he won't take no for an answer, so say thank you very much, Peter."

"Thanks, Michael, Jesus, a hundred notes. New exhaust system no problem! Anytime you want a driver, Michael, I'm your man!"

"Now Peter", his mother interrupted, "you and I will away into the kitchen and let Michael phone Canada in peace. Take as long as you like, Michael, and don't think of leaving any more money, you've been far too generous, as it is."

Assuring her that the call wouldn't take more than a few minutes, he dialled the Cascade. This somehow seemed more of a duty than a pleasure.

"Hi, Mabel, are you missing me?"

"Sure am, Mike, why in God's name did you allow that old fool to run the bar? He thinks he still owns the place."

"Now Mabel," he replied with a chuckle. "That's no way to talk about your husband. How is Jake anyway?"

"He's a wreck; I'm suing him for divorce, so I'll be free to marry you!" "Mike, how's your family?" her tone now serious.

"They're fine, but I'm going to stay with them for a while, there's a lot to get sorted out, a few weeks should do it, will you manage?"

Michael didn't need her positive reply to convince him that the Cascade would survive without him. Her answer to his next enquiry, however, resulted in a strange sensation of relief tinged with guilt. "No, she finished around midnight and went for a drive."

He paused for a moment. "Okay, will you let her know I phoned and could you remind John to represent me at the Tourist Association Meeting next week?"

"Sure Mike, but he doesn't need any reminders, he's been working on his speech since you left."

Although Michael laughed he was all too aware that Mabel's sarcasm was well placed. His junior partner moulded and encouraged by himself now benefited from the enthusiasm he had lost. Tammy, unfortunately, was probably on the same wavelength.

As he concluded his discussion with Mabel, in her capacity as his personal accountant, Michael pictured his girlfriend driving along the mountain roads, listening attentively to John rehearsing his speech. Strangely the thought didn't create feelings of anger or jealousy, only guilt passed through his mind; it wasn't just the Cascade he had slowly lost interest in. Difficult decisions would have to be made on his return to Banff, however uncomfortable for both of them.

Secure in the knowledge that her visitor was now closing the garden gate behind him, Ina Andrews, ignoring her son's complaints, immediately deducted fifty pounds from his recently acquired car maintenance fund. "Did you hear that Peter? Represent him at the Tourist Association. And would you believe how much money he's having sent over? Mary Murdoch's son. And that poor woman's no' even got a telephone!"

Relieved that his first task had been completed with relative ease, Michael felt slightly more relaxed as he walked towards the new scheme. He must, as promised, try to get the pigeon clock back, and perhaps he could persuade Jamie's old friend to reveal more to him than the "investigations are continuing" response given to his mother.

Carefully following Mrs. Andrews's eagerly relayed directions to 189 Forbes Avenue, the ten-minute walk through the housing estate his father had built, further concentrated his determination to seek some answers.

He was at least rid of the weariness, which had yesterday curtailed his capacity for clear thought. A sound sleep in his old bedroom had resolved that inconvenience. Not that it now resembled anything like the room he remembered from his youth. Recalling how apologetic his mother had been last night when she showed him the fold-down bed that now took up temporary residence in her husband's study.

Apart from the view overlooking the back garden and pigeon loft, everything else in this small apartment had changed out of recognition. Gone were any reminders of his own past. His father had obviously seen to that, probably soon after he had left for Canada.

Now, in place of his own memories, Tam Murdoch's presence was everywhere. Armchair and hand-built bureau at the window. Framed photographs of Murdoch and Sons favourite pigeons, proudly decorating the opposite wall; including, of-course, the wee Mealy Hen, taking up centre position. Constructed with similar expertise and care as the bureau, a beautiful piranha pine trophy cabinet adorned the corner facing the door, displaying the impressive array of silverware associated with their success. Although of no great surprise his disappointment deepened when he failed to identify any trophies, and there had been a few, won by Murdoch Brothers.

Interrupting these thoughts his mother spoke quietly. "He spent so much time in here Michael, sometimes with Jamie, but mostly he liked his own company. He used to say it gave him the chance to think in peace. What he was always thinking about I don't know, but I'm sure it was often you."

"Maybe, mum, and maybe not." He retorted instantly. "But he certainly showed his opinion of me clearly enough! Not even a trophy left with my name on it."

Realising that any further attempts to relieve her son's bitterness would be unsuccessful, she left him silently examining his father's library.

He now realised how intense Tam Murdoch's interest in racing pigeons had become. Dozens of books neatly filled each of the white pine shelves, without exception, referring to the same subject. He didn't remove any, unwilling to disturb the orderly rows. Below the books, two wider shelves containing large ring binders with his father's handwriting on the spines describing the contents of each.

"Race Results - Rosyth P.C." "Race Results - Fife Federation." "Breeding Programme - 1973 -88." As he expected, every last detail of Murdoch and eldest son's involvement in the sport, in precise chronological order. Just the way Tam Murdoch liked things. Everything in its proper place, newspaper at his chair, meals on time, his sons following his pre-planned future, everything neat and tidy, just like this room.

He picked up the binder containing this year's monthly Racing Pigeon Pictorials, recalling how he used to admire the photographs and eagerly devour every word of their glossy pages. Flicking through several until he came to the latest edition. Gracing the full front cover for July, Jamie's "Blue Boy". Now at least he knew why his brother kept going on about this particular pigeon. It might not be quite worth two million pounds but in winning four nationals in a row, it had to be the best in the world.

As he admired the beauty of this Long Distance Champion his sympathies strayed towards his brother, a fully-grown man stranded with the imagination of a child.

Mrs. Andrews's description of Ian and Linda Miller's home was as accurate as her directions. He saw it almost immediately after turning into Forbes Avenue from Dixon Way.

Michael hadn't failed to notice other bought houses as he walked through the still predominantly council owned estate. It amused him to see how each of the new owners had attempted to change the appearance of their properties to make them look private.

24 Bryce Walk had its oak panelled door with brass accessories.

120 McGonigle Place, double, lead inlaid, glazing.

30 Dixon Way, sandstone roughcasting with matching leyandii hedge.

189 Forbes Avenue, everything the other three had with the addition of a dormer extension to the roof.

Although, in itself, obviously more impressive than its near neighbours, it seemed just a little too pretentious. Perhaps, he thought, when the rest of the houses in its terraced row were purchased by their tenants and improved, the Miller residence would blend in a bit better or maybe, unless Ian has changed, that's when the Millers would sell-up and move.

Linda opened the door before he could reach for the brass knocker.

Although obviously older and perhaps even slimmer than he remembered, she was still the Linda Morrison who had arrived all these years ago at the Murdoch home, arm in arm with Jamie. His brother adorned in his off-white three-piece suit, with favourite floral tie and his fiancée to-be, shyly but unsuccessfully hiding her beauty behind those gorgeous auburn locks.

She now masked her nervousness behind a welcoming smile. "Michael Murdoch! I knew it was you as soon as I saw you coming round the corner."

Michael kissed her on the cheek and followed her into the freshly re-decorated lounge. "Beautiful home Linda, were you expecting me?"

"We like it Michael, it's been hard work, especially for Ian but we're getting there now.   Just the conservatory to build at the back.   And of course we were expecting you, Ian thought you'd be paying us a visit at some stage, but it was the phone-call from Ina Andrews that pin-pointed exactly when."

Their laughter relieved some of the discomfort they both had tried to hide at the doorstep.

"Apart from your hairstyle, Linda you haven't changed a bit, still as pretty as ever."

"Of-course I have," she responded happily, enjoying his hopefully honest compliment. "Fifteen years and two children have made sure of that!"

As they passed under the alcove, which separated the lounge from the rear dining area, Linda directed him to a chair at the window.   Explaining, in a now distinctly nervous tone, that while she made them a coffee he could keep an eye on "those two rascals playing in the back garden" To ensure, however, that their conversation was not interrupted she, immediately on entering the adjoining kitchen, opened the sliding door of the serving hatch.   "De-caffe or regular, Michael?"

During her next appearance at the hatch she took the opportunity to express the Miller family's sincere condolences. "Your dad was so well respected, Michael, he didn't deserve...well you know what I'm trying to say."

Acknowledging his appreciation of her kind words and also noticing she'd said "respected" instead of "liked", he changed the subject. "Linda, I was so surprised when I heard Ian was a policeman, I'd really like to thank him for the way he's dealt with things over the past few days, it's been a real comfort for Mum and Jamie."

Her response was as welcome as the coffee she now served. "Ian won't want any thanks until this is all over and he'll probably tell you that himself when he comes downstairs."

Observing that her husband's presence in the house had obviously come as a pleasant surprise to her guest, Linda continued in explaining how difficult the past few days had been for Detective Inspector Miller.   "He's hardly been home since it happened; he's so determined to find out whoever would do such a terrible thing. You know, Michael, he didn't get to bed till two this morning, that's why I haven't disturbed him, but he's getting picked up at ten so I'd better make breakfast, not that he's eating much at the moment."

On her return to the kitchen Michael took the opportunity to admire the skills being displayed by the two young lads playing headers on the drying green. Although his view was partially restricted by a row of washing, the proficiency, particularly of the tallest, in keeping the ball in the air, was most impressive.

He didn't spill his coffee however until the ball bounced out of play towards the house.   For a few seconds he couldn't move just stared open-mouthed at the blond haired youth running to retrieve it.

Linda was at his side in an instant frantically wiping the stain from the arm of his chair.

Although he now found the ability to stand, the power of speech didn't return until she grasped his arm tightly, re-affirming the reality of the situation. "Is it that obvious? I hoped you'd have forgotten what Jamie looked like at that age, he's a good lad, Michael, brilliant with a football, Ian's so proud of him."

"D...does Jamie know about this Linda?"

She had anticipated his response, its abrupt delivery, however, took her by surprise, her voice now shaking with anger and guilt. "No. And we haven't told Daniel either, but your mother certainly knows, she hasn't spoken to me, since he was born!"

It was only when he was standing immediately behind them that they became aware of Ian's presence. Both turning instinctively, their mutual discomfort clearly apparent.

"I can assure you Michael, when we're confident Daniel's ready, he'll be told, but not before then. Do you understand?"

The visitor smiled and responded with a warm handshake. "Of-course I understand Ian, it just came as such a shock, I honestly had no idea. How are you? Linda tells me you've been working so hard."

Linda quickly ushered them away from the window. "I've a table to set for breakfast, so the pair of you better away through to the lounge and have a blether."

Taking their places in the brown leather armchairs at either side of the ornate log effect fire, Ian seemed smaller than he remembered him and his waistline distinctly thicker. The most surprising change, however, was his now obviously receding hairline and the silvery grey streaks intermingled with what remained of his once dark mass. It was the policeman, however, who took the opportunity to pass comment on his guest's appearance. "Well Michael, I see from the scar you didn't give up the fighting after you left."

Conscious that an honest reply wouldn't suggest the image he was keen to portray, Michael hoped the cheerful tone of his lie would confirm its authenticity. "Trust a detective to come to that conclusion! No, Ian, that was nothing to do with fighting, just an accident at work." Noting no immediate response, he continued. "We all change with time, who'd have imagined Ian Miller becoming a policeman, and a Detective Inspector no less?"

"Yes, I suppose you're right, Michael, I was just saying to Linda the other day, apart from me and yourself, of-course, the rest of the lads from the scheme ended up in the Dockyard and most of them have been made redundant now. By the way, how do you earn a living? I know you were always keen to be a joiner."

This was not the time to disappoint, explaining truthfully how, despite considerable effort, his desire to take up his father's trade had, unfortunately, been unsuccessful. "So after a short career as a bin-man in Toronto, I moved to a place called Banff in Alberta, picked up a job in a bar and I've been there ever since." As he spoke Michael noticed Ian relaxing further into his armchair, obviously now enjoying the company of a lesser achiever than himself. "It's good to see you've done so well Ian, beautiful home, Linda and the kids, and dressed as if you're on your way to a boardroom meeting."

Any fears that Ian's police training and career enhancement may have resulted in positive benefits to his character, fortunately proved groundless. To Michael's satisfaction he was as vain as he remembered him in his youth, responding with increasing enthusiasm to every compliment. "Yes, and as far as the meeting I'm holding this morning is concerned, they'll soon find out who's chairman of the board! I'm gathering my whole incident team together for a full briefing on the case. This one's important to me Michael, and although I can't reveal details of my investigation, I can assure you I will not rest, nor will my lads, until the bastards are behind bars!"

Tempting, as it was, to immediately pursue the detail of the investigation he had, in fact, just revealed, Michael instead freely expressed his gratitude and complete confidence in Ian and his colleagues, adding that his main concern was to re-unite Jamie with his pigeon clock.

"Unfortunately, at this moment in time, that's one thing I can't do Michael. As I've explained to your mum, we need the clock for evidence."

Ian didn't need a verbal reply. The look of abject dismay on his visitor's face removed any lingering doubts. Jamie's young brother would not interfere with the case; his priorities were obviously limited to lesser achievements for his family. "Leave it with me Michael; I'll have a word with Jock Turner, the Club Secretary. I'm sure one of the members will have a spare clock, don't worry, I'll not let Jamie down."

Neither will I, Michael thought, as his smile returned.

Apart from responding with the occasional nod of agreement, he made little contribution to the conversation available in the remaining few minutes before Ian's breakfast. Content to listen to the success story of a Detective Inspector until Linda requested her husband's presence at the dining table.

Michael politely refused another coffee and took this opportunity to say his farewells, thanking them again both for their kindness. He waited until Ian was accompanying him to the door before pursuing his final question, delivering it in a relaxed tone as if just an innocent afterthought. "I got the impression, from something you said earlier, that you're still looking for my father's killers, but Peter Andrews seems to be convinced there was only one and you've already arrested him?"

It was of no consequence to Michael whether it had been the timing of his enquiry or the mention of Peter's theory that sparked Ian's indignant reply. "The Pie should spend more time looking for work than interfering with police business! I can assure you Michael, there have been no arrests, I did pull an individual in for questioning, but I'm convinced he wasn't involved, although he probably knows more than he's saying at present. Mark my words though Michael, if he does I'll find out sooner or later!"

Michael responded with a smile. "I'm sure you will Ian, as I've said my only worry is getting Jamie's clock back and you're kindly seeing to that as well".

Linda watched him through the window until he turned the corner into Dixon Way. "Wasn't it nice to see him again Ian? You know, I'm still surprised how well he took what you said about Daniel, he's changed so much."

"He's older that's all," her husband retorted instantly, "An accident at work - I should have seen through him then. The bastard knows as much as I do now!"

CHAPTER 9

On his return home, Michael spent the remainder of the morning with Jamie and the young bird team.

Unlike yesterday, Mary could clearly see he now needed no encouragement from her to visit the pigeon loft. Both he and Jamie were obviously enjoying each other's company again, and Michael seemed more relaxed today, particularly after his morning walk. She had been surprised how early he'd got himself out of bed and organised. Downstairs at seven-thirty, fifteen minutes behind herself, showered, shaved, smartly dressed in tweed jacket and brown cords and ready for breakfast.

For over an hour they had enjoyed the luxury of uninterrupted conversation, until a pyjama-clad Jamie arrived, grinning between his yawns. "Michael, you'll get to see the young-birds to-day. After I've been for the messages, that's my first job Michael, isn't it mum?"

"Yes of- course it is, Jamie," she replied with a smile. "After you're dressed and had your breakfast, I'll give you the note."

When he happily disappeared upstairs again to get changed, Mary explained how Jamie always looked forward to his morning routine. "As long as I give him a list to hand over and there's a sweetie on it for himself, he's delighted. It's only round to the corner shop, and the girls are very nice to him, he enjoys a blether with them, and anyone he meets on the way."

Michael sadly knew exactly what she meant. In their boyhood he and Jamie used to be sent to the corner shop on alternate mornings before school, carrying a note, no money just a note, usually with a sweetie on it. For him, however, this was just a distant memory, for his older brother, much more! His first job of the day, and the inevitable reality of his tomorrows.

When both her sons had departed on their separate ways, Jamie with his note and Michael to thank Ina Andrews and Peter, Mary busied herself with the breakfast dishes. Despite the events of the past few days she now allowed herself the pleasure of reflecting on their earlier conversation.

Even her most optimistic expectations of her youngest son had been exceeded. Although putting most of his achievements down to luck, his modesty didn't lessen the extent of his success. It amused her to recall how, until she asked him directly, he hadn't mentioned anyone special in his life, apart from Jake and Mabel. *He's still shy when it comes to girlfriends,* she decided with a smile. *But Tammy sounds like a lovely girl and they've been together for almost five years! I wonder how she feels about him staying here until the funeral. That won't be for another two or three weeks yet, what with the post-mortem and everything.*

Her mood immediately changed with the memory of the visit to the police morgue on Saturday morning. She regretted now not staying longer, they had kindly asked her if she wanted to, but she hadn't coped well when she saw Tam lying there.

Ian had done his best to comfort and prepare her in advance of this dreadful obligation. Unfortunately, it hadn't helped. For a few seconds she had not recognised him as the man she still loved so dearly, despite their past difficulties. Slowly, however, the appalling reality was confirmed. The awful results of his head injuries couldn't hide his true identity, "Yes, Ian, it's my Tam." Her tears said the rest.

Stopping for an instant to gently touch his cold hand, she then turned towards the door. "Ian, I'll need to get home before Jamie wakes up, I don't want anyone else telling him."

As she dried the last fork and placed it neatly with the others in the cutlery drawer, her thoughts returned to the present. She still had Jamie, and although Michael would have to return to his own life in Canada, his father's death had brought him back to her again. Perhaps on his next visit, and he'd promised there would be many, he would bring Tammy. Her smile returned. "He can certainly afford to, what with his business doing so well and the wee surprise I've got for him."

Jamie found it difficult to contain himself during lunch. Michael, as promised, had arranged with Ian Miller to get a clock and following careful examination of the young birds had agreed with his own opinion of them. "They would all win big prizes." Best of all though, was the big bag of toffees awaiting him after he finished his custard. The girls at the shop had put it in his bag, and it wasn't even on the note. Although pleased he had contributed to his brother's high spirits; Michael's thoughts were now focused towards the other goals he wanted to hopefully achieve today. "Mum, I'll have to go into town this afternoon, remember we talked earlier about getting a telephone installed? I can't keep bothering Mrs. Andrews, so I'll see to it to day. There's also some money being sent over from Banff, Mabel should have arranged its transfer to the Royal Bank."

Mary happily acknowledged their earlier agreement. His mention of the Royal Bank was, however, an added bonus. "Fine son, it was your dad who didn't want a phone, why not - I'll never know. It would have been so handy especially during the pigeon season, but you know how stubborn he could be after he made his mind up." Observing the effect of her last comment, Mary attempted to conclude their discussion on a brighter note. "And we'll be able to keep in touch so easily, Michael, and I'd love to speak to Betty again. The poor soul, she misses Bert so much, but she was so pleased to see you at the funeral; she sent a letter all about it."

"I was happy to mum - well you know what I mean, they were so kind to me when I stayed with them. I suppose it was a way of showing my appreciation."

"Poor Bert, imagine ice-skating on Lake Ontario at that age, and they warned him it was too early in the year."

Michael replied with as much solemnity as he could muster "Yes mum it was tragic, everyone in Toronto knows that the ice isn't safe in early December, but seemingly he just wouldn't wait. "Did Aunt Betty tell you I had the privilege of holding one of the cords at the graveside, opposite Louise's new husband? Really nice guy - Louiggi."

As he spoke, Michael couldn't fail to notice the speed at which Jamie devoured his custard. Now pushing the empty bowl towards the centre of the table as he sprung proudly from his seat. "All done, mum. I've got lots to do, see you later Michael, Mum, where's the toffees?"

Sharing a smile they watched Jamie, toffee bag gripped tightly in his left hand, happily marching down the path, towards the pigeon loft.

"He'll be out there for the rest of the afternoon Michael, unless he's sick, with eating all those sweets." As she spoke she left her seat at the table, glancing at the wall clock above the fireplace, before persuading her son to do likewise. "If you want to catch the next bus, you'd better hurry; they only come on the hour nowadays."

Mary waited patiently until he had his jacket on and was heading for the door before removing the brown envelope from her apron pocket. "Michael, did you say you were going to the Royal Bank, in the High Street?"

"Yes Mum, Alberta National will have contacted them by now, they should be expecting me."

Her temptation to say: "They've been expecting you for fifteen years," was impeded in apprehension of his likely response. "Take this, there's a letter in it for Mr. Prentice, The Manager, he's a nice man, you'll like him." He didn't have time to question her instruction. "Look, Michael, there's the bus now, you'd better hurry!" Seeing the red double decker slowly but steadily appearing larger as it trundled down the street, he quickly placed the envelope in his inside pocket and ran to the gate, shouting his farewell as he slipped open the bolt.

Pick up enough money for the next two to three weeks, a thousand pounds should do it - buy some clothes. He had been in such a rush when he left Banff he'd forgotten even his black tie. *Arrange for the telephone to be installed. Pick up some peanuts for the pigeons.* He'd noticed that although Jamie still had a healthy supply of the birds' staple diet of tic beans, maple peas and maize, he was quickly running short of their favourite treats. *And, of-course, sweets for Jamie, he'll probably be through the toffees by the time I get back.*

The bank, however, was the first priority, and to ensure there would be no hindrances at the counter, he re-examined the contents of his inside pocket to re-assure himself that all was in order. *Passport, drivers licence, banker's cards - and a small brown envelope for Mr. Prentice.* It was unsealed. *Perhaps,* he thought, *I should have a quick glance just to make sure I'm on the same wavelength as the bank manager.*

For the remainder of the journey Michael found it extremely difficult to control his emotions. Astonishment and anger merged eventually with a desperate feeling of frustration and finally a sombre acceptance of the cold reality.

The hard blue cover of the account book had forewarned him of its content. "Royal Bank of Scotland - Premium Account." "Mr. Michael Murdoch per Mrs. Mary Murdoch."

His displeasure increased as he flicked through the pages of neatly tabulated figures.

"11th April 1973 - pay-in £642.95p: withdrawal - nil: balance £642.95p."

Apart from the occasional line indicating that Premium Interest had been added, each page told the same story. Every penny he had sent to his mother via aunt Betty had been paid into this account, no withdrawals - all pay ins. Half way down the seventh page, the most recent transaction confirmed precisely what this had cost the Murdoch family, in security, well being and comfort over the last fifteen years.

"20th May, 1988 pay-in £432.18p: withdrawal - nil: balance - £100,786.92p."

He shook his head in disbelief. *Over a hundred grand! And she didn't spend a penny of it, not even on Jamie.*

Any hope that her letter to Mr. Prentice would explain her reasoning was soon dashed.

("Dear Mr. Prentice, this is my son Michael I've talked to you about, and he'll be taking care of the account from to-day, yours sincerely Mary Murdoch")

To his surprise the double decker now shuddered to a halt at its allocated space in the central bus terminal.

"At last we meet Mr. Murdoch, please come into my office and take a seat. Would you like a coffee?"

By the time their coffee cups were empty, Michael had relaxed in the knowledge that his mother's statement about Mr. Prentice had been accurate. This quite-spoken, be-spectacled and efficient elder statesman of his profession was also an exceptionally "nice man."

"It came as such a shock, when I read Monday's Scotsman. I personally have never met your father, but Mrs. Murdoch is such a lovely lady, and one of our best customers. Please pass on my staff's sincere condolences."

Business then commenced and within thirty minutes, was concluded to their mutual satisfaction. "Yes, as you say Mr. Murdoch, this account must have come as quite a shock. To be perfectly honest, it often surprised me that your mother didn't make any withdrawals, but I could not and, of-course, wouldn't influence her. I have a rather old fashioned attitude to banking Mr. Murdoch," he added with a smile. "I still prefer people to bank with us, rather than us with them. If you know what I mean?"

Michael knew exactly what he meant; it was the way he had run the Cascade since he took it over from Jake, nothing borrowed, everything he had achieved, paid for out of the profits of his hard work, not even a "nice" bank manager breathing down his neck.

Mr. Prentice did, however, offer one piece of advice when they finally shook hands. "Mr. Murdoch - Michael, I hope you won't take offence, but please don't be too upset with your mother for all of this, I suspect she had good reason to arrange things in this way."

Before Michael could voice his thoughts they'd been partly answered.

"However, circumstances have now changed, and I'm sure she'll be happy with the arrangements we've agreed."

As he left the premises, Michael considered the bankers last few words. He was right; she had good reason - Tam Murdoch! Circumstances, however, had changed, and as tragic as they were, he'd at least now seen to any financial concerns.

Perhaps now he could concentrate on other pressing family business.

"Before you start Michael! I've had too much upset in the past few days, to cope with your bad temper as well!"

To her relief he replied with a smile, "Okay mum, we're not going to fall out over money, but dad's not here now, so please listen to what I have to say."

Within minutes a compromise was reached. Michael explained that he had cancelled the money from Banff. "Instead we'll use what's here already, you and me both mum. I'll use it when I visit and you can spend as much as you like in-between. I've arranged cash cards for both of us, they're easy to use, I'll show you tomorrow!"

She nodded her head in cheerful agreement. "Fine son, we'll soon spend it between us, I'm starting to-morrow with a new apron! Now let's have a cup of tea before Jamie comes in and sees those sweets."

Michael noticed, however, that when she joined him at the table with her cup, her mood seemed more serious. "Michael, did Ian Miller tell you anything about your dad's death. Are they any further forward?" Before he could give a dishonest reply, she continued, "Ina Andrews came round to see me this afternoon, she said Peter and you saw that McLagan yesterday, why would they let him out Michael? Maxwell saw him walking down Kings Road, just after your dad, it must have been him!"

"Don't worry mum, Ian didn't say much, but we've got to have faith in the police. If this McLagan did it, Ian will prove it. The Pie says he's a real bad one, but you know how he tends to exaggerate."

She shook her head. "Peter's not exaggerating when it comes to Francis McLagan. He's evil, Michael, evil! You know Ina was telling me, as soon as he got out of jail, yesterday; he went home and gave that poor girlfriend of his a terrible hiding. At least this time she's seen sense and gone back to her mother's in Burnside."

He touched her hand and immediately changed the subject. "That's dreadful Mum, how is Maxi? I was thinking of maybe visiting him tonight, to see if he would still help Jamie train the young birds."

Mary agreed fully with his suggestion. "He'll be so pleased to see you, Michael, he was always your dad's closest friend, and you're in luck, this is Isobel's bingo night."

Francis McLagan was not in the best of moods.

The inevitable effects of a most disappointing day and several recently consumed large red wines at the Palace Arms were clearly witnessed by the unfortunate elderly couple and their Poodle now passing him on the pavement. "Who the fuck are you two looking at? Aye, piss-off, before I lose my temper, and if that fucking dog barks at me again, I'll cut its fucking throat!"

Even the Poodle needed no further encouragement. Their pace quickened noticeably as they silently increased their distance from him, regretting instantly the decision to take their pet for a late night walk.

Despite this temporary boost to his confidence and the increasing burden of the white plastic carryout bag in his right hand, he avoided taking the shortcut through the garages.

Without exception, nobody now ventured near the lock-ups after dark.

This inconvenience would of course be resolved by the end of the week, following the Budget and Allocations Committee Meeting on Monday morning. To the delight of the tenants' delegation, waiting impatiently on the lawn outside the Council Chambers, an immediate re-allocation of funding was announced by the Chairman. "In light of what has tragically occurred at the Park Crescent lock-ups, at my request, my fellow members have unanimously agreed to reduce this year's representation at the Scottish Cultural and Business Exhibition in New York. And as the Director of Roads and Lighting will not now be joining us, the resulting saving in expenditure will allow him to complete the necessary illumination works by Friday of this week."

Ignoring a question from the local press as to whether the tenants' threat to stop paying the £50 rental had influenced this decision, he immediately retreated to the comforts of the members' lounge.

Turning into Park Crescent his anger increased as he stared towards number eleven. This was the second night he'd come home to a house without its lights on, and he did not like it.

"Why did that bitch have to ruin everything? A wee row and she fucks off; after all I've been through! I'll give her till the weekend, - if she's no' crawled back by then, I'll go to Burnside and sort her out! Mother or no fucking mother!"

Francis, however, had no regrets about his own actions over the past few days. Friday night's entertainment, although terrifying at the time, had started things off nicely. Particularly when he realised who the victim was.

Saturday and Sunday were even better, he was used to police interviews and an occasional night in a cell, but this had been special, big league. Thankfully, it had been that stupid bastard, Miller, who was running the show. "What a tosser - couldn't even find 'Stanley' and it only took me five minutes. I hope the bastards never find out, Murdoch deserved what he got, so they'll get no favours from me!"

He cursed loudly as he fumbled for his front door key; there was nothing worse than coming home to an empty house.

When he entered the lounge and switched on the light, shock propelled him backward against the television, smashing the screen and the two bottles of red wine he'd attentively carried home. "Who - what the f...?"

The visitor took the opportunity of his host's confusion to rise from his chair and move slowly to the door, effectively blocking any means of escape. He spoke calmly, "Hello Francis, sorry to give you such a fright, looks like I've ruined your evening's entertainment."

"Who?"

"My names Michael, Michael Murdoch, you knew my father. Don't you remember Francis? The old man you murdered on Friday night."

He didn't reply he had one choice only; one response could free him from this nightmare.

His right hand reached slowly into the pocket of his leather jacket.

CHAPTER 10

Having spent their evening in silence, Maxwell and Isobel Clark, although completely unaware, shared their first common thought and reached total agreement. She should have gone to the Bingo!

Isobel had not missed her Tuesday night's entertainment at the Tradesman's Club for as long as she could remember. It had become more than just an enjoyable routine; it was now veering towards a passion she almost lived for. Meeting the girls at eight in the ladies lounge, a good hour before the first call. A few gins to liven things up nicely and then through to the main hall in plenty of time to claim their lucky table at the corner near the bar. Best of all though, the hushed anticipation and excitement experienced as the hallowed words were amplified by the stage microphone. "Ladies and Gentlemen. - Eyes down for the first house!"

Despite admitting to herself that the decision not to go had been hers alone, she couldn't resist a growing feeling of resentment. *Of all the nights. It had to be when the snowball was up to three hundred pounds and it's not as if he's even appreciated me being here. If that Jessie Martin wins it, I'll die,* she decided with justified dismay. *That would make it three times this year and not so much as a gin out of the old bitch. Mind you,* she recalled with her first smile of the evening, *I've won it a few times myself, but never as much as three hundred, and that lovely fur coat sitting in Wylie's window, wouldn't that give Jessie something to think about?*

Unfortunately, even this single pleasant thought was interrupted when she noticed what her husband was up to. "Maxwell, for goodness sake, another whisky's not going to help, you should be in your bed, not sitting there staring at the screen, and you've not said a word to me all evening, I would have been as well going to the Bingo, for all the use I've been here."

To her despair his only response was to continue filling his glass. He seemed to be beyond caring and that's what worried her most.

Maxwell usually always did what was asked of him, but in the past few days this had all changed. He was now so quiet, so deep in his own thoughts and what was worse he had hardly eaten since Saturday; almost nothing with the exception of whisky had passed his lips. In a way this wouldn't have been so bad if it had helped to cheer him up, or at least get him talking. Unfortunately, it had completely the opposite effect. In all her years as a nurse, Isobel prided herself in persuading and, if necessary, bullying patients to get better and stop feeling sorry for themselves. So far she had failed miserably with her own husband.

Tears now filled her eyes as she attempted a final plea. "Please, Maxwell, you've got to realise, Tam's gone and there's nothing you or I can do to bring him back, and you'll be next if you don't snap out of this depression." If she'd learnt anything in recent days it was the knowledge that the mention of Tam Murdoch would, at least, guarantee a reply. Perhaps this time it would hopefully be more positive.

He spoke in a whisper, the whisky glass noticeably shaking in his hand. "Isobel, do you not understand how much his friendship meant to me, and I let him down so badly. All I had to do was to make the effort to get off my arse on Friday night and ask him in for a wee dram. Isobel, he'd still be alive to-night, you'd be enjoying yourself at the Bingo and Tam would be sitting here going on about the wee Mealy Hen topping the Fed from Sartilly!"

She now, with visible regret, decided to leave him alone with his grief. He'd repeated the same remorseful account since Saturday and she didn't have the energy to argue with him. As she lifted herself wearily from her chair and turned towards the kitchen she curtly announced her intentions. "Well, if you've not got the sense to go to your bed, I have, and if you're no better to-morrow, I'm phoning the Health Centre, maybe a doctor can give you something that I obviously can't." As she switched off the kitchen light, the doorbell rang.

For a few seconds they could only stare at each other, acknowledging their second shared thought of the evening.

Whisky spilled freely from his glass as he left the security of his chair, automatically switching off the television as he rose. "Isobel, don't answer it." The urgency of his instruction clearly confirming that his mood of despondency had now been replaced by abject fear! "I'll look through the curtains, if it's McLagan you phone the police".

Although surprised that Maxwell, in his present state of mind, was capable of taking the initiative, Isobel silently indicated her agreement with an anxious nod. She was all too aware what her husband had told Ian Miller about the events of Friday night. Not that his statement had apparently made any difference. McLagan was out and about again, he'd passed her on the street this afternoon and his evil grin clearly showed he knew who was responsible for his two nights in jail, and who else could it be at a quarter to midnight on a Tuesday. Unless of-course it was Ian Miller back to ask more questions or even Jessie Martin popping in on her way home to announce she had won the Snowball again.

Isobel relaxed slightly at the thought of giving the Detective a piece of her mind about the progress of his murder investigation or better still telling Jessie where she could melt her snowball. Unfortunately, her husband's initial reaction, as he peered through the narrow gap in the curtains, seemed to confirm their worst fears.

Maxi's gaunt face instantly went from pale to ashen as his eyes became transfixed in an unblinking stare. She lifted the phone off its hook and pressed the first "9" before he stopped her, and although not revealing all she wanted to know. "Isobel, put the phone down it's not McLagan." was more than enough to provide the relief she'd been praying for.

It was not until the visitor had been warmly welcomed into the hallway by her now grinning husband that she realised who it was. "Michael Murdoch. What time of night is this to be calling on people? Do you know that silly old bugger nearly had a stroke? And no wonder, you're the image of your father, now come away into the living room and I'll make us all a cup of tea."

He smiled nervously. "Mrs. Clark, Maxwell, I'm so sorry, I planned to visit you earlier in the evening but I got involved in other company, and I know I shouldn't be coming here now but Isobel, I'm afraid I need your help."

She had realised instinctively, before he stopped talking, that all was not well with Tam's son. Sweat was trickling down his brow and his eyes expressed more than the discomfort of a nervous guest. He was in pain, and unless she had been too long away from nursing, she knew that the source of his problem would be revealed when he removed his left hand from his jacket pocket. "Come through to the kitchen son and show me that hand you've got so well hidden." As he slowly revealed it, tightly wrapped in a red-soaked dishtowel Isobel didn't hesitate. "Maxwell Clark. Stop staring at the poor lad and boil the kettle, and no more whisky; I might need what's left. Now Michael, lets get this filthy rag off your hand and see what you've done to yourself, and don't think of telling me any tales, I need to know exactly what happened."

As she slowly unwrapped the temporary bandage from her patient, Michael removed the Stanley knife from his right hand pocket and placed it carefully on the kitchen table. This and the depth of the cut crossing his palm told enough of the truth to keep Isobel from enquiring further. "Michael, it's awfully deep and you've lost a lot of blood, I think Maxwell should phone the hospital, I'll drive us there."

He responded with a quiet firmness. "I'm afraid that's impossible Mrs. Clark, - - please Isobel, all I'm asking is for you to do what you can."

Before she could re-argue her case, Maxwell broke his stunned silence. "Isobel can you not see what's happened? That's McLagan's blade on the table, Michael can't go near any hospital!" Placing a comforting arm around his wife's shoulder he continued, "Isobel Clark, you're better than any damned doctor when it comes to sorting cuts, now what do you need?"

To her patient's visible relief, only hesitating for long enough to gently pat her husband's arm, she returned to her duties. "Well then Maxwell. First things first, you'd better get yourself up the stairs and find my wee medical box; it should be at the back of the wardrobe in the spare room. If I'm not mistaken there should be enough bandages to do us, and remember what I said, no more whisky, what's left is for Michael's hand, not your throat!"

Satisfied that her husband was now out of earshot and once again doing what was asked of him, Isobel treated herself to a wry smile. "Michael, despite what that silly old bugger says I'm no doctor and it's a long time since I've done anything like this, so if you've got any sense at all, you'll change your mind."

He returned the smile in reassurance. "Isobel believe me, coming here was the most sensible thing I've done tonight, and you'll never know how glad I am that you didn't go to the Bingo."

Within thirty minutes she was returning the depleted contents back into the medical box with the satisfaction of a job well done. She would now leave them both, in the certain knowledge that Maxwell would find out what had happened and tell her everything in the morning.

As she bid them goodnight before carrying herself slowly up the stairs, a final thought helped to lighten the burden of her physical weight. *If the Snowball's no' been won tonight, it'll be up to £350 next week!"*

"Were in luck son, there's just about enough left for a dram each." Maxwell poured what remained of the whisky into two glasses and joined Michael at the kitchen table. Noticing his young guest seemed preoccupied with the bandage adorning his hand and lower arm, he continued, "Don't worry Michael, you saw how good a job she made of it, a couple of weeks and you'll be boxing again."

Michael's smile couldn't hide his anxiety. "It's not that Maxi, Isobel was wonderful, it's the bandage. Ian Miller's going to be asking some pretty awkward questions, when he sees it."

It was Maxwell's turn to smile "Don't you be worrying about Ian Miller, the man's a bloody idiot! How he managed to become a detective - God knows! Find a murderer. - The man couldn't find the haddock in a fish supper!" Noticing that either his words or the whisky seemed now to be relieving his guest's discomfort he continued, "As far as the Police are concerned, Michael, you've been here all evening, and naturally after all these years we had to have a few drams. It's just a pity, you're such a clumsy bugger with a drink, breaking your glass, and giving yourself such a nasty cut."

Accepting reluctantly that he had no better alibi, he agreed.

"Okay, Maxwell, but you'd better know the rest". His voice now lowered to a whisper as his eyes moved from the bandage to the Stanley knife. "You were right, this does belong to Francis McLagan, but he didn't use it, or anything else to kill my father. I was pretty sure before I met him tonight that he probably wasn't involved, but I had to find out if he knew anything, and he does, Maxi, he saw it happen!"

Maxwell had too many questions to ask, to interrupt.

"I was genuinely on my way to visit you, Maxi, but as I got closer to McLagan's house, I just became more determined to have a talk with him. "It was just getting dark, and once you're in his garden, the height of the hedge helps make things pretty discreet, so I wandered round to the back door and before I could change my mind, I was in his kitchen."

The pleasure Maxwell gained from the remainder of Michael's story was plain to see, his smile widened and his eyes seemed to gleam with enjoyment. "Michael, your dad would be proud of you. That bastard deserved what he got, and don't worry, it sounds as if he won't be telling much to the police for a while - so what exactly did he say to you?"

"Not much, Maxi, but I'm sure it was everything he knew. Seemingly on Friday night the visibility from the fence to the garages wasn't very good. However, he saw three men attacking my dad; one used something like a metal bar or a piece of wood." His voice although continuing in a whisper, was now shaking with emotion. "He was the one, Maxi. Not McLagan. He had a Geordie accent and apparently he was in charge, the other two didn't speak. One of the guys - Terry - couldn't. Seemingly my father broke his nose."

Maxwell's smile disappeared. "I should have known, Michael, a shite like McLagan wouldn't have troubled Tam, it took three of the bastards, but he still gave them something to think about. But imagine McLagan just sitting there, watching what they did to your dad. Michael, even if he didn't do it, he deserves what he got tonight, so don't you be regretting what's happened."

Michael regretted many things in his life, his relationship with his father, what happened to Jamie, leaving his mother and home for so many years, but not his meeting with Francis McLagan, that in comparison had been a pleasure.

It still, however, slightly surprised him how quickly the so-called hard-man of the village went to pieces when he realised his Stanley knife had let him down. Perhaps on its previous outings one cut had been enough.

To McLagan's despair, however, Michael had not even seemed to notice it. He'd just kept moving silently towards him, crashing his right fist repeatedly into his face, stopping only to pick up the knife and place it gently against his throat. Then, between the pleading and the whimpers he had tearfully told Michael all he knew; instinctively acknowledging that anything less would not be acceptable.

When his visitor was satisfied with the truth he removed Stanley from his throat. Then persuaded him not to mention their little discussion to the police. The final blow broke his jaw removing several of his front teeth.

For several minutes they sat together in silence each reflecting on the evening's events and in particular what Francis McLagan had revealed.

"Maxi, we'll talk about this again, at the moment were both too tired to think straight, so please thank Isobel for me, I hope she doesn't mind the broken glass."

"Don't worry son, it was worth it, and I did wait till it was empty, so no harm done." As he helped him on with this jacket Maxwell's final question to his guest was delivered in an almost embarrassed tone. "Michael, you'll probably think I'm daft but can I ask you something about Jamie? It's probably got bugger all to do with your dad, but everything seems crazy at the moment".

"What is it Maxi, what could Jamie have to do with all this?"

"Oh, nothing Michael, but has he mentioned anything about a pigeon?"

Michael grinned, "Maxi, he never stops talking about pigeons, I think its time you got to your bed."

"No, Michael, not one of his own, a champion pigeon, Blue - something or other - !"

Michael turned instantly, "Yes, Maxi, Champion Blue Boy, he's read about it in his pigeon magazines."

"He's done more than read about it Michael. Tam didn't say much, but Jamie had that pigeon in the loft about a fortnight ago, and your dad, for some reason was most upset, going to cause all sorts of fuss."

"Maxwell Clark. Did I hear one of my crystal glasses break? Get yourself to bed now - or..."

CHAPTER 11

Despite the confidence he'd gained making his own life, he still felt like a scolded child when confronted with Mary Murdoch in full flow.

Michael was now realising, to his cost, that time had not succeeded in tempering his mother's most effective means of tackling the misdeeds of her children.

The potent tone of her voice, merging irritation, indignation and most cutting of all, bitter disappointment, always reached their target. "Oh, Michael! I honestly thought you'd have changed, but obviously that was too much to expect from you, - you're just the same, aren't you? Just when Jamie and me need you most, you let us down again. It didn't do us any good in the past, so what do you think you're going to achieve by it now?"

He would not interrupt; his mother was accurate in everything she said. The last thing he wanted was to let down the family again, but what else could he do? Remorseful, as he now felt, for causing her more distress, sitting back watching Ian Miller and colleagues stumble through his family's personal tragedy, was nevertheless not an acceptable option.

At least he'd had the sense not to lie to her, what would have been the point? She'd always seen through him before, inevitably making an unhappy situation even more exacting.

"And what's worse Michael, when Ian visits us next, you're expecting me to just stand here and listen to you telling him you broke a whisky glass at the Clarks? You might not think much of him, you never did. But he's not a complete fool!"

Even this comment didn't tempt him into a response. This was not the time for further argument, and if he was sure of once certainty in his life it was that his mother, despite her protestations, would support him through this, even if it meant lying on his behalf.

In the intensity of their discussion, Mary Murdoch pacing the lounge floor and Michael sitting head bowed at the dining table, nervously picking a wayward thread from his otherwise tightly secured bandage, neither realised that the complexity of their current predicament was radically deepening.

Unfortunately, for once, Jamie had not charged into the house in his usual exuberant manner. Returning from the pigeon loft to the kitchen was not normally part of his mid-morning routine. Today, however, he had his own crisis to deal with; all was not well in the young bird compartment.

A grandson of the Old Pied Cock, the picture image of the old stager, was, even at the tender age of four months, expressing its grandsire's other major characteristic, ensuring it was to be the main player in the young bird team.

Dissatisfied with the confines of its own comfortable perch, it had decided to expand its territory by attempting to evict an immediate neighbour, an equally aggressive but less determined Red Cock. The resulting conflict, although successful, earning him now the choice of two perches, had its inevitable downside. Several missing feathers and a badly scalped head.

Although an annoyance to his master, it was nothing that a wee dab of his mothers Germoline wouldn't quickly sort out. With the pigeon safely secured in his left hand Jamie quietly prised open the kitchen door. Luck having it, mum was busy giving Michael a telling off so she hopefully wouldn't interrupt his illicit use of the household's one and only medicinal product.

Unfortunately, with only one hand free the tin lid proved difficult to open and after slipping along the kitchen worktop it clattered noisily against the dishes on the draining board before continuing its journey to the tiled floor. The resulting disturbance combined with an "Oh bugger it!" from Jamie, effectively confirmed his assumption that the game was up and he would be next to receive his mother's wrath.

With a child's instinct however he made his best attempt to divert the attention from his failed exploit. With an exaggerated expression of anguish he strode through the lounge doorway. "Mum, Michael! Look what's happened to the Young Pied Cock, he's hurt himself fighting. Just like you did Michael, with the bad man that killed my Dad!"

With a fleeting glance they both acknowledged they now had another major problem. Although their mother voiced a spontaneous warning that he must not say a word, to anyone, about his brother's injury, she knew it was pointless, particularly if he was questioned by his old friend, Ian Miller.

As a grinning Jamie, pigeon and Germoline tin in hand, retreated to the loft his younger brother also decided this was a good opportunity to escape. "Mum, I think I'll go out and give Jamie some help with his pigeon, and please try not to worry about this, I promise from now on I'll leave everything to the Police."

She didn't grace him with a reply; her look was enough to express her lack of confidence.

As he closed the kitchen door behind him she didn't immediately return to her household chores, sitting for a few minutes to reflect and regret the enormity of the crisis affecting her family. Her husband was now lost to her, Jamie's future held so many uncertainties and now Michael, would he ruin all he had achieved in his life just for the satisfaction of trying to revenge his father's death?

Jamie Murdoch, had none of these concerns, his priority was to ensure that his favourite young pigeon received prompt treatment. But with Michael holding it securely in his good hand while he lovingly administered the healing ointment, this problem was now being satisfactorily resolved.

"Yes, he's a nice bird, Jamie, just like his granddad. I'm sure he'll win lots of prizes. Now what's his ring number again?"

Jamie smiled, "Young Pied Cock SU/88/F5649."

"That's amazing - how do you remember all these numbers without looking?"

He concentrated for a moment and then grinned. "Because I'm a bit clever, Michael, a bit clever."

Michael couldn't allow his instant feeling of remorse to put him off track. "Jamie, when I got home last night I couldn't get to sleep so I read some of your pigeon magazines, they're very good, lots of nice photos especially of your favourite, Champion Blue Boy, isn't he a beauty? I think I remember his number - is it EHU/85/X2520?"

Jamie chuckled, "No Michael, you've no' got a good memory like me, have you? It's Champion Blue Boy EHU/85/X2220 and guess what Michael, I know his other ring number as well."

"What other ring number?"

"His race ring, Michael, his race ring."

In his confusion he took a moment to realise the significance of what his brother had just said. A pigeon's metal ring gently squeezed over its toes and knuckle when only a seven day old baby, remained for the rest of its life its only permanent means of identification. The rubber ring however, temporarily placed on its other leg by the race basketing secretary had its number concealed to everyone except the official himself. Until the pigeon arrived home from the race no one, and particularly the bird's owner, would have the benefit of its secretly coded details.

Jamie hadn't failed to notice Michael's attentive reaction. "It was a yellow rubber, Michael, number 5995. I would have kept it, but dad told me to put it back on its leg and then - silly bugger! - I let it out with the young birds and it flew away home. It wasn't my fault Michael, I just forgot - I just forgot!"

"Of-course it wasn't Jamie, now why don't we just sit here on the bench for a little while and keep an eye on the young pied of yours to make sure it doesn't start fighting again. You can tell me all about Blue Boy."

In Tam Murdoch's view, "Hold-overs were a bloody nuisance!" Although the partnership had experienced more than a few over past racing seasons, this did not lessen their sense of frustration.

The Murdoch and Son team of six carefully selected candidates, together with several hundred competitors from other Fife lofts had not been released earlier that morning from Stafford, some two hundred and forty miles south, the programmed race point for Saturday 25th June.

Tam had received the half expected, but still unwelcome news, just before lunchtime from young Billy Dow, the son of a neighbouring pigeon fancier. The telephone message from the Club's secretary having been received with equal annoyance at the Dow household only fifteen minutes earlier.

It was of no great consequence to Billy, as he cycled frantically towards Park Crescent, whether the pigeons were released or not. All he had to do was memorise the message, say thank you for the 50p and, if Mrs. Murdoch was in, an extra thank you for his wee bonus, maybe if he was lucky, a Mars Bar. "Mr. Murdoch, they're no' letting the pigeons up today, too much fog, maybe tomorrow if it clears, is Mrs. Murdoch in?"

"No. Here's your 50p, now make sure you're back here to-morrow as soon as your old man hears anything."

As he returned to the back garden to relay the bad news to his son, his interest in what little the remainder of a hold-over Saturday had to offer, was now rapidly waning. Race Saturdays were special and what with Jamie having to spend half his Sunday at Church with his mother, even if the birds were up to-morrow, it wouldn't be the same. It spoilt their routine, Tam sitting comfortably in his hand-made slatted garden seat, mug of tea in hand, and Jamie pacing up and down the narrow concrete pathway, eyes scanning the sky for their first arrival. The anticipation merging instantly with unparalleled excitement when a pigeon was spotted in the distance. Knowing automatically it was a racer, but unsure if it was one of theirs until seeing its wings fold backward, skimming down like a stone. One triumphant circle round the house roof then into the loft and timed.

Whether it was to be a winner or not, at that moment, was of no consequence. As always, although the first pigeon was of critical importance they wouldn't worry about its time until later when the committee checked the clock. For the next hour or so they would relax, enjoy each other's company and the pleasure of hopefully witnessing the arrival of the remainder of their candidates, whenever they turned up.

The stragglers wouldn't be treated with less favour, especially by Jamie. They all tried their utmost to return home as quickly as possible despite the effort and risks involved.

Murdoch and Son prided themselves on their returns, even in a 'smash' when, occasionally, due to bad weather or unknown circumstances, the majority of birds got lost, the Murdoch pigeons seemed to have that additional ingredient to see them through. Today, however, they had to put up with a hold over and as irritating as it was Tam had to admit that the Federation's Race Controller made the right decision, it was far too foggy.

Even in June the North Sea haar could build up in the Forth Estuary and creep inland overnight, taking the residents of Fife unawares until morning, when they couldn't see to the end of their streets. It would probably lift in the afternoon, but the weather forecast had not guaranteed that, Sunday would have to do.

Explaining this fact to a grim-faced Jamie standing in the back garden, they heard the rattle of the doorknocker echoing through the empty house. Tam told Jamie to answer it, whoever it was would hopefully take his mind off pigeons for a while.

Although he didn't know her name he recognised her as someone he occasionally met and said hello to on his way to the shop. She was around thirteen, tall for her age, with mousy hair straggling to her shoulders; a white mud-splattered tracksuit matching her dirt engrained training shoes. If Mary Murdoch had not been at the town the visitor wouldn't have been permitted to enter the house and cross her clean carpet. Jamie, however, in his excitement, didn't share her concern - she'd brought a pigeon to him and that's all that mattered.

Grinning widely, he ushered her through the lounge and kitchen then into the garden to meet his father.

She explained proudly, that when practising her long-jump technique across her favourite spot of the Park Burn, just as she landed successfully on the opposite bank the pigeon dropped at her feet. Without hesitation she had gently picked it up to confirm it was alive and then immediately ran towards the Murdoch home presuming the poor wee thing was one of theirs.

Although Tam confirmed, with less than a glance, that it wasn't, she wasn't to leave their garden disappointed. A pat on the shoulder, 50p in her pocket and a Mars Bar, now replacing the pigeon in her hand, were accepted gratefully. Also accepted, without undue concern, the parting advice Tam used to give to his own boys at that age. "And for goodness sake lass, keep away from that damn burn it's infested with rats!"

To their relief the pigeon didn't appear too traumatised, following its obvious collision with the telephone wires bounding the Park Burn. The wires had been the cause of injury to more than a few of the Murdoch birds over the years. Tam, on his part, had at least attempted to seek a solution to this unnatural hazard; however his increasingly irate correspondence to British Telecom had been to no avail. The manpower costs in the relatively simple task of attaching corks to the wires for the pigeons to see as they approached remained a low priority for the now privatised company. Their priority for some considerable time had been to try to persuade Mr Murdoch to install a telephone in his home. "Perhaps then, Mr Murdoch, when you're one of our customers, the noted concerns relative to your pigeons will be further considered."

"Bugger off!" Although this economically worded response from Tam wasn't totally unexpected, its clarity confirmed that any further persuasion would be given the same priority as the corking of the Park Burn wires. In the thickness of the fog to day, however, Tam had to agree that even with them corked, the pigeon wouldn't have seen the approaching danger.

It was now fully conscious, the dull parlour in its eyes caused by the shock of the collision had cleared and as Tam held it securely in his large hands its bold blue head turned inquisitively, as if carefully examining its new and unexpected surroundings.

Unlike many of the strays that had been brought to them by well-meaning neighbours or entered the loft on their own accord, this one was different. It didn't show any physical signs of distress, feathers silky and tight and its flesh and muscle as firm as the fittest pigeon in the Murdoch team. What's more it was beautiful, in their opinion it even beat the Old Pied Cock for looks. They examined it carefully, initially for any signs of injury and to their satisfaction it seemed in good health.

To many pigeon fanciers, stray racers were nothing more than a nuisance, but as far as Murdoch and Son were concerned, the little effort required in allowing them the comforts of their loft before regaining the strength and determination to continue their journey home was of no great burden. Should the occasional one not disappear after a few days, Tam would report its ring number to the Racing Pigeon Authorities, and the owner, when traced, would send money for its care and carriage. In doing this, he had made several good contacts with fellow fanciers throughout the country and, of-course, a little profit for his trouble.

Before placing it into the security of the loft, one more routine task, just in case it had to be reported. "Right, Jamie, listen." His voice, however, indicated more than a little interest as he slowly read out the letters and numbers embossed on its metal ring. "E.H.U......... Jamie, it's an English National Bird, must be a North-Roader, I think they're flying from Fraserburgh this weekend. Imagine letting them up in this weather - silly buggers."

Having dealt with a couple of English strays before Tam was reminded that the ring details he had relayed to his son would not, in this case, be the bird's easiest means of identification. Unlike their Scottish counterparts, all English race birds had to have the name, address and telephone number of their owners stamped on the last two flights of one wing.

Tam quickly spread open its left. No ink stamp, almost a perfect wing - just one flaw. The long barbed quill of its outer primary feather, unlike the other nine, was not hollow and translucent. It was filled with liquid red.

Tam's eyes focused. "Well you might be a lucky wee bugger but you didnae get off scot-free, altogether. Look Jamie. A blood flight. Must have got it hitting the wires."

Jamie gaped, nodding his head in agreement "He'll be okay, won't he Dad - won't he?"

His father smiled, "Aye Son. One blood flight's no' going to stop him getting home and by the end of the year, he'll have moulted it out, no harm done. Now let's have a wee look at the other wing."

As predicted earlier, in dark blue indelible ink, all was revealed: -
Stenway and Pearce
Foxhole, Kent
Tel. 01233 5431
Even Jamie immediately recognised the importance of the name but it was his father who voiced their excitement. "Jesus, Jamie, it's a Stenway Pigeon! Imagine

that my lad, we've got ourselves a bob or two here." Transferring the bird urgently to the security of his son's hands, Tam then instructed him to put it in with the young birds. "And take a quick look at the rubber ring number; I'm going to have a wee look upstairs for something."

Jamie immediately did as he was told, and after memorising and then replacing the race rubber, carefully placed the stray on to a spare perch, confident that even the Young Pied Cock would not dare disturb its new companion.

He would have happily sat for long enough on his bench in the corridor, admiring the visitor, but he couldn't ignore his father's next urgent instruction from the kitchen door. "Jamie! Check that pigeons number again and then come in here. As quick as you can now, I've got something to show you."

As he entered the kitchen, he was told immediately to sit at the table beside his father and repeat the ring details again. As he spoke, Tam, with an unusually shaky hand, penned the letters and numbers down in a small lined notebook and in a vain attempt to conceal his excitement, lowered his voice. "Now Jamie, my Lad! You're not going to believe this, no bugger will. But look at the top of this race result, what's the number of the pigeon that won the last English National?"

He spread the Racing Pigeon Weekly June 10th Edition opened at the third to last page, in front of his bemused son. This page and the next listed line below line, The England Homing Unions, Thurso National Race Results, flown on Saturday 4th June. Details of ring numbers, ownership, distances flown, velocities and prize money for the 9542 competing pigeons were concisely tabulated in descending order. For Tam and Jamie, however, their eyes couldn't move from the top of the page.

Position	Name	Flight Time	Distance	Velocity	Ring No.	Prize Money
1	Stenway & Pearce	10.38.05	540.1664	1492.3	EHU/85/X2220	£11,582.04p

Unbelievable although it appeared, the fact couldn't be denied, Tam Murdoch and his now extremely excited son had in their possession, probably the best and most valuable racing pigeon in Britain. If not the world!

As soon as Jamie had accurately confirmed this as reality, his father retrieved the magazine and flicked to the front page, stuttering as he read the headline: -

"CHAMPION BLUE BOY WINS THIRD NATIONAL,
WILL HE MAKE IT FOUR?"

He then gripped his hand on his son's shoulder and laughed, "Not this week he bloody won't - not this week!"

Confirming, with a glance at his watch, that Mary wouldn't be back for another hour or so, Tam decided that a wee celebratory dram was now in order. He didn't often drink at home, only on special occasions like winning a race or when Maxi paid an evening visit. He was well aware that although Mary didn't mind him his Friday evenings at the Club, she did not fully appreciate more than his very occasional domestic tipple. Acknowledging that she may also not be over impressed with his intended proposals for Blue Boy, he persuaded Jamie that "For the time being son, this'll be our little secret." The plan was perfect, Blue Boy would be kept discreetly in the Murdoch loft for a week or two, just long enough for Mr. Stenway and his partner to become sufficiently desperate about the loss of their champion and major source of income. They would then, of-course, be obliged to admit its disappearance and post a substantial reward. Tam would then nip round to Mrs. Andrew's and phone Mr. Stenway with the happy news, that his pigeon had just entered the Murdoch loft that very morning.

The afternoon's excitement and his third glass of whisky were now taking their inevitable toll. "Jamie, I'm going through to my chair for a wee nap, just till your mother comes home. Will you put the bottle away and wash the glass?"

By the time Jamie had happily completed this chore Tam was embedded in his armchair dreaming of a day he would never forget.

Unfortunately, unlike his father the quality of Jamie's memory, apart from recalling numbers, left a lot to be desired, he also got bored quickly. Tam had been sleeping for ages, his mother wasn't home yet with his sweeties, and this week's edition of the Dandy had been read from cover to cover, three times. But at least the fog was clearing; he could let the young birds out for a fly.

Tears ran freely down his cheeks as he told Michael the remainder of his Blue Boy story.

His brother tried to comfort him. "Don't worry Jamie, it wasn't your fault, you always let the young birds out in the afternoon, you just forgot. The main thing is Blue Boy must have got home safely, I read in this month's Pictorial that he's won four Nationals now."

"Aye, Michael, and when dad found out, he was much more angry at Mr. Stenway than he was with me. He called him a big cheater, and he is Michael, he's nothing but a big cheater!"

"And why did dad think that Jamie?"

Jamie released and exasperated sigh; "Blue Boy couldn't have won that big race, Michael. That was the day he was mine!"

Michael's mouth opened in disbelief. "Are you sure it was the same day?"

"Well if you don't believe me dad's got it all written down in his wee notebook so he could tell the polis or somebody."

"Jamie, of-course I believe you, now where's the notebook."

CHAPTER 12

As she reached the final stages of preparing lunch, Mary treated herself to a smile. At least some things were consistent. When she gave her boys a telling-off they still kept out of her road to lick their wounds for a while. Confident, however, that the aroma from her soup would soon break the deadlock, she set the dining table in readiness for their re-appearance.

It was of no great consequence that Michael, after leaving Jamie in the pigeon loft, had then immediately retreated to the confines of his room. Perhaps, after all, he had taken some heed of what she had said and would now see sense and let things be.

His first words, as he came back downstairs, seemed to confirm this view. "Mum, I've being doing some thinking. I know I've just arrived, but would you mind if I made myself scarce for a little while? Just two or three days, to keep out of Ian Miller's way. I'd really like to hire a car and go for a little tour around, you know, apart from Fife, I haven't seen much of the country - I've never even been across the border."

Before she could voice her disappointment, his expression had changed from enquiry to concern as he gently placed his right hand on hers. "I really must get my mind off what's happened and I just can't give you any more worries."

She had to agree. A few days would soon pass and hopefully allow him the space he obviously needed to put all this behind him. "All right, Michael, if that's what you think's best. But before you go, you'll have to teach me how to use that auto-bank contraption, I've some spending to do before you get back." Although smiling, her final say on the matter was also more than a request. "And of course, the phone should be getting installed to-morrow, so you'll be able to speak to us, every day!"

Clearly relieved, he took the opportunity to casually re-affirm his intentions. "Mum, do you remember Les Fenton, from Seaham, do you ever hear from him? I thought I might pay him a visit, maybe pick up a pair of nice young birds for Jamie, that's if he still keeps pigeons."

Her smile widened. "He does, Michael, he does, and we still get a card from him every Christmas with a nice wee letter. He's married now, of-course, but the last we heard he was out of work, now that all the mines have closed, and three children to look after, poor souls."

Although Michael indicated his genuine sympathies with a frown, the fact that Les remained in the Durham area and was still involved in pigeon racing brought a glint of satisfaction to his eyes. It was a long shot, but perhaps his old friend could be of help. If there was to be any answers to what his father had penned in the notebook they would most definitely be found in Foxhole, Kent, but perhaps also around two hundred miles further north. Hopefully close enough to Seaham to make his visit worthwhile. If not it would at least be a pleasant stop-off on his journey to meet Mr. Stenway and his Partner.

Further discussion on the matter was, however, abruptly interrupted. He guessed who it was before his mother had answered the door. *My God*, he thought. *He even knocks on a door like he's important.*

"Good morning - no - I should say good afternoon Mrs. Murdoch, we were just passing, and I decided to call in to see how you were all bearing up."

Mary ushered them both in with a nervous smile. "Come in Ian, my goodness, this one's taller than you, and so slim and smart in her uniform."

Unlike her superior, the young dark-haired policewoman took obvious pleasure from this accurate but completely innocent statement, particularly as she knew, without doubt, her Detective Inspector would be livid.

Changing the subject immediately, Ian curtly enquired whether Michael was at home. His mother's hesitation prompting her son to walk through smiling from the kitchen. "Nice to see you again Ian, would you like a bowl of soup? You've got plenty to spare, haven't you mum? A few bowls of mum's soup and you'll end up as tall as your young colleague."

Unlike his mother's comments, this deliberate attempt to put the detective off his stride failed miserably. "No Michael, but thank you anyway, as I was saying we're only here to see how you all are and, of-course, keep you up to date with events. Which I'm afraid have now become a trifle more complicated."

Michael couldn't avoid noticing that Ian's now piercing eyes had fixed on his bandaged hand.

The Detective's face seemed to redden instantly. "Well, Michael, what have you done to yourself? At a guess, I'd say you'd been fighting, but of course you've given up all that - haven't you? Must have been another accident!" With the satisfaction of seeing Michael's smile quickly dissipate he didn't allow him the opportunity to reply. "As I said, things have become slightly more complex. My main witness, much like yourself, Michael, has also had an unfortunate accident and won't be in a position to speak for a few days. And would you believe our bad luck, he never learnt to write, probably too busy getting into trouble when he was a boy, not like you, of-course, you were always such a smart trouble maker." Despite his police training it was now clear that his anger was increasing towards the bounds of control. "Isn't it such a coincidence that this kind of thing seems to occur so often when you're around. Your hand - Francis McLagan - and of course, there was Jamie. If you can call what you did to him an accident."

Michael clenched his fists tightly, his eyes clearly expressing the rage now sweeping through his body. The sharp pain from his left hand however instantly brought him back to some sense of reality. This was not the time to respond with his fists, he must regain his self-control, somehow talk his way out of this.

The Detective, although concentrating his attentions on her son, hadn't failed to notice Mrs. Murdoch's anxious intake of breath when he'd mentioned Jamie. Perhaps it was the reminder of past unpleasantness, perhaps more recent concerns. Buoyed by the fact that he had obviously hit an extremely raw nerve, Ian allowed himself a self-satisfied smile. "By the way, how is Jamie? You know I haven't had a good blether with him for a while. He'll be out at the loft of course, P.C. Matheson, come and meet Jamie, you'll learn all about racing pigeons and, you never know, maybe a lot more."

Without inviting or waiting for a response Ian brushed his way passed Michael into the kitchen, leading his now confused assistant towards the back door. The last thing she wanted was to see the inside of a pigeon loft, particularly as the tall Canadian seemed quite interesting.

Michael glanced apologetically towards his mother. "You're right Ian; Jamie will be so pleased to see you. Why don't you tell him how well young Daniel's coming along at his football. Probably as good as he was in his youth - must take after him, don't you think?"

In her astonishment P.C. Matheson stumbled sideways, as her superior immediately slammed closed the kitchen door and spun round towards Michael.

The two men stared at each other, now unable to conceal their mutual contempt.

"Murdoch! I've come across some bastards in my time, but none of them come anywhere close to you, and to think Linda thought you'd changed."

Michael knew instinctively not to respond in kind. It had been the cruellest of bluffs and no matter what Ian thought; he wouldn't have gone through with it. He also realised it had succeeded, so he could now retrieve his smile. "Well it seems your opinion of me hasn't changed Ian, but don't worry, I'm going away for a few days so you can forget about me and get on with 'your' investigation."

He didn't speak to Michael as he passed by him, preferring to direct his parting words elsewhere. "Mrs. Murdoch, I'm sorry if I've caused you any upset, but you must understand no-one is going to interfere with my case - no-one!"

She had faced a catalogue of upsets over the last few days, but at least she had been half prepared for this one. What she hadn't expected was the level to which both Ian and Michael had stooped. She did, however, accept the apology and as she showed them out, even managed a sympathetic smile for P.C. Matheson.

When she returned Michael was sitting at the table staring out towards the loft. In an attempt to hide his shame he didn't turn his head. "Mum, I'm so sorry; I didn't think it would have come to that."

"No Michael, you're quite right, - you didn't think. How could you bring his boy into this? No matter what Ian said about Jamie's accident."

He turned his head slowly and spoke almost in a whisper. "As you know, all too well mum. Daniel's not Ian's boy - he's your grandson, and sooner or later you and Ian are going to have to accept that."

"But your father, he wouldn't...!"

"Have anything to do with him.".
Her tears showed he was correct.
"Well that doesn't matter too much now mum, does it?"

CHAPTER 13

"No' bad. - Michael - no' bad. - You'll no' win many races with it, but it's no' bad. Me, I'd have gone for the white one, put a flashing light on the roof and drive up the backsides of some of they Sunday crawlers, wind them up a bit. - Just, like the polis!"

Michael wasn't entirely sure why he'd opted for a Range Rover, but it didn't include trying to emulate Peter's little fantasy.

With a smile as genuine as any former car-salesmen, the grey haired and suited Lease Company Rep. strode purposely across the tarmacadamed forecourt, blue plastic folder in one hand, cigarette and keys in the other. "As I was saying, earlier sir, an excellent choice, particularly if you're doing a week's touring. Now should you have any difficulties, and I promise you won't, just phone our nearest agency in the brochure and they'll replace the vehicle without question."

As he accepted the keys, information package and cash receipt, Michael thanked him for his prompt service and the complimentary road map. "It's really appreciated, and I reckon I'll need it with all the changes."

"Of-course you will sir, what with you living abroad for so long. But don't worry it's the latest edition. Oh! - And just one other thing, and I hope you don't mind me reminding you." As he spoke his right index finger picked at a tiny tar spot on the otherwise highly polished bonnet. "We still drive on the left here, I would hate you to forget and have an accident."

Realising instantly that the Rep's concerns were not wholly attributed to his client's well being, Michael replied with a smile. "Don't worry, Peter's been showing me how to drive in Scotland nowadays. But as you said, if something does go wrong, and I promise you it won't, I know who to phone."

Only the Pie and Michael were now smiling, as now grey faced, the Rep glanced towards Peter and then the Escort, proudly sporting its black Go-Faster stripes, before returning less confidently to his office.

"Peter thanks again, and I hope you don't mind, but here's a little something for all your extra running about. And, as I said, I'd really appreciate if you would occasionally pop into my mums and keep Jamie company."

The Pie confirmed by his wide grin and the speed he stuffed the notes into his back pocket, that no offence was taken. "No problem, Michael, but the old witch'll be raging if she finds out you've given me more money, so maybe we won't tell her, eh?"

A fleeting sensation of sadness, tinged with envy, interrupted his thoughts as he shook his young friend's hand in agreement. If only his own mother had so little to concern herself with.

The dark-green Range Rover initially felt slightly bulkier than his own Cherokee; however, there was no doubt that its power steering was effective, the driving wheel creating no noticeable discomfort to his weaker left hand.

In the short time it took to leave the outskirts of Dunfermline and reach the southbound carriageway of the M9 Motorway he felt totally in control. It was certainly comfortable and its height on the road, combined with the large front and side windows, would allow him the opportunity to view parts of the country he had, in his youth, only imagined from his father's recollections of journeys in the passenger seat of a work's van.

Having crossed the impressive expanse of the Forth Road Bridge, leaving Fife behind him, he increased his speed to a steady seventy and headed south-east skirting Edinburgh towards the A1. Less than three hours, he thought, should see him to Newcastle and then a short drive down the Durham coast to the former mining town of Seaham.

Michael couldn't deny his sense of relief as he steadily distanced himself from the past four days. He hadn't expected his return home to be easy, if he had any choice he'd still be in Canada. But of-course there hadn't been a choice. Sooner or later he would have had to come back and although, on reflection, he probably wouldn't have acted any differently, his regret in once again adding to his family's burden, allowed him little comfort. The drive, however, would hopefully help.

Although successful in many ways, his life in Banff hadn't always been easy and, on occasion, when the pressures of running the business seemed impossible, he would pack his holdall and disappear for a day or two. Driving his Jeep to nowhere in particular, as long as it took him as far from the Cascade as time and a resolution would allow. It gave him the peace to think things out, refresh his enthusiasm and then return usually with a solution and always a smile.

He recalled how Tammy hated when he just took off. She never seemed to understand the need for him to separate himself from everything, including herself. "Mike, why don't we both go for a drive? We can think things through together."

Although he took no pleasure in her disappointment it didn't stop him going.

For five years they had been almost inseparable but occasionally, and particularly over the past few months, he was conscious of needing a little space. Perhaps if he was being totally honest, more than a little.

His first clear decision of the drive was now made, whatever happened in the next few days he would phone her and talk things through. He was acutely aware, however, that any lack of communication hadn't been Tammy's fault; she'd been trying to pin him down about their future for a long time. Although genuinely wanting to, he had resisted. He wasn't sure if they had a future together and at the moment that also applied to the Cascade. For some reason it had recently become somewhat less than his major reason for being. Unlike the early years when, despite the hardships, it was everything.

That's when his closest friendships had been formed, when his achievements had real meaning.

Jake Matthew's, however unwittingly, had been the catalyst. In Michael's view, a father, in everything except blood.

Why the old man had taken to him so readily, he wasn't completely sure. Perhaps he was the son he never had; perhaps, in different ways they were both running from their pasts. Maybe it was as simple as Jake often repeated. "The place was getting too much for me, I needed cheap labour!" Whatever his reasons, the night they ended up in Banff General, Michael with his scar and Jake, his busted calliper, witnessed a critical turning point in both their lives.

At the outset, there was no doubt that cheap labour was the extent of Jake's requirement from his young protégé. Michael, however, had few complaints, and soon settled down to his new career as Jake's only assistant barman and general message boy. "Mike, get round to Gopher Street and pick me up a carton of Marlboro Full Strength. Mike, we've run out of Jack Daniel's, pick me up a quart at the market, - put it on my account. Mike, I said Full Strength - get your ass back to Gopher Street!"

Although, at times, he was sorely tempted to remind his employer that a little occasional exercise would do the lazy old bastard no harm, as with Uncle Bert in Toronto, he knew where his "bread was buttered."

Even his frustration in being refused permission to open the Cascade's gates, did not impede their growing friendship. "Mike I'm not having just any nosy buggers wandering about the place, picking through the junk like vultures. The stuff either gets burnt or stays under that tarpaulin. When a serious buyer comes along and I've got fifty grand in my pocket, he can do what he likes with it." Jake wouldn't admit it, but even with the dance hall cleared of debris and the vast floor brushed clean, it was far from a pleasant reminder of its once resplendent past.

Although not renowned for his sensitivity, as its curator for more than two decades, even Jake would rather avoid the embarrassment of showing the outside world what little he had done to prevent the Cascade's sorrowful fall from grace. This, however, did not diminish his confidence that the place would be "snapped up" within a week of the 'For Sale' signs going up. Two months however, languishing in the Prime real-estate page of the Banff, 'Crag and Canyon' indicated to his young assistant at least, that Jake's prediction may have been just a tad over optimistic.

So far only two prospective purchasers had applied for a guided tour.

The first, Ms Phoebe Trimble, an extremely heavily built and enthusiastic representative of the Town's Cultural History Society, took the opportunity as soon as she strode through the wrought iron entrance gates, to joyfully declare her mission statement. "My vision, Mr. Matthew's is to create, in our own little corner of Alberta - a place, where even the most latent of potentials can be unleashed!"

Jake smiled politely, *if she wanted to open it up as another one of the Society's home-made craft and knitwear outlets that was up to her.*

Unfortunately, within minutes of entering the hall Phoebe's vision disappeared, as did her right leg, through one of the Cascade's several rotting floorboards. Her only mission then was to reach Banff General, supported by an extremely embarrassed young barman and a visibly expanding sprained ankle.

The second, honest Tom Norton introduced himself with a gold engraved calling card and a smile as authentic as his blonde hairpiece.

Although Jake wasn't over-concerned that the Cascade might be demolished to facilitate the 'Biggest and Best' car dealership in town, he didn't fully appreciate the three hours of deliberation and the salesman's final offer, of less than half the asking price. Thankfully, Michael was at hand to retrieve the wig and prevent the old man from also adding Tom to the hospital's casualty statistics.

Unlike his employer, Michael wasn't too upset. The longer it took to sell, the longer he had cheap accommodation in his tiny, but now comfortable, apartment behind the stage. He'd also been given time to devise an even more profitable plan for the contents of the tarpaulin. All that was needed was a lot more money and the courage to ask.

For now he contented himself with the fact that the Cascade had yet to impress anyone other than himself. And, in addition, trade had started to pick up nicely in Jake's Bar.

Unlike its owner, the bar, through his assistant's efforts, was now looking less decrepit. Floor cleaned daily, toilet facilities now more hygienic than the bar counter used to be, and ash-trays, including Jake's, emptied on a regular basis. The result - wall-to-wall lumberjacks and to Jake's initial displeasure the occasional lost tourist.

Michael had to admit, of-course that the old man had also unknowingly contributed greatly to the increase in takings now happily flowing into the cash register.

As in all events of any consequence in the world of timber, word had soon cheerfully spread throughout the yards, following the almost unbelievable dispatch of Ginger McQuire and Big Joe Lindey at the hands of an old cripple assisted, seemingly very ably, by a young Scots kid.

Lumberjacks, as Michael soon found out, loved stories, particularly first hand and exaggerated, and who better to tell this one, than the main-player himself. "As I was saying, young Mike was flat-out cold. That's when I decided to step-in!" Jake's story, of-course, became more romanced at each telling and soon took its place in the annals of local lumberjack folklore.

His assistant, on the other hand, offered little contribution to the tale, responding only with a smile as he poured another drink or placed another few dollars in the till.

As the summer progressed even the daytime trade increased beyond their expectations, following Jake's surly acceptance of Michael's suggestion. "Why don't we, just for a couple of months, cut the price of the beer during the day and serve soup and sandwiches? There's money to be made out there Jake, if we don't frighten the tourists away."

Jake stubbed out his cigarette in the otherwise spotless ashtray. "Okay, son! You've got yourself two months. I'll cut the beer prices - the rest's up to you."

Next task, despite the pub's reputation, to encourage more than the occasional tourist through its newly varnished door.

Thankfully, Mabel, never one to miss-out on a little earner, enthusiastically accepted his public relations proposal. An advertising campaign to make her youth hostel guests aware of the welcome awaiting them at Jake's Bar. "It's got to be high profile Mabel, how about a 'Jake's Bar' poster on every second tree?"

The youngsters, of-course, couldn't avoid the posters and when they eventually found the bar, enjoyed the prices and genuine backwoods atmosphere. To Michael's delight the unlikely merging of the two cultures, back packers, and lumberjacks, proved much easier than either group could have imagined. On occasions, after a few Jack Daniel's, even Jake got in on the act, repeating with ever evolving detail, the now legendary fracas with Ginger and Big Joe. After that, it usually became a free-for-all, stories of the road from the young travellers and amazing tales of log rolling, forest fires, snow-bound winters and, of-course, Grizzly's from the woodsmen.

Of all the subjects, Michael noticed with amusement, anything associated with bears seemed to enthral the tourists, especially if delivered by Joe Caskie, one of the bar's now almost permanent customers.

Joe, a retired woodsman, always sat at the far corner of the bar counter, unnoticed by the tourists, until persuaded by his knowing companions that the present group were now adequately primed for a 'Grizzly Tale'.

It was only, however, when he turned slowly on his stool, towards his young audience, that they realised this particular story would merit more than a casual interest.

Although in his late seventies, this was not a man to place in any category other than 'Hard'. The leathery face, solid build, and the immense size of his right hand told their own story.

His steely eyes fixed momentarily on each young face, ensuring beyond any doubt he had their undivided, and now slightly uneasy, attention. He spoke in a growl, the left arm of his woollen plaid jacket hanging loose and empty at his side. "Well, if you really want to know kids, it was a Grizzly, - the biggest mother I've ever seen!"

Complete silence now prevailed - Michael wouldn't even use the cash register in case the atmosphere was disturbed.

"It was back in the Spring of fifty seven. I was on a dollar-a-tree contract in the foothills of Robson, just north of Jasper. Four children and a Blackfoot squaw to support. Beautiful country up there, you should have a look-see. But crawling with bear, so be careful."

The foothills of Mount Robson were now instantly struck from his young listeners' sightseeing itinerary.

"As I was saying - dollar-a-tree, and believe me, they were big suckers. Lucky if you could drop twenty a day. It was nearly dusk, the rest of the squad had left for camp, but I thought, - just one more! I was halfway through it. - No chainsaws in these days, just muscle and an axe."

He paused to allow the other elders of his profession within the bar to voice their approval, "Yep, Joe, just muscle and an axe!"

"I didn't notice I had company till it was almost tapping me on the shoulder, must have come at me downwind. Just turned round and there it was, - three metres high by two across - solid as a brick shit-house, and the meanest eyes I've seen in any bear, and I've seen a few, - believe me."

The open-mouthed expressions confirmed - they believed.

"I tried to run - downhill of course, remember kids, if you're running from bear, always run downhill. But, I was too slow, in seconds it was on me! Still had my axe though, and gave it my best swing - but it just took its big grizzly paw and ripped my arm off, clean at the shoulder." Joe was obliged at this stage to patiently wait for the vocal expressions of anxiety and disgust to settle. "That reminds me, I hear there's a bear, nearly as big, wandering round your tents at nights! So remember what I said - downhill!"

"Now, where was I? - Oh yeah! - No arm and nearly passing out. All I can remember was its great big jaws round my boot, dragging me through the snow and a bright red trail leading back to my arm. You know my hand was still holding the axe and I could swear it was still moving. I dunno how long I was out, maybe only a few minutes, but when I came to I was lying flat-out in a big cave, on a stinking pile of fish-bones. - What a stench! Haven't eaten a salmon since. It was darker than hell, and for a while I thought I was alone, till I heard them shuffling closer, and saw the whites of their eyes. Three of them, two adults and a cub, stooping over me - ready for the kill!"

In an effort to conceal his emotions, the old lumberjack turned back towards the bar as he reached the dreadful finale. "And then - and then - it was curtains!"

As always, Michael, Jake and the Bar's regulars waited in almost unbridled anticipation for a spokesman of the now completely perplexed tourists to voice the group's abject confusion. "But Mr. Caskie! How do you mean it was curtains? You're here, - telling us the story!"

He took a welcome sip from his glass, before turning again towards them, grinning widely. "Yep. - Curtains. - Bedroom curtains. - My wife opened them. - Woke me up from the worst god -damned nightmare I ever did have!"

As practised to perfection, just as Joe finished either Michael or Jake would involve themselves in the endplay, "That'll be a dollar fifty for the beer Joe."

Joe would then immediately slip his hidden arm out from under his jacket and pay for his pint.

If there was anything Jake appreciated more than a good story it was hard work, particularly when carried out by others, on his behalf. After two months in his employment, and without prompting, Michael's wage was increased by two dollars an hour and more surprisingly the rental agreement for his accommodation cancelled. "The room's yours Mike - for as long as you work for me anyway, and the bloody place isn't sold."

Michael happily agreed. With the amount of hours he was now putting in behind the bar, his recently opened account at Alberta National Bank was looking healthier by the week. Rather, however, than send any more money home via Aunt Betty, he had decided, for the time being, to accumulate as much as possible in Banff. Just in case his now all-consuming dream for the Cascade met with anything other than an expected "Dream-on!" from its owner.

By the end of September most of the rucksack-laden youngsters had disappeared, giving up their temporary freedoms, to return to their studies. Jake's regulars, however, kept things ticking over nicely and Michael now had the spare time needed to take the first practical steps towards reaching his goal. His mind and efforts were now concentrated on little else, but a major hurdle remained. *If only I can find the bottle to ask the old bugger.*

In the vast solitude of the dance hall his speech sounded so impressive. Practised to perfection, Michael was positive it couldn't fail to convince any fair-minded person. Sadly, he had to keep reminding himself that its intended recipient was an awkward old bastard!

To his complete surprise, after weeks of anxiety and deliberation it was the old man who came to his rescue. "Okay, Mike. For God's sake, sit down for a minute; I've had enough of you moping around the place like a bear with a sore paw - that's my job! Now, I'm going to pour you a glass of your favourite, and you're not leaving this bar till I know what's wrong."

Jake poured two glasses, his usual closing time Jack Daniel's and a large Canadian Club with American Dry. "You want ice, Mike?"

"Okay Jake, if you can find any more room in the glass for it."

They sat facing each other over the bar counter, allowing themselves a moment of silence to experience the pleasure of the first few sips.

"Well son, you ready to tell me?"

Whether it was the genuine tone of concern in Jake's voice or the soothing sensation of the alcohol now reaching his brain, Michael accepted that his moment had arrived and further delay would benefit no one. "Jake, I've been meaning to speak to you for a while, but I keep putting it off, - in case you think I'm crazy."

The old man responded with a smile. "Don't worry son, I know you're crazy. You've been working for me for near-on six months, how else you gonna be?"

In his anxiety Michael couldn't return the smile, his future relied so heavily on what was to be said in the next few seconds. "I've got an idea. It's about the Cascade. If it works, and I know it will, you could have enough to retire on in two or three years."

Before he could say any more Jake again interrupted. "Two or three years, eh?" His smile had disappeared as his lips now narrowed in readiness for a final deep draw from his cigarette. They both stared at each other in silence, until the stub was crushed dead in the ashtray. "That sounds fine to me son. It's all yours! - And so are the losses, if there's profit, and I doubt it, we split fifty-fifty. That's the deal - no arguments!"

An ice-cube freed itself from Michael's shaking glass and skimmed across the counter as he stammered his confused reply. "But, Jake, How can you...? You don't even know what my plan is."

He answered with a wide grin. "I might be old son, but I'm not stupid. Do you think I don't know why you've been spending all your spare time grafting in the hall, fixing the floor, and painting the walls? And don't tell me the one about making it more presentable for my next buyer, that's as believable as Joe and his story about the Three Bears!"

His embarrassed silence confirmed Jake was right, if the Cascade had a future Michael wanted desperately to be part of it and he was now being given his chance. Bewilderment however still restrained his growing feelings of delight. "But Jake. Do you know I want to set it up as a restaurant?

"Yep, I know that too, Mike. You're forever under that tarpaulin, fixing the chairs, counting the plates, it doesn't take a genius to suss out that you want to give Macdonald's a run for their money. Oh. And one other thing son, you're gonna have to quit talking to yourself - good speech though! You should buy yourself a suit and join the Tourist Association."

CHAPTER 14

He had to check his wristwatch against the dashboard clock before fully accepting over two hours had passed. The border crossing over the River Tweed was now fast approaching and although memories of happier times had diverted his attention from present concerns, he still felt slightly cheated that his journey, so far, seemed to have been condensed into what felt like only a few minutes.

Michael had to reluctantly accept, however, that this was not a day for enjoying the scenery. The low cloud and now torrential rain had put paid to that pleasure.

With just over sixty miles still to drive and the windscreen wipers continuing their valiant struggle to let him see the road ahead, he decided that a coffee break at the next service station seemed a sensible option. It would hopefully give him the impetus to re-direct his thoughts to the task ahead and, if not, would at least ensure he wouldn't arrive in Seaham earlier than expected. He had said on the phone "around five-o-clock" and although Les and Ruby probably wouldn't mind him turning up over an hour early, he had no intentions of inconveniencing the Fenton family more than was necessary.

Although embarrassed by it, he couldn't prevent the smile as his thoughts strayed to Uncle Bert in Toronto - *God rest his soul in Lake Ontario - if he'd said five-o-clock he'd be annoying the hell out of his hosts by two.*

His smile remained as he recalled the previous evening's conversation with Les. There was no doubt in his mind that he would be a welcome guest, his old-friend had seemed so genuinely enthusiastic. "Christ - man. A thought you were dead. One minute your about to gee Bobby McLay his first bloody winner's belt in years an' the next your buggering off to Canada, an' no' a word heard from you till now. A thought it was something a'd said about your chances in the finals, - but how could it 'ave been? A'm such a subtle bugger!"

Realising with some embarrassment that, like himself, his mother hadn't told Les what had caused the sudden chaos in their lives, in an attempt to change the subject; Michael promised he would explain everything when he paid his visit. Hopefully, when they met, discussions on other more recent events would take precedence.

The remainder of their short chat confirmed what Michael had hoped, resurrecting their friendship, even with the loss of so many years, had not been a mistake. The natural and almost instantaneous bond they had formed in their youth still seemed as strong now as it was when they first met over sixteen years ago and knocked hell out of each other.

For three short winter months the Kings Road Amateur Boxing Club hosted a star. Not only was he a superb boxer, his humour and enthusiasm radiated its influence throughout the Club and eventually, after a slightly awkward start, even Bobby McLay learned to appreciate it. "Right lads! Stop what you're doing - no' that your up to very much you lazy buggers. Gather round here I've got someone to introduce to you. This young man calls himself 'Les the Bam Fenton' and he says he's the best light middleweight to come out of Geordie land since Mickey Turner, and that was a fucking long time ago. So - he's either good or a complete bloody chancer like the rest of you's. He's up here for three months on some work exchange with a lad from the Valley Field Pit - so even if he is a complete waster we know that Geordie land's still getting the worst of the deal. Well, Les the Bam - get yourself changed and we'll see what you can do - unless you want to say something?"

The newcomer hadn't given the impression he was at all interested in what had just been said. His bright-blue eyes had been scanning the dingy gym, his smile indicating no embarrassment or unease, just amusement.

Michael, of-course, acted no differently from the rest of Bobby's Boys. His initial interest related to the stranger's physique - and although his height didn't over-impress, for a light-middle weight five foot ten was on the short side - even in his duffel coat and jeans, they could tell he was built for the business.

Michael, for one, couldn't wait to get into the ring beside him.

"Well, ta very much, Mr. McLay for your kind words. A'm no' one for gabbin, a usually let ma fists do the talking for me, But a must say this. Your gym's reputation is well known in Seaham, but despite that a'm willing to gee you the benefit o' the doubt. Just ca' it Geordie charity if you like."

Although most of them, including Michael, appreciated the humour no one dared upset their trainer more by laughing. As Les walked casually towards the locker room Bobby whispered to Michael through his now tightly gritted teeth.   "If I get into the ring with that cheeky little bastard, I'll kill him, so he's all yours Michael. Now he's a couple of years older than you, but don't worry, just make sure you welcome the wee shit to Fife!"

Although, at sixteen, he wasn't the most experienced boxer in the gym, he was the right weight and had his trainer's confidence that what he lacked in skills was compensated for by his strength and determination.

After what appeared to even the idlest of Bobby's Boys, as the most dubious of warm-ups, Les completed his thirty seconds of skipping and almost lethargically entered the training ring smiling broadly through his mouth-guard to Michael and then the expectant young faces below. Bobby, as referee for the three rounds, inspected their gloves and reminded them both that it was, of-course, only a training session, before winking to Michael as he pointed them to their corners.

The first round went smoothly for both of them, little more than light sparring, each assessing their respective strengths and styles. Michael found him slightly awkward; Les was a natural south paw, his left arm benefiting from a reach which belied his stature. He also seemed very capable of hiding his head so effectively behind his gloves. At the moment, however, nothing much to worry about; Michael was setting the pace, his confidence steadily increasing.

The second continued with the same predictability, Michael doing all the work, content that if this was a competition bout he would be well ahead on points. His only disappointment was his opponent's apparent lack of enthusiasm, which was now being clearly mirrored by the now less attentive audience.

With less than ten seconds left he felt bold enough to carry out his trainer's instruction.

As the newcomer's glove lifted for another lazy and easily avoided swing, Michael immediately stepped in close and replied with a sharp left uppercut to the jaw, its force instantly jolting his opponent's head upwards, for a split second breaking his concentration, allowing his right fist to follow through cleanly with a crashing blow to his forehead. Its precision and power leaving the self-proclaimed pride of Geordie land sprawling on the canvas.

Although the referee succeeded with great difficulty to mask his delight, the rest of the gym erupted. Les, however, got to his feet just as the bell rung and to everyone's surprise grinned widely as he ambled to his corner, apparently oblivious to the pandemonium his come-uppance had created.

The final three minutes, unfortunately, didn't go quite as Michael planned - or the audience expected. As soon as the bell rung it seemed as if his opponent was there. Even Bobby was amazed by the speed the Geordie crossed the ring. Before Michael fully realised what was happening he'd received four searing blows to the body, their force almost doubling him up as his back collided against the corner post. For a two-minute eternity the corner became his prison, the viciousness of the punches raining in, effectively preventing any hope of escape. In his pain and confusion all he soon had left was a desperate yearning to stay on his feet.

Bobby, thankfully, didn't believe he was capable of even that and on the false pretext that Les had thrown an illicitly low punch he intervened, giving Michael the respite his body craved. The few seconds rest gave him the chance to clear his head, he knew he wouldn't survive going back into the corner again, he also knew he couldn't box his way out of this.

There was now no choice; if he had to go down he would give his last efforts to wiping the grin from the Geordie bastard's face.

As they touched gloves to resume what everyone now accepted was a one-sided battle, Les approached with the assurance of an easy victor, straight into a barrage of punches from both his opponent's fists! Michael was no longer restrained by the disciplines of his training; he was now doing what came naturally. Street-fighting! Although the majority of his flailing attempts missed their intended target, some didn't and from the expression on his adversary's face, they hurt.

Les responded in kind, their bodies now almost stationary at the centre of the ring, punching hell out of each other for a horrific twenty seconds, neither prepared to accept defeat.

Having seen the damage they were doing to each other, the referee pushed in-between them, taking a stray punch for his trouble as he prematurely halted the proceedings. "Okay lads. - I'll tell you how bloody awful you were later. - And if I find out which one of you buggers hit me, it'll be me you're against next time."

Bruised and exhausted they allowed themselves the solitude of their own thoughts until their sweat-damp training clothes were packed into their holdalls.

As they slumped opposite each other on the locker-room benches, heads-bowed, Les eventually broke the silence. "How old are you - man?"

Michael lifted his blood-shot eyes and answered quietly - "I'll be seventeen next month."

"For fuck sake. - Michael, is it?   - Well me bonny lad, a'll no want to be around when your nineteen. - A think afore then, a'll gee this game up and stick to me bloody pigeons."

Michael grinned as Les' words filtered through his memory. There was no doubt they had cemented their friend-ship, 'boxing and pigeons' - what else was there in life?

He eased the Range-Rover through the puddle-strewn lanes of the rest area car park until he found the closest space available to the garishly painted complex. Although some thirty metres away, he could see clearly into the restaurant, noticing, with satisfaction, that despite being reasonably busy there were still several unoccupied tables. Removing the holdall and road map from the passenger seat he locked the doors, dropped the keys into the pocket of his tweed jacket before lifting his collar and making a dash to the entrance foyer.

Before going into the restaurant he briefly visited the compact but surprisingly well stocked 'all you need to keep the kids quiet shop' and left with a ribbon bound box of milk chocolates, black pen, pocket calculator and the biggest jar of Quality Street he could find.

With both hands full and the plastic handle of the carrier bag reminding him that his cut had not fully healed, he gently nudged open the Little Cook's glazed door and found the most convenient table beside the window.

He was slightly surprised that like the Cascade, it was table-service only. Apart from that, however, there were few similarities.   In the Little Cook plastic was in season - not an inch of wood to be seen, and although bright and wipe-down clean, the atmosphere was as sterile as the waitresses' expression. "You're not intending to have a meal sir, only a coffee?"

He smiled politely. "Yes, that's right, black please, and as large as you've got, and I'll maybe have another if the rain doesn't ease-up."

Only the slightest raising of her eyebrows, as she scribbled down his order intimated either inconvenience or a suspicion that maybe his meal was to comprise coffee and the contents of the large jar of chocolates protruding from the carrier bag at his feet.

When it eventually arrived, its taste held no surprises, nevertheless it was coffee and his brain welcomed it like an old friend.

He had almost an hour to spare and apart from a cup and the menu, a clear table in front of him. Unzipping the side pocket of the holdall, Michael removed the notebook. He then found the calculator and pen in the carrier bag and placed them together with the map on the table. All he would hopefully need to re-assess the information his father had painstakingly gathered about Champion Blue Boy.

To the waitress and probably anyone else in the restaurant, with as little interest, he was just another sales-rep fine-tuning the embellishments to his mileage expenses. In truth, if Tam Murdoch's theory could be proved, the extent of this fraud would reduce to insignificance even the most successful of salesman's life earnings.

Of the dozens of lined pages in the notebook only ten had been filled. Although Michael was pretty sure that every detail from the first page was securely held in his memory he quickly scanned each line in confirmation.

Blue Cock - EHU/85/X2220 - Champion Blue-Boy
Yellow Rubber No. 5995 - Blood Flight (Last Primary - Left Wing)
Stenway & Pearce, Foxhole Kent, Tel. (01233 5431)
Racing Pigeon Weekly, England National Result
Fraserburgh - Released 9.15a.m. (8,542 birds) - Saturday
25th June - Light North Westerly

Position	Name	Flight Time	Distance	Velocity	Ring No	Prize Money
1	Stenway & Pearce	9 hrs 15 mins	472.103 yds	1498	EHU/85/X2220	10,572.05P

25th June	- 9.15a.m. - Race Liberation, Fraserburgh
	11.20a.m. - Blue Boy brought to house
	4.20p.m. - Escaped from loft
	6.30p.m. - Timed in Kent?

1st July - Phoned Stenway
1st July - Phoned Major Lockwood, EHU General Manager
1st July - Letter to Major Lockwood, EHU, HQ, 18 Upshire Rd., Waltham Abbey, London.

Even without the benefit of the next nine pages of neatly pencilled long division and multiplication calculations, there was no doubt in Michael's mind that his father was right. *No way could any pigeon, let-alone a champion, fly from Fife to Kent in just over two hours.*

It was, however, the rest of his father's, albeit, carefully considered assumptions that he still had some difficulty in accepting as fact.

For the next half an hour, between sips of coffee and pressing almost continuously the buttons of the calculator, he checked each arithmetical sum. As he confirmed their accuracy, one by one, Michael became conscious of an intensifying admiration of his father's obviously undiminished sharpness of mind. Each conversion from miles to yards, hours to minutes and then the division of the many thousands of yards by the hundreds of minutes had been completed with only a pencil and a brain. Even with the calculator, Michael had taken now over thirty minutes to reach the same conclusion. Expressed in the Racing Pigeon Authority's Imperial Velocities of Yards per Minute, the speeds worked out by Tam Murdoch showed clearly that Blue Boy, flying at his official recorded winning velocity of 1498 yards/minute, almost 51 miles per hour, could, after spending five hours in the Murdoch loft, only have reached the North of England.

All he had to do now was somehow prove it.

His father, possibly to his tragic loss, had posed the questions; his son had to find the answers. Whether they lay in the corrupted hands of two pigeon fanciers in Kent or in a yet unidentified pigeon loft in County Durham was still to be established.

His visit to Seaham might not grant him more than the pleasure of resurrecting an old friend-ship. If that was the case he would welcome it with the gratitude it deserved. Michael hoped, however, that Les could help him find more. Somewhere much closer to Seaham than Foxhole, Kent, a racing pigeon dropped from the sky and entered the temporary security of a loft. Had its race ring removed and won its Fourth National with less than half the effort and risk its competitors had faced.

They had struggled on southwards, exhausted by their honourable endeavours to return home, many beaten by the distance, fog, wires, hawks and guns and even the luckiest and best, finally defeated by dishonesty. - Dishonesty perhaps so profitable that was worth an old man's life to conceal.

CHAPTER 15

When the "Welcome to Seaham" sign came into view, Michael gave up wondering if the rain would ever stop. He was satisfied, however, that the road map had kept him on the correct route and despite the driving conditions, his timing couldn't be better. *Four-fifty-two - perfect!*

According to Les, less than ten minutes should now get him to Sixty Daphne Row. All he still had to negotiate was the town centre and a few side streets. "Turn right at the bottom of the High Street, along Deneside Road, under the railway bridge, keep going till you get to the pit gates, then a sharp right."

As he slowed down to take the sharp right, the imposing wrought-iron gates of Seaham Colliery dwarfed the Range Rover. Although much grander in scale, they reminded him of the first time he saw the Elk Street entrance gates to the Cascade, closed and pad-locked, their ominous presence barring for ever, if they could, the dormant potential inside. Unlike their Banff counterparts, however, the livelihood of generations had depended on the colliery gates staying open and he felt a genuine sadness for Les and the many others who no longer passed through them.

The brick-built housing scheme now facing him re-focused his attention. "Stay on the main road, the fourth street to your left should be Daphne Row. If not, you're lost, you daft bugger, you'll need to ask someone." Thankfully that wasn't necessary, as the Daphne Row sign, attached to the frontage of the first house of the fourth street, now confirmed.

Unlike Park Crescent the terraced row of two storey houses had no front gardens, their doors opened straight on to the pavement and, although making the street appear narrow, there was still ample room to ease past the parked vehicles lining its route.

"Sixty's near the middle, look out for me white and rust Transit."

He drove slowly along the street, realising with a smile, when he reached his destination, that his old friend's sense of humour hadn't deserted him. When Les said rust - he meant rust. Apart from the roof, every panel of the white brush-painted van was covered in it. In a way it complimented the flat tyres. Thankfully, there was a space available immediately behind the Transit, just wide enough to reverse into.

He switched off the engine and glanced to his right towards the curtilage of the Fenton residence only a pavement width from his seat. Four faces peered up at him from the floral curtained window, three with their open mouths almost touching the glass. Two boys and a blonde, curly-headed little girl. Only the fourth, the tan and white Jack Russell in her arms, appeared less than awed by his arrival.

As soon as Michael had acknowledged their presence with a smile they disappeared. As he stepped down to the pavement, however, the door of number sixty flew open, allowing the Jack Russell to escape through the legs of its grinning little mistress. Scampering straight through a puddle before leaping into the Range Rover. Before Michael could voice his annoyance, it was frantically burying its head into the plastic bag on the passenger seat. · The blonde eight-year-old now clambering in after it, expressing his feelings almost to the word.   "Get out o' the man's motor you nosy little bugger, your feet's filthy-dirty."

As she struggled to separate the dog from its quarry her sparkling blue eyes turned towards him. "You got chocolates in this bag mister?   Jock loves chocolates!"

Michael laughed. "Yes, but they're not for your dog. Maybe you should take the bag; I don't think he'll let me near it."

With a wide grin she pulled the Jack Russell out on to the pavement and grabbed the carrier, quickly eyeing its contents as she scrambled down from the driver's seat. "Your ma da's mate, Michael, aren't you?"

"That's right, and you must be Susan, and I take it this is Jock, is he from Scotland like me?"

She watched him remove his holdall and lock the door before answering in a matter of fact tone. "No, we saved him from the Houghton pound when he was a little puppy. Ma da' ca'd him Jock, cos he's no' even scared o' big Alsatians, an' he licks beer off the floor."

Michael was still chuckling when Ruby came to the door, grinning widely. "Susan, that's no way to welcome our guest. Just because he's from Scotland it doesn't mean he licks beer off the floor. - You don't do you, Michael?"

They both laughed openly as they warmly shook hands, Michael instantly recognising that Les had found the ideal life partner. She was about his own age, around Les's height and although veering towards plump, her pleasant rounded face seemed to exude friendliness.   As his friend had confidently stated on the phone; "Don't worry Michael, you'll like ma Ruby, she's a gem."

As she led him into her home, he noticed that the twins had retreated from the window to the couch, their eyes now fixed on the television, trying to retrieve the dignity of their thirteen years by attempting to ignore all the fuss. Their apparent lack of interest, however, changed abruptly when they noticed their sister pull the jar and box of chocolates from the carrier bag.   "The box must be for you mam, and the Quality Street'll be for me."

"Susan, get those sweets back in that bag right now. Have you no manners girl?"

Smiling, he interrupted on her behalf. "That's okay Ruby, the jar's for the kids to share, I couldn't think of anything else, and I hope you like milk chocolates?"

"Thanks Michael, they're ma favourites, you don't have any children - do you?"

Puzzled, he shook his head; "Why do you ask?"

"Well, wait till you see what trouble that jar o' sweets is ganin to cause in this house." Her expression now changed to a scowl as she turned her attention towards her arguing children. "Right - you lot! Tak' three paper bags from the drawer and share them out equally - no cheating now. An' remember, none for that dog, a'll no' have it being sick over ma good carpet." Her mouth curved back into a smile. "Michael, we best get into the kitchen for some peace an' quiet."

For the next fifteen minutes they enjoyed the pleasure of a coffee pot and uninterrupted conversation. Despite meeting Ruby for the first time, he was surprised how totally relaxed she made him feel. As they sat opposite each other at the Formica topped breakfast bar, which took up most of the space in the tiny kitchen, he soon also realised she seemed to have the knack of making even the most direct question appear like a casual enquiry. Without, in any way, feeling his privacy was being invaded she became a party to information that he would normally only have sparingly released to the closest of friends. "No - Ruby, I'm not married yet, I do have a girlfriend, but to be perfectly honest, I'm not sure if I'm ready to commit myself to anything final at the moment, if you know what I mean."

"Aye, Michael, of-course a do; now about your poor da', was he ill for a long time?"

Sharing even this personal trauma didn't cause him the degree of discomfort he would otherwise have expected.

Ruby, although clearly shocked by the circumstances of his return, didn't express more than genuine sympathy and, to his relief, did not question him further. "Well, Michael, if there's one thing certain, life's no' easy, is it? One minute, everything's running along nicely, then out-o-the blue, something terrible happens an' you wonder if it'll ever be the same again."

He echoed her sympathies, when she explained how difficult life in Seaham had been for her family since the pit closed. "I'm no' saying Bam loved the job, Michael, far from it! - But there's more to it than that. Supporting the family means so much to him, he's never really adjusted to the way things are now, not many o' the men have, mind-you." The faintest trace of a smile came to her lips as she continued. "He tries his best to joke his way through it, but a know him too well, he can't hide anything from me."

Ruby's acute perception of her family's behaviour was now further confirmed, as the trouble she had predicted earlier tearfully exploded through the kitchen door.

"Mam. Joe's stoled one o' ma sweeties, a red one, an' he won't gee me it back - tell him mam, tell him."

Ruby grinned wryly towards Michael before placing a comforting hand on her daughter's heaving shoulder. She then marched through to the lounge, and despite the barrier of the kitchen door her voice could clearly be heard by a more than slightly embarrassed guest and a now less than upset little girl.

Despite the protestations of innocence particularly from Joseph, both he and David were forced to each hand over a red-wrapped chocolate to their mother. Jock, perhaps thinking he should follow their example, also decided to give up the chocolates he had surreptitiously received from his young masters. Within seconds the door again flew open, allowing a still retching dog to escape through the kitchen and out, thanks to Susan, via the back door into the brick-walled back yard, where it threw-up the remainder of what it had deposited on the lounge carpet.

Michael glanced across to the little girl, both their expressions clearly showing they were on the same wavelength. This may also be a good time to follow the dog's example, and get out as quickly as possible. When, a now irate, Ruby returned to the kitchen, he nervously apologised for his part in the proceedings, suggesting he may pay her husband a visit at the gardens.

"Now, don't be blaming yourself, Michael. All you did was bring the sweets, these little buggers did the rest, an' he'll be so pleased to see you. That's why he's no' here, he's been round there all day getting the place spick-an-span."

Michael smiled as he thought of Les, spending his whole day; scraping out the pigeon loft and tidying his allotment, just to ensure his visitor would be suitably impressed.

"Susan, you show Michael the way and tak' that little bugger we you. Tell you da' it's no' getting back into ma house till it can control itself and never mind what he says about him stealing his pigeon eggs."

Before they left, Michael gratefully accepted Ruby's offer of her husband's spare waterproof jacket. As she removed it and Susan's yellow plastic raincoat from their pegs attached to the back door, she reminded them that their meal would be on the table at six-thirty. "An' tell your da' no' to be late, your Auntie Julie an' me are ganin dancing tonight. Oh, an' Michael! You best tak' your bag, save you carrying it later."

He automatically picked up the holdall from below the breakfast bar before fully realising the significance of what she'd said.

Noticing his now obvious confusion, Ruby, although still smiling, was unable to conceal the embarrassment in her voice. "Michael, did that daft man o' mine no' tell you about the sleeping arrangements? You must think a'm terrible, tellin' you to move your bag, wait till a get hold o' the devil. We'd love you to stay here Michael, but there's just no' the room. Bam's sorted it all out though, a just wished he had the gumption to tell you!"

Seeing that her embarrassment wasn't lessening, he lied; "Ruby, don't worry, it's probably my fault, we talked about so much on the phone last night, that's the last thing I would've remembered."

Although unfamiliar to him, he soon realised that the companionship of an eight-year-old had its pluses. Unlike most adults, including himself, the concept of saying exactly what came into her mind was so refreshing. It wasn't a happy comparison, but listening to Jamie, was the closest he'd come in years to such freedom of expression.

With Jock now fully recovered, following close at her heels, she guided her new friend along the brick alleyways, splashing through each puddle in their way. To his amazement, as soon as the rear windows of number sixty were out of sight she halted mid-puddle, stared up at him, with the most innocent of blue eyes and retrieved a red-wrapped chocolate from up her sleeve.

Michael attempted but failed to prevent the grin crossing his face. "I see you've managed to find the sweetie Joseph stole from you."

She casually unwrapped the chocolate; bit it in two, keeping one half in her mouth, placing the other in the dog's, before returning the grin. "He smacked me at ma breakfast, this morning, for nothin'!"

Michael accepted her reasoning with the credit it deserved. As he bit his tongue, however, he wondered what little "nothin'" she had got up to this morning over the cornflakes.

For the remaining five, all-too short, minutes, any further enquiries he had intended stayed unasked. His full attention was needed to find acceptable answers to the barrage of questions now flowing happily from a chocolate smudged mouth.

"Michael, are you a boxer, like ma da' was?"

"I used to be a long time ago."

"Why have you got that scratch on your head and a sore hand then?"

"Oh - em. - - the scratch was a just a little accident at my work and I cut my hand on a broken glass a couple of days ago."

"Michael, how old are you?"

"I'm, thirty-three - two years younger than your dad."

"You'll be married then?"

As he answered he couldn't avoid observing the same glint that had crossed her mother's eyes, when she had asked the same thing only minutes before.

She paused for a moment's silent thought before continuing with a wide grin. "Michael, guess what. I know a secret and I'm no' telling you it."

"Okay, Susan, you're quite right not to tell secrets."

The grin immediately disappeared.

As they turned left out of the alley she pointed to the gardens no further than two hundred metres away. They were nothing like he'd expected. Picturing them much the same as the Council's allotments in Rosyth, an area of open land sub-divided into small, patchwork plots, with the occasional wooden shed or pigeon loft breaking the landscape. If there were any similarities he couldn't see them. In front of him a vast city of multi-coloured wooden doors stretched side-by-side for as far as the distant railway embankment would allow.

As they got closer Michael saw that the approaching barricade wasn't totally intact, as in any maze there was an entrance leading to its hidden interior. The Jack Russell scampered ahead towards the narrow opening, and Michael soon realised, without his two companions he would probably never have reached his destination through the mud-covered passageways criss-crossing their route.

Occasionally, as they advanced, he heard voices or a dog barking behind the wooden walls and, despite their similarity, he noticed that the occasional door was hinged and padlocked, realising its legitimate purpose.

They had walked nearly halfway into its centre, turning two rights and a left, before an excited Jock, announced with a chorus of yaps, their arrival at the Fenton allotment. Susan turned the brass knob and shoved open the blue-painted door with her shoulder, before loudly declaring their arrival. "Da'! I've brung your mate, you should see his motor, we thought it was someone important."

As he stepped through the threshold, Michael re-experienced the sensation of astonishment he'd encountered when Jake Matthew's turned the Cascade's lights on. This surprise, however, was so pleasant in comparison. The place was beautiful, calling it a garden did it no justice, he'd never seen anything quite like it, Les Fenton's answer to Shangri-La!

In an area no bigger than a good sized tennis court his friend had created an oasis. Climbing roses, yellow honey-suckle and a dense cushion of ivy provided an exquisite backdrop for the spectacular array of plants and flowers bedecking the white-stoned rockery, defining its entire boundary in resplendent colour. In the centre, row upon row of vegetables, Michael counted around ten different varieties. Each separated by neatly pointed crazy paving footpaths. Although the limits of his own horticulture expertise was being able to mow a lawn, he saw enough, particularly from the size of the leeks and onions, to seriously consider placing a bet on the winner of Seaham's Annual Growers Show. The freshly creosoted pigeon loft, with its louvered-doored frontage and green trellis-topped roof, blended in perfectly with its surroundings. Between it and what looked like a rose-covered port-a-cabin, which he took as being Les's equipment store, an aluminium framed green-house and mesh fronted rabbit hutch completed the impressive row of garden real-estate.

At the entrance of the now open cabin door, the proud master of all he surveyed, Les the Bam Fenton, - sporting a dark blue boiler suit, checked tweed bonnet and a grin as wide as his girth. Despite the burden of his weight he leapt from the top of the three wooden steps to the path, gripping Michael's shoulder as they warmly shook hands. "Well - well. Michael Murdoch! You've no' got any better looking, and you're still bloody fighting. When you ganin to realise you're past-it man?"

Michael relied on his laughter to prevent the need for further explanation.

For all of five minutes they stood together, ignoring the rain, talking and laughing like two school chums renewing their fellowship after the summer holidays. Attempting but failing to get a word-in, Susan decided for the moment, that her pet rabbit would provide better entertainment. As she approached the hutch, she expertly pulled a large lettuce from its neat row, shook the dirt off it before loudly announcing her intentions. "Tea-time, Snowy! Me and da's got a big secret, Michael doesn't know it yet, but a'll whisper it in your ear."

Michael noticed a flush of red cross his friend's cheeks as he darted an irritated glance towards his daughter. "Em- - Michael, did Ruby mention where you'd be staying tonight?"

"No, Les, but don't worry, I know you don't have the room at home. Have you booked me into a hotel or somewhere?"

"No, not exactly me bonny lad." Despite his obvious embarrassment, he couldn't avoid a devilish grin as he pointed towards the port-a-cabin. "Welcome to the Seaham Hilton, an' don't thank me, it's the least a could do for you."

For a few seconds Michael stared open-mouthed at its dark green door, hoping it was another of Les's jokes. Susan happily confirmed his fears. "Tell him the rest o' the secret da', tell him!"

Les acknowledged his daughter's enthusiastic interruption with a chuckle. "No yet Suzie, - the poor bugger's still in shock."

Before his bewildered guest could find the words to express his feelings, Les had carried his holdall up the steps and through the cabin door. "In you come, bonny lad, you're in for a little surprise."

In stunned silence Michael followed him up the steps, his brain not yet capable of clear thought. It was only when he was fully inside the door that his power of speech returned. "Les, I just can't believe it - I thought you were winding me up, it's just - - it's just beautiful!"

"Aye, it is me lad, he replied proudly, better than any hotel in Seaham anyway. Electricity, running hot and cold, shower, T.V. and all for twenty five pounds a night."

Michael acknowledged his friend's joke with a grin, soon realising, however, that if he wanted to get into the self-catering business, the standard of accommodation on offer would more than merit the price.

Snowy in her arms and Jock at her heels, Susan happily joined them for the guided tour.

Although smaller than most, the port-a-cabin had been skilfully converted into what compared favourably with the finest of Canadian mobile homes.

The entrance steps led directly into a compact, but surprisingly well appointed, white surfaced kitchen. Facing them in a neat row, an electric cooker, fridge and stainless steel sink, with a double set of cupboards conveniently positioned at eye-level against the sky blue wall.

To their right an open doorway revealed a deceptively spacious lounge, its brown thick pile carpet merging comfortably with the lime painted walls. A large deerskin rug elegantly cloaked the centre of the floor, embraced at opposite edges by a rust patterned couch and matching easy chair. In the far corner, a small T.V. and equally compact stereo system bedecked a mahogany-shelved unit, angled snugly against the adjoining wall.

What surprised him most, however, was the array of books, including several leather-bound tomes, lining the dark stained pine-shelves surrounding the coal-effect electric fire. Although realising immediately that, unlike his father's library, their contents did not include, "How to Breed Better Pigeons," before he could take a closer look, Les had ushered him back through the kitchen into a narrow adjoining corridor. Mid-way along its short length he opened a connecting door, proudly introducing his still awe-struck guest, to the pink tiled toilet and shower compartment. Noticing that his visitor seemed suitably impressed, Les broke the silence.

"Nice, isn't it, you could, lick beer out o' that bowl, no' that a've done it, a'm a Geordie no' a Jock."

Michael grinned as he pointed to the door at the end of the corridor. "And I take it, this is the bedroom Les?"

His friend's smile matched his slightly nervous reply. "Aye, it is Michael, but you'll be sleeping in the lounge. The couch folds down to a good size bed." Seeing that his daughter was about to interrupt, Les glowered towards her. "It's ma sister's room Michael, she stays here when she's at home. But I'll explain all that later, it's time you feasted your eyes on the finest pigeons this side o' Durham Castle."

Dissuaded by her father, Susan turned abruptly on her heels and marched to the lounge. Switching on the T.V. before placing herself firmly on the couch. Her scowl plainly expressing the extent of her annoyance.

For once the Jack Russell didn't follow her, opting instead to accompany Michael and Les back out into the rain. Unfortunately, his persistent attempts to join them in the pigeon loft proved unsuccessful, leaving him wet and whining miserably outside the sliding door. "Whatever you do Michael, don't let that thieving little bugger inside ma cree, he's taken to stealing ma eggs. Picks them up in his mouth, as nice as you like, sneaks off behind the rabbit hutch, an' licks them out dry. You know, the little bugger, got one from right under ma top stock pair last week, worth a bloody fortune, that egg, more than ten Jack-bloody Russell's! He'll be spending his days at the house keeping Ruby company, till he learns to mend his ways."
Michael didn't reply, allowing only a frown to indicate his sympathy and un-expressed desire not to be around when Les and Ruby next discussed the matter.

For the next half an hour he enjoyed a learning experience, "How to race pigeons, Ont' widowhood." Although in his youth he had read about the Continental system of pigeon management, no one he and Jamie had known in the sport had even considered attempting it. As Les explained, however, at least in England, times had changed. "If you want to win, especially in this part o' the country, it's the only way."

The theory seemed simple enough. "Keep the cocks away from the hens all week. Then, just before they're getting basketed for the race, put the hens back in the nest boxes with 'em for a few minutes. Just long enough to get 'em nice and excited like. Now only the cocks gan to the race, never the hens, an' the quicker they fly home the quicker they get their nookity-coo. Ruby's threatening to put me ont' same system, reckons it'll get me home for ma tea on time."

Although agreeing that widowhood racing certainly seemed to have its merits, Michael couldn't help silently acknowledging why his father and Jamie hadn't succumbed to the modern way. Despite its undoubted advantages, there was something discomforting about disrupting the natural way of things. Pigeons, like most creatures, were happiest with their mates and what a waste of good racing hens, never getting the chance to see the inside of a race pannier.

As Les nevertheless expressed, with justified enthusiasm, the system worked and apart from a few of the old guard, nearly every fancier in the northeast now practised it.

As they moved along the corridor facing each of the four compartments, Michael couldn't deny the obvious health and vitality of the occupants.

Each section was different apart, of-course, from their immaculate state of cleanliness. The ten widowhood cocks each had their plastic fronted boxes to wait patiently in, for the occasional visit by their mates. The stock compartment with its four happily mated pairs, was more like the Murdoch loft; sand covered floor with large open-doored nest boxes, each containing a clay straw filled nest-bowl. Michael couldn't fail to notice the two lovely red youngsters sitting snugly together in the top right box.

"That's a fine pair of squeakers Les. Would you be prepared to part with them? I'm looking for a nice pair of young birds for Jamie."

"Jamie's welcome to anything in this cree Michael, you know that, but they'll no' do him any good, they're out-an-out sprinters, everything here's off Belgian stock. Fly like bullets up to three hundred miles, an' then the buggers gee up the ghost. Jamie an' your da' are distance flyers; you'd be doing them no favours with my stuff, no matter how fast the buggers go."

Michael nodded his understanding. Jamie now had enough problems racing his pigeons without adding to the burden by diluting their inherent long distance qualities. There was, however, something in what Les had just said that perhaps had more relevance to the immediate traumas affecting his family. The difference between sprint and long-distance pigeons.

Having now had the opportunity to compare his friend's sprinters with the present Murdoch team, he was confident that their physical appearance didn't allow any clues to their racing ability. Unlike their human counterparts, the hundred-metre athlete and the marathon runner, physical stature although important wasn't the major factor. Racing pigeons, both distance birds and sprinters, came in all shapes and sizes. The critical differences were hidden from view, in the heart, brain and blood. Unseen characteristics enhanced through generations of manipulative breeding techniques by their masters. The Murdoch birds contained nothing but distance blood, even if they wanted to, they couldn't fly 'like bullets'; something in their genes told them to pace themselves, for the long miles ahead. The most successful of distance-men knew this and succeeded in merging it with the strength and determination required to produce a long distance champion, - a Champion Blue-Boy. Unless, of-course Blue-Boy was just a good sprinter, that would lead the field for a while and then, like Les's birds, "gee-up-the-ghost" and stop-off near Durham for an extremely profitable rest. "Les, I've got something to ask you. Have you heard of a Pigeon called Champion Blue...?"

Their conversation was noisily disrupted by the yapping of an extremely excited Jack Russell, alerting them, and probably anyone else within a hundred metres, to the visitor's presence. Their view, restricted by the louvered doors, didn't allow them to immediately identify who it was. Susan, however, now bounding down the port-a-cabin steps, cheerfully announced her father's worst fears. "Auntie Julie! - Auntie Julie! - Guess what? - A've got a big - big - secret!"

Les's face instantly turned pale as he whispered, "Michael. There's something a've forgot to mention, just stop in the cree till a tell you to, a've got a little explaining to do with ma sister. "

Before he could voice his reply, Michael found himself abandoned and confused in the narrow corridor.

Peering through a gap in the louvers he noticed the outline of the slim shape drifting past the loft. Her voice, however, was much clearer and at the moment she didn't sound overjoyed. "Tell me your little secret, when I'm inside, out of the rain, Susan. I'm absolutely soaked; look at my tights they're covered in mud. Les. When on earth are you and your useless mates going to do something about these paths? They're a disgrace!"

As she led her giggling niece and mumbling apology for a brother up the steps, Michael caught a fleeting glimpse of the back of her blonde, briefcase, covered head. The extent of his predicament now fully dawning. Les's sister stayed in the portacabin when she was home and she was most definitely now home. Les knew it. Susan knew it. - Even the bloody Jack Russell knew it. And to make the situation now even worse, she remembered her pretty little niece had a secret to tell. "Okay Susan, but I hope it's a happy secret, I've had an absolutely horrid day."

Michael could recall dozens of uncomfortable moments in his life - this rated with the worst. As he closed his eyes in anguish, the eight-year-old finally had her say. "There's a big mate o' ma da's hidin' in the cree. He's from Scotland, got a scratch on his head an' a sore hand. An' guess what, Auntie Julie? - he's sleeping we' you tonight!"

The portacabin door slammed closed, thankfully sparing him the specific detail of the muffled but extremely heated conversation inside.

Not yet daring to move he tried in someway to come to terms with what was happening, succeeding only in increasing his feeling of hopelessness. "Last week I was in Banff, running a business worth over half a million. Neat log cabin, neat jeep, neat friends - hardly a care. - Now I'm hiding from a woman in a pigeon loft, in the middle of a bloody Seaham maze, it's pissing rain, my father's dead and all I'm interested in is a fucking blue pigeon and a bed for the night." Despite his friend's instruction, he couldn't just "stop in the cree." If he still had his bag he would have quietly left the allotment, found his way out of the muddy labyrinth and booked into the nearest hotel.

Ensuring that the sliding door was secured behind him he walked nervously towards the cabin, climbed the steps and knocked. The voices inside immediately stopped and although it felt like an age, less than five seconds passed before the door flew open.

For a fleeting moment, as they faced each other, her blue eyes staring into his, they both seemed to lose concentration. Michael, however, eventually managed to stammer. "I'm M - Michael. D - Do you think I could have my holdall?"

Her lips parted slightly but she didn't speak. One hand then flicked back her straggling rain soaked hair as the other slammed the door in his face.

Michael stood open-mouthed; eyes fixed, a strange weakness in his legs preventing him from moving. When he saw the handle turn again he expected his holdall to be joining him on the steps. This time, however, it was Les, his face beaming red. "A'm really sorry about all this Michael. In you come, Sis an' me were just having a little chat. She's gone to her room to get changed, so come away in an' mak' yourself at home."

He reluctantly crossed the threshold and nervously glanced into the lounge, satisfied that apart from the presence of a white rabbit, Jack Russell and grinning little devil-child, it seemed safe to enter.

Susan, patting the couch cushion at her side, gleefully invited him to join her happy trio. "Come in Michael - ma da's sorted it all out. You're sleeping on the couch and ma Auntie Julie's no' ganin to speak to him, ever again!"

He turned an unsmiling face towards his old friend. "Les. I know you mean well, but I just can't impose on your sister like this. Look at the bad feeling it's caused already. To be perfectly honest I've had my fill of family problems over the years and I don't intend to create any more here. I'll just find a hotel or something."

"Look Michael, believe me man, everything's okay. A haven't seen Julie since yesterday so a didn't get the chance to tell her you were coming. An' despite what you've seen, she's a good lass. - Just gets a bit annoyed at me sometimes. - God knows why?"

He glanced towards the bedroom door before finally accepting the Fenton hospitality. If he was being completely honest he would have to admit that his expressions of reluctance had been slightly exaggerated.

Behind the door an extremely annoyed, beautiful young woman was changing out of her wet clothes. Michael's memory raced to a Spring evening and a youth hostel tent in a forest clearing outside Banff.

Over fifteen years had passed, but his memory of his one night with Becky Harris remained intact and, until now, he hadn't met anyone quite like her.

CHAPTER 16

"Ruby, it was delicious! If I can persuade Stan the chef to retire, do you think you could be tempted back to Canada with me?"

Satisfied that her beef hot pot and husband's fresh vegetables had impressed even the owner of a restaurant, she replied with a smile. "An' leave all this, Michael. Ma nice little home, all paid for. Ma three adorable children, ma handsome Bam. - Okay, gee me five minutes to pack ma case!"

"Can a come too, Michael, an' Jock as well? A would help ma mam in the kitchen, an' he could eat up all the scran from under the tables."

As the laughter around the breakfast-bar subsided and they made a start to the sherry trifle, Michael imagined the little dog eagerly patrolling the Cascade. Although the Public Health Department probably wouldn't appreciate his efficiency, even with beer spillages. What a godsend for the Highways Committee. Sort out that argument they've been having for weeks, what to call the new road? Yes, 'Jack Russell Street' had a certain ring to it.

After dinner he was ushered to the lounge with a mug of coffee and instruction from Les to enjoy some "Peace and quiet for a few minutes - The Fenton family had things to do." He, for one, following Ruby's request was seriously considering returning to the gardens. "Bam. - A'm ganin upstairs to get ready. So get yoursel' round there right now and tell her a'll no' take no for an answer. A've been at her for weeks to gan dancing, so no excuses from either o' you."

Although Michael could not see the children, their voices and the clattering of dishes could be heard clearly as they earned their pocket money. Sipping slowly from his mug he contented himself in the atmosphere of his friend's family home. As his mind wandered, however, seeds of sub-conscious thought steadily sprouted to the surface. *The Cascade, the closest of friends, even Tammy aren't enough. There must be more - maybe not exactly what Les has - but perhaps close.*

A smile crossed his lips as he relaxed back into the comforts of the easy chair, with the thought of Ruby, Susan and Jock arriving back with him to the Cascade. - *My God! Wouldn't it be worth it, just to see the look on Stan's face.*

"Yep! Mr Murdoch, this is the first spell I've been unemployed in near-on thirty years. I've been in near every cook-house west of Calgary - so if it's experience you're looking for, Stan Daniels is your man."

Although slightly nervous, Michael was warming to the task of his first staff interview and unknown to Stan, however it went, the job was his.

After a Winter of extremely hard work and the anxiety associated with impending financial ruin, 'The Cascade Bar and Grill' was due to open its gates the following week, with only one prospective chef having answered his increasingly desperate call. "Yep, Mr Murdoch, I personally taste everything before it's plated, if it's not perfect, it's out with the garbage."

Michael did not feel he needed to question him further on this particular point - his twenty-five stone testified to it perfectly adequately. He was around fifty-something, complete bald and built like an over-weight Grizzly. But what was important, he could provide his own chef's hat and whites.

"Okay, Stan that sounds fine." His nervousness, however, now noticeably increasing. "There's... em... just one thing I don't understand. Your... em... last employer, Canadian Logging, they dispensed with your services without even a letter of reference?"

Michael thought his reply would never come. When it did it was hardly audible. Stan's face was now bowed towards his shaking hands. Michael noticing that even the top of his head had turned a flushed red. "Okay, Mr Murdoch, this here's a small town, so you'd probably find out sooner or later."

He now expected the worst, dishonesty, a drink problem, some dreadful food borne infectious disease. "The truth is Mr Murdoch, the Foreman, Mr Peterson, he didn't like my dessert and it's my speciality, fruit pudding and custard, took me years to get it just right."

Michael responded with more relief than sympathy. "That's terrible Stanley; you were fired because he didn't like your fruit pudding? That doesn't seem fair. - And Stan - no-one calls me Mr Murdoch, Mike's fine."

"Well... em... Mr Murdoch - Mike, I'm afraid there's a mite more to it than that, you see I have a slight problem coping with criticism, especially about my fruit pudding."

"You resigned then?"

"No, I threw Mr Peterson out the cook-house window, I tried to apologise! God knows, Mr Murdoch, I tried!"

It was now his prospective employer's time to delay his response, slowly considering what Stan had just said, as the same time recollecting that it was the same Mr Peterson who had rejected, with a curt "Piss-off Scotty." his own eager ambitions to become a timber-hand. "I see Stan, well at least you tried to apologise. Now let's talk money. How about a dollar an hour over the rate, and no criticisms from me about your fruit pudding?"

Within two months of opening, even Jake had to admit to everyone except Michael, that: "The boy done good!" Basic as the facilities were, few of the ever increasing volume of customers were over concerned. The concept was simple; three course menu, soup of the day, steak, French fries, vegetables and the chef's speciality - fruit pudding and custard. Eight dollars for as much or as little as you could eat. Two choices 'take it or go hungry?'

The beer, Labbats Blue, sold by the pitcher, ranging from a pint jug to a gallon and, of course, free entertainment from any talented customer willing to step up on the stage for a half price meal.

Stan's contribution far exceeded his employer's initial expectations, the busier they became the happier he was. In the Cascade - quantity was King. And his years in timber camp kitchens had adapted him ideally to his new role.

By the end of their first Summer Season, although exhausted, neither Michael nor his chef opted for even the shortest of breaks before the snow arrived. "Mike, if you're prepared to spend the profits improving my kitchen, I'd be happier staying put to help get it just right before my skiing customers turn up."

His generous offer was, of-course, willingly accepted, and in Michael's view, "If anyone deserved a better kitchen it was Stan." Without complaint he had struggled through the Summer Season with only the occasional destitute back-packer for assistance. How he had managed to produce the quantity and quality of food demanded, amazed his employer. Particularly as the best that could be said about what lay behind the hurriedly erected, pine clad partition at the far end of the hall, was - 'It couldn't be seen by the customers.' "Okay, Stan it's a deal. Now tell me what you need."

"Well, Mike, running hot water would sure be appreciated."

As November, and the early skiing parties arrived, the chef was proudly inspecting the finishing touches to his white tiled and completely re-furbished domain. "It's perfect, Mike, just perfect, wait till the Public Health people see it. They're sure to lift that threat of closure."

Thankfully, Stan's predication was accurate. The Banff Council's Health Officials were now suitably impressed, and to his delight, so too were the Cascade's new Winter clientele.

The vast majority, although wealthier that their Summer counterparts, appreciated the place for what it was - 'Cheap and Cheerful', perfect for après-ski food and entertainment. The little money required for their generous meal allowed a seemingly endless flow of cash to be spent on beer. The more discerning, treating themselves to the comparative luxury of a wander through the narrow corridor to Jake's Bar for an aperitif and the pleasure of a lumberjack story.

Apart from the occasional comment about the choice of food on offer, few complained, and these were normally placated with an understanding smile and a promise from their host that, if he could persuade Stan, the menu would be enhanced before next season. "Unless, of course, you'd like to speak to the chef in person?" Few accepted the offer.

Saturday nights were busiest. Even the townsfolk were steadily recognising, if they wanted a good steak and a fun evening, the Cascade was the place to be. Although it often resembled Bedlam, Michael seldom had to deal with anything more difficult that the occasional drunk needing a supporting shoulder to the door. Anything more serious, like the first party of Texans, then assistance from the kitchen would be requested and eagerly given.

Michael never found out where in Texas they were from, but he guessed from their conduct it was probably Waco; and despite his best attempts they wouldn't comply with even the politest of requests to curtail their unruly behaviour. "Please gentlemen, everyone knows you're here! Do you really have to dance on the table? There's a young man up on the stage trying to sing, why don't you settle down and give him a chance to earn a half price meal."

"Fuck-off, sonny! We're from Texas, and if we wanna party, we party! Now run-off and get the manager of this shit-house, so he can explain why the beer tastes like piss-water." Before he could explain that it was, in fact, the manager they were presently insulting, Michael received what remained of a gallon pitcher of beer over his shirtfront. A smile, however, came to his lips as he stared up to them "Okay lads. You've made your point, now enjoy what's left of your evening; I'll go pass on your complaint."

Despite the discomfort of the beer-soaked shirt the smile didn't leave his face as he walked casually towards the kitchen.

"What's the problem, Mike?"

"Oh, it's nothing, Stan, just a little misunderstanding with some lads from Texas, the three wearing the cowboy hats and dancing on their table. But don't you be worrying about it, Stanley, whatever they say - your fruit pudding's not crap."

CHAPTER 17

He wasn't sure which one of the twins brought him back to the present. "No way! You little bugger, are you getting out o' this kitchen till you've finished the last pot. An' remember, we've no' forgotten about the Quality Street, so greet as much as you like, you're staying in here till you've done drying."

Despite the crying and banging from the other side of the kitchen door, Michael decided it was best not to interfere. Confidently predicting that the little girl creating the rumpus would, no doubt, seek her revenge at the earliest opportunity.

In the commotion he didn't hear the front door open or Julie Fenton's light steps as she hurried up the stairs. As Les entered the lounge, however, his grin revealed that all seemed well. "Well, Michael, you'll be pleased to know she's calmed down a bit, an' even better, she's away upstairs to get dolled-up for the dancing. An' what with the twins staying at their mate's house tonight, you, me an' Susie can settle down for a good blether. Now, what the hell's ganin on in that kitchen?" The grin disappeared as he strode towards the adjoining door. "Right lads, let her out o' there. Do you two big bullies no' realise she's only eight?"

Grudgingly the door handle was released, allowing a glowering, red-faced eight year old to march through to the lounge. "A'm nearly nine, da'!. Big enough to sort those two buggers out if a wanted to."

"Susan Fenton. A've just about had enough o' your cursing, now get up that stair an' annoy your mam an' Julie."

She hesitated, hands behind her back, only long enough to acknowledge her father's reprimand with the demurest of smiles. Then, running happily towards the hall door unseen by Les, but all too obvious to Michael, two of her angelic little fingers lifted in a farewell salute to the twins.

Pleased that his daughter appeared suitably influenced by his words, Les retrieved his grin and relieved Michael of his empty mug. Soon returning from the kitchen with two pint glasses of beer. "No more coffee for you tonight bonny lad. It's bad for you! You're in Geordie land now, an' it's brown-ale time; so get this down your throat - help lubricate that Canadian drawl of yours, an' you can tell me why you're really here."

Michael, aware that his friend's expression could not mask the piercing intensity in his eyes, replied with an embarrassed smile. "Okay, Les, the truth is, I'm on my way further south. It's a family matter and I can hardly believe it myself but it involves a pigeon, and I'm here for your advice."

Although the tone of his guest's voice concealed any impression of anxiety, Les noticed Michael's pint glass shaking as he brought it to his lips. "Well, Michael, I think we'll leave what you have to say till later, but if it's advice you're after, you've come to the right man. The same Bam who taught you how to box properly can tell you anything you'd ever want to know about pigeons, an' as far as families are concerned, do you know anyone with the respect that a'm given from ma lot?"

Michael almost choked on his brown-ale before responding with a grin. "Very true, Les - very true. I was so impressed with the way you dealt with your sister. Is it seven or seven-thirty tomorrow you're making a start at the paths?" His expression, however, faded at the fleeting memory of Julie. "To be perfectly honest, Les, I'm still very uncomfortable about what she thinks of all this; have you really managed to put her mind at ease?"

"Of-course a have, man, an' between you and me she could do we' a bit o' company - spends far too much o' her time with her head buried in those bloody books."

"Yes, Les, I was going to ask you about that, what does she do? I guessed probably a student."

His host's answer contained more than a trace of pride. "No, well no' anymore, Michael, she's a lawyer, and a bloody good one! Fully qualified M.M.L.B. Honours, out o' Bristol University. You know, in the year she's been working, she's sorted out more compensation cases than all the bloody Union so-called legal experts put together."

Michael listened in silent admiration.

"Top student in her year, an' if she'd any common sense she'd 'ave followed her fancy-man down to London. He offered her a junior partnership in his da's firm, big-league stuff - but no, she gees him the heave. Rather come back up here, stay in a port-a-cabin an' do some good, an' that's her words, Michael, no' mine, - daft as they bloody are!" Les was just getting into his stride when the kitchen door re-opened. "Now what do you two rascals want?"

By the time the twins had persuaded their father to hand over their pocket money and then immediately announced their farewells for the evening, Michael was contenting himself with his second pint of brown-ale, at the same time eagerly awaiting the rest of the Julie Fenton story. He was conscious, however, that his principal train of thought must not be diverted. With all that was going on in his life, the last thing he needed were the kind of feelings which had repeatedly entered his mind since his experience at the allotments.

The problem was he couldn't deny them. She was upstairs getting dolled up to go out dancing. Why that made him feel uncomfortable was beyond his reasoning but, inexplicably, it did. What was certain, he was desperate to see her again, even for another few seconds; would she deign to allow him that opportunity?

As the lounge door slowly opened, Michael's hopes and heartbeat reacted instantly. How she'd negotiated the stairs, in high-heels of that size, amazed both of them, especially with the additional tripping hazard of the black sequinned dress, its hem trailing well below her ankles. The bright red handbag, which matched the shoes, and the over-generous layer of red lipstick, completed the picture perfectly. "Da'! Tell mam an' Julie a can gan dancing too, tell them da'!"

With a valiant effort to keep a straight face, Les, after complimenting her on how grown up she looked, reminded her gently that even at almost nine, she wouldn't make it past the doorman at the Social Club. "An' what's your mam wearing, Susie, now that you've pinched her good dress?"

"She couldn't get into it da', her bum's got too big, so it's mine now. She's wearing her black trousers an' a boob tube. An' you should see Auntie Julie. She's brought a lovely blue dress, it's no' got a back, an' it's that short when she bends over you can see her knickers - they're blue as well!"

Les, for once, was momentarily speechless. His voice only returning when Ruby and his sister, answering Michael's silent prayers, eventually made their entrance. "For God's sake! The pair o' you. You canna leave the house like that, you'll be arrested. Michael, what do you think, is that no' shameful?"

Les had to repeat the question before his open-mouthed guest had the ability to stutter a response. Although since coming into the room she hadn't once glanced his way, on his part, his eyes had been transfixed almost trance-like, oblivious to everything else, except the pounding in his chest. "Em - well. You both...erm - look really great, and I'm sure you'll not be missing out on many dances. But Susan wins first prize, must be the sequins."

Thankfully, Les couldn't delay an irritated interruption. "Miss-out on dances! They'll be round the pair o' yous like flies round..."

"That's enough, Bam! An' Michael's quite right, a should 'ave put on ma sequinned outfit, it's ma favourite, but a just felt like a little change."

Not even Susan dared to pass comment.

"An' don't be expecting us home early. It's licensed till one, an' it's turning out a beautiful night - so we'll probably no' bother we' a taxi. Kissing her red-faced husband she now gleefully added to his burden. "An' don't you be fretting dearest, a'll tak' good care o' your little sister, unless the talent's too much to resist - eh Julie?"

Until now she hadn't spoken or diverted her blue eyes from Ruby or Les, allowing Michael to doubt his host's earlier assurances that all had been forgiven. She at least appeared more relaxed, and although he'd doubted her perfection could be improved, her smile now proved otherwise. "Don't worry Les, Ruby and I won't embarrass you, not that you don't deserve it." Michael was taken by complete surprise as she turned towards him. "Oh, and that reminds me, could you please leave the cabin's outside light on. I don't want to be stamping all over my brother's prize onions, until you've gone that is."

He could only voice a flustered, "Okay - it's a pleasure." Before Julie turned on her long, gorgeously shaped legs, and accompanied her giggling sister-in-law to the door.

Within seconds Susan, reminded by her now less agitated father, stumbled eagerly to the back door to retrieve Jock from his enforced exile in the back yard. It was not, however, until they were both happily snuggled together on the couch, sharing what little was left of her chocolates and watching a Disney video about a talking dog, that

Les turned his full attentions to his guest. "Okay! - It's a pleasure! - You get one chance to speak to the bonniest lass in County Durham an' that's all you can come up we'? My God man! - No wonder you're still single."

Michael could only muster an embarrassed smile and a mumbled excuse that he'd other things on his mind.

To his relief, his friend accepted his statement with a sympathetic nod. "Aye, a know you have lad. An' it's time you told me what a can do to help."

He spoke quietly, only the strained look in his eyes giving any clue to the depth of his feelings.

Les sat in silent concentration.

Michael took him through it, step by step. The telegram, his return, Peter's dreadful news, Francis McLagan, Ian Miller and finally Jamie's Blue Boy story. "So that's about it, Les, apart from what my father put down in his notebook."

"Aye, Michael, the notebook. If it's as you say, an' believe me a don't need much more convincing, don't be losing it, do you have it with you or is it at the cabin? A must read it Michael."

A relieved smile crossed his face. Les wouldn't have bothered even asking about the notebook unless he was sure there was some truth in what he'd said. "It's in my jacket pocket Les; I think Ruby hung it up in the front hall."

"Right lad, you get it while a put ma little angel to bed. Look at the two o' them, dead to the world; you know she hasn't seen the end o' that film yet." The little girl's eyes didn't stir as her father lifted her gently to his shoulder and quietly edged open the lounge door, before slowly climbing the stairs.

Michael, having followed them into the hall, retrieved the notebook and noticing the telephone on its ledge at the bottom of the stairs, waited until Les came back down. "Here it is, Les. I wonder, when you're reading it, could I use the phone? I promised mum I'd give her a ring."

His host grinned his agreement as he snatched the notebook. "Of-course, Michael. Tak' as long as you like, a've got some serious reading to do. Oh! An' mind tell her how well you're being looked after."

"Hello, Rosyth 58649, Jamie Murdoch speaking!"

"Hi! Jamie, how are you?"

"Is that you, Michael? Guess what! We've got a phone now and it's my job to answer it."

Michael delayed his response. "I know, Jamie, I was at home this morning when the men came to install it."

"Oh, aye, I forgot, so you were. Michael! The Pie's taking me for a run in his motor tomorrow, after I've been to the shop and seen to the pigeons. He's been round here all day."

"That's nice, but remember, tell him not to be speeding."

"Don't fret, mum's telt him already. So he knows I'll spew if we go too fast. I'll have to go now, Michael, it's past my bedtime and I'm going for a run in Peter's car tomorrow. Here's mum, cheerio!"

"Hi - mum! Jamie sounds pleased with himself, how are you?"

"Oh, fine son, it's been a bit of a day, though."

"What's happened?"

"Well, Michael, the police have been to the house again, not Ian though, just that nice lassie. She's saying your dad's remains won't be released till probably the week after next. That's a dreadful long time son; I just want him laid at rest."

"I know mum, but there's probably not a lot we can do about it, maybe I'll have another word with them when I get back."

His mother's confidence in the degree of influence her son had with Ian Miller and his colleagues prompted her to immediately change the subject. "There's some good news though, you'll never believe who I've just been on the phone to! - Aunt Betty! I found her number in one of her letters. It was so nice to talk with her again, must be more than thirty years since we last had a blether, and she's just as cheery as ever. The main thing is Michael, and I can hardly believe it myself, she's coming home for the funeral, maybe stay for a month or two."

She couldn't see his smile. "Great mum! She'll soon cheer you up - and you never know, if you haven't spent all our money on new aprons, you could pay her a visit some day."

"That's right son, I hadn't though about that, but, as you say - you never know. Now how's Les and his family keeping?"

"Fine mum, he's asking for you. They're all like him - comedians. I haven't laughed so much in a long time."

"That's good son, you were right to have a wee break and you'll be pleased to know, Ian Miller seems to be getting somewhere at last."

"Oh."

"Yes, and don't sound so surprised - as I've said to you before, he's not a complete idiot."

He now made his best attempt to sound relaxed. "Sorry mum - you're quite right, what has he found out?"

"Well, the young constable lassie was telling me, they're making lots of enquiries about a dark blue estate car - a Ford something-or-other, Siesta, I think."

"Would that be a Fiesta or a Sierra?"

"Yes, that's right, a Sierra, definitely a dark blue Sierra Estate car, with three men in it. Seemingly they were driving round in it for two days before your dad's death and it hasn't been seen since."

"I see mum, well, it sounds as if Ian's maybe on the right track, has he got its number?"

"No, she didn't mention that, but they're definitely not locals, they asked someone for directions and they were English."

"I see - well let's hope Ian's lucky and at least he hasn't got me to concern himself."
"That's right Michael, and mind make sure it stays that way."

He returned to the lounge where he found a re-filled pint glass at his chair and Les Fenton pacing the floor like a pigeon man waiting for his first bird to arrive. "Well Les, what do you think - am I wasting my time?"

His deep frown clearly expressed the soberness of his reply.

"It sickens me to say this Michael, but John Stenway, his side-kick Pearce an' Jamie's champion fucking Blue Boy, are complete bloody frauds. Your da' found them out an' paid a price no one deserves, except those bastards! Sit yourself down lad, it's ma turn to do some talking."

Michael did exactly what his now clearly agitated friend requested, slowly sipping his beer as the facts, as Les saw them, were affirmed with the coherence only a keen knowledge of the subject could dictate.

"Right, let's start at the beginning. On Saturday 25th June, the day of the E.H.U's Fraserburgh National, Blue Boy turns up at your da's. He's locked in the cree for five hours an' then Jamie lets him out. Two hours later - six thirty - he's supposedly timed in at Foxhole, no fucking way Michael, it's impossible. Now at the speed he was doing, 1498 yards a minute, he could only have flown about 110 miles south o' Rosyth. Near enough to here to persuade you to pay me a visit after fifteen bloody years."

Although he saw from Les's smile that the truth had created no bad feelings, he couldn't prevent the flush of embarrassment now colouring his cheeks.

"A'm in no doubt Michael, Blue-Boy was timed in no' far from here, an' then some bastard put him an' the clock in a motor and belted down to Kent before the clock checking. Now that sounds simple, but it's no', or plenty more cheating bastards would have tried it."

"How do you mean Les? It sounds straightforward enough to me; they've just got to train a good sprint pigeon to drop to a loft half-way home, where it knows it's going to get food and rest?"

"Aye lad, an' maybe if it's on't widowhood, its nooky as well, cos that's where his hen'll be! But you've been too long away from the sport man, that's no' what a'm getting at. Can you no' see? The whole bloody scam relies on Stenway an' his mate knowing exactly when to put the rubber ring in the clock."

Noticing Michael's sate of confusion, Les took the opportunity to sit down and take a welcome mouthful of brown ale. "Now lad! First of all, forget about the Fraserburgh Race for a minute. They would have been in such a panic, with Blue Boy no' turning up for five hours, as soon as he got there at six-thirty, he'd 'ave been timed. An' they were bloody lucky; they didn't win the race by much, five yards a minute - if it was that. But as a say, forget about that, what about his other wins? If they timed him as soon as he dropped he'd be so far in front o' the rest; he'd be disqualified -

impossible velocity! No, the bastards are too cute for that, that's why it's so bloody perfect. They don't time him till just after the first pigeons are arriving north o' London. All they need is a quick phone-call from somebody in the know, an' with the extra distance he's supposed to be flying, he'll beat them every time."

Michael was now realising the debt he owed to Bobby McLay for putting him in the ring with Les-the Bam-Fenton.

"Now what else do we know? The week after the Fraserburgh Race, your da' reads his pigeon papers and sees the results. He phones Stenway, causes a hellava fuss an' isn't happy we' what's been said, so he's right back on the blower to the General Manager o' the E.H.U. Major Lockwood, no-less. What's been said we don't know, but he's obviously been told to put it in writing. It's a bloody pity we don't have a copy of his letter, but never mind." His voice began to rasp with emotion. "The following Friday night, you da's murdered by three dirty bastards, an' it sickens me to say it, but they're maybe Geordies. Well at least one o' them is - another's ca'd Terry, an' it sounds as if he's got a sore nose for his trouble. Michael, that's about all a'm sure about, unless there's more you're no' telling me?"

"Yes, Les, there is. My mother's just told me they may have been driving a dark blue Sierra Estate."

"Right lad, that helps. The facts are all here, now all we have to do is prove them."

"No, Les! I've go to prove them. You've given me the advice I asked for, and I can't thank you enough for that, but this is my problem and you're not to get more involved - okay?"

Their stares fixed on each other.

"Sure, Michael! If that's what you want, but if you're so pleased with ma advice a've got some more for you. First thing tomorrow morning you should get in that fancy motor o' yours an' pay a visit to the E.H.U. Headquarters, an' have a word with Major Lockwood before Saturday."

"You've lost me Les, why?"

"Why, you daft bugger, do you no' read your Pigeon Press? Because Blue Boy's racing again this weekend. From Thurso, that's bloody why!"

Michael's fists gripped tight as he slowly realised the full significance of what had just been said. "Les, this is my problem, not the English Homing Union's, and it's up here that the pigeon's been timed in, so what good would I be doing in London tomorrow?"

His friend returned a sympathetic smile. "A know what you're saying bonny lad, but you've got to realise it's no' just your problem. There's thousands o' decent, honest pigeon fanciers being shafted by these two bastards, an' at the end o' the day, despite what you think, only the police or the Homing Union can sort this out properly. Now a appreciate your no' wanting to involve the police yet, an' a can understand your thinking, they'd probably make an arse o' it an' Stenway would get off scott-free. But if the E.H.U. can prove what they've been up to, the bastards'll get life. Now a know you want more than that, an' maybe in your shoes A'd want the same, but think about it Michael, it's the only way."

As he considered the sincerity of his friend's words, Michael released his grip and forced a smile before quietly responding. "Okay Les, I appreciate what you've said, but I just thought I'd be better up here, trying to prove where Blue Boy is timed in, before telling the authorities".

"Aye Michael, an' most folk would believe your intentions, but I bloody don't! A know you too well. Listen, even if a did agree with you, tomorrow's Friday - there's just no' the time to find out anything up here. You're better in London, they're probably already investigating the whole thing, a'm told this Major's a right stickler for the rules."

Michael finally nodded his agreement. His friend, on balance, was probably right. He would allow the Racing Pigeon Authorities the opportunity to assist and if they couldn't, well, their headquarters in Epping Forest was close enough to Foxhole to pay the Stenway Stud a little visit on Saturday. Maybe buy a pair of squeakers for Jamie.

What now remained of their evening passed in comparative relaxation. As they enjoyed the last sips of their third brown ale, realising it was close to midnight; Michael yawned his intention. "I'd better get some shut-eye, Les. We've gone over it enough for tonight and thanks to you I've got an early start and another long drive tomorrow."

"You're right, Michael, an' you're no' the only one that's knackered. It's no' often a have to use ma brain nowadays and it's tired me more than a twelve-hour shift. No' that a'm doing many o' these this weather."

A feeling of guilt added to the burden of fatigue now nagging at his mind. He'd sat there for over four hours, so wrapped up in his own problems, not once having the decency to ask how Les was coping with life. "I know, Les, it can't be easy for you, especially when self-centred buggers like me turn up without even asking how you're managing to get by."

He responded with a tired grin. "Oh, don't you be fretting about me, bonny lad; you've got enough on your plate. A'm fine. An' you can see what a lucky bugger I am, so a'll no' be on the dole for ever." Before his guest had the chance to reply, Les lifted himself slowly from his chair and gently prodded the sleeping occupant of the threadbare couch. "An' you're in luck too ma lad! Jock could do we' a walk, so he'll show you the way, keep you nice and cosy in that fold-down bed o' yours".

As Michael and his happy companion shared the pleasure of their star-clear stroll, despite all the words spoken, his thoughts were concentrated on the grinning importance of his friend's parting statement. "An' for God's sake man. Remember to leave the outside light on or you'll never get the chance to say more to her than: 'Okay - it's a bloody pleasure!' "

CHAPTER 18

She lay on her side, naked and motionless. Only her eyes disputing the brain's message to the rest of her body - she should still be asleep!

With confused resentment she stared at the second hand of the small travel clock as it moved relentlessly around its full circle indicating, with uncompromising precision, that another precious minute of unconsciousness had been lost.

Three minutes past seven! Like clockwork she always woke at seven-thirty, ready to prevent the alarm ringing before it had the audacity to interrupt her morning's tranquillity.

Why not this morning? It should be no different. Same clock perched on the same bedside table; same room, same cosy duvet to snuggle under, same intoxicating aroma of freshly percolating coffee... Percolating coffee! Her brain staggered into action, initially to comprehend what was going on and then slowly and deliberately to mull over her options. Either snuggle back under the duvet for less than half an hour of fitful dozing or see what her brother's friend was up to in the kitchen.

"Morning! I see you've found my coffee, I don't suppose I could trouble you for a cup?"

Her yawning introduction, as she slowly lifted her slim figure onto the high-backed kitchen stool, was acknowledged with a nervous smile. "Okay, it's a pleasure."

As he poured a fresh cup and topped up his own, Michael hoped she was too tired to notice his shaking hand. He was also now in no doubt - another major problem had entered his life. Sitting opposite him, cross-legged on the stool, in a beige towelling dressing gown with matching fluffy slippers, Julie Fenton, dishevelled blonde hair, bleary eyes and not a hint of make up was, without question, the most beautiful woman he'd every met.

They shared the tiny kitchen and several sips in silence before he recovered his concentration. "Em... how did your evening go - dance till you dropped?"

A smile slowly widened her lips, instantly bringing the comfort he craved. "Almost! Yes it was great fun. It couldn't be any other way when Ruby's on form." The smile was now displaced by a giggle. "She's such a party animal. You know, she had all the girls doing a Conga right through the gentlemen's lounge, ruined their dominoes tournament. Wait till Les finds out, he's been so keen to get on the Club Committee."

Michael responded with a grin. "Well at least, with all your dancing, you shouldn't have much of a hang-over."

Following a moment's self-assessment her smile returned. "No, that's true. I don't feel too bad, and just as well, I've an extremely busy day ahead. How was the couch? Even with it folded down, your feet would be hanging out the bottom."

"It was just fine, slept like a log, didn't even hear you come in and, of-course, I had company, so it was nice and cosy."

"Company?"

"Yes, the last I saw of him he was outside staring into Les's pigeon loft. You know, he wouldn't quit licking my ear till I got up and opened the door."

"Licking your ear? Oh! - You mean Jock? - You had me worried there for a moment."

As their laughter filled the portacabin he relaxed in the confidence that the animosity of yesterday seemed to have totally disappeared. "Michael - em - look. About yesterday, I was a bit short with you what with slamming the door and everything. It was just one of those days I'm afraid, and all I needed was Les making arrangements without telling me, so..."

"Before you say anymore, Julie, I'm the one who should be apologising. I understand completely. The last thing you'd expect is to come home to find a complete stranger looking for a bed for the night. If anyone should be saying sorry it's me."

She returned an impish grin. "No Michael, you've picked me up wrong, I wasn't going to apologise, I was going to ask you for twenty five pounds B & B!"

As they shared the pleasures of the remaining, all too brief, minutes, he noticed occasionally that her now sparkling blue eyes perhaps hinted something potentially more encouraging than merely the enjoyment of a pleasant interlude with a mate of her brothers.

"I hope you don't mind Julie, but I flicked through one of your books last night. The Law of Contract, pretty heavy stuff, certainly helped get me to sleep though."

She nodded her agreement. "It used to have the same effect on me. It's all the legal jargon of-course, its there deliberately to confuse anyone who's not in the business, but I suppose it helps keep us in a job."

"Yes, Les was saying you've been busy with compensation cases. I take it that's with all the mines closing?"

"Mostly, the majority of lawyers find it pretty tedious work, but most of the time I actually quite enjoy it. You wouldn't believe how many workers accepted their redundancy packages without question. The problem is it seemed like a fortune at the time. But in too many cases it's less than their due entitlement and, of-course, that's not often realised until after the papers are signed and the money spent."

Realising instinctively that he'd struck the right chord, Michael smiled sympathetically. "So, you're left to sort out the mess, it can't be easy?"

As she flicked a wayward strand of hair from her forehead the full extent of her frown was revealed. "Not always! Especially when it turns out like yesterday, another of Les's mates of-course. Six months I've been working on his claim, Tribunals,

Appeals, all the usual hassle, and finally yesterday I hand him a cheque for over five thousand pounds."

"Was he not happy with the amount?"

"No, that's what makes it more annoying, he was ecstatic! He'd blown his redundancy within three months at the Social Club. All the family had left was a weekly Giro and a pittance of a pension and you should see the way they're living. So, I hand him the cheque and within minutes he's on the phone to his pals, arranging to go quarter share in a race horse, Durham Folly or something equally appropriate."

The noise of the alarm ringing from the bedroom immediately curtailed his response.

"My goodness, seven-thirty! I'd better get organised, I'm supposed to be at the Magistrates Court by nine. If you're in town this afternoon, and as a loose end, pop into my office, it's above the betting shop. Coffee's around three."

"I'd love to, but I'm heading off this morning. I've to meet someone in London." Noticing what he hoped was a flicker of disappointment as she raised her cup for a last sip, he smiled nervously. "Em - if you don't mind though, I might stop-off on my way back up to Fife, maybe we could - em - go out for a meal or something?"

"Maybe."

Unknown to each other, both smiles remained intact as they separately busied themselves for the day ahead. Michael folding up the couch before packing his holdall. Julie enjoying the pleasure of the pink-tiled shower. Disappointed slightly that she couldn't show him off to Marlon, her secretary. *But, a meal, that'll make up for it nicely.*

Within five minutes, Michael was ready for the road and his first decision of the day. Either shout a farewell through the shower-room door or relax in the morning sunshine for a while on Les's garden bench, just to keep Jock company and perhaps chaperone Julie through the allotment paths.

The wait was worth each of the twenty minutes. Closing the cabin door behind her, she turned on the wooden step and took his breath away. Black pin-striped suit, the hem of her skirt a demure inch above the knee, black tights, matching lace tie, white blouse, dark tan briefcase, all that and a flick of her flowing blond hair as she approached the bench. Even the backless number instantly became a distant memory.

She stood facing him, her eyes acknowledging that his wait had been appreciated.

As she spoke, however, the softness of her voice betrayed the importance she placed on the question. "Michael - I hope you don't mind me asking, but Ruby told me about your father's death, and I know it's none of my business, but you coming here and now going off to London - it has something to do with it, hasn't it?"

By the time his brain caught up with his mouth it was too late to curtail the terseness of his reply. "What makes you think that? Has Les said something?"

Her response, although momentarily delayed, mimicked his tone. "No, Les hasn't said anything. Not that he would, my brother might be an annoying devil, but his loyalty can't be faulted!"

Michael's irritation was now totally directed to himself. "I'm sorry Julie, what I said wasn't called for, it's just such a personal matter, I'm really uncomfortable about others becoming involved. But what I'm doing - is it so obvious?"

Sitting down on the bench beside him their eyes met, sharing each other's apprehension. "I'm a lawyer, Michael. I get paid for being nosy. Your father's murdered, you come back from Canada after fifteen years, and then - after a couple of days and a sore hand - you leave your family to go off touring the country! It just doesn't make sense. Unless you're a callous sod, and I don't believe that, or more likely you're getting yourself involved in something better dealt with by the police."

"Well - em! - As I said, it's a family matter but maybe you're right, perhaps I have made it too personal. Les and I had a long talk about it last night though, and all going well, I'll soon be able to put it behind me without any more fuss. Then I can tell you all about it over dinner, that's if you've made your mind up yet?"

Accepting with a wry grin, the skill with which he'd changed the subject, Julie gripped the handle of her briefcase and stood up. "Before I say yes or no, do you know anything about Lurchers?"

"No, they're some kind of dog - aren't they?"

"Okay, it's a date."

Before he could voice his confusion, she chuckled. "The last friend of my brother's who took me for a meal turned up at the door with his Lurcher. Not that I had anything against the dog, it was more interesting that its owner. Did you know the best Lurcher for hare coursing is a cross between a Greyhound and a Border Collie? I learnt that and a lot more over a pie and mushy peas at the Hare and Hound. I probably know more about Lurchers than Les knows about pigeons!"

In the time it took to walk to the boundary of the allotments and say their farewells, Julie having explained that a few minutes of well-worn short-cuts would take her to the town centre, he felt he'd known her for years. Striding purposely towards Daphne Row, he tried to rationalise why. - Why? With a girlfriend sharing his life for five years and more than a few, albeit, casual relationships before that, should he feel this way about the sister of an old pal he'd known for less than a full day. He also reminded himself that apart from this morning, the remainder of their time together hadn't exactly been overburdened with friendship.

It was around eight, and all was quiet at number sixty, curtains drawn and no hint of activity inside. Michael decided not to disturb Les and his sleeping family. If he was to achieve anything constructive today, time was at a premium.

Following a quick check he was satisfied he had all he needed. *Holdall, car keys, wallet, notebook and, of-course, one added essential - the promise of a date with Julie Fenton.*

CHAPTER 19

With over three hundred miles of motorway ahead, the Range Rover gathered speed and its driver his thoughts. Unbelievable as it seemed, only four days had passed since getting off the plane at Prestwick. Only a fleeting moment, just long enough to experience a lifetime's emotions.

Shock - anger - guilt - frustration - joy, had raced through his being. Until yesterday revenge was leading the field. Now he wasn't so sure if its grip was just as strong. He felt guilty that grief hadn't even entered the race yet. Sadness for his family - yes, but no more. Perhaps there hadn't been time to grieve; maybe it would sneak up on him when the others had ran their course. Perhaps, where Tam Murdoch was concerned, he was no longer capable of such sentiment. Since talking to Les and Julie, however, other considerations were now becoming focused in his mind. Foremost, his family's future - his own future. His determination to play a part in achieving justice, some kind of satisfactory settlement for his father had not lessened. *But if others could help, allow them their chance.*

Today, two priorities would need his full attention. Meeting Major Lockwood, he would play by ear. If the Racing Pigeon Authorities could help get to the truth, fine. If not, Stenway and Pearce may still receive a Canadian visitor to their famous pigeon stud.

The outcome of his first task he already knew, and as soon as he found the resolve and a telephone, he would hopefully put it finally behind him. Tammy should have finished work and be back at his cabin overlooking the Sulphur Springs. How she would react to him selling the Cascade and Jake's, he wasn't entirely sure, but if anyone should be first to know it was her. Perhaps she'd already guessed the inevitability of it. Although she still shared his bed, their once shared enthusiasm for the Cascade had steadily widened. She was increasingly finding solace in John's company and Michael didn't entirely blame her.

In five short years his partner, since being offered and eagerly accepting a stake in the business, now seemed to have no bounds to his youthful ambitions. Both John and Tammy had that in common, if there was more, Michael hadn't noticed, not that he'd recently concerned himself to look too closely.

A wry smile crossed his lips as he recalled how different it all used to be; their minds - their passions had been as one. Unfortunately, both had failed the test of time.

Unlike his relationship with Tammy, a decade together had proved the strength of his bond with Jake Matthews.

On paper they were no longer business partners - Michael owned everything. Jake, on his part, was the wealthiest part-time barman in Alberta. Turning up when he felt like giving a hand, helping himself to the Jack Daniels and entertaining the timber hands and tourists to his heart's content.

Despite the pressures of running the business, at twenty-seven Michael, at last felt he'd gained the stability he'd yearned for. Financial security, close friendships and the added bonus of becoming well respected in his adopted community. His Wednesday evenings off - seeing him, tweed suit and attaché case, strolling along Banff Avenue towards the Tourist Association HQ. to chair the weekly meeting. Afterwards, joining Jake for their regular steak dinner back at the Cascade. Nothing interfering with his routine, the ordered smooth-running lifestyle he had created for himself and the old man. "You what? --- You devious old bastard! --- Getting married! --- Mabel! --- After all you've said about her!"

"Now Mike! Anything I might have said about Mabel was in the past and I don't want it repeated again, you hear? And whatever you think, we've grown kind-a close in the spell she's been here and it's about time I settled down."

"About time. You're eighty-three, you daft old bugger!"

"That's right son, and I'm not getting any younger. And what with not having to concern myself with this place. Not that you're capable of running it properly without me, spending good money on toilets that served me perfectly well for thirty years. I want to see my last years out with a good woman."

"Sorry Jake, you're right, and she is a good woman. I just don't see what she sees in you. My God, it's all coming home! That's why you've tidied yourself up over the past few weeks and you're never away from the office. I thought it was just too nosy at the profits I've made since buying you out - and to think, this time last year you didn't want her near the place. What was it you kept whining? 'No way Mike, the woman's a crook; her hand'll never be out of the till.' Seems to me, Jake, her hand's been occupied somewhere else."

"Mike! - That's enough. If I thought you'd take it this way I wouldn't have bothered telling you, least-of-all ask you to be my best-man."

For what seemed like an age he stared at his old friend in stunned silence. Slowly, however, the shape of his mouth altered to accommodate the widest of grins. "Best-man! Me. Do you really mean it Jake? What can I say. --- I'm delighted for both of you! - Best-man, eh."

"Yep, Mabel and me had a long talk about it. We need someone presentable, a good organiser, someone who can string a few, well-chosen words together. But we can't come up with anyone, so you'll have to do. Now we want to get hitched next month and as best-man you'll have one or two little chores to take care of, and don't try to tell me you're too busy."

"What little chores, Jake?"

"Well, there's the transport, flowers, entertainment, the food of-course - and a cake; do you know anyone who can make us a wedding cake? Three tiers, Mabel wants the works!"

Michael's grin immediately disappeared, displaced again with the open-mouthed silence.

"Stanley, surely a chef of your ability can make a wedding cake. Is it not just your fruit-pudding recipe with a few wee additions - you know, icing, ribbons, that kind of thing?"

Leaving Stan proudly polishing his baking utensils in preparation, Michael slowly warmed to the task and as the days progressed found, that organising a wedding provided a welcome change from his normal routine.

It wasn't the easiest of undertakings, particularly as it involved the almost constant interference from an expected but still exceedingly frustrating source of annoyance. The more, however, he saw of Jake with Mabel, giggling together like school kids or hand in hand leaving the bar, the more he realised, despite their age difference, how perfect they were for each other. What he still found extremely difficult to understand was how radically Jake's opinion of his intended had altered since Mabel's early retirement from the Youth Hostel Association and her new career as the Cascade's accountant.

Michael, on his part, hadn't shared the old man's vociferous lack of confidence in her character and had no hesitation in offering her the job. She had the qualifications and experience required and he couldn't help admire the way she had fleeced the Association for all these years. And probably would have continued doing, if her cousin hadn't been on sick leave.

Perhaps if Mabel had been at the camp when the two gaunt, be-spectacled visitors paid their unannounced call, she may still have talked her way out of it. Unfortunately, she was in Jake's bar, collecting the monthly envelope for her Public Relations Work.

To add to her problems, the girl she had left in temporary charge wasn't over-burdened with common sense. "Nope!" Mabel's not around. You'll find her in Jake's Bar, Caribou Street, unless you want to wait for a couple of hours?"

"Oh! Yes, Jake's Bar - adjacent to the Cascade Bar and Grill?"

"You know the place then?"

"No. However, we couldn't fail to notice that almost every tree within the Hostel's boundary is advertising the delights of both establishments! And you, young lady, are you employed by the Association?"

"Nope! I'm just staying here for the Summer. Mabel said it would be okay if I didn't tell anyone, paid cash in advance and helped around the place."

"Mmm - in that case perhaps you could give Miss Lawrence a ring. Just inform her the auditors are here and would appreciate her immediate presence. Now, if you don't mind, until she arrives, I think Ms Fletcher and I will have a little look around."

"Nope! Carry-on, just be careful you don't step on any bear-shit, I haven't done my rounds yet."

"Well, what do you think Ms Fletcher? Apart from the bear droppings we can't question the tidiness of the place?"

Dabbing, with a white lace handkerchief, the stream flowing from her piercing, hay-fevered eyes, she voiced, what she hoped was a suitably efficient reply. "True. Mr Thorogood, however, the unauthorised advertising of licensed premises and leaving the Hostel under the charge of a non-association employee should, in my opinion, merit a written warning."

Mr Thorogood raised his eyebrows in a gesture of professional admiration. "Agreed! Now where are we? Yes, tent number ten - after you Ms Fletcher."

In the time it took to bring his colleague back to semi-consciousness, man-handle her to the office, find her a chair and a glass of water, Mabel was driving through the camp's entrance, her face almost as pale as Ms Fletchers.

"Miss Lawrence! Before you explain leaving you post in the dubious care of a cash-in-advance Summer guest, to spend your afternoon in a bar, the delights of which are illicitly displayed throughout the camp. Before that, Miss Lawrence, and prior to producing your accounts - which I assure you, when Ms Fletcher fully recovers, will be examined in finite detail! Please, Miss Lawrence, would you kindly explain why a young gentleman from Kentucky, wearing nothing but a smile and a Davy Crocket hat, as he succinctly put, is 'hunting beaver' with two Italian females in tent number 10!"

Although Mabel's mouth opened, closed and opened again, the power of speech had deserted her. Her final memory of Mr Thorogood was the cold sarcasm in his smile as he delivered his verdict. "Miss Lawrence, how can I explain your situation in terms you can't fail to understand? Yes! You either retire immediately, without severance pay and pension, or we meet you again - in Court!"

When they'd gone, Mabel's books secured in Mr Thorogood's briefcase - "As further evidence if required." she cleared her desk, too traumatised to cry let alone contemplate a future out with the Association.

The tears didn't flow until she reached the Cascade. Michael, realising instantly her state of shock, rose from his office chair to meet her. "Now, just sit yourself down Mabel. I'll get you a gin, my God. You look as if you need it."

"Mike, it's dreadful, I've --- I've been fired. They're calling it enforced early retirement but no pension! No severance pay! No nothing! After the years of dedicated service I've given them."

The time, of-course, wasn't appropriate to remind his good friend that even without the official severance package she should surely get by on her own little pension fund she'd been discreetly building up over the years. "Don't you be upsetting yourself, Mabel. We'll work something out, Jake and me won't let you down."

"No-way, Mike! She's a crook! You, me and everyone else in Banff knows it. If you want her in the Cascade that's your problem but she's not getting near the bar's books or my cash register till you've bought me out. And I'll tell her that right now, if you wont!"

"No, Jake, she's upset enough as it is. But whatever you think, I know she won't let me down. So I've made up my mind, she works for me!"

Almost a year to the day, sitting at their usual Wednesday night table at the quietest corner of the restaurant, once again in deep conversation about the ever approaching wedding, the old man needed no further reminders of the accuracy of Michael's words. "And of-course, Jake. There's the added bonus she's going to free me of a burden I've had to carry for years!"

"Okay, you cheeky young bugger, enough's enough! Now, have you got yourself a partner yet? No self-respecting best man turns up without a partner."

To the old man's delight, his words had produced the acute embarrassment they'd intended. "Em, not yet Jake. You know how busy I've been, but the cake's finished; Stan spent days on it, it's beautiful, so for God's sake - remember to thank him in your speech, eh."

"When it's eaten and nobody's ill, that's when I'll thank him and not before. Fruit pudding in a wedding cake! I'm making you personally responsible for this Mike. Now what's next? The cabs, have you booked...." To Jake's annoyance he was now being completely ignored. The young man's attention had suddenly diverted towards the stage.

Carrying a battered acoustic guitar, black iridescent hair flowing to the slimmest of waists, the prettiest Canadian Indian he'd seen was nervously walking up the access stairs, her head bowed as if attempting but failing to conceal her beauty. She perched herself on the wooden stool before slowly raising her brown eyes, gracing the audience with a smile, then lowering them again to tune her guitar.

"Sorry, Jake! Could we hold things a minute? Look at that girl on the stage, she's gorgeous - do you know her?"

The old man strained his irritated eyes in the direction his young friend was gaping. "Nope! Not from this neck of the woods, looks part Cree. You're right though, ain't she a little honey. Now where were we? The transport!"

Despite his protestations, Jake was forced to accept that, for the time being at least, his best man's concentration was completely lost to him.

Tuning now completed to her satisfaction; she lifted her eyes again and with the demurest of smiles, as she gently tapped the microphone, introduced herself quietly but clearly to the now attentive diners. "Hi! My name's Tammy Hobbs and I'm proud to say I'm a native Canadian from the Cree Nation." Encouraged by the polite ripple of applause, her smile widened. "I wasn't always known as Tammy Hobbs, I changed it from Tam-a-Lay-Hobos, which for anyone who doesn't speak Cree, means two dogs fucking."

Michael felt the wave of shock from the floor reverberate against the pine-clad wall at his back. "Jake! - D... did she just say what I think she did?"

The old man allowed the drop of his steak knife and a single animated nod to state his confirmation.

If anything, her smile now took on an added sweetness. "I guess I can't complain - being the last of seven sisters. You see - my father, Chief One-Arrow Missing, couldn't think of another girl's name. So he shared a pipe or three with the Medicine Man, who told him to call me after the first thing he saw when he left the Tepee."

In the explosion of laughter, few heard her now grinning introduction to "Big Yellow Taxi". Within seconds, however, of the Joni Mitchell song echoing beautifully around the vast hall, little encouragement was needed for the majority to join in. The audience's reaction merely confirming what Michael hadn't doubted - her voice matched her looks.

Although his young friend was too enthralled to notice, even Jake was suitably impressed, tunefully tapping the floor with his good leg.

The cries of 'Encore!' 'More!' and the crescendo of rattling cutlery when the song ended didn't, however, immediately gain their desired effect. "Thank you so much. I'd love to sing another, but I'm told, no matter how many I do, a half price steak is the best this place can offer!"

Michael waited until the audience started stamping their feet in unison before attracting his headwaiter's attention. "John! Ask her to do two more, and the meal's on the house."

Two songs later, acknowledging the standing ovation with the most comely of smiles, she was ushered, celebrity-like, back to her now lace covered, candle lit table, to await the first course.

"Nice touch John!" - Michael grinned his silent appreciation, before receiving the full sharpness of a bony elbow to his rib cage.

"Well, son! You can take that idiot look off your face and get over there right now! That's who I want singing at my wedding. And don't be offering her any of my money - she'll be coming as your partner."

Although the glowering response clearly expressed his annoyance, he needed no further encouragement to leave his table.

"Hi, I'm Michael - Michael Murdoch, I thought you were great up there. Do you mind if we have a little chat?"

She glanced upwards, her brown eyes straying casually over her tall, nervous admirer. The coolness of her smile betraying her answer. "Well thanks - but I don't think so. You see - I'm expecting the owner of this snake pit to come over soon and offer me a job. Is it true he's a mean old bastard with a limp?"

As he parked the Range Rover opposite the row of telephone kiosks, the vivid memory of their first words and the embarrassed confusion on her beautiful face almost made him turn the key again and drive on.

As her arm stretched slowly to place the bedside phone carefully back onto its onyx receiver, she couldn't prevent the tears welling in her eyes. Using the edge of the black satin sheet to stop them trickling down her cheeks, she lay silently for a moment, reflecting on each word. *Three thousand miles away and in fifteen minutes he says more than he's done in months.*

Before turning towards the centre of the bed, she pushed her elbow side-ways, nudging the hidden shape beside her. "John! Get your head out from under there. Everything's okay, so you don't have to make out you're still sleeping."

Slowly a forehead and a pair of anxious eyes emerged from the security of the darkness. His mouth, still hidden, voiced a trembling whisper. "Are you sure Tammy? Did you - d... does he suspect anything?"

"No, I didn't tell him, not that it matters much now, what's important is he's prepared to offer you the business for half a million."

Her partner freed the sheet from the remainder of his head. My God! Half a million! You were right - he must be losing his grip. Pass me the phone honey; wait till my father hears what a bargain I've struck!"

The tears forgotten, a wry smile crossed her mouth as she watched him frantically press the code numbers for New York, her hand now free to meander its way down his body.

"Now, honey! Make sure you tell your daddy it's not just the business that's included in the deal."

CHAPTER 20

Michael predicted the coolness of his reception as soon as he turned into Wing Holm's tree-shaded driveway.

The disdaining stare from the stone-frozen pigeons, perched regally on each of the marble entrance pillars, expressed less than an open welcome. He returned them a nervous glance in the rear-view mirror. *This looks like the last bloody place to play things by ear.*

He accepted grudgingly, however, that time for regret was no longer available to him, nor was the opportunity to prepare his thoughts for his meeting with the Major. That had been lost soon after speaking to Tammy. His feelings of relief, as he's driven quickly away from the telephone kiosk, had lasted less than twenty motorway miles. The remainder of the journey too filled with memories.

Until he reached Waltham Abbey, the Range Rover, as if responding to his needs, seemed to have been travelling on autopilot. Michael had pointed it south; it had taken over from there - Cruising effortlessly down the outside lane, it had reached the northern boundary of the capital in less than three hours. Then easing eastwards on the M25, until within minutes, veering north at the Waltham Junction towards Epping Forrest.

As it approached the village centre he realised he had to think for himself and almost immediately got lost. The address in his father's notebook didn't give him many clues - E.H.U. - H.Q. 18 Upshire Road, Waltham Abbey, could be anywhere. If he was in luck, hopefully in the main street, maybe like Julie's office, above the betting shop? Circling the village centre three times, before reluctantly accepting he'd have to ask someone, he found a parking space opposite the Post Office.

"Upshire Road? Yes, keep going north, straight past the cross for about a mile. It's a long road though. Who is it you're looking for?"

When he told her, the elderly Postmistress couldn't resist a wry smile. "In that case you can't miss it. You'll come to a set of big pillars with two grotesque birds stuck on them. He's calling it Wing Holm now. The Major thinks his place is too important just to have a number. Causes us all sorts of inconvenience!"

Five minutes later, as the tyres crunched loudly over the drive-way's deep layer of grey stone chippings, Michael slowed the Range Rover to a crawl, for a moment wishing he was still lost. Wing Holm was most definitely no cramped office above the "bookies".

Skirted by an impressive boundary of ancient oaks, its dark sandstone façade seemed to demand admiration. The parallel lines of the freshly cut lawn at both sides of the driveway, adding to the building's Victorian formality. He guessed it may have been built as a Manse, perhaps for the near-by Abbey. It wasn't enormous, maybe eight rooms, but as its two storeys drew closer he was confronted with a disturbing sense of inferiority. The imposing stone stairway adding to his now growing apprehension. Although realising, that apart from the black-painted balustrade, the steps were probably no grander than the Tradesman's Clubs. The property they served was in a different league, and unlike the Social Club, tradesmen would almost certainly be obliged to enter by the back door.

The driveway led him almost to the bottom tread then swept left below a large white-framed bay window, towards the car park - sign-posted for staff and visitors. The four staff spaces were occupied, one by a Range Rover, a similar model to his, but metallic black, its wax-polished chassis glinting in the mid morning sunshine. As he passed it, Michael noticed what looked like a Regimental Sticker on the rear window, also observing, with little surprise, that the visitors' parking area was empty.

He checked the time - 11.25am - switched off the engine and sat for a moment in pensive silence. Before he'd phoned Tammy he'd come close to turning the key again. That option was, once more, begging serious consideration - but he'd come this far. What was there to lose?

The opaque reception window rattled across its wooden runner, revealing a stout woman in her mid-forties. Secured by a silver chain, her half-rimmed spectacles balanced comfortably on her ample chest. Accompanying them a rectangular identity badge firmly pinned to her white high collared blouse. "Yes! Can I be of assistance?"

Michael immediately recognised the facts now facing him. Her name, Miss Florence Simpkins. Her position in the Organisation, Personal Secretary. Her clear intention - to be of as little assistance as possible. He offered her the politest of smiles. "Em - hopefully. I've travelled down from Scotland to see Major Lockwood, I don't have an appointment but I'd really appreciate a few minutes of his time."

Miss Simpkins responded with a withering stare, unable or unwilling to return the smile. "You don't have an appointment?"

Michael's face flushed with embarrassment. "Em - No. But it's very important I speak to him, maybe you could let him know I'm here, the name's Murdoch."

"Out of the question, I'm afraid. Major Lockwood is extremely busy." Placing her spectacles in position as she spoke, she reached along the narrow counter, sliding a red covered register into closer view. "Now, let me see. Yes! Monday morning 9.30am - what did you say your name was?"

Although his smile had disappeared, Michael struggled successfully to retain a degree of calm. "Murdoch. But don't trouble to take a note of it for Monday, you see - it's imperative I see him today and I'm prepared to wait for as long as it takes." He was too pre-occupied with Miss Simpkins to notice that the two younger secretaries, typing furiously at the Bay window, were now taking more than a casual interest in the proceedings at reception.

"You've obviously not fully understood what I've just stated Mr Murdoch. Whatever you're prepared to do or say, you will not be seeing Major Lockwood today. Do you realise this office is preparing for a National Race tomorrow? Of all days to arrive without the courtesy of making an appointment!"

Michael's eyes fixed on hers, irritation straining his voice. "Okay, but maybe you could do me one little favour. Could you let him know I'm here? I'll be sitting in front of the black Range Rover, I guess it's his. Oh! And would you also mention that my father, Tam Murdoch, wrote to him recently and a few days later he was murdered."

He turned to leave; narrowly avoiding the indignity of the reception window slamming closed in his face.

Sitting on the grass, shaded by the Range-Rover's bonnet, his tweed jacket beneath him, he felt like a complete fool. Even the vivid memory of hiding in a pigeon loft from Julie Fenton compared favourably with his present predicament. His teeth clenched. *At least that hadn't been of my making, Les caused that fucking fiasco. And then last night persuaded me to waste my bloody time coming here.* By the time, however, he heard the footsteps scattering the gravel on their path towards him, the blame had been re-apportioned squarely on his own slumped shoulders.

Thankfully it wasn't Miss Simpkins but one of her young typists, wearing the shortest of orange skirts, matching tights, and the cheeriest of teenage grins. As she approached he got to his feet, picking up his jacket, at the same time brushing it free of grass cuttings. "The Major's prepared to see you now, Mr Murdoch, if you'd like to follow me."

He replied with a relieved smile. "Thanks for coming out to let me know, I hope I haven't caused you too much trouble?"

"Don't worry about that, Mr Murdoch, it was a pleasure to get out of the place, you could cut the atmosphere with a knife in there. I'm just glad it was me she sent, poor Lorraine, she's still in there listening to Florence bleating on."

"Oh; I've obviously upset her then?"

"'Fraid so! And not just Florence, the Major as well. He just went ape-shit! - Gave her such a bollocking, me and Lorraine could hardly keep our faces straight."

"He sounds like a bit of an ogre, your Major?"

"'Fraid-so! But not usually with Miss Simpkins, if you know what I mean?"

As they neared the steps she slowed her pace, hesitating before she spoke. "Em - Mr Murdoch, please don't take offence, but - you're not retarded - are you?"

He halted, mid step. "What do you mean? - Retarded."

"You know. Not the whole radio, batteries not included, that kind of retarded?"

He couldn't resist a bewildered grin. "Well. I don't think so, should I be?"

"I'm not sure, but I didn't think so. Neither did Miss Simpkins, but, the Major, he's convinced you are. Kept ranting on about having to waste his morning entertaining a six year old."

His grin immediately disappeared, unable to reply, only to understand.

They passed the reception window in silence before being ushered to a wide wooden stairway. As he followed her up the polished steps, he transferred his jacket to under his right arm, allowing his bandaged left hand to hold the oak banister, unaware that even the tightest of grips now held no pain. His attention was drawn to the gilt-framed oil paintings adorning the stair wall. He glanced at each of them in turn, six former champions of England, each proudly displaying its reverent place in Racing Pigeon history.

Noticing his slowing pace and obvious interest, his young companion delayed her progress, voicing her opinions in a whisper. "The Major paid a fortune to get these done, copies from old photographs. Imagine that! A wall full of dead birds and the old sod won't let me pin-up my poster of Richard Gere."

Michael's sympathetic smile was short lived. As they neared the stair-head the striking elegance of the blue, white flighted pigeon in the last portrait, brought him to a stop. He gazed admiringly as its classic features. Standing almost surreally in a sky blue backdrop, its noble presence seemed to claim respect. As he read the inscription of the brass plate below the bottom frame, his mouth opened wider.

Champion White-Wing - EHU/53/R4879
1956 - 1st Nationals Fraserburgh/Thurso
1957 - 1st Nationals Thurso/Lerwick
1958 - 1st National Thurso
British Long Distance Record Holder
Bred & Raced by F. Little, Maidstone, Kent

Until now his mind had blocked-out even the slightest whisper of doubt. But, five Nationals, *my God. It can be done!*

Afraid he might stand gaping at the silly bird all day, the typist gently tapped his shoulder. "Best not keep him waiting too long, Mr Murdoch - believe me - he won't appreciate it."

Michael followed her along the narrow corridor, his anxiety increasing with each slowing step.

She arrived at the General Manager's door two paces in front of him, paused and straightened her skirt before knocking.

"Enter!"

The abruptness of the voice, the fleeting image of the large room, Michael's studied first impression of Major Lockwood, held few surprises. As he crossed the carpeted floor towards the mahogany desk, their eyes met - neither willing to blink until their examinations were complete.

The Major pushed his chair backwards, extended his thin frame to its full imposing height and stretched a long black-blazered arm across the desk.

"Welcome Mr Murdoch. Or should I say Jamie. Please take a seat."

Michael smiled, shook his hand, sat on the nearest chair and said nothing.

"Now, old chap. Shall we get you a little refreshment? Perhaps a Coca-Cola? Miss Berry!"

"Major Lockwood, I think there's been a little misunderstanding. I'm Michael Murdoch, Jamie's younger brother."

The older man's frame immediately stiffened to attention, his staring eyes narrowing with each mystified blink. The ill-timed interruption from the doorway adding to his visible dilemma. "Do you still want me to get Mr Murdoch a Coca Cola Major?"

"No! Miss Berry! I'm sure you have more pressing duties to attend to, now please leave us!"

She turned to make her smirking exit.

"Oh! And Miss Berry! Remind me to speak to you once again about your mode of dress. Orange mini-skirts and fluorescent legs are not considered appropriate attire in this organisation."

Michael, now immediately conscious of his own sartorial deficiencies, faded cords, open necked checked shirt, the grass specked jacket resting on his knee, shared her embarrassment, but did not avert his eyes from the source of the reprimand.

When the door closed sharply behind her, Major Lockwood returned his attention to his visitor. "The Youth Training Scheme, Mr Murdoch, the bane of my life. Two years in the army, that was the youth training in my day. Now where were we? Oh yes. I'm due you a sincere apology."

Michael was momentarily bemused by the Major's brisk transition from intense irritation to apparent composure. "I was under the clear understanding, Mr Murdoch, that your father had only one son and he is - well - how can I put it...?"

Michael quickly came to his assistance. "Retarded?"

"Well, yes! That's precisely the impression your father conveyed to me on the telephone and I must say, in his correspondence." As he spoke he flicked open a brown file cover, taking up central position on the desk.

Michael immediately noticed his father's neat handwriting on the top page. His face flushed. "I suppose, Major Lockwood, it's kind of understandable, you see - I've lived abroad for so long and not had the chance to keep in close touch with my family. I only came back for the funeral."

"Yes, old-chap! Miss Simpkins has informed me of your father's tragic demise. Please accept the Homing Union's sincere condolences. Murdered you say? How dreadful. But surely you don't think his death was in any way associated with the concerns he raised with this organisation?"

Michael's eyes fixed solidly on the older man.

"Yes, I do and I'm looking for your help to prove it."

The Major returned his gaze. "Mr Murdoch, do you realise how serious these allegations are? Seeking out criminals of that sort is a matter for the police, what do you think I can achieve?"

"I'm not sure, maybe if it can be proved that Blue-Boy and its owners are frauds, it can also be proved they're involved in my father's murder, and when I'm sure of that.... well.... then I'll go to the police."

Major Lockwood's grey eyebrows raised in an animated gesture of unease. The cold determination in the young man's voice - the hesitation - the now unmistakable scar on his forehead, clearly expressed his intentions. "I see. Well in that case, if, and I must re-iterate it's against my better judgement, if you think I can help clarify matters in any way, I'm prepared to do so."

Michael nodded his appreciation.

"Now what information do you require?"

"Well, maybe your file holds some details I don't already have - for a start, my father's letter. I have his notes but I haven't seen the letter."

"Yes! Of-course, you're most welcome to read it, and, if you wish, peruse the file. I can assure you that every detail of the Union's Investigation is held within it."

"Investigation?"

"Of-course. Old-chap, allegations such as your father's are taken extremely seriously by my organisation, particularly this one. I don't know if you're fully aware of how long and highly regarded the Stenway name has been associated with the sport? In fact, his father, John senior was past President of the Union - if I recall - 1953 to 1958. And as for Champion Blue-Boy, it's become national news, and not just in the Pigeon Press. Only last week the Mirror had its photograph in the Sporting Pages."

Realising instinctively that the young man seemed surprised by his words, he continued. His tone reflecting a growing confidence. "I can therefore assure you - old chap, any concrete proof or wrong-doing would be rooted out. No matter how, let me say, temporarily inconvenient for the sport. Integrity! Mr Murdoch takes the highest precedence in my book. Now the letter, would you care to read it?"

Michael nodded, confirming his gratitude with a smile. Major Lockwood slid the letter across the desk, retaining the file for his own brief re-perusal. They both sat in concentrated silence, the younger man's head bowed towards the single page.

211 Park Crescent
Rosyth
Fife

1/7/88

Major Lockwood
General Manager
The E.H.U.
18 Upshire Road
Waltham Abbey
Nr. London

Dear Major Lockwood

You told me to put my complaint in writing, so I have.

As I said on the telephone, the pigeon called Champion Blue-Boy, Ring No. EHU/85/X2220, was brought to me by a wee girl on Saturday 25th June at 11.20am, the same day as your Fraserburgh National.

My son, Jamie, put it into our loft and took its rubber ring number, which I've still got a note of.

This so-called Champion got out of the loft at 4.20pm.

Now. Major Lockwood, how could it have been timed in by John Stenway in Kent at 6.30pm? It's not on Major. Impossible!

The pigeon must have been timed in the north of England somewhere.

When I saw the result in the following Saturday's Racing Pigeon, I phoned Stenway and he had the gall to call me and my boy liars! That's why I contacted you. How can I be a liar when I know the Race-Ring Number?

Stenway and his partner are crooks, Major! And you'll need to sort them out, or I'll be going to the Pigeon Press!

As I said to you, I'm an honest man, all me and my wife have is our son, Jamie, and all he has is his pigeons. As I said on the phone, he might only have the mind of a six year old, but like me he's honest and no way is a cheating so and so like Stenway going to call him a liar!

Yours in sport

T. Murdoch

When he'd finished reading it, his eyes remained lowered for a few seconds. His father had told it as it was; only a couple of facts were missing. The race ring number that seemed a sensible precaution. He hadn't mentioned the blood-flight, probably forgot. What cut him to the core, however, was not what he'd missed, but what he'd stated, with unambiguous conviction. - Tam Murdoch had one son and no capacity in his heart to accommodate another.

He took a deep breath before returning the letter and his full attention to the Major. "Well, there's little in this that I didn't already know, but it seems plain to me that my father uncovered their con and paid the price for it."

His host slowly shook his head. "You're his son, old-chap, and in the circumstances I can fully understand your train of thought. But I must be frank with you; my investigations have not endorsed what you're alleging."

"How do you mean, not endorsed?"

"Well, before I explain further, do you have a note of the race-ring number? There's no point in wasting each other's time if the number is not accurate!"

The time-wasting remark adding to his growing aggravation, Michael immediately retrieved the notebook from his jacket's inside pocket. "Yes, I do have it!" He flicked it open to the first page. - "Here it is. It was a yellow ring, Number 5995."

The Major's long, bony fingers burrowed through the file, retrieving a small white envelope, which had been pinned to the second last page. He opened it, turned it over, allowing a yellow race ring to fall silently onto the desk. "Yellow Ring 5995 - correct Mr Murdoch. I'm now in do doubt that the pigeon in question did arrive at your father's home on Saturday 25th June."

"So, Major Lockwood, does this mean we're on the same side?"

"No, I'm afraid it doesn't. I'm in the middle - playing Devil's Advocate - if you like. As I have stated, I will assist you to clarify matters. However, I have also a principal duty, as General Manager of the English Homing Union, to do my utmost to protect members against false accusations."

"I don't understand, Major, what are you trying to tell me? Do you believe me or not?"

"Now, old-chap, let's not get overwrought - let me explain. Notwithstanding the Race Ring, one critical doubt remains which, I'm afraid will be extremely difficult to resolve, particularly in a Court of Law." His visitor seemed too confused to reply, allowing him to continue uninterrupted. "The precise length of time Blue-Boy was held in your brother's pigeon loft. Now, your father claims it was there for five hours. But tell me, Michael; is it not possible that Jamie may have - lets say - become confused? Perhaps by all the excitement. Particularly as he is, unfortunately, mentally handicapped. Perhaps Blue-Boy escaped within minutes and, of-course, a racing pigeon of its calibre could still win a race of that distance."

Michael sprung to his feet, his eyes stabbing towards the older man. "Thanks for your help, Major. I appreciate your frankness but you're wrong. And I aim to prove it. By myself - if I have to!"

As he headed for the door he couldn't witness the intensity of thought in his host's piercing eyes. He reached to turn the brass knob, only to have his progress intercepted by the most amiable of commands. "Please, Mr Murdoch, sit down! As I've said, I'm merely playing Devil's Advocate. Now between you and I - I have certain, how can I put it - misgivings - about the Blue-Boy scenario, and should these be confirmed beyond doubt, I can assure you, radical action will be taken."

"So, you're prepared to help then?"

"Yes! Within the limits of the Union's Rules of-course. However, the need for discretion must be paramount."

"I appreciate that Major, but so is the need for speed. I understand that Blue-Boy's racing from Thurso tomorrow."

"Yes, exactly! Discretion and expedience - that's the order of the day. Now, on that vein, it's nearing lunch time, I can recommend the Waltham Arms. Perhaps if you'd be so good as to return later. I may have a little proposal to put to you. But I'll explain all that after you've had a good lunch and I've made a few phone-calls. Shall we say 2.00pm - sharp?"

In other circumstances he would have enjoyed the atmosphere in the Waltham Arms. It reminded him a little of Jake's bar, low ceiling above, relaxed conversation around him. All it needed was a cantankerous old barman with a limp - choking the customers with a constant cloud of Marlboro Full Strength. At the moment, Michael was sorry it didn't.

He spotted a bottle of Canadian Club on the bar gantry but resisted the temptation. "A coke, please, with ice." He had to retain his full concentration for 2.00 p.m. - sharp.

As he sipped slowly he tried to make some sense of the day so far. He hadn't come across anyone quite like Major Lockwood and wasn't sure how to take him. *At least he's a straight-talker,* he decided. *Maybe it's just his manner? But - tearing a strip off that young girl - well, that just wasn't called for.*

"I see we have something in common, Mr Murdoch."

"Oh?"

"Yes. Punctuality of-course." As he spoke, the Major turned in his chair towards the velvet-curtained window. "Yes. Here she comes, as regular as clockwork, three minutes late! If she doesn't take a leaf out of our book I'm afraid the remainder of her Youth Training will be spent in a knit-wear factory."

Michael didn't respond. The Major probably wouldn't appreciate his answer, and at the moment he had his own concerns. "How did your phone calls go?"

"Most satisfactorily old chap, most satisfactorily. By the way, how are you placed tomorrow - late afternoon - evening?"

"Why?"

"Well, Michael, the little proposal I mentioned before lunch, it may just resolve this whole business to our mutual satisfaction."

Michael listened in anticipation.

"As you correctly stated this morning, Blue-Boy is competing in our Thurso National tomorrow. I've just been in contact with my Race Convenor and the transporter, containing Blue-Boy and 6,235 others, has now safely arrived at the Liberation Point. What's more, according the M.E.T. Office the weather tomorrow should be conducive so, old chap, the race is on.. Now how would you like to be my official witness?"

"What exactly are you getting at, Major?"

"Rule 67 Subsection B of-course! In my capacity as General Manager I have a statutory right, for corroboration purposes, to enter any competing loft, without prior notice, during or within 48 hours of the race.. And Michael, what's of crucial importance, my witness does not need to be another Union Official.. That's what the legal 'bods' have just clarified. So what do you say to that old chap?"

"So what you're saying is, we turn up at Foxhole tomorrow unannounced and wait for Blue-Boy to arrive?"

"Yes! Exactly!"

"Won't Stenway and his side-kick be kind of upset?"

"That's as may be, but no more than I will should there be the least hint of impropriety. If so, Stenway and Pearce will be subject to the full extent of my displeasure!"

Michael smiled his silent agreement. *Mine too, Major - mine too.*

CHAPTER 21

If he hadn't felt so tired he may have enjoyed becoming a Canadian Tourist for what remained of the afternoon. He'd never experienced the city and the break from the traumas of the past few days might have given his brain the respite it was now nagging it deserved.

As he drove back towards the village, Michael mulled over the choices. After his meeting with the Major, the pleasure of viewing London's famous landmarks seemed like a well-earned bonus. Either that, he yawned, or point the Range Rover north and take Julie out for the evening.

Although the warm anticipation of seeing her again filtered through his mind, he knew, for the time being, it had to be discounted, grudgingly accepting it was just too far. A second wider yawn now physically expressing his immediate needs. *No. Find somewhere to rest-up, make a few phone calls, and then maybe take in the sights. - - - That pub was okay, wonder if it's got rooms?*

The Waltham Arms had five rooms with one still available.

"Unfortunately it's rather compact, sir, and immediately above the bar, but I can assure you it's comfortable."

As he locked the door behind him, a quick glance corroborated the barmaid's words. Although tiny, it was comfortable, with the added bonuses of an en-suite shower and window table with a telephone.

Michael placed his holdall at the foot of the single bed, eased off his jacket and shoes and lay down on the top cover, slowly moulding his body into the soft mattress. For less than five minutes he considered his two remaining options - *The City - or sleep?*

When he woke his eyes strained towards his wrist watch. Seven-thirty-five. In his confusion he wasn't sure what it was telling him. - Was it evening or morning? He was positive of only one thing as he lifted himself from the bed. He'd lied to Julie about her fold-down couch. On this bed, for either four hours or sixteen, he'd honestly slept like a log.

When his eyes gave up looking for clues, his ears came to the rescue. Although muffled by the carpeted floor, the base beat from the bar's music system and the occasional chink of glasses confirmed his wishes beyond doubt. *They don't serve drinks at seven-thirty five in the morning.*

He quickly undressed, knowing instinctively that the benefits of his sleep wouldn't be fully realised until he was showered, shaved and changed.

The pleasure of the warm spray flowing through his hair felt like an indulgence he could enjoy forever. It seemed to permeate through his scalp clearing the last remnants of fatigue from his brain. He decided to remove the bandage, it was now saturated and he hoped it wouldn't have to be replaced. Gently peeling it off under the shower, Michael smiled as the final layer was released from his hand. Isobel hadn't lost her knack. The cut, although still clearly visible, was clean, allowing him to clench and open his fist with no discomfort. All it needed was a plaster, maybe - if he asked nicely - from the bar's first aid box.

The reminder of what was under his feet, particularly the bottle of Canadian Club, hopefully still awaiting his acquaintance, spurred on his progress, delayed only momentarily by the removal of a fresh shirt from the hold-all. Only his mother could fold shirts that neatly. Years working for extra housekeeping money in the Parkside Laundry had seen to that. Michael glanced nervously towards the phone - could he lie to her again?

Thankfully the pub wasn't busy. The staff were just preparing for evening bar meals and the selection now being sketched on the chalkboard put even the Cascade to shame. He ordered a Canadian Club - as a starter - a sirloin steak and then asked nicely for a plaster.

All three were provided with the friendly efficiency he'd come to expect from his own staff, apart, of-course, from the part-time barman he'd left in charge. A frown suddenly crossed his fore-head as he acknowledged the reality of his thoughts. Lying to his mother would be bad enough, but Jake - could he find the courage to tell him the truth?

He consumed his meal with the haste its excellence didn't deserve. He had three phone calls to make and he wouldn't relax until the first two were behind him.

Noticing him rising to his feet so soon, the barmaid met him with an inquisitive smile. "Enjoy your steak, sir?"

"Yes, it was great, but I'm afraid I had to kind of rush it, there's a couple of phone calls I must make. Em, I don't suppose I could buy what's left of the Canadian Club and take it to my room, maybe with some ice and a can of American Dry?"

"Of-course sir, you're most welcome, now let me see, there's about three glasses left in it - shall we say ten pounds, including the American Dry?"

Unsure if he'd received a bargain Michael accepted the deal gratefully.

When he got back to his room he immediately mixed himself a drink, placed it carefully next to the phone, then drew up a chair. He checked his watch - five past eight, roughly twelve noon in Banff. Jake hopefully wouldn't have left for the bar; he should catch him before Tammy had the chance to give him the news.

"Yeah! Who is it?"

"Who do you think it is Jake? Who else would want to speak to a cantankerous old bugger like you?"

"Oh! It's you, Mike? What time of the day is this to phone? I've got a bar to open in twenty minutes!"

Michael couldn't prevent his hesitation.

"Mike! You still there? How are you son?"

"Fine Jake, but things aren't working out too smoothly - I'll explain it all when I get back, but there's something you've got to know now."

"Okay son, but if it's about you selling up the business, there's no point in spilling your guts over the phone, I know all about it."

"You what? Has Tammy told you already? I only spoke to her a few hours ago - I thought she'd still be in bed."

"Tammy's told me nothing, Mike! Me and Mabel - we sussed it out ourselves."

"But Jake, I only decided myself last night."

"If that's what you want to think son, that's okay with me, but when you gonna realise I'm smarter that you. I could see it coming weeks ago; you've been disappearing too much lately in that Jeep of yours.."

As relief displaced confusion, his voice slowed as he asked the next question. "Well Jake, if you're that smart and you've known all long, what do you think, are you disappointed?"

"Tell me how much you're getting for the place, then I'll let you know if I'm disappointed."

Michael answered in a whisper.

"Half a million! Shit son, I know I was being over-generous when I sold it to you for a pittance, but its worth more than half a million bucks, and you know it.."

"That's right Jake, but over-generous isn't exactly how I saw our deal. The main thing is I want it wrapped up quickly, so I need to speak to Mabel, if she hasn't seen sense and left you."

"Okay Mike. But before you get me off this phone I'm gonna tell you straight.......!" Jake's deep inhalation of cigarette smoke took just enough time for Michael's anxiety to return. "You've got my full blessing son. So you can think about that when you're spending my money!" Ignoring his young friend's curses he called across the room. "Mabel! We were right; you'll soon be spending all your time concentrating on me."

Michael relaxed again when he heard her voice. "Mike, please don't tell me you're selling up. The old fool's gonna drive me crazy, and I didn't plan on retiring till he was good and buried, then I would a' spent the time persuading you to marry me."

Michael chuckled as he listened to his friends sharing a parting kiss. "Sorry Mabel, but you don't have to retire, just write yourself into the deal."

He immediately recognised a new seriousness in her tone. "No way, Mike! As Jake said, we reckoned it was coming, and to be perfectly honest, despite what I say about him, we want to spend more time together. He might be an old fool, but he's mine. Well, you know what I mean."

She couldn't see his smile. "Sure Mabel, I've got the picture, but if you change your mind, get the lawyers to put it in the contract, that's what I need you to help me with. Could you arrange to have something drawn-up, nice and simple, I don't want John's father complicating things."

"So John's the lucky guy then?"

"Yes, Mabel, he's already got five per cent and you've got to agree - he deserves more. And Mabel, I'm sure he can find half a million."

"You're sure his daddy can find half a million, Mike. But don't worry, no matter how big a New York accountant he is, he'll soon find out I haven't lost my knack. How about a one-liner: The Cascade and Jake's Bar - half a million bucks. - Take it or go screw yourself - sign here!"

His laughter filled the room.   "Sounds fine Mabel, could you hand it to him today. Now that Jake will have reached Banff Avenue, John'll probably be the only one in town who doesn't know yet."

She bit her lower lip, attempting, but failing, to mask the sarcasm in her voice. "Oh, I don't know Mike, I'm sure Tammy's been in touch with him by now........she'd be keen to give him the good news. How'd she take it herself - Mike?"

"Okay Mabel, but that's another story that I don't really want to get into at the moment."

Mabel slowly replaced the receiver, lines creasing her forehead. Mike was right. When it came to Tammy, there definitely was another story to tell. Like how easy it would have been for her to get in touch with John! Her irritation in not saying anything, nevertheless, soon merged with a begrudged acceptance, it was Mike's business - not hers. She had a job to do for him today. A fancy New York accountant to deal with, and unlike some, she wouldn't let him down.

He sat staring out towards the street lights, his thoughts three-thousand miles away. Fifteen years and it's all wrapped up in a phone call. He still had his friends though, that was the main thing - and the cabin. He wasn't selling the cabin. Tammy should be getting up by now. He wondered how long she'd take to pack her cases and close the door behind her.

Filling his glass again he returned his attention to the telephone - murmuring to himself quietly. - "Yes - good friends and family, at least I've still got that."

"Hello, Rosyth 58649."

"Hi mum. I thought it was Jamie's job to answer the phone?"

The sharpness of the reply almost visibly confirmed the sourness of her mood. "Yes Michael and he would have enjoyed a wee blether with you. Wait till I get a hold of that boy of Ina's. A good skelp with my dish-towel, that's what he's needing!"

"Is Jamie okay?"

"Yes, but no thanks to that Peter Andrews though.   He's still feeling a bit squeamish, so I put him to his bed early with his pigeon magazines and a glass of Lucozade - he'll be fine tomorrow."

"I take it the Pie took him for a drive then - did you warn him not to be speeding?"

"I did, Michael, but I don't think his head can be buttoned up the back. Jamie was telling me they were doing eighty miles an hour on the way home. No wonder the poor soul spewed all over the front window."

Michael replied with a sympathetic smile. "Well, tell Jamie I'm asking for him. All going well I'll have nice pair of squeakers for him by the time I get home."

"Good, that'll cheer him up no-end. Now how are you, are you still in Seaham?"

"No……..I'm in London…….I thought if I was in England I should do some sight-seeing in the capital."

"London! - That's a terrible distance away Michael, I didn't expect you to be going that far. I thought you and Les would have spent more time together."

Reminding himself instantly that few could equal Mary Murdoch's ability to make him feel guilty, he stammered.

"W…we will mum. I'm stopping off on my way back. I just wanted to see the city - that's all."

"Well if that's all Michael, fine, but make sure it is, I don't need anymore worries at the moment."

"Has something else happened?"

"No, it was just something Maxwell Clark said when he came to see Jamie this morning about training the young birds."

"What did he say?"

"Well, when I told him you were off touring around for a few days, he wished you the 'best of luck!' But it was the way he said it. Does he know something that I don't?"

He gripped the half-empty glass with a tightness nearing its breaking point. "No mum. It's as I've said, I need the break that's all. I must have mentioned looking for a couple of pigeons for Jamie, that'll be why he's wishing me luck. I want to find a couple of really good ones."

"Well if it's as you say, I believe you, but with everything that's happened, your dad, the police and everything, I can't help worrying."

Michael's grip relaxed slightly, he'd hopefully passed the worst of the lying stage. "Mum, leave the worrying to Ian Miller, that's what he gets paid for; I'm sure he'll sort it all out."

"Maybe! Michael, but when? Goodness knows! And he's not been near since…well…the two of you had words. I just can't credit it; Ina Andrews seems to know more about what's going on than me."

"Oh. What's she gossiping about now?" He hoped the casual delivery of his reply had hidden his acute interest.

"Well, she was round again this afternoon…"

"To give Jamie a telling off about throwing up in Peter's car?"

"No son, she might be a bit of a battle-axe, but she knows how far she can go with me."

Michael nodded, his smile silently verifying her words.

"She was telling me the police haven't found the blue car yet and you'll not believe this Michael, they've been interviewing Jimmy Thomson from Lochgelly!"

"Jimmy Thomson, I think I remember him, doesn't he race the pigeons?"

"That's right Michael. And he won the Sartilly Race last week, after you're dad's Mealy hen couldn't be timed in."

"So they think he set this all up so he could win the race?"

"Yes son, I'm not saying your dad had much time for the wee weasel, - but have you ever heard of anything more ridiculous?"

"No mum, not really."

He drained the glass and immediately refilled it, with the satisfaction that its soothing promise was now at last being delivered. He reconciled himself with the fact that the two difficult calls were now behind him and they could have been a lot worse. Jake and Mabel had seemed genuinely happy for him and his mother, yes he lied to her, but what else could he do? Tell her he was paying a visit to a couple of pigeon fanciers tomorrow. The ones that probably murdered her husband, so they could win a few races.

He'd one last call to make, this one held no misgivings, and if his luck was still holding, maybe Julie would be around, she might even be the one who answers the phone?

"Aye, what do you want?"

He accepted his misfortune with a wide grin. "Hi Susan, its Michael, shouldn't you be in bed by now?"

She ignored his question. "Michael, when are you coming back, is it tomorrow?"

"I'm not sure Susan, maybe, or maybe Sunday, why?"

"I've run out o' sweeties, will you be bringing me some more?"

"Okay, I'll try not to forget, how about some more Quality Street, but have you been behaving?"

"Aye, Michael. But don't be bringing any for that other two; they've been smacking me again!"

Michael struggled to adjust his voice to a sympathetic tone. "That's a shame Susan, and you behaving yourself so well, by the way, is you dad at home?"

"No, he's away at Murton with his pigeons, he says he's ganin to win the race tomorrow, but he always says that. Ma ma's in though, do you want to speak to her? Ma! - It's Michael. - Michael are you Auntie Julie's boyfriend?"

The directness of her whispered afterthought shocked him into an honest reply. "Well, I'd like to be - but that's our little secret Susan, so promise you'll keep it. Why did you ask?"

"Cos, she quite likes you Michael an' you're takin' her out for dinner. She told ma she'd be wearing her blue dress, the one that's that short, when she bends over you can see..."

Michael interceded with a chuckle. "Okay Susan, I know which one you're talking about."

"Here's ma! Ma! Guess what? Michael's bringing me more sweeties an' he wants to be Auntie Julie's boyfriend!"

The laughter from Ruby, as she approached the telephone, warned him his embarrassment wasn't to be short lived. "Michael, I'm so sorry. The little devil, she just puts words in peoples' mouths, so don't be takin' any heed o' what she said."

"She sure does Ruby, you should see my face - it's like a beetroot."

"Aye, Michael, but no' as red as my sister-in-law's when I tell her you want to be her boyfriend."

"Ruby. Please tell me this is a wind-up?"

"Aye, Michael, of-course it is - we'll let you tell her yourself over that candle-lit dinner you've got her so excited about."

He took a deep breath hoping it would help retrieve some degree of calm in his voice. "Now Ruby! That's just a thank you thing for letting me stay in the portacabin. I take it she's not around - I was going to ask her if Sunday night suited?"

"No Michael, you're out o' luck, but I'll tell her you phoned. Bam should be home shortly though, if you want to phone back in half an hour?"

"No, that's okay Ruby, I'll see him when I get back. If you could just tell him that I'm in Waltham Abbey and things are going pretty good, and the advice he gave me last night - it was really appreciated."

"Okay Michael, that'll be to do with finding a pair o' nice pigeons for your brother?"

"That's right Ruby, that's right."

The barmaid's calculations had been accurate, three glasses and the bottle was empty. One more would have been perfect. Michael listened to the sounds permeating through the floor a few feet below. People were enjoying themselves, enjoying companionship, enjoying another drink.

He was alone in a tiny room with a telephone and an empty whisky bottle.

He stood up, stared for a moment at the door then closed the curtains. "Julie Fenton quite likes you." Her little niece's words tasted better than the smoothest of drinks. He knew now he didn't need another, he had what he wanted right here. A soft bed for the night, and time to plan for tomorrow - perhaps beyond tomorrow.

CHAPTER 22

As the black Range Rover hurtled up the driveway, spraying stone chippings over the lawn, Michael checked his wristwatch and silently cursed his luck. *Another fifteen seconds and there'd be no more crap from the bold Major about punctuality.* On his part he'd made sure of reaching Wing Holm well before the pre-arranged deadline of, "Shall we say 4.00p.m. - sharp old chap?" He waited for the Major to draw up before acknowledging his presence with a smile.

With the engine still running, the driver immediately leaned over to open the passenger door, his face flushed with irritation. "In you get Murdoch, absolute disgrace these Caravan Club people, not the slightest courtesy for others! Ten minutes lost, sitting behind one of their blasted convoys! I'll be telephoning their secretary first thing Monday morning, mark my words!"

Michael forced a sympathetic reply as he climbed aboard. "Well at least you got here in time, and as I said yesterday, I really appreciate your help."

"Yes, quite! Now! The Thurso scenario. I've made the necessary phone calls, the pigeons were liberated at 0600 hours and, as expected, the weather conditions right down the line are excellent. However, the light headwind, ten to fifteen m.p.h. from the south-west will, no doubt, slow their progress somewhat?"

"So when do you think the leading birds will make it into Kent, Major?" Noticing the older man's greying eyebrows raise further with each word, Michael regretted his interruption before he'd finished making it.

"Well, they're not coming home by train, so we can't rely on time-tables - can we?" He paused for a sigh. "However, if we must take a guess, if I was a betting man I'd wager a speed of just under forty m.p.h. Now John Stenway's pigeon is flying five hundred and forty miles, give or take a yard or two, so shall we say thirteen hours to be on the safe side. E.T.A. around seven p.m."

"E.T.A. - Major?"

"Yes! Rather a self-evident term I would think - estimated time of arrival - of-course!"

The loftiness of the tone now clearly confirmed what Michael suspected. Today, the General Manager of the English Homing Union was intent on pulling rank and no mere upstart of a temporary witness was going to interfere with his agenda.

"Now, where was I? Yes, E.T.A. seven p.m. - that's if you're still convinced of your father's conspiracy theory. If that's the case, according to him, the game's afoot even as we speak. By now Blue Boy will be ensconced in some mysterious pigeon loft in the wilds of the North Country and our little sojourn will, undoubtedly, uncover the whole dastardly plot!"

If he hadn't mentioned his father so sarcastically, Michael would probably have put up with his arrogance until they reached Foxhole. He spoke slowly, his eyes fixing firmly on the older man. "Durham's not exactly in the wilds of the north. But you're right, that's where Blue Boy is and the same bastards that murdered my father will be deciding when to put its race rubber into the clock. Just like you major, they'll have worked out the E.T.A. As you say - a dastardly plot and I wish it was some kinda game, but you've just reminded me it isn't. So how about we cut the crap - old chap - and get started?"

For the briefest of moments his chauffeur's face matched the starched whiteness of his shirt. He stared in outraged silence. No-one spoke to him like that, he should have seen through him yesterday. This chap Murdoch was more than just a trouble maker, he had an insolent streak and it could prove extremely awkward. "I say old-boy. No need for any unpleasantness between ourselves. Let me assure you, I'm fully aware of the seriousness of the situation. Perhaps I sounded a trifle flippant, but please don't underestimate the gravity of my concerns."

Satisfied his presence was now being accepted with a degree of equality, Michael offered a smiling apology. "Sorry Major, I don't doubt your concerns, I'm just a bit on edge that's all. How do you think we should play things when we get there?"

The colour had now returned to his face. "Don't worry about that Michael; I've had a lifetime's experience of conflict situations - so please bear with me. It's essential, of course, in my position of authority, that I take the lead."

"Fine major!" Michael grinned, "Next stop Foxhole - eh?"

As they drove from the car park Michael quickly realised his grey-flannelled, stripe-tied, chauffeur, seemed extremely keen to change the subject. "Damn nice vehicle you've got there, same model as this one I see. Excellent machines the whole family of them. Spent most of my life in the passenger seat of a Land Rover you know."

Michael didn't know, but had a strange feeling this wouldn't be the last time he'd be reminded of it. "Yes Major, I picked it up on rental a couple of days ago, always liked the look of them, but a bit on the expensive side, I would think."

"Worth every penny old chap, reliability's the important thing; quality comes at a price, that's my motto."

His passenger accepted the statement with an agreeing nod, at the same time wondering how many more mottoes the Major lived his life by.

"Find a suitable billet, old chap?"

"Yes thanks, went to the Waltham Arms and I was in luck, they'd one room left."

"Excellent.......Excellent! Not the most luxurious of accommodation I understand, but comfortable, so my regional people say. I book them into the place when I call my monthly briefing meetings. In fact, if you'd let me know, as my official witness, a five per cent discount would have been perfectly in order." So how did you while away the hours, take in the city?"

"No, I'd have liked that, but to be honest, I spent most of the time sleeping, felt great this morning though. Had a nice wander round the Abbey, and then did some shopping. Picked up some neat gifts." As he spoke his thoughts strayed to one particular gift, the little reminder of Rosyth he'd picked up a few days ago for someone particularly deserving. The gift, he now realised, he'd left back in the glove compartment at Wing Holm, under the small framed portrait of a lurcher he'd bought for Julie.

"Excellent, Michael, excellent! Yes, it's not often nowadays one gets the opportunity to relax, and what - with recent events - a bit of R. and R., who could blame you."

"R. and R?"

"Rest and Recreation old chap! The best antidote for battle fatigue. Seen it all before, as soon as the problem's spotted, act! That's my motto. Allow the men and hour's shut-eye and a brew-up, even a sing-song, always did the trick. You obviously weren't in the Forces, Michael? Pity, you look the type."

Now fully realising where the conversation was unremittingly leading, he accepted the inevitable with a wry smile. "No, Major, 'fraid not, but my father was, did a couple of year in Palestine, National Service I think."

"No. I must correct you there, if your father was in Palestine he wasn't doing National Services, no - old chap, he was like me, a regular. He was in the Army when the country was needing men like him, not just feeding them! Yes Palestine. Damn messy business, didn't know who the enemy was, glad I missed that one. Now the Falklands! Different story altogether, knew exactly what we were up against and we sorted the blighters out! ....I remember......"

By the time they'd merged with the M25 east bound, travelled over thirty miles around the north-eastern boundary of the city and reached the Thames at Dartford Tunnel, Michael felt he'd experienced a life-time in the Army.

He listened politely, answering only when expected to with an "Oh, really" or "Is that so".   Malaysia, India, Burma, Oman, Northern Ireland. Apartment from Palestine, this old soldier had led his men, from the passenger seat of a Land Rover, into every conflict since the Normandy Landings, and my God, he loved talking about it.

On another day he'd have relaxed, probably enjoyed the major's expedition down memory lane. He was used to listening - he'd worked in Jake's Bar, worked with Jake! But he wasn't there now, smiling patiently as he poured drinks to another lumberjack story, he was less than an hour away from Foxhole. A tiny spot on the road map between Maidstone and the English Channel, a spot he'd stared at for an age before falling asleep last night. Foxhole, Kent, the answer must be there. But before they arrived he needed to know more about John Stenway and his partner Pearce. If he could just get the Major to change the bloody subject! "Major Lockwood, sorry to interrupt, but with your background, fighting for your country and all, what made you get into this game, did you keep pigeons when you were young or something?"

As he briefly returned Michael's glance, a wide grin crossed his clean shaven face. "Well old chap, close I suppose - poultry!. The family had a battery hen business, not that I was much at home to get involved with it. Between you and I, never kept a pigeon in my life. Not that it mattered, just waffled on at my interview about my inherent love of all creatures feathered, and more importantly, my determination to drag the sport into the twentieth century. Worked a treat, so here I am now, five years down the line and how can I put it without sounding somewhat immodest -- they've never had it better!."

"But I was under the impression, what with the mines closing and everything, there's less people involved in the sport nowadays?"

"True, unfortunately, very true, and that's a trend I'm determined to reverse. But the quality, Michael, the quality, has improved immensely, and I don't just mean the calibre of racing pigeon. The days of the cloth cap are disappearing; we're at last becoming a serious sport. Professionalism, that's where the future lies, believe me."

"So, Major, this Blue Boy con., I suppose that's the last thing you need at the moment?"

He waited and watched as the driver's eyes narrowed in preparation for the response now straining his voice with displeasure. "Mr Murdoch. If it's as you so eagerly suggest, a conspiracy, yes of-course it would be most unfortunate but please, let's not jump to rash conclusions. My earnest desire today is to confirm the validity of this pigeon and, of-course, the reputation of John Stenway, and what I would appreciate is your full co-operation. I can fully understand the intensity of your suspicions, old chap, but you must be prepared to be open minded and, as I've already stated, it's essential you follow my lead. The truth will prevail, that's always been one of my mo....."

"Sure, Major, anything you say, but how exactly are we going to play it. I've been thinking, if they know who I am, will that not put them on their guard? Maybe we shouldn't mention right away that I'm Tam Murdoch's son."

In a despairing gesture the Major shook his head. "We most certainly will Mr Murdoch. Honesty has always been the only policy in my book. We play this strictly by the rules; meet the problem head-on, no deviations. John Stenway's going to find our visit difficult enough without us appearing other than completely above board."

"Sorry Major, you're quite right, we'll play it your way. Now, Stenway I've heard about him, he was well known in the sport years ago when me and Jamie raced the pigeons. But this partner of his, this guy Pearce, where does he fit in?"

"Now that, old chap, is a more appropriate question. Can't say I know him too well, more of a silent partner really. I think he bought into the business a few years ago, made quite a difference to John's luck though. Poor chap's not as able as he used to be, dickie heart you know. Then Raymond Pearce turns up, injects a bit of capital and now he's back where he belongs. Top of the tree!. One of the premier pigeon studs in England - if not Europe."

"So you don't know the guy then?"

"Well I have met him of-course, but as I say, he's rather low profile. Ex army I understand, but definitely rank and file material, not the most - how can I put it? - sophisticated of chaps. However, it takes all sorts, don't you think?"

Michael nodded answering softly. "Sure Major, all sorts."

CHAPTER 23

With the county town of Maidstone and the motorway now behind them, Michael at last had the chance to fully appreciate the advantage of being chauffeured in a vehicle that allowed a view over the hedgerows.

His first two days since leaving Rosyth, even if he'd been intent on seeing the country, hadn't provided much to tell his mother and Jamie about.

On Thursday almost the whole journey to Seaham had been shrouded in mist and rain. Yesterday morning the sun won through, but speeding down a motorway at over eighty miles an hour hadn't entirely imprinted his soul with a picture of England's green and pleasant land.

Kent was now doing exactly that, and in some style. He'd heard or read somewhere it was known as the Garden of England. A fact he was now realising that no one, except maybe Les Fenton, could argue. It was perfect; narrow rose hedged roads, lush pastures, tree-lined avenues, orchards of red apples and what looked like ripening cherries, scenting the inside of the now slowing Range Rover with their sweet fragrance.

They eased their way through tiny villages, each more picturesque than the last. Black and white draped houses with ancient red-tiled roofs. Each cluster either protected by the tall steeple of a honey-coloured church or an equally imposing wide-sailed windmill.

Observing that his young passenger seemed suitably enthralled, Major Lockwood intervened with a contented sigh. "Yes, the Kentish Weald, God's little garden. I'm a Berkshire man myself, you know. Grew up just north of Sandhurst. But pleasant as it is and, of-course, handy for reunions, I've always preferred Kent. Every turn of the road seems to produce another reason to like the place. - "Here we are old chap, The Stenway Stud, what do you think?"

His passenger's mouth dropped open. The Berkshire man was right, every bend in Kent had something different to offer, but nothing, he imagined, quite like this.

The driver grinned. "Somewhat impressed old chap? As I said, one of the premier studs in England, and expanding by the day!"

Michael swallowed hard. "Expanding by the day, Major. How much bloody bigger can it get?"

If it wasn't for the large, freshly painted sign, proudly displaying a blue pigeon, with the words *'The Stenway Stud'* above and *'Home of the Champions'* below, he might have mistaken the place for an up-market chalet park, Holiday luxury with the added extra of prison-like security!

Built on an incline, almost a hill but not quite, and surrounded by green pasture, its high chain link fence, topped with barbed wire, enclosed over two acres. In the centre of the vast compound, partially secluded by a border of beech trees, a traditional two storey Kentish Farmhouse, with what looked like a more modern extension to its left gable, seemed now to be struggling to compete with the changes in the landscape it must have once dominated.

Encircling the brick dwelling, row upon row of identical timber pigeon lofts. Michael estimated over fifty, each about the same size as Jamie's, but with double pitched red pan-tiled roofs. And the Major was right; the Stenway Stud was most definitely expanding. Dwarfed only by a mountain of rich earth, an enormous yellow excavator stood like a motionless sentry in what remained of the field immediately adjacent to the impenetrable meshed barrier.

Smiling freely, Major Lockwood found the words his opened-mouthed companion seemed incapable of uttering. "Yes old-chap, we're looking at the future, all this and over a thousand top class pigeons, and there's more. Wait till you see the exhibition room. As for next year, well, a coach park, children's play area, cafeteria and of-course the multi-purpose sales hall. Birds, loft equipment, feed stuffs, all the discerning fanciers needs under one roof. Impressive what?"

Michael didn't answer. Not that he could disagree. He just hadn't been prepared for the scale of the remarkable business enterprise two pigeon fanciers had created, and he, a gaping-eyed day visitor, was here with the sole intention of ruining. Until now, Jamie's Blue-Boy story, his father's notebook, his conversation with Les, had primed his determination to do just that, seek clinical retribution for the wrongs Stenway and Pearce had inflicted on his family. Imagining the type of justice he wanted had been so easy, but now seeing the place, seeing what had been achieved, flooded his brain with uncertainty. Could the Major's grinning vision of the future be correct? If anywhere had the capacity to produce a Racing Pigeon to grace the stairway of Wing Holm next to Champion White Wing, where else, but here?

As they drove in to the empty car park and stopped opposite the metal framed entrance gate, Michael was forced to grip his knees tightly to prevent his hands from shaking.

"Are you all right, old boy? You seem somewhat agitated"

"Yes...I'm fine Major, I'm...em...I'm just a bit surprised by the size of the place, that's all, and there doesn't seem to be much sign of life, does it always close so early?"

His innocent afterthought brought a quizzical glint to the older man's eyes. "No old chap, and that's a perfectly valid observation. Normally it's open until 9.00p.m. seven days a week. However, John has a strict policy during National Races, absolutely no visitors after 2.00p.m. and the same goes for his staff, they're all sent packing!"

Michael grasped his companion's words like a life-line, his voice tinged more with relief than accusation. "So, major, they don't want anyone around to see what's going on, surely that proves they've got something to hide?"

The driver switched off the engine, loosened his seat belt and leaned over to the back seat, lifting his blazer and the brown file concealed beneath it. "Perhaps, Michael, perhaps not. However, you may recall I mentioned a certain misgiving yesterday." As he spoke he flicked the file open to the last page before handing it to his bemused passenger. "If you care to read this old chap I think you'll find we're not totally askew in our thinking."

Michael read eagerly and under the typed heading, 'Comments' focused on what he presumed was the Major's bold handwriting.

The Stenway Stud closes at 1400hrs sharp, during National Race events. Is this, as John Stenway suggests, a sensible precaution against distraction, or for reasons of somewhat greater significance?

A few sparse words, just enough for his confidence to now re-emerge almost unscathed. As he returned the file his mouth curved to a narrow smile. "Thanks Major, after we've proved what they're up to, I'll maybe get the chance to read the rest of it, eh?"

Major Lockwood blinked twice before replying in a murmur. "Of-course old chap, of-course, now shall we proceed?"

As they approached Michael noticed that apart from supporting a white-grill fronted box and a closed sign attached to the mesh above, the gate was barely discernible from the perimeter fence it secured. His companion now officially attired in his black blazer, with the investigation file tucked under his left arm, halted immediately in front of the box. "Excellent security system, watch this." He pressed a small red button located below the grill.

Michael watched and waited - nothing happened.

After the second press and wait, the only change he witnessed was the growing similarity between the colour of the older man's flushing cheeks and the button. Following a muffled curse and a failed third attempt he changed tactics, keeping his thin index finger firmly in place until his determination finally succeeded.

A voice came from the grill, its tinny resonance highlighting the speaker's obvious state of annoyance. "Can you not read? The sign says we're closed, and that means, and I'll say this slowly, we - are - not - open!"

Major Lockwood took a deep breath before positioning his now quivering chin closer to the box. "Yes John, I can read perfectly well. Now be a good chap and open this infernal contraption, it's Major Trevor Lockwood on official E.H.U. business."

Unlike his companion, the delay, as it lengthened, added to Michael's growing confidence. John Stenway had good reason for his silence. He didn't like visitors during national races, particularly ones on official E.H.U. business, and now, he needed time to panic.

Just as the Major was returning his exasperated attention to the intercom button an electronic whirring sound came from the gate's locking mechanism. Michael watched attentively as the heavy metal bolt securing it to the fence, slipped backwards allowing the barrier to slowly open inwards. Neither hesitated in accepting the reluctant welcome and as they walked up the central pathway he soon became aware of having to lengthen his stride to keep up with his scowling companion's impressive marching pace.

At regular intervals they met similar shrub-edged pathways reaching out at both sides. Each serving a row of five horizontally clad, ship-lapped pigeon lofts, built with the joinery skills he knew even his father would have found difficult to criticise. Securing their full frontages, ground to ridge weld-mesh aviaries and facing each aviary, a wood slated garden bench.

Michael frowned thoughtfully before gazing upwards. A clear blue Summer's sky and nothing but a single black crow circling high above the home of champions. His lips tightened. Luxurious as these lofts were, none lacking the space, day-lighting and natural ventilation essential for optimum breeding conditions, they were prisons, allowing their captive inhabitants the hint of freedom, but no more. He shook his head. If this was the future Major Lockwood enthused about, he was confident of at least one pigeon fancier who wouldn't want to be part of it. *Leave Jamie Murdoch alone in the Stenway Stud,* he mused, *and within an hour the last thing the crow would have to worry about was the lack of company.*

Michael smiled as he pictured his brother relaxing back into one of John Stenway's benches, whistling contentedly as a thousand racing pigeons saluted his compassion with the sound of their wing-beats.

"Damn good idea the seating arrangement, what?" I prefer standing myself, but not all John's customers are blessed with my fitness. As he quite correctly states, look after your customers and they'll look after you. Excellent motto to run a business by, don't you think?"

Michael nodded. The Major now having apparently recovered his composure was quite right, but he'd run his own business for long enough to realise there was more to the benches than that. Each one was conveniently positioned facing directly into an aviary. Yes, John Stenway knew exactly how to look after his customers. Time and opportunity to relax...take in the atmosphere, discreetly re-check the hard-earned contents of their wallets and at the Stenway Stud, sit on a garden bench for as long as they liked, peering through the mesh-wire of an aviary at racing pigeons, anyone of which might just have the potential to become a champion - another Blue Boy!

When they reached the shade of the beech trees, the farmhouse doorway less than twenty metres away, Major Lockwood slowed his pace, interrupting Michael's silent concentration with an abrupt whisper. "Now old chap. I trust you don't need reminded, but what we're about to undertake is an official English Homing Union investigation, and your role is that of my witness.... Just that.... And nothing more!"

Michael delayed his reply hoping, as their eyes met, his reassuring smile would portray some semblance of honesty. "Sure Trevor, anything you say."

Fortunately, before his glowering companion could verbally express the lack of faith he had in him, the farmhouse door swung slowly open.

Since talking with Jamie on Tuesday, every mention of John Stenway had added to the imaginary picture he'd created of the slightly built man now leaning precariously on a walking stick and directing his scowling gaze towards them.

For some reason Michael had moulded him in the likeness of the Museum Curator back in Banff. Piercing beady eyes...bald head...hawk-nosed...a man incapable of the least hint of humour. Apart, of course, for the fun time he'd given everyone during his trial. Explaining to a packed court-room how, when caught in the taxidermy room in an extremely compromising position with a dead elk, his stumbling excuse that he'd: "Merely been employed in some out-of-hours stuffing!" Had given them all a good laugh!

Realising, with each step closer, apart from the walking stick, how accurate he'd been, allowed him little satisfaction. If anything the scolding tone of Stenway's waspish voice adding to Michael's pre-determined disapproval. "Lockwood! You know my policy on race days, so this better be important." He glanced accusingly towards the younger man. "And who's this you've brought with you? If you're here to buy pigeons, you can come back tomorrow. I've had to chase more than a dozen punters away from the place already this afternoon."

Before Michael could translate the coldness of his stare into words, the Major, as if predicting the outcome, intervened with an amiable smile. "Of course it's important John. Now why don't we discuss it inside, by the way, is Mr Pearce available, I'd also like to have a chat with him?"

During the moment's hesitation, Michael's eyes narrowed as he watched the sallow skin tighten on John Stenway's brow. "Em...no major, he's...visiting his mother in hospital...won't be back till later this evening."

The younger man's wry smile seemed to compliment the casual delivery of his question. "Would that be a hospital in the Durham area, Mr Stenway?"

Their eyes locked in a frozen stare. "No, Maidstone! But what damn business is that of yours?"

Michael's smile widened. *You're either an obnoxious bastard Stenway, or you're rattled, now which one is it?*

Major Lockwood struck both of them in turn with a rebuking glance. "Now, gentlemen! There's no need for unpleasantness. If you'll be so good as to lead the way John I'll explain everything indoors and introduce my young...rather impetuous companion. How are you keeping old chap, pacemaker still ticking away nicely?"

Until he'd successfully manoeuvred his thin frame through the hallway, into the dimly lit lounge and then onto his leather upholstered armchair, he allowed his guests no more than the discomfort of silence. Pointing his brass handled stick towards the couch he now matched the sarcasm in his voice with a narrow smile. "Well Gentlemen, take a seat if you must and I'll sit back and listen to the important official business you're no doubt going to tell me all about." Both opting to stand, the Major straightened to attention. "Well John, I must warn you that what I'm about to say may be rather upsetting, so please try to relax. We don't want your blood pressure going sky-high, do we?"

"Okay Lockwood, but as you're well aware this isn't exactly a day for relaxing. I'm expecting Blue Boy back within the hour, so let's get on with it; I've another National to win."

Major Lockwood cleared his throat. "Yes...exactly John, and that's why we're here...but before I explain further, let me introduce you to my witness, Mr Michael Murdoch."

They acknowledged their belated introduction with the coolest of glances.

"Murdoch...Have I met you before? The name sounds familiar."

Michael's hands gripped tightly. The casualness of Stenway's enquiry seemed almost insulting. His eyes narrowed, this was maybe the right time to up the stakes a little. "No Mr Stenway, we haven't met, but you're acquainted with my father, Tam Murdoch, from Fife. I'm sure you'll remember him, he sussed out your Blue Boy con. and....!"

"Now old chap, that's quite enough."

The sharpness of the Major's protest confirmed his readiness to make it, his chin quivering as he continued. "Yes, John, Mr Tam Murdoch, he spoke to you on the phone, he claimed he had Blue Boy in his possession for five hours on the day of the Fraserburgh National."

Their host leaned forward in his chair, gripping both his shaking hands over the handle of his walking stick. "Yes, Major! I remember now. He'd the nerve to call me a cheating bastard! So you're his son? Well in that case you can tell your old man to put a stop to these lies or he'll be hearing from my solicitor."

Michael's face flushed with anger, his throat tightening. "As you're well aware Stenway, my father's dead...so let's you and me sort out who's lying?"

"Mr Murdoch! I'm quickly regretting bringing you here. This investigation is to be carried out my way, so please, no more foolishness!" The Major lowered his voice. "John, what has been put in such an unfortunate manner, is sadly true. Mr Murdoch's father was murdered last Friday night and although I regret saying this, he is convinced you, Raymond Pearce and your pigeon, Blue Boy, are implicated in the whole sorry tragedy."

Pushing his stick to the floor, he levered himself out of the armchair, the yellow pallor of his face deepening as the words escaped hoarsely from his throat. "So that's it. The pair of you have come here to accuse me of fraud and ...murder! My God, Lockwood, you can't be serious. ...And as for you Murdoch! My biggest disappointment isn't your father's death...that's got nothing to do with me, no; it's that Ray Pearce isn't here to listen to your crap. You might be able to upset me, you big scotch bastard. But Ray doesn't have a weak heart, far from it my friend, far from it!"

Michael forced a smile, replying softly. "As far as your partner's concerned, Stenway, I share your disappointment. But the day's not over yet, so maybe I'll get the chance to make his acquaintance, when he gets back from Durham."

"Gentlemen please, that's quite enough! ...Mr Murdoch, if it's your intention to make a mockery of this investigation, you're undoubtedly succeeding...and John, no matter what your opinion, neither I nor the E.H.U. are accusing you of anything. However, you must accept, four National wins with the same pigeon is bound to create doubts in some quarters. ...So please sit down and we'll try to resolve all this with some degree of civility."

Although their bulging eyed host had clearly no intention of returning to his chair, the Major's commanding words seemed to have lessened the severity of his agitation. He shrugged his undersized shoulders. "I suppose you're right major, but wait till it's five wins. And you never know next week's the big one - Lerwick. What if Blue Boy wins that, are you going to order the bloody S.A.S. to break down my door?"

Neither guest replied as they watched him shuffle his way across the lounge floor. "Murdoch. If you came here to upset me, you have, so I'm not taking back anything I've said, apart from about your old man. I meant him no harm, but I want to show you something. It proves nothing, but I want to show you just the same."

In other circumstances Michael would have felt sorry for him. There was no doubt he was burdened with ill health; the time he took to reach the adjoining door proved that. Although he looked much older, Michael guessed he was probably in his mid-sixties. Much younger than someone else with a limp he'd taken a dislike to when they first met. He also was now sure John Stenway hadn't murdered his father, not personally anyway, he just wasn't physically capable of it. Whether he was malicious enough to arrange it, he now had few doubts, and one way or another they would be confirmed.

As their host reached into the darkened room for the light switch, the Major motioned with a raised eyebrow that they should follow. It was larger than the lounge and although it had no windows, only a partially glazed door on the opposite wall, three double fluorescent units provided more than sufficient light to reflect the now astonished glare in Michael's eyes.

He realised instinctively that they were standing in the extension he'd noticed from outside; an office, more spacious that the Cascade's, with two wood veneer desks facing each other at the glazed door, supporting identical word processors, telephones and neatly stacked grey plastic In and Out trays. Unlike Mabel's paper strewn domain, this looked the model of administrative blandness. With one conspicuous exception, at least in Mabel's office you could see the walls.

Michael had wondered what the Major had meant by the exhibition room, now - all was revealed. Wall to wall glass fronted cabinets, laden with trophies, silver plated cups, shields, prize certificates, every conceivable memento of sporting triumph. Over the years he's had the privilege to gaze admiringly at similar honours. His own families, like these, for pigeon racing, Jake Matthews for ice hockey, Bobby McLays for boxing. With the exception of Jamie's football trophies they'd always produced warm feelings of pride, recognition of past achievements. But four walls full and every one engraved permanently with the name Stenway now produced nothing but intense resentment.

"Well Murdoch, I hope you're impressed, because you bloody well should be! Fifty years, me, and my father before me, have raced pigeons and won at the highest level, without having to con anyone or murder an old man. So take your time, have a good look and then leave me in peace. I've got another trophy to win today and I don't need a cheeky, interfering bastard like you, ruining the pleasure!"

Staring into the cabinets, his young visitor seemed too pre-occupied to reply, allowing the Major to speak on his behalf. "Yes John, I'm sure Mr Murdoch is suitably impressed, and I'm of-course well aware of your family's outstanding contribution to the sport, but, I'm afraid that's not the current issue and although I appreciate your desire for privacy, I must stay to corroborate Blue Boy's arrival. Do you understand?"

"No, I don't bloody understand! Blue Boy's as honest as I am, he's won four bloody Nationals, the clock's proved that. And he'll do it again today, unless he's stopped off up in Scotland for more than the few minutes he did last time. Because that's all it was Lockwood, not five hours, only a few minutes, and he still won the bloody race!"

Michael immediately turned from the cabinets, his stinging look matching the lack of charity in his smile. "Neat trophies Mr Stenway, you and your father sure did your share of winning over the years, but I can't help notice from the dates that you had a bit of a lean spell. What was it, ten years with nothing to show for them till, of-course, Blue Boy put you back in business?" His smile widened. "You know, I'm really looking forward to seeing you time-in this champion of yours, that's of course if the clock's here, or has your partner taken it to the hospital in Maidstone by mistake?"

Major Lockwood interceded with an indignant scowl. "Yes John, rather indelicately put, but a valid question nevertheless. If you would be so good as to show me the timing clock, I understand it's an S.T.B. Quartz, am I correct?"

Michael's smile narrowed as he waited for the pleasure of seeing John Stenway break into a sweating panic. With the Major's help he'd forced him into a corner and now he'd have the satisfaction of seeing him squirm his way further into it.

"Well major, you've obviously done your homework, that's exactly what it is, an S.T.B. Now where did I put it? Oh... yes, on the patio table... care to see it Mr Murdoch?"

Michael swallowed hard, but couldn't answer. *The timing clock, how could it still be here? It should be up North somewhere with Raymond Pearce.*

Even the early evening's sunshine, warmly embracing him as he stepped out onto the flag-stoned patio, failed to dislodge his frigid stare. It didn't make any sense, but there it was. Sitting squarely on the white circular plastic tabletop, shaded by a large multi coloured sun umbrella. A red, metal cased timing clock.

According to the major an S.T.B. Quartz. He hadn't seen one before, but he couldn't argue it was definitely a pigeon clock. Although almost half a century more modern that the wooden cased Benzing Imperial he and Jamie had struggled to save

£30 for - second hand, it couldn't be mistaken for anything else. The same solid box shape, the large clock dial on its front face, its black hands now pointing to quarter past six. The rectangular window in its left side, displaying a taught white band of printing paper. The metal turning key, protruding from its hinged top. Inches away from the key and separated by the leather carrying strap, a thimble sized hole, open and empty, waiting for a race ring... Blue Boy's race ring.

Michael hardly noticed the conversation around him had resumed. "Excellent timing devices John, and extremely popular nowadays, do you mind if I take a closer look?"

"If you must, but I don't want your friend touching it. You know how easy the security seal can be broken. Instant disqualification Major, your rules - not mine. And I trust him less than he trusts me!" He turned his gloating eyes towards Michael. "Take a seat Murdoch; you look as if you need one... So you thought it wouldn't be here? Well I wonder what little notions are going through your slanderous mind now eh? Maybe the same thoughts as the bold Major's having. There's hundreds of S.T.B.'s and they all look the bloody same, so why doesn't John Stenway keep a spare one at home? Just in case some nosy bastards from the E.H.U. turn up to see it." He paused momentarily, his eyes baiting Michael to speak. "No, I doubt you've got the gumption to think of that Murdoch. And even if you did, you'd be wrong, isn't that right Lockwood?"

The Major, now seated on one of the two plastic chairs, his file spread open on the table, delayed his reply until, with Michael peering wide-eyed over his shoulder, he'd finished checking the clock's metal security tag numbers against the exact duplicates penned in large black ink on page eleven. "Yes John, the seal number 81279, corresponds precisely with that noted and duly recorded during last night's official clock setting." Turning his head, he glanced sympathetically towards his young companion. "Well, Michael. As you see everything appears most satisfactory. Now why don't we try to enjoy what remains of this pleasant evening, in something closer to harmony? My goodness, all this fuss and nonsense has left me quite parched. I think a wee dram all round would be quite in order, wouldn't you agree John?"

"Whatever you say Major, but if you insist on staying here and drinking my whisky, you and your friend are going to have to listen to me for a while. What do you say to that Murdoch? Nod, if you can't speak."

Michael slowly shook his head, unable to mask the lack of conviction in his murmur. "Forget the whisky, but yes, I'll listen to you while we wait for your so-called champion to turn up and your partner, I'd still like to meet him."

"Don't worry Murdoch; you'll meet Ray all right, unless his poor mum's had another relapse. Cancer - poor soul, riddled with it. Surprised she's lasted this long. Yes a bit of a rough diamond is our Ray, but a heart of gold when it comes to his mother. Have you met him Major?"

"Yes, John, last year's Presentation Ceremony at Wing-Holm, quiet sort, I understand you had to force him to be there? Imagine not wanting me to present him with two National Trophies."

The grin spread further across their host's nodding face. "Yes, exactly major! A heart of gold, wanted me to take all the credit, that's Ray Pearce. Now Major, let's see to that dry throat of yours, still enjoy your whisky with a splash of water?"

Noticing that his companion seemed keen to spend the time before his drink arrived jotting notes in the file, Michael opted to leave the patio, wandering aimlessly down the neat garden towards the pigeon loft. The shock of seeing the timing clock still numbed his concentration. He'd been so convinced his father had been right - but the clock was here. If only he could get his mind focused again, there must be a rational explanation. If anyone knew the answers, it was Stenway, but what good was that? This wasn't like having a chat with Francis McLagan; he couldn't beat the truth out of an invalid. The Major, well, he was playing it strictly by the rules, and who could blame him for wanting John Stenway to be innocent? There was nothing so far to arouse more than the slightest of doubts. All he had was a dead man's notebook, the word of his retarded son, and a pigeon fancier's craving for privacy on race days!

He stopped on the pathway in front of the loft, both fists now tightly clenched deep in his jacket pockets. It was much smaller and considerably older that the fifty or so others now hidden from view beyond the garden's high latticed fence, and to his surprise, it was shabby in comparison. If this, he thought, was the home of the finest racing pigeon in the country, it deserved much better.

Felted roof, a broken trellis along its front, with the black creosote and oil mixed finish of its wall panelling faded in patches to grey. Compared to the aviary-fronted palaces over the fence it looked almost derelict. He peered through a narrow gap in the heavy sliding door. The inside was no better, one compartment - no perches. Just six-doweled nest boxes fixed precariously against the back wall. As his eyes adjusted to the restricted light, he saw that all but one held a single blue pigeon behind its bars. Michael guessed, by their size and the bold shape of their heads that they were cock birds waiting patiently for a visit from their hens. Even is his continuing state of confusion he now realised Les had been right. John Stenway raced his pigeons on the widowhood system. The same method his friend practised with his sprinters, the ones that flew like rockets for up to three hundred miles and then gave up the ghost. A spark of hope flicked across his eyes. There was something wrong here. If he could only work out what.

"Well Murdoch, impressed with what you see?"

Michael turned instantly. "No, should I be?" He walked slowly back to the patio and his smirking host.

"Are you thinking you wouldn't use that loft to house street pigeons, Mr Murdoch?"

Michael forced the thinnest of smiles. "Yes, something like that."

"Well in that case, you've got something in common with Ray. He's forever pestering me to have it demolished, but it's staying exactly where it is, in memory of my father and the races he won from it."

Major Lockwood lowered the whisky glass from his smiling lips. "Admirable sentiment old chap, most admirable, and I'm sure John senior would be proud of your recent achievements. But getting back to Raymond Pearce for a moment he... well... how can I put it tactfully...?"

"Put it anyway you like Major, I know you don't think much of him and to be perfectly honest neither did I when he first turned up at the door. But beggars can't be choosers, good motto eh, Major? What with my bad heart, the place was getting too much for me, and as for winning races, your friend Murdoch here's quite right, not a trophy in ten years. The punters stopped coming, and who could blame them. You know, I was less than a month away from paying off the staff and filing for bankruptcy."

"Yes John, How extremely fortunate for you. Ex army I understand? But, if it's not too indelicate to enquire, where did he get his capital? He certainly doesn't give the impression of being inherently well-heeled, and I know how much the army pays."

"Security Major. When he left the forces he set himself up as a Security Expert and he's a bloody good one. There's not been one bird stolen since he put the system in, and my God there's been more than a few attempts since Blue Boy started winning."

"And made you and this guy Pearce a lot of money in the process?"

His eyes flashed towards the source of the interruption. "Yes Murdoch. And he's going to make us a lot more, there's no crime in that is there? I don't know how much you've got to your name, but the day you can dream of owning a pigeon like Blue Boy is the day you've got two hundred and fifty grand in your pocket; and then I'll still ask you to apologise for your bloody cheek, before I tell you to piss-off!"

"Come now, John! I know he's - well - a bit special, but quarter of a million pounds, is that not stretching things a tad?"

He lowered his tone to a throaty whisper. "Not after next week it's not. Six Nationals Major, that's what we're going for, no more - no less. Thirty years I've been waiting for a pigeon to beat..."

"Champion White Wing's record?" Michael's interruption produced a momentary silence. "Yes Stenway, I saw his picture back at Wing-Holm, but that was in the days when pigeon racing was a genuine sport. Seems to me, looking around your place, it's come a long way since then."

Their eyes locked as his host spat out his answer. "Genuine! My God Murdoch, you've got a lot to learn. - Yes, White Wing was a genuine champion, but don't tell me his owner was straight. A devious bastard - that's what Fred Little was!"

Major Lockwood tapped his empty glass against the tabletop, expressing his bewilderment with a deep frown. "Sorry old chap, what exactly are you getting at?"

"Major, I haven't told you this, only Ray knows, but why do you think my father resigned the presidency of you fine organisation?"

"I've absolutely no idea John, that was before my time, but didn't he suffer like yourself, from a weak heart?"

"A bloody broken heart more like!" His voice now sounded as shaky as the walking stick he was pointing towards the foot of the garden. "That loft you're so impressed with Murdoch, that's where White Wing was hatched and reared. It was a Stenway pigeon, not that that bastard Little would ever admit it."

"But surely John, if your father bred the pigeon his contribution would have been rightly acknowledged by the recipient?"

"Yes Major, that's what we thought, but no-way. Little swore blind it was off his own stuff, and bloody useless as they were, everyone believed him. Made a fortune from that pigeon, and what did it cost him; bugger all, that's what Major. He came to my old man, cap in hand, nothing but a pigeon ring in his pocket, begging for a quality youngster and they were old pals, so sure enough, he bred him one off his best stock pair. And the rest of the story, well that's up on your stair wall. Turned out a bloody champion and as for my old man, he never got over it. Within six months of White Wing winning his fifth National he was dead!"

"My goodness old chap, how simply dreadful for you. But John, that was over thirty years ago, what possible relevance has it to do with the present?"

His chin quivered noticeably as he forced an answer through his now tightly gritted teeth. "Everything Lockwood. Can't you understand - everything."

The Major shook his head --- Michael slowly nodded. "So that's what this is all about. Whatever it takes you're going to make sure Blue Boy beats the record?"

"Yes my friend, exactly! Whatever it takes, except bloody fraud and murder. And I know you still don't believe me, but what happens when I prove you wrong. What are you going 'o say then?"

What surprised Michael most about the question was that his mouth immediately had an answer for it. "If you prove me wrong Stenway, I'll buy a pair of squeakers from you, for my brother."

The grin immediately returned to his host's face. "A pair of squeakers eh? Well that'll cost you £500 for the cheapest I've got."

The Major raised his bushy eyebrows. "My goodness, your prices have certainly gone up John. Are you sure that's sound business practice?"

His reply was accompanied by a hoarse chuckle. "Major, the punters are queuing up for them now and some of the paying a lot more than that. The Japs, well they're offering £15,000 for youngsters directly off Blue Boy - grandchildren £5,000. So don't tell me £500 a pair for the same bloodlines, no matter how diluted, isn't a bloody bargain! And as for selling the Boy himself well, I hope you didn't get too excited when I said that earlier Murdoch. I was winding you up, not that you've got the sense to realise it. - Blue Boy stays here! After Lerwick next week, he'll be retired to stud. A whole breeding loft to himself and a dozen top class hens to keep him company. - The Bull system Major, you've probably never heard of it, but it works. Up to a hundred squeakers off him a year." He squinted a cutting glance towards Michael. "Yes, it doesn't take a financial genius to work out what that means, and if you take in the profits from the new sales hall, we're talking over ten million a year. So that's the story Murdoch, like it or not, John Stenway's back in business, and you, well, you - can go to ..."

CHAPTER 24

If it was Hell John Stenway meant, before he was stunned into silence, Michael quickly accepted that it couldn't be much worse than where he was now. He hadn't noticed the bird skimming down from the cloudless sky. Until its presence couldn't be avoided - no one had. It now circled in plain view, over the house and trees, reducing its height with every slow blue wing-beat.

"John is it... John - old chap... are you all right?"

The stark urgency of the Major's words wrenched Michael's gaze from the sky to the slumped figure gasping for breath over the table. Reaching his side in time to catch the walking stick as it slipped from his trembling fingers; he could then only stand gaping while his companion propped their host's sagging head upright against the chair-back, quickly unloosening his shirt collar. To their visible relief it seemed to help. Although ashen faced and still heaving for air, he managed a rasping whisper. "Major... White tablets... Kitchen cupboard... Above the fridge... For God's sake, hurry man!"

As the Major darted towards the patio door, Michael instinctively placed an arm round Stenway's shoulder. Their eyes met, and straining with the effort, in a hoarse choking voice, he spoke again. "Murdoch... Let Lockwood worry about me... You've got a pigeon to time in, and make sure you don't make a bloody hash of it!"

Michael instantly turned his head, focusing his glaring eyes towards the loft and the pigeon walking back and forth on the pathway in front of it. Seeing the timing clock had been bad enough, but he now realised that had merely been a gentle hint of the nightmare now immersing him. What Stenway demanded would only add to his self-inflicted burden.... But what could he do? Ignore the desperate, perhaps, last wishes of an ailing man?

When the Major finally re-appeared, unscrewing the bottle top with his long fingers as he hurriedly approached, Michael was still rooted beside their now semi-conscious host, his anxiety mounting with each lost second. "Major. - He... he wants me to time in his pigeon."

His cool-eyed companion gently prised a single white tablet between John Stenway's lower lip and teeth. "Well, old chap! I think we can rule out John being able to. And even if I knew how to catch a pigeon, which I don't, as you see - I'm rather busy. So if it's not too much trouble, why don't you put your prejudices to one side for a moment and show a little compassion!"

In a vain attempt to hide his acute embarrassment, he turned away from the table, pushing his fingernails deep into his tightly clenched palms, then walked towards the loft. The pigeon, as if oblivious to the crisis unfolding on the patio, had stopped for a moment to nonchalantly preen itself, before returning its patient attention to the closed sliding door.

Michael nervously narrowed the distance between them, forcing the conflicting images from his brain with each step. He knew exactly what was expected of him. With Jamie at his side, they'd shared the exhilaration of the task too many times in the past to forget.... Walk quietly down the garden... slide open the loft door... gently shepherd the pigeon inside... catch it. Remove its race rubber... squeeze it into the thimble... drop the thimble into the clock... turn the key... and pray you'd timed a winner!

A bead of cold sweat trickled down his creased brow. It all sounded so straightforward. Compared to the enormous undertaking the bird had just completed, so easy. Nothing to worry about except his own lack of confidence and the thought of walking back up the garden empty-handed after making a complete bloody hash of it. He edged closer, halting only for a moment when its proud head turned towards him, returning his stare with a single inquisitive blink of its gleaming eyes.

Michael couldn't avoid the Major's brusque words stabbing into his back. "For pity's sake old boy - we don't have all day, and whatever you do, don't take its race ring off, just catch the damn bird and bring it over to me, do you understand?"

He understood, but didn't answer. Less than five paces away all he could think of was it taking fright, flying over his head or round his shoulder to the sanctuary of the farmhouse roof. Why it didn't, just waited patiently for him to join it on the pathway, seemingly unperturbed by his anxious presence, was a puzzle he didn't have time to dwell over.

He leaned his shaking arm over it, slowly sliding open the heavy door. To his amazement before the gap opened to his own width, the bird had crossed the metal runner and with an effortless flap of its wings, rose from the floor to the narrow wooden ledge of the vacant nest box.

Michael manoeuvred himself into the loft, closing the door immediately behind him. He leant towards it, the gap between his hands slowly narrowing, and then instantly scooping forward with a speed, half as fast would have ensured the same success. With the bird secured safely in his right hand, he opened the door and ran up the garden unaware of the smile spreading across his face.

"Well done old chap. Now quickly, remove the rubber, read the number to me and then it's into the clock with it!"

Easing the red ring over the pigeon's scaly left knuckle and toes, Michael was satisfied, by its apparent lack of concern, that he'd caused it little discomfort. Before quickly transferring the ring into the Major's outstretched hand, he fixed his eyes on the black printed numbers and whispered urgently, "4826 - Major." Then watched eagerly as his companion placed it into a tiny plastic capsule, held in the long fingers of his other hand, dropped it into the round hole in the clock's lid and turned the key.

As the ring disappeared into the clock, Michael's smile followed. He looked down at the pigeon now nestled in the security of both hands, the stark acceptance of the truth glazing his eyes with torment. Two weeks ago his father's callused hands had cradled the same bird and for a fleeting moment it had allowed them to share, to retrieve, the bond they'd broken. Michael now realised how hopeless that longing had been; he'd achieved nothing... nothing but the cold resignation of failure.

"Now Michael, if you would be as good as to read out the details of its metal ring, before I telephone my race controller."

Despite the pointlessness of the Major's smiling order, he obliged. Accepting before he looked, that the letters and numbers permanently encircling its right leg were the same ones Jamie had imprinted in his memory. He repeated them in a subdued murmur. "EHU/85/X2220"

Major Lockwood found it hard to conceal his delight. "Excellent... simply... excellent! Its Blue Boy all right, now be a good chap and keep an eye on John while I get on the blower and confirm what's what."

Conscious that too long had passed with his thoughts distracted from the plight of their host, Michael couldn't mask his guilt laced reply. "How...how is he Major?"

To his astonishment the answer came in a sluggish drone from John Stenway's colourless, but now sneering lips. "Never been bloody better! And Murdoch, before you give me back my pigeon, take a good look at it. You might still not believe me, I don't bloody care, but you're holding a champion and remember you and the Major timed him in... not me."

Before he attempted a response, his fingers gently manoeuvred down the bird's firm body. He thought of Jamie proudly watching him when he'd examined the old pied cock just after its return from France and almost weightless with the effort. Blue Boy was different, light, but its muscles still hard and strong. He opened out one wing, not one of its silky feathers out of place, on the second to last flight (Stenway and Pearce, Foxhole, Kent) and a phone number, stamped in dark blue ink, against the light blue background. He opened the other, no name, no address, almost perfect, just one blemish. The single red filled quill of a Blood Flight.

He swallowed hard, clearing the tightness in his throat as he transferred the bird into Stenway's small sweating hands. "My father... my brother... they're not liars, Mr Stenway. The Blood Flight's enough to tell me that, but they were mistaken and so was I. Your pigeon didn't spend five hours in their loft, much less, so you're due my apology. I just hope you can accept it?"

The sneer widened to a grin. "That depends."

"On what?"

"On you handing me a cheque for £500... remember the deal Murdoch? I'll be sending two nice squeakers up to Scotland next week."

When Major Lockwood started the engine, Michael turned towards him, his eyes betraying the gravity of his mumbling voice. "Wha... what can I say Major?"

"Nothing old chap, nothing you haven't already said most eloquently to John. Poor chap, I'd hate to see him having a serious attack, but all's well that ends well, that's my motto. And as for you Michael, well you've had the pleasure of witnessing what looks to be the winner of five Nationals!"

Michael nodded reluctantly. "I can't say it was a pleasure Major, but you're right, less than twelve and a half hours against the wind, and my God, it handled as if it hadn't flown a hundred miles, least of all over five hundred and forty."

"Precisely why it's a champion old boy. Bred for the distance and as John says, a few days rest and its back up to Scotland for the final challenge. Lerwick, over six hundred miles, then perhaps John, poor chap, can put the past behind him."

His passenger didn't reply, opting to retreat into a frowning silence as they drove from the car park. Could he do the same? Put the past behind him?

In the cruellest of ways maybe John Stenway had done him a favour. Shown him, if allowed to continue, how crippling the burden could become. Blue Boy might win Lerwick, beat White Wing's record, but at what cost, a life consumed with bitterness?

Michael knew for his own sake, for his family's sake, he must stop this now. Somehow come to terms with things and look to the future.

A white Mercedes saloon turned in from the main road, slowing to a halt beside them. Its dark tinted window glided downwards; the Major's reluctantly following suit. "Mr Pearce! John tells me you've been visiting your poor mother in hospital, how is she bearing up?"

Raymond Pearce delayed his reply long enough to fix his disapproving stare and tight-lipped smile on the Range Rover's silent passenger. "Aye Major Lockwood, she's doing just fine, but what's brought you all the way from London. A'll wager John wasn't too pleased to see you?"

The Major hesitated slightly. "That's true Raymond... very true... in fact he took a bit of a bad turn when Blue Boy arrived... all the excitement you know. And my friend Mr Murdoch here had to time him in. But don't worry, he's fully recovered, and what's more it looks as if the pair of you have another National win under your belts."

The smile remained, but his stare seemed to harden, become more threatening. "A hope no-one's been upsetting him Major? A don't tak' kindly to folk upsetting him."

During the Major's reassuring reply Michael studied every visible detail of the man John Stenway had accepted as a friend and partner. Little, as the restricted view beyond the Mercedes door allowed, it was enough to confirm what Pearce's voice had hinted. He was more than a rough diamond... much more. What he could see of his solid build, his muscled upper arms and neck, presented a clear portrayal of his physical strength. His dark brown, short-cropped head, almost touching the car's ceiling, indicated his size. The tattoo, half hidden beneath the sleeve of his navy blue T shirt, with a horse shoe shaped inscription encircling its base, meant something to Michael, but he didn't know what. What meant everything was the look in his grey-blue, impaling eyes. No matter his concerns for his partner, his visit to his sick mother in hospital, Michael was convinced of one thing, Raymond Pearce wasn't burdened with a heart of gold.

"And I can assure you Raymond, he's now more than happy we paid our visit, and I hope to see you both at the presentation ceremony. Perhaps you'll choose to accommodate the photographer this year?"

The smile merged to a sneering grin. "Maybe. Major maybe. Now tak' care now and you too Mr Murdoch. Timed in Blue Boy, eh? Maybe a can do you a favour in return someday."

Michael spoke softly; slowing his reply to make sure it was understood. "Sure Mr Pearce... if I ever need a favour... I know where to find you."

Both windows glided upwards.

"Major you didn't tell me he was a Geordie!"

"You didn't ask old chap, but as I said earlier it takes all sorts, don't you agree?"

When the Range Rover reached the junction with the main road its driver gave up waiting for a reply.

CHAPTER 25

"Amazing what you see when you don't have you're your gun, - what?"

Michael turned his eyes to where the Major's bony trigger finger pointed over the steering wheel. To their right, silhouetted by the last streaks of sunlight filtering through the lower branches of the oak border, two dappled brown roe deer raised their heads from Wing-Holm's lawn. Within seconds of seeing the vehicle approach, their white rumps were disappearing into the safety of the tree line.

Michael now knew his companion well enough to realise what he'd just said, he'd said in earnest. "You don't shoot them do you Major?"

The driver replied with a quizzical grin. "Of course, that's what they're there for. Epping Forest's teeming with them. Out of season at the moment, unfortunately, but bagged a lovely stag last winter, from the office window. And not with a rifle, Webley revolver, first shot! Did you notice its head mounted on the wall, overlooking my desk?"

He had but shook his head in silence.

"Fine trophy, everyone visiting my office agrees, except, of course, Miss Berry. Silly girl got herself most upset. Apparently she used to share her lunch with it; damn thing was almost as tame as a Labrador."

Michael didn't know whether to laugh or cry, so he did neither, just stared ahead for the remaining few seconds it took to reach the car park. To his relief the Range Rover was still there awaiting his escape.

"Why don't you join me upstairs for a quick dram before you head North old chap, get a final chance to admire that stag of mine?"

He forced a muted smile, repeating his earlier intention to make his way home as quickly as possible.

After the obligatory farewells and another apology about wasting the Major's time, he breathed a deep sigh of relief as he switched on the engine. His speed, exiting the car park, indicating clearly the need to distance himself from the day's hapless misadventure.

He gripped the steering wheel, cursing his stupidity, praying by the time he'd reached Seaham, the all-consuming feelings of guilt and shame would have lost some of their edge. At the moment he doubted it. The picture of John Stenway, ashen face, purple lips, gasping for air, seemed permanently fixed in his mind. He gritted his teeth, wondering how he could have been so sure of himself. He'd wanted Stenway to be behind his father's murder, wanted his pigeon to be a fraud. What was worse, even when these certainties were proved groundless, one look at his partner Ray

Pearce, - a hard-man with a Geordie accent, and his desperate need for retribution had been aroused again. Thankfully it had only lasted for a fleeting moment; the Major had put things rightly into perspective. So Pearce was a Geordie, - so what? Michael didn't particularly like either of them, Stenway or Pearce, but he'd nothing more than the vagaries of Jamie's memory to base his suspicions on. His brother was adamant Blue Boy had been his for five hours, but the facts said otherwise. Who else, other than a guilt-ridden fool, could argue it hadn't been more than five minutes?

Despite several grimacing reminders, the drive slowly eased the sharpness of his self-inflicted pain. A resigned numbness filled the vacuum. Broken, only after over a hundred miles, with a stray thought. *"Bloody shame. All she wants is a little respect and a photo of Richard Gere above her desk, and what does she get? Her best friend at Wing-Holm, staring down at her every time she's got the bad luck to be summoned upstairs."*

The flicker of a smile then crossed his lips as he imagined the frustrations the Major and his Webley would have to contend with if they lived in Banff. Smack in the middle of a National Park, where the animals, by Law, were considered as important as the residents. More important if they'd been lucky enough to be born an Elk. Wandering about the town as if they owned the place. His smile widened as he re-called how the only part of town they seemed to avoid had been the immediate vicinity of the museum, until of course after the court case.

Now their territory held no bounds. One, an old Bull Elk, even having the temerity to turn up at the wedding. What with the photos being taken, no-one had noticed it ambling into the marquee, until it was too late and the whole top tier of Jake and Mabel's cake was devoured.

Michael's smile turned to a grin. If he and around a dozen other guests hadn't been able to haul Stan the chef away from it, there was no doubt that the new museum curator would have had to accept another glass-eyed resident. But all's well that ends well…. Even Jake had to agree, when he'd calmed down. The Elk had been right about the cake… it was delicious.

Michael was now realising, as always, the road was coming to his rescue… He wasn't totally useless….! The wedding he'd organised for his good friends had been, apart from the uninvited guest, a great success, and in so many ways a turning point. Jake and Mabel betrothing their futures…. In Jake's case probably less of a long-term commitment than Mabel. John, after a private chat in a quiet corner of the marquee, agreeing, if he could persuade his father to finance him, to a 5% stake in the business. And Tammy… yes Tammy… she'd stolen the show. And it wasn't just her low-cut dress. She'd sung, she'd joked, she'd teased, and ended the perfect day in his bed… what a performance!.

His grin instantly disappeared. If his thoughts dwelt on Tammy his mood would sour again, he had to change track. Yes the wedding. His gift to Jake, not the official one… no, that had been well received especially by Mabel. She'd never slept in a water-bed, not, as she announced to her husband's embarrassed discomfort, had she much intention of doing any sleeping in it for the next few nights.... No! The other gift, the little surprise he'd worried about for weeks, the one he'd planned for years but hadn't found the courage to go through with.

Mabel knew, of course. "Do it Mike! And if he gets so riled he has a heart attack, I'll be a rich widow, free to marry you next."

On the pretext of having to nip to the bar for half and hour to see how the stand-in staff were coping, he'd persuaded Jake to accompany him. "Just for a wee Jack Daniel's, for old time's sake, Jake, and it'll give me the chance to talk over a few ideas I've got for the place."

"Like taking John on as your junior partner... eh?"

"What...? You old bugger.... Do you know bloody everything before it happens?"

In the five minutes it took to stroll in the warm Summer's evening from the marquee in the Public Park, along Banff Avenue into Caribou Street to the closed door of Jake's Bar, his anxiety had reached stammering point. "Em... th... there's something... em - I need to show you, Jake." His hands shaking almost uncontrollably as he fumbled the keys into the lock, pushed open the door and switched on the lights.

"I thought you said the place was open...stand in staff...what you up to son?"

They reached the bar counter with just enough time for Michael to take down the Jack Daniel's and a Bottle of Canadian Club from the gantry, before the old man realised things had changed in Jake's Bar.. To his right, on the corner wall, the Formica topped shelf, which for years had supported well-thumbed copies of the Woodsman's Journal, had disappeared. In its place a new dark pine, hand moulded cabinet and behind its tinted glass frame, the resurrection of a now gaping eyed, old man's youth. "Jake Matthews, Lynch Pin of the Edmonton Oilers 1921-27." Three varnished shelves glinting with cups, shields, silver framed photographs and press cuttings. "Jake Matthews, National Leagues Top Goal Scorer... three years running"...

Michael prised a full glass of Jack Daniel's into his friends trembling hand before whispering nervously, "Jake, don't blame Mabel or anyone else for this. It was my idea and if you're unhappy, well, I've got room for it in the cabin. But whatever you say, I wouldn't destroy them years ago and I'm not about to now."

The reply took long enough to start adding stupidity to his list of silent regrets. *Why did I have to choose today of all days...? Why on his wedding...? Why didn't I tip them with the rest of the junk...? Why doesn't the old bastard say something?*

Jake didn't move his eyes from the cabinet until, after one long swallow; he'd finished the whole glassful. He then turned back to the bar, staring through his tears towards the younger man. He spoke quietly, gripping his empty glass on the counter. "Mike, I've never said this, and probably wouldn't have ever got round to it. But what you've done here, kinda forces me to... I've never had a son, too selfish maybe, but if I had... well... we're not blood Mike. But you've given me more than any father could ask for..." He paused; allowing Michael's face to reach an even deeper red then pushed his glass across the counter and grinned. "... Well, next to Mabel, this place and that photograph of me picking up my third top scorer's award... Now fill this up again, son, all these damn surprises are making me thirsty!"

The picture of Jake in his mind, as his eyes glanced the road sign confirming 12 miles to Durham, at last brought the comfort he'd driven so far for. His hands gripped the steering wheel now with determination, not anger. *We might not be blood, but I've been a son to Jake... What I've got to do now is be the same... The same for mum, and a brother to Jamie... When I get back to Rosyth, that's what I'll be... No more crazy ideas... No more looking for trouble... A son and a brother.*

He loosened his grip. *But before that - Julie... wonder if she'll wear her blue number?*

CHAPTER 26

The light fingers of mist greeting his arrival on the outskirts of Seaham, now in the town centre, clasped the Range Rover in a thick glove of damp fog. He pushed the heater control to red. He hadn't far to drive but the coldness had filtered inside, slowly spreading a shiver from his neck to his shirt covered spine.

Michael peered ahead. What little the dipped headlights and glass-smearing wipers allowed him to see, was enough to reverse his decision to head straight for the gardens instead of Daphne Row. *Damn fog...! There's no way I'll find my way there without a torch or a Jack Russell.* A resigned smile parted his lips. Les would hopefully provide both, and if he was in luck a brown ale and a sympathetic ear. *But only for half an hour, I don't was to miss Julie.*

The curtains were closed tight at 60 Daphne Row. Their thin material, combined with the fog, allowing only the faintest glow to filter to his parking place opposite. He got out of the car quickly, only the keys in his hand. The gifts he'd bought in Waltham Abbey would wait until tomorrow. The kids would be asleep by now, so the three individual boxes of Quality Street could sit in the car till after breakfast.... *Hopefully prevent open-warfare this time.*

Two steps took him to the door; he knocked as quietly as he could. Loud enough to alert Les or Ruby, quietly enough not to disturb the whole household. He waited, knocked again with the knuckle of his index finger... still no answer... not even a yap from Jock. Regretting he hadn't phoned to tell them roughly when he'd arrive, he was about to opt for a tap on the living room window with the car keys when the door opened. When he realised who it was a wide smile crossed his face, followed immediately by the palm of Julie Fenton's right hand! Like slow motion, he'd seen it coming, but was too surprised to avoid it. He stood, an open-mouthed statue, both cheeks reddening more in shock than pain.

"I hope that hurt... you conniving bastard...! Now, why don't you turn round, get back into your status symbol on wheels and leave my family alone!"

Although incapable of replying, he knew, from past experience, what was about to happen next, just managing to reach the door's speedily, narrowing gap with his right foot. The force of the collision jarring against his shoe, instantly added excruciating physical pain to the verbal abuse he'd just received from the girl he needed to like him... more than like him.

Michael circled the pavement in a left-footed hop until a message from his brain finally reached his grimacing lips.

"Christ, Julie!.... What's wrong...? Either something's happened or you're bloody crazy... And I don't know what you've done to my toe... probably broken it... but I'm staying put till you've told me what the hell's going on!"

She stared through him. Her tied back hair revealing the coldness of her eyes. Her static body barring the door, daring him to take one hop closer. When she spoke again her voice seemed more controlled, more cutting, more like a lawyer... removing the last remnants of dignity from a guilty child molester! "You want to know what's happened...? Well, how can I put it to you so you'll fully understand...? In less than two days you've managed to rope my brother into some personal disaster of yours and succeeded in getting him almost killed... And, of course, my little niece, you certainly charmed her with your Canadian drawl and the sweets. I bet you've brought some more with you, pity she won't be able to share them with Jock this time. Now that she's had to help me bury him behind her rabbit hutch."

Michael shook his head, attempting but failing to dislodge the mass of confusion. "You know, you look genuinely surprised, must be the years of experience, conning people like us to do your dirty work!"

Her tone - disgust laced with mockery, finally cleared the fog. His eyes flashed towards her. "Julie... I... don't know what you're talking about... Now... for God's sake, tell me.... Tell me... is Les okay... Where is he?"

Julie paused for a moment, taken aback by the passion - the determination in his voice. "No... he's not okay. but if you're so concerned, why don't you go see for yourself. Pop into Intensive Care, Sunderland Royal... on your way back to Scotland. Maybe you can con him into feeling better."

The door closed slowly, he didn't attempt to stop it. Staring at the letterbox, the cold shiver he'd felt before was back, stretching down his neck, numbing any movement. Only his brain seemed unrestrained. *Sunderland Royal! Intensive care! Oh my God, what the hell have I done?*

He was met at the reception counter by a young, more emaciated than thin, male nurse. The lines of fatigue surrounding his eyes betraying the yawning routine of his reply. "Les Fenton, Intensive Care... are you family?"

"Yes... his brother."

"Okay, he's been transferred to a general ward... let me see... yes - 27b - second floor. You don't sound like family?" By the time his eyes had lifted from the register he was too late to get his answer. Michael was yards away, heading for the stairs.

Ward 27b wasn't large, maybe ten beds. Between each, a wall mounted radiator. He felt the sickly wave of warmth and disinfectant as soon as he stepped through the swing door.

It was, thankfully, nurse-free, giving him the time to scan each bed as he passed. His apprehension increasing when he realised instinctively, that the one furthest to the right, with the curtains drawn round it, was undoubtedly where his friend would be found.

He drew the grey plastic drape across its rail, stepping backwards with the shock. If it wasn't for Ruby, sitting on the nearest chair to the bed, holding a bandaged hand, the person lying there, without a single sheet covering him, could have been anyone. Michael stared in silence, slowly comprehending the dreadful extent of the injuries the bandages must be covering. His head, his arms, his chest, his legs... all bandaged. A drip of some sort, pumping red liquid into the back of his hand, another, pumping clear liquid through his tightly closed lips. What he could see almost turned his stomach. His face was bruised and swollen beyond recognition. The skin around his closed eyes blackened like pummelled lumps of coal. Matching them in colour, a three-inch row of tiny burnt weeds, stitching a vertical wound on his cheek.

Ruby's tear-stained eyes turned from her husband. "Michael, thank goodness you're here... he keeps asking for you."

He placed his shaking hand on her shoulder.

"Ru... Ruby, how... how bad is it?"

She rubbed her eyes. "Bad enough, Michael, bad enough. At one stage they'd thought one o' his broken ribs had punctured his lung, but it hasn't so he'll live... till a get the silly bugger home that is!"

"What happened Ruby... it's my fault, isn't it?"

The hint of a smile crossed her lips. "You've been speaking to Julie, haven't you?" She didn't need an answer, the expression in his eyes confirmed he had. "Whatever she says, its no' your fault, Michael... Well no' all your fault.... He woke up two hours ago, told me everything... an' that you'd warned him no' to get involved... but you should know him better... he's an interfering sod, Michael. A should 'ave seen through him this morning, he wouldn't rest in peace. A thought he was just excited-like about the pigeon race... little did a realise he was getting himself involved in..."

"My problems?"

"Aye, Michael... your problems... but I'm no' blaming you or Bam, that's just the way he is." She lowered her voice. "Between you and me... a've been here before."

Before she could continue, they noticed Les's eyes flicker to half open. His lips followed suit, spitting out the end of the clear plastic tube. Ruby tightened her grip of his hand. It seemed to help focus his straying vision. His voice, when it eventually came, sounded like a distant whisper. "Michael, me bonny lad... see what a mean, ma Ruby, she's a gem... ganin to kill me when a get home. What more could a man ask for?"

Michael stepped closer but could only nod, allowing Ruby to fill the silent vacuum. "Of course a won't kill you, dearest... that'd be too kind. It's your pigeons a'm ganin to do away we', and a'll mak' sure you watch, as a neck every bloody one o' them." She then leaned over the bed and gently kissed his swollen lips. "Now.... A've to catch the last bus home, its leaving the main door in five minutes, so Michael - he's all yours. A'll have one of his brown ales waiting for you at the house.... A think you'll need it."

"But... Ruby, do you not want to stay, I'll drive you back?"

She responded with a tired smile. "No Michael, a've heard his story and a don't want to go through it again. It's your turn, a've a sister-in-law to sort out... stop her running to the police. She's as daft as him you know, and as protective as a mother hen. But when she gets riled she can be as vicious as a Jack..." In an attempt to hide the tears welling again in her eyes, she immediately turned from the bed. "An'... an'... there's Susan and the twins... a promised a'd wake them up, tell them their silly da's on the mend."

Michael stood watching her as she walked slowly down the ward, noticing her nod sympathetically to another woman visitor sitting silently at a bedside. They were probably strangers, he thought. Probably only one thing in common, the inherent strength to support their loved ones through even the worst crisis. His cheeks flushed red. His own mother had been here too, years ago with Jamie. Not in this ward... not in this hospital, but here... like Ruby... a gem. Too precious, too perfect, to be placed in the same cluster as a worthless fool. And that's exactly what he was... a hapless troublemaker. Julie Fenton was quite right. He'd dragged an innocent friend into his own personal disaster, and what was worse, it wasn't going to end here.

He slowly closed the curtain again and sat in the chair Ruby had left. Leaning over the bed, only inches from his friend's battered face, he whispered gently, "Les, how bad is it - Les - what happened?"

Less than an hour later, almost midnight, sitting in a cold Range Rover in a hospital car park, watching as another ambulance approached the patient's entrance, as another stretcher rolled through the sliding doors, Michael slowly grasped the truth. A fractured jaw, six broken ribs, severe bruising, multiple bites. As Ruby had said, "Bad enough".

Les, of course, had played it down. "Don't be fretting about me, bonny lad, a'm on the mend, but how did you fare down in London? Better than me a think, there's no' a mark on you."

"I got nowhere, Les, there was nothing to prove. I saw Blue Boy come home with my own eyes, helped time the bloody bird in. And Stenway, he's just a bitter, sick man, and as genuine as you or me."

Before he'd finished Les had tried to raise his head from the pillow, rasping heavily with the effort. "Genuine....! Genuine....! He's a bloody crook man... the bastards - they've stitched you up... They're fucking ruthless, Michael - ruthless. An' you and me are ganin to sort them out... as soon as a can get out o' this bloody bed. But before that there's a story to tell an' don't bloody well interrupt, unless it's to tell me what a bloody hero a am!."

CHAPTER 27

"Ruby. This is the last bloody time a'm ganin to Murton on the bus... Money or no money a'm getting that Transit through its MOT if it bloody kills me."

Ruby, as always, accepted his declaration with a knowing smile. "Aye, whatever you say Bam, then you can trade it in for a Rolls Royce... or maybe swap it for that fancy motor o' Michael's. Or then again, you could do something sensible, like phoning the Scrappy an' getting the bloody heap towed away from ma front door."

Les hated getting on a bus with a basket of pigeons. It always caused hassle. If it wasn't the driver complaining about wood shavings littering his floor, some equally awkward passenger would claim they had an allergy to birds and between sneezes, demand he moved them further up the aisle.

"Ruby! If Michael phones, tell him a'll be back around eleven. Tell him a've got a good feeling in ma water about tomorrow's race... tell him a'm putting ma six best widowers... tell him..."

"A'll tell him Bam... tell him you're as daft as a bloody brush. You've no more chance o' winning the Murton Open as me winning Miss Wet T Shirt at the Social next Saturday night."

He turned from the doorway, his eyes focusing on the ample contours of her thread-bare jumper. "Oh, a don't know pet?" His lips now curved into his best impression of a leering grin. "Finest pair o' turnips this side o' Durham Castle. In fact, if you're willing to hire them out, a could use them for the Grower's Show next month, sit ma prize cucumber between 'em."

"Prize cucumber, eh? Well maybe, if you don't down too many brown ales at Murton, a'll gee you a chance to show me it later... now bugger off... or you'll miss your bus!"

Tonight Les Fenton felt lucky... a promise from Ruby... and an empty bus. Even the driver turned out to be a fellow pigeon man. "In you get, bonny lad. So, you're having a crack at the Murton Open, eh? Well in that case a'll drop you right at the Club door."

It turned out to be the wrong door. Murton Social Club had two. The main one, leading to a newly carpeted entrance foyer with a sign:
'PIGEON FANCIERS WITH BASKETS, PLEASE USE SIDE DOOR - OFF THE CAR PARK'
Whistling softly, as he made his way around the brick building, basket in one

hand, pigeon clock in the other, the anticipation of tomorrow's race, the £500 first prize, the glory of winning the Murton Open, almost saw him walk past the blue Sierra Estate. He stopped whistling, stared at it for a moment, then shook his head. "No... it canna be... loads o' bloody blue Sierra's." He walked on for a few yards then turned, fixing his eyes on it again. "But no' many owned by pigeon men!"

The Gentleman's Lounge, large as it was, was almost full to overflowing, dominoes in one corner, darts in another. In the middle, a long row of pigeon baskets and their owners, leading to a two-man table. Behind it and its two bespectacled occupants, a dozen large wicker race panniers, already half-filled with race-rung birds.

Les first visited a side-table, paid his entry fee and handed over his clock for setting, before joining the basketing queue. Thankfully they knew how to organise a race at Murton, he didn't have to fidget for long. Less than ten minutes and his birds were through the ringer and into the panniers. He watched intently as each one was gently dropped through the hinged wicker top, to join their competitors. If his luck held he'd see them all again tomorrow, hopefully nice and early. A one hundred mile sprint up from Selby... *No problem... and the wind a light south-westerly... right up their tails.*

He smiled confidently as he placed the empty basket under a bench seat at the side wall.

Next stop, the bar.

It was three deep in pigeon men, all like him, with a thirst and a dream.

Topping the Murton Open from Selby.

"'Scuse me... 'Scuse me." Ignoring the more than muttered protests, he pushed to the front.   "Barman...! There's a couple o' young tykes out in your car park eyeing up a blue Sierra Estate... best tell the man that owns it, eh?"

Although the barman wasn't big - around 5 feet 4, he was blessed with the voice of a foreman lumberjack. "Right you lot....! Whoever belongs to the blue Sierra Estate, best go have a gander... before its wheels are gone."

For less than three seconds silence prevailed, followed by a loud curse from the far end of the counter. "Fuckin' toe rags! Terry! Get out there an' sort the bastards out."

Les stared through the crowd, now fully re-occupied in their quest for drink.

Terry sprang from his stool, spilling half his pint glass in the process. As he hurried to the door Les's eyes narrowed as they followed each step of the tall, denim clad figure. *The man ca'd Terry... owner o' a blue Sierra Estate... an' a dirty grey plaster covering his broken nose.* He then turned again to the bar, grinning widely. "A brown ale... ta." *Thirsty work,* he thought, *sorting out cheating bastards.*

Within minutes Terry was back on his stool, arguing with his big brother. Les, now only two yards from them, reckoned it couldn't be anyone else. They were almost identical, apart from the nose plaster: matching less than handsome looks; matching denim jackets; matching respect for each other. "That's the last fucking time I'm losing half ma pint just 'cos you're too lazy to get off your fucking arse. There's no one out there... waste o' fucking time!"

"You'll do what a tell you, you flat nosed tosser. Now sup what's left o' your pint... before a lose ma fucking temper!"

"'Scuse me, bonny lads. A'm looking to buy a good pair o' stock birds, and they tell me you're the best flyers in these parts... fancy another pint?"

They turned on their stools in perfect unison. The biggest spoke, examining the source of the interruption with an unyielding stare. "Who telt you that crap...? Haven't won a race for three fucking seasons."

Les tried to conceal his discomfort with a nervous smile. "Em... some lad at the other end o' the bar... he was pissed like... said you were the Stoker brothers."

"Stoker brothers...? Never bloody heard o' them. Vincent's the name. Best flyers around, eh...? No man... we've got other talents. So why don't you piss-off or we'll gee you a fucking demonstration!"

Les's smile merged to a wide grin. "Fine, lads, sorry to be bothering you. Barman! Two brown ales for the lads, an' all the best for tomorrow... a've a feeling your luck's changing."

The barman silently poured the drinks, watching Les's progress as he ambled to the opposite end of the counter. When the opportunity arose to return his change, he motioned him to whispering distance. "You're takin' a chance, lad... winding up the likes o' the Vincent brothers... you got a death wish or something?"

Les grinned. "Aye, something like that. Who are they anyway, no' exactly Brothers in Love."

"Brothers in Love....! More like the Brothers bloody Grim! They're evil bastards, man... run a scrap business at the back o' the reservoir, beneath the old railway line. Used to be four bonny allotments until they scared the other tenants out an' took over the bloody lot."

Les checked his change and smiled. "Thanks for the advice, a'll no' forget you when a win the race tomorrow, a'd buy you a drink now, but this is ma bus fare home."

Saturday morning couldn't come too early, he pulled open the curtains at just after six, greeting the day with an exuberant grin. "Ruby! Wake up lass, look at that sunshine, they'll be up at seven, home by nine and a'm feeling lucky."

Ruby tugged the quilt cover over her head. "Lucky! You're lucky a don't break that cucumber o' yours... a never got a wink o' sleep last night we' it prodding into ma back!"

He leaned over, pulled the cover down slowly and kissed the back of her neck. "Well pet, you would be snoring your head off when a got home. We could have sorted out that little problem in ten minutes."

"Ten minutes… ten seconds more like. Now before you gan out, mak' me a cup o' tea, an' remember to tak' the dog with you. It's no' staying in ma house for the whole day, no' after what it did on ma good carpet!"

What with a Jack Russell constantly trying to sidle past him into the open cree and the sight of two pigeons dropping into Joe Fishers in the next allotment but one, the morning now, wasn't going as well as he'd planned. *Ah well, there's bigger fish to fry… two big sharks… one we' a broken nose.*

At last a bird came. Dropping like a stone, right onto the loft floor. "That'll do nicely," he mused as he turned the clock key. "Maybe no' a winner… but there's more to life that topping the Murton Open… like sorting out a wee problem for a Scotsman!"

"Ruby! Six out o' six… no' bad, eh?"

Ruby smiled. "Aye, no' bad Bam… pity they decided to walk home. You'd be better sending Jock; he could do we' the exercise."

A flush of red darkened his cheeks. "Aye, Ruby, that reminds me… a'm ganin to Murton again this afternoon, a'm told the railway embankment's teeming we' rabbits. Let's see how many Jock can catch for our tea."

She watched him leave, brown hessian rabbit bag over his shoulder, Jack Russell at his heels. *My God… he's bounced back quickly…. He's up to something… a don't know what, but a bet he's no' back here we' a rabbit.*

It was all going perfectly to plan. Jock sitting quietly at one side, rabbit bag at the other, the flask and sandwiches still inside. *But no' the binoculars…they'll be needed any minute now.* He glanced again at his watch, two thirty five. *Aye, any minute now.*

The E.T.A. had been worked out in his head as the kettle boiled for Ruby's cup of tea, seconds after phoning the E.H.U.'s Race Release Service. "Good morning and welcome to Race Release. The convoy of six thousand two hundred and thirty five pigeons competing in the English Homing Union's Thurso National have been liberated today, Saturday 16th July, at six a.m. into a light south westerly wind. Best of luck to you all!"

As he lifted the binoculars from his chest, he was forced to take a deep breath. Anticipation had now merged with the first stirrings of apprehension. He scanned the sky to the north of the reservoir. *Aye, any bloody minute now.*

He couldn't have found a better vantage point. Dry ground, tall grass and a gorse bush, half way up the railway embankment, and the view… perfect. Right down to the reservoir and the allotments; set back less than a hundred metres from its south bank.

Where he knelt - facing the corrugated iron compound - he could almost see right into it. Almost… if it wasn't for the corrugated iron. *Worse that bloody Fort Knox.*

His lips widened to a nervous grin. *These bonny lads have definitely something to hide.*

He re-focused the binoculars, following the rusting stockade until it reached its corrugated gate, then over it. Not much to see - a trellised pigeon loft roof and what looked like the top of a large black creosoted shed. Outside, a waste ground, cluttered with junk. Apart from allowing a space for parking, the debris of the scrap yard pushed to the very edge of the dirt track leading from its entrance.

In the puddle strewn car park - two cars, a blue Sierra and a white saloon. His eyes fixed on its dark tinted windows then down its bonnet. "Jock!. ... Looks like a bloody Merc. In good nick too... the bastards must be entertaining someone important."

Jock replied with a whine and bulging eyed stare towards the rabbit bag.

Grinning, he lay down the binoculars on the grass and searched through the bag, soon producing two ham sandwiches from their tin-foil wrapper.

Les was just about half way through his, and seriously contemplating opening the flask, when he saw them coming. The sandwich dropped from his shaking hand, caught before it landed by a delighted Jack Russell.

A team of about forty racers was approaching from the north. Les knew instinctively they were racers, they were going like trains. He grasped the binoculars, just in time to catch them around one hundred feet up, crossing the water towards him. Suddenly one peeled off, folded back its blue wings and dropped without a circle, right into the high walled compound. A trickle of sweat seeped through his brows temporarily blurring his vision. His shaking left hand gripped the binoculars as his other frantically wiped his eyes.

When they were back in place, their metal rims pushing tightly against his eye sockets, there was nothing to see. What was happening behind the corrugated iron he could now only imagine. "It's Blue Boy. Fucking Blue Boy... Jock, we've caught the cheating bastards. Now you sit here. A'm ganin for a closer look."

As he reached standing position, the compound door flew open, bouncing on its hinges as it crashed backwards against the wall. Les was immediately on his knees again, parting the pricking branches of the gorse bush for a better view.

A man, with a large black Alsatian running at his side, hurried towards the white car. In his left hand a small wicker basket, in his other... nothing. Even without the binoculars Les could see his right hand was empty. *Where the fuck's the clock?* The answer flashed through his brain with the same speed. *Christ. It'll be in the motor, he's ganin to time it in - on the way home... clever bastard.* Following a swift kick to the dog's side, the Mercedes door banged shut. In an instant its wheels spraying water and mud over the chasing and now barking Alsatian.

Les automatically turned his glare towards Jock who was already off his backside yapping as loud as a Jack Russell *who's no' even sacred o' big Alsatians.* "Shut the hell up, you daft bugger, you'll get us both bloody killed!" Before the words escaped from his rapidly tightening lips, he saw the Vincent Brothers standing at the open gate pointing to where the Alsatian was running... straight towards him.

In blind panic he got to his feet, scrambling up the banking towards the railway line. He'd almost reached it, and the mesh link fence beyond, when he realised Jock wasn't with him. As he spun round, his arms automatically raised themselves in defence. The Alsatian was only three metres away and closing. He crouched low as it leapt from the ground. The next second seemed to take forever. A lingering blur of white and tan immersing itself into the thick blackness of a throat. Les' eyes had narrowed too thin to notice where the Jack Russell came from. The Alsatian did notice, but was still in the air, as it sprung from the deep grass below. The pain... the shock in its fearsome eyes, expressed the howl it couldn't make. Jock's teeth gripped its throat with the ferocity of a hungry polecat, forcing his prey to roll sideways as it fell. They tumbled back down the embankment, the tiny dog sometimes clinging... sometimes hanging from its neck. They didn't separate until they crashed against a boulder.

Les scrambled down after them, knowing he'd be too late, Jock had lost his grip and he was too slow... too slow to stop the butchery now begun.

He watched the little dog attempt another upward spring, but his slavering foe knew what was coming, its gaping jaw flashed sideways, snaring the Jack Russell's spine in its brown stained teeth. Les heard the snap of bone, screaming as he closed the gap. The Alsatian, busy crunching more bones with its snarling teeth, didn't realise he was there until a steel toed pit boot hammered against its flank.

The Vincent brothers saw it all... saw their dog, Satan, "The best fucking Alsatian we ever had." Snarl, bite, gore its heart out, as its head was being punched to a bloody pulp by the cheeky bastard who bought them a pint last night at Murton.

When they reached him, Les was bleeding and exhausted, barely able to rise to his feet, turn towards the biggest and break his nose with a single left hook.

For the Vincent's, however, the party was just starting. Terry smiled a quick thank you for his brother's nose job, then pounded Les to the ground with four venomous kicks to the ribs. Les curled up tight, knowing he couldn't retaliate, only survive. He'd done the same once in the boxing ring... curled up, lost, but survived. But then it was only one pair of fists crushing his body. Now there were two, and their boots, steel toe capped like his own, pummelling against his legs... his arms... his head.

He woke up in a tree-lined lane, his broken arms draped around a dead Jack Russell.

Les heard the voices of the two boys, but could only raise his eyes to the rim of their bicycle wheels. "Mister! You got any money on you? Gee us a pound each an' we'll phone a' ambulance."

In the space of twenty minutes Michael watched another four ambulances turn up at the patients' entrance, watched six stretchers and a wheelchair roll their blanket wrapped carriages through the sliding door. He knew each one bore a story with it. Perhaps less traumatic than the one he'd just heard, perhaps worse. But it was Les's story he'd written the script for, Les's story he pictured over and over in his mind.

His decision was now made. In truth he'd made it as soon as he'd pulled back the plastic curtain. The same decision, but now somehow different, now it was re-affirmed with a calmness, a coldness, only the distant look in his eyes disclosed.

His stare reached beyond the patients' entrance, far beyond… to a racing pigeon stud, over two hundred miles away in Kent. He paused momentarily to allow the faces of John Stenway and Raymond Pearce imprint themselves permanently in his vision. When they had, he smiled and slowly turned the ignition key.

CHAPTER 28

The baseball bat rattled along the inside of the perimeter fence, making a dull chiming sound against the chain-link. When it reached a metal post the noise sounded stronger, more alive... more in tune with his feelings.

Ray Pearce couldn't sleep. He needed to think things through, and a stroll around the fence always helped. He enjoyed the freedom of it... walking in the early morning dark inside a security fence... outside if he felt like it. It was his choice. His lips curved to a narrow smile... "An' no bastard could do a thing about it!"

For too many years fences had controlled his life. Borstals, Army Barracks, Prisons. But now it was different, he controlled everything... John and him together. He glanced up towards the house, almost lost in the blackness behind the beech trees. What little he could see of it, silhouetted in the skyline, looked so solid, so secure.

The thick muscles of his neck tightened as he nodded his head in silent satisfaction. John was asleep at last, his reading lamp was out. He sometimes read half the night, old dog-eared, tea stained pigeon magazines. Past glories, his and others. Ray could tell by his partner's mood in the morning who he'd been reading about. Anything to do with his father was okay, or more recently, Blue Boy. That always brought him hobbling down the stairs with a self-satisfied grin. But White Wing, Fred Little, or any other of his long dead adversaries, there was no speaking to him for at least an hour after breakfast.

A lingering grin crossed his face. *No worries about this morning though... breakfast with a smile... what with Blue Boy doing the business again, an' that little irritation finally out o' the way.*

The grin widened as he recalled how John had gone to bed so pleased with himself, barely able to contain his mocking laughter. "Ray! You should've been there... second thoughts... maybe not... probably killed the cheeky Scotch bastard. The bold Major sitting having a whisky... me having a fucking heart attack... and that stupid bastard Murdoch, timing in Blue Boy. Then, and you'll not believe this, the moron signs me a fucking cheque for £500 and apologises. Ray, it couldn't have worked sweeter. We're some team... Stenway and Pearce... some fucking team!"

He was right, they were some team. Three short years together and now only a week away from achieving everything they'd ever wanted.

In John's case it was simple... recognition. Six National Wins with one pigeon... The British Record. The name Stenway back where it belonged.

For Ray Pearce it couldn't have been more different, recognition was the last thing he wanted. What he longed for was a home, security, money, a successful...

legitimate business. *Yes... all o' that an' no bastard ever again telling me when a can or canna go for a walk in the dark.*

What they did share was the all-consuming determination to see things through to the end... no matter what. The awkward old bastard in Scotland had recently verified what Ray already knew, their partnership was solid. Even though, it still surprised him how easily John had come round to his way of thinking. "We either pack it all in now John, or make sure the old fool doesn't gan whining to the press... what do you think?"

He smiled as he remembered his partner's piercing eyes slowly raise from his pigeon weekly. "Well, Raymond, I think... I think... you and the Vincent boys should take a little trip up to Scotland, have a quiet meet with this Tam Murdoch, and then... kill the bastard! And if his idiot son's with him, do him as well."

His long fingers gripped tighter around the bat's smooth wooden handle. Unfortunately, the idiot son hadn't been there. *Neither had the fucking prodigal son from Canada... no bugger knew about him till it was almost too late.* Suddenly the baseball bat crashed against the fence. The feel... the sound of it, immediately easing the frustration of unfinished business. *Three strikes an' out! That's all we'd 'ave needed for the Canadian, eh Mat? Three strikes. Four for the father... three for the son.*

He'd named it Mat before even bribing the workshop screws to let him make it. "Honest, it's for ma young nephew, Mathew... mad keen on baseball. Now what is it you smoke...? Embassy or Silk Cut?" Silly tossers believed him. Believed he had a nephew... believed he'd any family that cared enough about him to accept his gifts. *Aye, Mat the Bat. Probably the most useful thing to come out o' Durham Jail.*

He gently massaged the striking end with his left hand, satisfied that its collision with the chain-link had done it no harm.

"Not a mark... aye you're made o' the best o' stuff, pure English willow... four coats o' varnish, an' polished every second day." The grin returned. "One careful owner... Ray Pearce. An' one use, aye Mat, one use... an' it's no' fucking baseball!"

The bat had been sitting snugly in the Merc's boot next to the empty wicker basket when the Major introduced him to the Canadian. He'd imagined more than a few times since, how nice it would have been to introduce them to each other. The words... his only words... still rankled. "If I need any favours, I know where to find you."

Cheeky bastard! But as John had said, over and over, it was a risk not worth the taking. "This time, we'll have to play it smart, Ray. Use the back-up plan, the one for nosy bastards! As soon as Blue Boy drops at the Vincents, get him into the basket and it's back down here like the clappers. Throw him up a couple of miles from here, somewhere quiet. The rest of them will be flying against the wind, forty miles an hour. We'll time him as soon as the Scotch fool catches him. Believe me, Ray, he'll still win the bloody race, and what's more... in front of the best two witnesses we could ask for."

John had been quite right, Murdoch had been fooled, and next week it would be back to business as usual. They couldn't rely on a head wind every week, nor a snarl-free motorway, without a speed patrol in sight. Yes! Back to business, they'd been lucky this time. Blue Boy had only won by fifteen minutes… less than enough time in hand for a speeding ticket. Next week, like his previous races, they wouldn't have to worry. Time him in at Murton. *Just wait till the competition's reaching London…* simple. He curled his lips into a smirking sneer. "Aye, even a retard like Murdoch could appreciate that… must run in his family… being a fucking idiot!"

He'd now reached the entrance gate. Pausing to check the lock was secure, at the same time mulling over whether to walk straight up the main pathway, back to the house, or do one more circuit. He knew the answer before his brain delivered it. "Aye, once more round the block… and why not?" Even in his T shirt it wasn't cold… "Summer in God's little garden… Ray Pearce's little garden."

He looked towards the east. The first hint of daylight was already testing the very edge of the darkness. Another hour, he thought, and the whole place would be alive again with the sound of pigeons… Stenway and Pearce's pigeons. Over a thousand of them, safe and secure in their timber palaces. Each one now worth more than a Durham screw's monthly wage packet. And after Lerwick… not a worry in the world. So why did he need another circuit? He thought for a moment. *The fucking Vincent brothers, that's fucking why. Everything's ganin so sweet an' they knock hell out o' a silly bastard who's only on the lookout for a pair o' stock birds. Terry! Fair enough, that's what a'd expect o' him, the gormless tosser. But Reg, what was he thinking o'? As soon as a've squared up their last ten grand a'm dropping 'em… mates or no mates, they're becoming a bloody liability. After next week a'm legitimate, an' they can do what they bloody well like. Gee 'em a year an' the daft bugger's will probably be banged up again in Durham, but there's no fucking way I'm joining 'em… no fucking way.*

Even Reg Vincent would have agreed. Six years sharing a cell with the same person, no matter how well they got on, seemed like a lifetime. The only respite they had from each other was Ray's time in the workshop and Reg's monthly visits from Terry. Out two years earlier for grassing on a mate from a previous job.

All Reg and Ray had in common was their keen interest in building societies, and the consolation of knowing they'd protect each other when things got iffy.
In her Majesty's Prison, Durham, a single hard man was just that. Two teeming up… different ball game - gave them the scope to do a bit of swaggering. Not too much, as to annoy the screws. Just enough to make sure the first timers smiled politely as they handed over their spare cigarettes.

The problem with Reg was he missed his hobby, and he went on about it endlessly. *Pigeons… pigeons… fucking pigeons.* It drove Ray up the wall. Until he told him the latest story about the young stray that Terry was going to neck the next time the silly bugger dropped into their cree. "Aye, Ray, it belongs to a fella Stenway down in Kent, he used to be a top flyer a few years ago. Owns a big pigeon stud... but canna race worth a fuck nowadays. The word is he's on his uppers." Reg then explained in his usual, monotone, prolonged, excruciatingly boring tone, how this particular young pigeon kept dropping into Murton, Saturday after Saturday; stayed for a few hours and then pissed-off home. "Well out o' race time Ray. A'm surprised either Terry or this bloke Stenway hasn't killed it long before now. The thing is though, Terry says it's so bonny... he's ca'd it Blue Boy... but a've telt him to neck it next time... no fucking use to anyone!"

Raymond Pearce was now pleased he'd decided to do a last circuit. *No fucking use to anyone.* Little could Reg have imagined how wrong he was. Blue Boy was worth a fortune in the right hands. He'd sussed that out in jig time and within a few months the whole scam had been planned to perfection. He was in charge; the Vincent boys would each get a healthy cut of the profits. All he had to do was wait till Monday, April 11th, 9.30am. *Get out o' this fucking hole, pay a visit to Foxhole, Kent an' put a little proposal to a near bankrupt, pigeon man.*

And right up to a fortnight ago it had all gone so smoothly... *Then the bloody Fraserburgh debacle.... Blue Boy hitting wires in the fog.* The desperate waiting at the Vincent's cree, until at last he'd turned up, still made him grit his teeth.

He breathed a deep sigh. Their luck had held. A cat, anything could have found him... but no, he ends up in a pigeon loft, fed and watered for five hours... thanks to the Murdoch family. He sighed again, this time with undisguised satisfaction. *Pity the old man was such an awkward sod. Aye.... an' he must a been a hard-case in his day, what with breaking Terry's nose an' needing four strikes from you Mat, to sort him out.*

As he glanced down to the bat, a stray thought clicked uneasily through his brain. *That nosy Geordie bastard couldn't 'ave been a pushover neither... geeing Reg a nose job an' killing the dog.*

He hadn't told John about it. He would just fret... ruin a good day. And Reg had seemed confident enough on the phone, not that he understood much of what he'd said... *Broke nose an' all.*

He was just about to take a shortcut back to the house, when he saw the lights. The car was coming from the north, speeding down the main road, much faster than safety demanded. He wasn't unduly concerned until it slowed with a screech of tyres just before the drive-way, turned in and sprayed its dazzling beam towards the fence. As it closed its distance he slunk back against the gable of the nearest loft, the bat head now raised to the palm of his left hand.

He'd guessed by the sound of its engine and the height of the headlamps, it was a four wheel drive... *Aye, a four be four, looks like a Range Rover.* As he whispered to the bat his malignant scowl rapidly merged itself into the bleakest of sneers. "Aye,

Mat, looks like we've another visitor... will we 'ave a wander down an' mak' him welcome?"

With the headlights switched off, the visitor was still adjusting his eyes to the darkness as he strode purposely towards the gate. Suddenly, just before he reached it, it swept open, making him reel back two paces with the shock. Out of the shadow a man stepped forward, leaning a baseball bat over his sturdy T shirted shoulder, carrying a grin across his face, too gratuitous to be anything other than dishonest. "Good morning to you Major Lockwood, the honour o' it! Two visits in one day.... But my goodness, some speed you were doing... you'll 'ave to learn to slow down. We wouldn't want you to have a nasty accident... would we?"

The Major, still stunned by the welcome, snapped a nervous reply. "Yes... Yes, Pearce... but I'm in a hurry, so there's no time for small talk. I must see John immediately... so if you'd be so kind as to move aside."

Raymond Pearce had no intentions of moving anywhere. He seemed to grow larger, the bat now doing a rolling motion... brushing gently against the stubble of his right cheek. "'Fraid you can't Major, he's fast asleep, had a terrible trying day... so a think it's best we don't disturb him. You wouldn't be looking for a bigger cut would you, Trevor?"

The older man hesitated; he hadn't expected Pearce to be awake, wandering around the damn place like an armed sentry. "No, I want no more damn cuts; I want this whole blasted misadventure stopped now, before it's too late. So Pearce, please don't be discourteous... I must speak to him."

Even before he'd stopped talking he knew, from the venom flashing from those pernicious, penetrating eyes, that something he'd said had caused acute offence. The answer was spat towards him. "Discourteous...! Now that's a word you've never ca'd me before, Major... scum, yes... villain, more than once, but discourteous? No Major, is it because a've stopped saluting you, like the old days... or maybe it's because you think a'm about to tak' this fucking bat an' crack your arrogant fucking head open we' it."

Major Lockwood immediately realised his predicament. He wouldn't get near John to persuade... plead with him to stop. What's more, he'd now got himself engaged in a more pressing, perhaps more perilous problem... The scum, Raymond Pearce, was most definitely in no mood for courtesy. "N...now, Raymond old chap, let's not be rash. I wouldn't have driven all this way, in the middle of the night, unless I was convinced this Murdoch chappie didn't still create a risk to our... to your... admirable enterprise.... And Raymond, despite our differences in rank, I always treated you fairly."

The response, although delivered with a smile, sounded colder... more threatening. "Treated me fairly, eh Major? No, you treated me like shit! Major Trevor Lockwood, Lord and Master o' the R.E.M.E. workshops, Colchester... Fighting experience... fuck all! Thieving experience... no bastard could out flank you.... Until of course a turned up, thrown out o' a real Regiment. Aye Major, an' a bet it still rankles you... The First Battalion major... the Paras....! Worse than a fucking prison sentence... a fighting man like me, demoted to a fucking grease monkey for you. By the way, do you still have the car sticker a gave you? Bet you have you old fraud.... That's right, isn't it Trevor you're a fraud, an' no bugger realised it till a turned up an' sussed out your scams. Losing a gear box here, an exhaust pipe there... ended up there was more Land Rovers in Colchester town centre than fucking taxis!" Unlike the stony faced recipient, Ray was now warming to his theme. "But you were always a smart bastard, must be the breeding, eh Major? A got the court-martial you got your pension. Is that what you mean by 'Treating me fucking fairly?'"

Major Lockwood didn't want to answer; he didn't feel fully capable of it. But the tone of the scum's question demanded it. "N... now Raymond... the past is the past... th... that's always been my mo...."

"The past is fucking everything for some o' us major. Especially for John Stenway... my friend... my partner! Who hasn't treated me like shit. So before you get the fuck out o' here, what's this crap about Murdoch? John says he's a tosser... in fact he reminds him o' you."

Despite his now desperate craving to retreat to the Range Rover without adding physical abuse to the verbal insults he'd received, the Major forced the words from his trembling mouth. "I... I didn't come here to be slighted like this Raymond. O... only to express that... that I'm extremely perturbed about next week. We're all ruined if Murdoch realises the deception we instigated today, and, of course, there was the unfortunate scenario with his father. I... I just wish you'd have informed me of that, before adding murder to our felonies. He's not a complete fool you know, and when you turned up, somewhat earlier than expected, I could see it in his eyes... he, how can I put it... he wasn't exactly over impressed!"

He closed his now sweat filled eyes when he saw the bat raise slowly off Pearce's shoulder. Suddenly he didn't feel afraid, now only a numbing coldness occupied his brain.

He opened them again when the cankerous derision in the laughter filtered through the chilling silence. "Over impressed... so the bastard wasn't over impressed eh? But a bet he was well impressed by you. Hero o' how man fucking battles? Why don't you piss-off home to Miss Simpkins Major. Gee her one for me, an' please, don't be upset that a don't salute you on your way. As you see, now that you've opened your eyes again, a've a bat in ma hand and a'm probably so fucking brainless a'd knock maself out we' it!"

The baseball bat rattled against the chain link. He'd more thinking to do, serious thinking. He'd wondered from the beginning if the bold Major would become a problem. He smiled wryly. *From a bloody Godsend to a liability in three years... oh well, that's life.*

Three years ago in a prison cell, listening to Reg Vincent, he couldn't believe his luck. "Aye, Ray, but we'll need someone in the know, someone to tell us when the first pigeons north o' Kent are being timed. We canna tak' any chances we' the English fucking Homing Union, they're as strict as hell, especially that Major Lockwood fella, he'll 'ave the law on us, the least hint o' a swindle."

Sometimes he still couldn't believe it. The same Major Trevor Lockwood who the Pigeon Fraternity thought the light of fair play and justice shone from his arse, was none other that the old crook he'd done time for in Colchester. "Aye, there is a God. An' we' your problem solving skills Mat, the Major might be meeting him soon."

CHAPTER 29

Susan Fenton hadn't bothered to check the time. The sunshine streaming over the smiling Teddy-Bear print on her quilt cover, was all the information needed. - It was morning and she'd very important things to do.

First, get dressed. Vest, pants, socks, pink jumper, blue tracksuit bottoms with the yellow stripe down one leg. Trainers - no! - Not the trainers, she didn't have time to bother with the laces. She'd wear her red wellingtons; slip them on at the kitchen door.

Second, have a pee. Then downstairs and out of the house without being noticed. Doing the toilet was an irritation she couldn't avoid. Washing her face, cleaning her teeth, brushing her hair yes. But not a pee. She purposely didn't flush it. The noise would wake the whole house up.

Leaving the silence of the bathroom behind her, she tiptoed along the narrow hall, attempting through tightly closed lips, to restrict the sound of her breathing. When she got to her parents' bedroom door she noticed it slightly open - open just wide enough - tempting enough, to stop and peek through. A flicker of hope momentarily brightened the blueness of her dark circled eyes - *Could he be home? - Could it all have been a nasty dream?* Peering through the narrow gap, reality returned with a single glance towards the bed. Only one sleeping mound under the covers. It was no nightmare. Her dad was in Sunderland Royal - her little Jock was dead - *killed by a big Alsatian!*

A single tear slowly slid from her left eyelid. Just like the ones that chaperoned her to sleep last night - a real tear. Not the kind she could turn on and off like a tap when the twins were annoying her and needed a severe telling-off from their mother. She quickly wiped it from her cheek, her eyes narrowing - she'd things to do.

The thought of how angry the twins would be brought the first smile of the day. Despite the ferocity of her objections they had demanded the responsibility, the honour, of seeing to their father's pigeons. *My job,* she confirmed silently. *My job - far too important to be left to two useless buggers like them.*

As she negotiated the stairs, the delicious prospect of returning home, waking them up, announcing what she'd done then listening to their howls of rage as she bolted to the safety of her mother, brought her, smile intact, to the living room door.

She eased it open, pausing for a moment while her eyes adjusted to the half light of the curtain shrouded room. She wasn't immediately aware of why, but her smile suddenly went missing, lost in the uncertainty of sensing something unfamiliar. She moved forward, but even the softness of the carpet beneath her socks seemed to betray a false comfort. Four paces on, her eyes straining towards the darkened corners of the room, she stumbled against the settee and saw it. Something! --- Somebody! --- Very big was stretched, from armrest to armrest, covered by a grey blanket - the grey blanket. The one taken from the airing cupboard every winter to cosy the twins and her under as they watched T.V. What was worse, the grey blanket was moving, slowly - but definitely moving.

She could have screamed, one of her best screams, but instinct told her not to. A scream would wake up the twins - wake up the something. Too terrified to move, she forced her gaping stare along its full length, before fixing her eyes on the far arm. Where the grey blanket ended, two brown, woollen socked feet - big feet - pointing up to the ceiling feet - stuck out into mid air. Below them, tucked neatly beneath the overhang, the clue her eyes were longing for - a brown holdall, and standing in a neat row on the carpet next to it, three cartons of Quality Street! Her face instantly beamed. Michael - Michael was back.

She stepped closer, reached over and gently lifted the cover from his head. His eyes were closed. She saw how peaceful he looked, how his face was lined with tiredness. *Poor Michael,* she mused. *Sleeping like a log - you look knackered - must 'ave had a long journey - must 'ave got here too late to go to bed with Aunt Julie - poor soul.* She then bent down to his shoulder, brought her mouth to less than an inch from his ear, and shook him with the ferocity of a Jack Russell killing a rat. "Michael. Get up you lazy bugger. We've a cree to clean and flowers to put on Jock's grave. He's dead Michael - a big Alsatian killed him! An' ma da' - he's in the Royal!"

His eyes flashed open. Of all the bad dreams the past hours had produced, this one seemed so real - the grinning face so clear. He had to shake the confusion from his head before he realised why. A hoarse whisper escaped. "Susan - what time -?"

"Time you got up you lazy bugger, we've a cree to clean out!"

He raised his watch arm to his bleary eyes. "But Susan it's not six o'clock yet, is it not a little bit early to be…?"

"No!" She interrupted with an irritated scowl. "An' if you're too lazy a'm ganin maself, all the way down the back lane and through the gardens - on ma own!"

Unlike their first walk to the gardens, they both seemed too deep in personal thought to get involved in willing conversation. Apart from expressing his sympathies for Jock and her father, Michael kept his concerns concealed beneath his strained look.

He glanced down to her, a little curly headed innocent, too tender to be part of this. Her pet Jack Russell dead, buried behind the rabbit hutch; her father lying broken limbed in hospital. His face stiffened. And what had he done to make things right? Bought her a box of Quality Street.

Why hadn't he kept driving last night? It had seemed so coldly simple. Turn the key, drive to Foxhole, determine justice with his fists. For Ray Pearce, natural justice.

For John Stenway, something even more equitable. Force him to watch as his life's achievement, the biggest - the best Racing Pigeon Stud in England, if not Europe, was torched to the ground.

Then drive back up to Murton and pay a little visit to the Vincent Brothers.

Unfortunately, less than three miles from the hospital, he'd remembered Ruby had asked him back to Daphne Row - more than asked. For a further two miles the thought of her waiting expectantly eventually persuaded him to call in. - *Just for a few minutes - explain exactly what's going on - she deserves nothing less. Then use the fast lane of the motorway to make up for lost time.*

"Michael, bonny lad, a'm so glad you came back. Now here's a brown ale. Ma daft sister-in-law's away to the gardens with a flea in her ear from me, the kids are in bed, so sit yourself down, nice an' relaxed - like an' start talking - 'cos you're no' ganin anywhere till a know everything."

Less than halfway through the brown ale, Michael realised, from her knowing nods, that Ruby had already got most of the story from her husband. What he did add about his meeting with the Major, their visit to the Stenway Stud, his determination to finish his business with them tonight, saw her stare intensify.

After a long silence she rose from her chair, glanced quickly at the wall clock and smiled nervously. "Em - look, Michael, am no' meaning to hold you back, but for the past fortnight a've had to pop along the street to see old Mrs Gibson at No. 94, she's had a stroke, poor soul, an' a have to mak' sure she's comfy-like. You don't mind waiting here for ten minutes? A canna leave the kids all themselves - poor wee buggers, they're so upset about their da'."

For ten minutes Michael had fidgeted on his chair, for the next twenty he paced the living room carpet. After an hour he gave up waiting, grudgingly accepting, with a yawn, that the settee now seemed too inviting to ignore.

The Seaham allotments, six o'clock on a Sunday morning, seemed so peaceful. Behind the rows of doors, no dogs barking, no pigeons flying, no clandestine huddles of gardeners chatting about their prospects at the growers show.

The chill fog of last night had long rolled back into the sea, leaving the place now bathing silently in a still, flower-scented warmth.

His eyes strayed back to his companion. "You like coming here, don't you Susan?"

The curve of her smile, immediately confirmed the apparent silliness of the question. "Aye! - Course a do - you'd be daft no' to like the gardens. A'm ganin to get ma own one when I'm old. Ma da's put ma name down on the waiting list. A'll have ten rabbits, fifty pigeons, three dogs, a goldfish pond an' ma own little house - just like ma Auntie Julie's."

He didn't answer, hiding his thoughts behind a nervous nod. Despite the competition, meeting Julie Fenton again seemed never far down his list of worries. When he thought of his mother or Jamie, there she'd be, smiling kindly in the back ground. Thought about Canada - The Cascade - he'd hear her soft re-assuring voice. Thought about Les, Raymond Pearce - Blue Boy - he'd feel the sharpness of her right hand crashing against his face! "Susan!" He whispered hoarsely, as she pushed open the blue entrance door. "Please, Susan - no noise. - Let's just see to the pigeons - then home, okay?"

The little girl's knowing chuckle didn't help. "Aye, Michael, we don't want to waken her - she gets so angry when she's wakened too early - specially a Sunday morning. Now a'll let the birds out an' you can start scraping."

Despite the sound of the cree's louvered doors rattling across their runners and the joyous flapping of Les's pigeons when they realised their premature freedom of the Seaham sky, Michael was reasonably satisfied, from his nervous glances to the closed curtains of the portacabin, that its occupant was probably still asleep. It was years since he'd cleaned out a pigeon loft - experienced the pleasure of turning a dust, feather, dropping-strewn mess into a housewife's dream. All with only a small triangular paint scraper, a brush, a garden hoe for the floor, and an old, rusting metal bucket.

As the minutes passed, he seemed to forget himself, forget everything. Twice he'd to stop his lips from breaking into a contented whistle. Although neither of them spoke, he knew instinctively that the little girl, happily refilling the water bowls, was on the same wavelength. Together they were doing something worthwhile, for the pigeons - for Les Fenton.

Within half an hour they'd finished and were standing side by side outside the cree proudly looking in. It looked so perfect, so spotless, everything in its proper place, everything ready and waiting for the pigeons to come home to, and happily mess up again.

A gentle tug on his shirtsleeve broke the moment. He turned. Her dazzling smile seemed somehow less genuine, less innocent than before. "It's time they were back in for their breakfast, Michael. That's ma job, so you have a sit on ma da's bench, nice and comfy - like, an' watch how fast a can trap them."

He did as she'd said, sat back into the slated bench, stretched one arm over its back rail, crossed his legs out in front of him, and relaxed for about five seconds before reality dawned. *Trap the pigeons. - She's going to trap the pigeons!*

Countless times he and Jamie had done the same. For pigeon-men, ensuring their birds knew the routine and followed it, was beyond necessity. A race could be won or lost by a split second and any delay in getting them into the loft, especially for Les's sprinters, was totally unacceptable. The trick was to immediately gain their attention as they streamed across the sky. Jamie and he had got it down to a fine art, with an old syrup tin half-filled with peas. As soon as they heard its resounding rattle, - down. - No hesitation, scrambling into the loft. Exercise over - feeding time begun.

Other pigeon fanciers used different methods. Some called them down. "Come on - boys! - Come on - boys!" Different techniques same common denominator, each was based on a familiar sound - a noise, the birds in flight clearly recognised - clearly heard.

Michael's eyes flashed towards the cree. There she was standing solidly beside the door opening, unzipping her tracksuit pocket, reaching in, grasping something small - something silver. He prayed it was a well-deserved Quality Street, he knew it wasn't. Panic roughened his urgent whisper - "Susan! - How - how - do you trap the pige....?"

"Pheee! - Pheee! - Pheee!" The whistle sound screamed through the air. The pigeons, dots in the sky, heard it, turned instantly, dropping like arrows towards Les Fenton's allotment.

Michael slumped further into the bench. *She traps them in with a whistle. A bloody whistle! And they heard it half a fucking mile away.* He then turned his gaping stare to the portacabin, repeating through tightly gritted teeth, his companion's earlier assurances.

"Aye Michael, we don't want to waken her, she gets so angry when she's wakened too early."

Unable to divert his eyes he hardly noticed the little girl skipping happily towards him then around the back of the bench. "Good whistle, eh Michael? Ma da' bought it from a policeman. Now, a'm ganin to put some flowers on Jock's grave - here - you keep it till a'm done." At the same time as the whistle flew casually over his shoulder, landing squarely on his lap, its chuckling employer was disappearing behind the rabbit hutch.

Every option for escape - running to the blue door - hiding in the cree - joining the devil-child behind the hutch, floundered haplessly before his unblinking eyes. All seemed abundantly preferable to what he was doing now - sitting, face flushed, incapable of movement, staring at the cabin door, waiting for the dreadful certainty of it crashing open.

Within seconds it obliged, surprisingly, with slightly less force than anticipated. The hinges, although badly bruised, remained intact "Susan Fenton! - Oh! - it's you." Realising instinctively, as she spoke, that the housecoat she'd thrown on in indignant confusion, was tied far too loosely, Julie Fenton's face colour instantly veered to as red as his own. She hurriedly pulled it firmly over her bare shoulders, then tightened the cord waist band.

"Em - I - didn't realise - it was - what time is it?"

Michael forced his stare down to his watch, then cleared the hoarseness from his throat. ""Em, its six thirty five - I've - we've been cleaning out the pigeon loft." A nervous smile stretched his lips. "I don't suppose there's the chance of a coffee?"

Her answer, when it came, was tinged with the vaguest hint of amusement. "A coffee? - No! - But there's a very good chance I'm going to take that whistle of yours

"Hi! - Auntie Julie, sorry he woke you up. I've been seeing to poor Jock's grave, an' now a'm ganin for ma breakfast, then to see ma da' in the hospital. Michael has to gan up to Molly's farm to get some bags o' pigeon corn. There's hardly a drop left. - You'll need to show him the way. - Bye."

They both watched in bewilderment as she skipped happily towards the garden entrance and disappeared. When their eyes finally met again they noticed each other smiling.

"Michael, have you ever had the strangest feeling that we're only on this earth to satisfy the whims of some superior being?"

He shrugged his shoulders and grinned. "Yep! - its just a pity we've had the bad luck to be chosen by the Daughter of Satan - have you ever checked her scalp for the 666?"

Julie's smile quickly faded. A new nervousness strained the softness of her voice. "No - I haven't - but that reminds me of something. Em - something I should probably tell you before you decide if you still want a coffee."

"Sure, Julie. What would that be?"

"I've - em - I've - spoken to the police." To avoid seeing his reaction she immediately turned round and disappeared back through the portacabin door leaving it open behind her.

Disbelief, as he sprung from the bench, rapidly veered to a surge of searing fury. Within seconds he was up the steps and through the doorway, his body shaking.

When she realised his closeness could no longer be avoided she turned from the worktop, the coffee percolator secured firmly in her trembling right hand. "Milk - no, sugar - or have I forgotten since yesterday?"

"You did what?"

The smile her mouth produced was too insecure to be genuine. "I phoned the police - well - a policeman friend - Sergeant Ron Adams, the previous owner of your whistle, you'll like him."

Michael's eyes stabbed deep into hers. "And…what damned right do you think you have to be interfering in my….!"

The force she used to push the percolator towards him like a loaded gun suddenly broke his flow. "Every damned right! As soon as you got my family involved - my brother in hospital - every right! - You might not be too concerned about our welfare, - I know you've no concern for you own - but I'm - we're not going to stand back and let you get killed. So why don't you calm down and let me explain."

As he spun from her, back out through the doorway, Julie felt her entire body shiver uncontrollably beneath the robe. Only her blue eyes remained static, fixing on his back with the sharpness of an arrow.

At the foot of the wooden steps he suddenly stopped. For what seemed an age, he stood there, motionless, his head bowed towards the crazy paving. When, at last, he slowly turned again, she saw for the first time an unfamiliar softness - a weariness in his eyes. His voice seemed so fragile. "Julie, - I'm sorry - so sorry - I didn't…." He closed his lips in an attempt to stop them trembling, making do with a despairing shrug of his shoulders.

Barefoot, Julie moved down the steps to the bottom tread, her hand gently reaching to his upper arm. "Michael - you've nothing - nothing to be sorry about. What you're trying to do for your family - to yourself is so sincere - and I know I shouldn't have said what I said - but I don't want to see you destroy yourself, and you will, Michael - you will, unless some interfering sod like me prevents you."

As she spoke, her fingers felt the taut muscles of his arm slowly relax. Their eyes fastened; hers - deep-blue - penetrating, waiting for the tear welling in his to escape down his cheek. Knowing if it did she wouldn't be able - wouldn't want - to stop herself gently wipe it gone.

To her surprise he blinked it back with a resigned smile. "Yes Julie, you're quite right. Just milk - no sugar. I think we could both do with one."

They didn't talk again until they were back in the tiny kitchen, sitting on the two stools, facing each other, coffee mugs cupped in their hands. When he did, the soft whisper couldn't mask its sarcasm. "Well, Julie. - You've spoken to the police - so what happens now. Are they going to arrest them, then cock-up the evidence - and let some smart assed lawyer get them off?"

She delayed, hoping that her tone would sound un-lawyer like, sound as genuine as he needed it to be. "No, Michael. - Not necessarily - but you're right, if we're not careful - if we don't catch them in the act, next week's Lerwick Race. Some smart assed lawyer like me will run rings round us."

His brow creased. "Julie, what do you know about the Lerwick Race? I haven't mentioned that to anyone - except...."

"Yes Michael, to no one except Ruby. You told her last night, and if you remember you also said you were going to drive back down to Kent, and then, goodness knows what. - Get yourself killed, or jailed for life."

"But...!"

She interrupted with a nervous chuckle. "But you thought Ruby was popping round to see Mrs Gibson at No. 94 - and she was Michael, six months ago anyway. She went there every night until the poor soul passed away. She came here, Michael, told me what was going on and then we'd no choice, we went to the nearest phone box and I spoke to Ron - and thank God, you must have still been at home when she got back."

His mouth twitched, but didn't open.

"And don't be worrying about Ron Adams, as I said, he's a friend - a client in fact. I'm dealing with his early retirement application. Believe me Michael, he's due me a few favours, and he agrees, right now you can prove nothing. It's your word - the son of the victim's word - against theirs. So they've won a few pigeon races - the Vincent brothers have a blue estate car - Terry Vincent's got himself a broken nose, that's not so uncommon in Murton. His brother, thanks to Les, has probably got one now. Michael, we've got to prove their pigeon's a fraud - and Ron agrees - catch Raymond

Pearce and the Vincents when Blue Boy arrives. Ron knows them - well he knows the Vincents anyway - he's convinced Terry'll panic - spill the beans. Seemingly he was famous in Durham Jail for it!"

Michael brought the coffee mug slowly to his lips; hoping that a sip from it would help him concentrate, find some flaw in what she was saying. "Julie - you don't understand. Despite what you, Ruby and now your policeman friend knows, none of you really understand what this is all…"

She leaned closer, close enough to allow a stray strand of her hair brush against his shirtsleeve. "No Michael, I don't fully understand - but the main thing is I care - believe me, it's the only way. You want justice for your father? I want the same for my brother and, and this sounds daft, for little Jock. But what's the point in your kind of justice if it causes more anguish for you - for me?"

Michael now realised something in her eyes, in the softness of her voice, her nervous smile meant more than she was prepared to say - she liked him - more than liked him. He wanted to place the coffee mug back on the worktop, reach his hand to her cheek, bring her mouth even closer. But what if he was wrong - he'd been wrong about everything else.

He gripped the mug tightly, clearing the delusion from his throat as he spoke. "Okay - you win - I'll go along with what you've said - it looks as if I don't have much choice."

His lips then stretched to a narrow smile. "So, Julie, where's this farm the Devil Child wants us to visit?"

CHAPTER 30

"No Michael, I'm not joking, as the pigeon fly's we've only travelled eight miles."

He shook his head in grinning disbelief, he didn't check the mileometer, didn't have to, sure that at least twenty meandering miles of narrow country roads had been negotiated in the last hour.

On his own, he was in no doubt, he'd have got lost, probably at the first junction, never found Molly's Farm, probably had great difficulty finding his way back to Seaham.

Fortunately he wasn't alone; he had Julie Fenton with him and was loving every minute of her.

"Well - Durham's answer to Tiger Tenzing - how much further? That's if we ever get by this herd of cows!"

She chuckled. He loved her chuckle. It was so fresh, so open - made her eyes sparkle even brighter. "Be patient, will you. Only another mile or so, then there's the farm track of-course. Just as well you've got such a nice new car, Les's Transit fell apart on Molly's track, had to be towed home, hasn't turned a wheel since. And the cows, why don't you just drive through them? They'll shift out the way."

It was Michael's turn to chuckle. "Not at home they don't, not cows though - Elks - the town's literally crawling with them."

He didn't notice the subtle change in Julie's smile. "Do you miss them?"

"Well, I try to - it's against the law to run them over."

"No! That's not what I meant, do you miss being at home, - you know - your mates, your business - your girlfriend?"

He turned his face towards her, a hint of red bursting to the surface. "Who told you about - oh? Of-course - what else has Ruby said?"

His companion's expression stayed firm. "Oh, probably everything you told her. But, getting back to your girlfriend, you must be missing her?"

Michael turned his eyes back to the road and the ambling back-sides of the cows, now only feet from the front bumper. "I - I haven't really had time to think of home too much - as for Tammy - well, I've sold the Cascade, so I'm pretty sure she'll want to stay with the business."

Julie felt herself blinking involuntarily. "You've sold your restaurant? Ruby didn't…"

Michael interrupted with a wide grin. "Ruby's a couple of days behind the times. I sold it on Friday and the Bar - over the phone. Sometimes I can hardly believe it myself, but to be honest I've been thinking about it for a while. Time to move on, that kind of thing."

As if heeding his words, the cows at last found a suitable gap in the beech hedge and were now tramping contentedly into a turnip field.

"Not far now, turn up along here at the "For Sale" sign. The farm's straight up that track, just beyond the brow of the hill."

Julie had warned it was rough, Michael now realised she hadn't exaggerated. Even with the benefit of the four wheel drive and the advantage of flicking the transmission into low ratio, he needed every bit of his concentration to negotiate the pot holes. When eventually they reached the brow, the sight of the stone-built farm, nestling in its bowl of green pasture, sheltered at three sides by gently sloping hills, forced him to place his foot on the brake pedal. "Julie - it's beautiful, and look at the view, is that Seaham in the distance?"

Julie nodded. "Yes, as I said, only eight miles. Les loves coming up here, he keeps saying when he wins the pools he's going to take it off Molly's hands - become a farmer, grow pigeon corn."

As she spoke, Michael noticed a figure standing in the washing green to the side of the house. At her feet an overflowing plastic basket, around her aproned waist a red cloth peg bag. They watched as she bent slowly to lift the basket, its weight buckling her shoulders with the strain. They then drove into the puddled forecourt, just in time for the old woman to reach the front door and place - almost drop - her burden on the red polished step.

She turned and faced the Range Rover with a scrutinising stare, her eyes straining against the sunlight. Michael guessed she was well into her eighties, built compact like his mother, with the same shock of white hair.

Julie was first to get out. "Hello, Molly, do you remember me?"

Molly Richardson brought her right hand up to shade her now perplexed eyes, then spoke. The frailty of her voice emphasising her indecision. "No pet - a don't think so, but ma memory's no' quite what it should be. Were you the lass an' her man that were up here last month, looking to buy the place? If you are, a'm really sorry, ma lawyer says a should bide ma time for a better offer."

"No Molly, I'm Julie - Julie Fenton - Bam's sister."

Molly moved closer, almost within touching distance, before breaking into a grating giggle. "Aye lass - a see you now! Well, well! Bam's little sister - my you've grown, but still as bonny as ever, an' who's this - your husband?"

Julie glanced towards Michael and waved him from the driver's seat with an embarrassed smile. "No Molly, he's just a friend - a friend of Bam's, we're here to buy some pigeon corn. Bam's - em-he's not able to get around much at the moment."

Molly giggled again. "No wonder, with that old van o' his, a told him it wouldn't last long on ma road. Now the pair o' you come away in. You're just in time for a cup o' tea."

Two hours, three cups of tea, a life's history and a guided tour of the farm later, Michael was happily loading the Range Rover with six 25kg bags of pigeon corn, while Julie said their farewells.

They managed half-way back down the track before the temptation could no longer be resisted. "So Julia - you were just like your pretty niece when you were little. 'Bugger this - bugger that!' And, of-course, there was the time Molly showed you the new puppies, got you so excited you wet yourself. Yep, we must visit her again - I haven't enjoyed myself so much for ages."

The scowl couldn't hide her acute embarrassment. "The name's Julie! And I'd be glad if you'd concentrate your sad mind on driving. At least I remember my childhood. When she asked you any questions you conveniently changed the subject." Satisfied by his silence, that she'd put a halt to his impertinence, Julie quickly regained her composure. "And talking about wetting yourself, you seemed pretty excited when she showed us round - thinking of becoming a gentleman farmer are we?"

"Probably not," he answered quietly. "But the place reminded me of something - something I haven't experienced for a long time."

The soberness in his tone instantly secured her attention. "What?"

"A challenge, Julie - a challenge! Did you see how run-down it is? Poor soul. She's not able for it. She kept going on about moving to nice cottage in the village - and so she should Julie, sell up and let someone else lick the place back into shape."

Another two miles passed before they wrestled themselves from their own thoughts.

"Julie - you and Les, you're so close - you'd probably do anything for each other?"

She gave him a puzzled glance. "I suppose so, but why do you ask?"

Michael hesitated. "Well, it was something Molly said - about your parents dying when you were so young and Les looking after you."

"And making such a bad job of it you mean?"

"No, quite the opposite, but is that why you came back here after university? He said you could have landed a great job with some top firm in London and maybe got married to the boss's son."

"My God. Ruby's not the only informer. Did my brother tell you I was about to marry Cecil Crowhurst? - Wait till I get to the Royal - he thinks he's in agony now."

Michael tried to stem his laughter, but failed. "Sorry Julie, I didn't realise his name was Cecil - no way could you marry a Cecil."

Her narrowing eyes tried to feign annoyance. "I can marry any name I like! - And what's more, Cecil proposed three times, not that it's any business of yours."

"So why did you come back?"

"I came back ...." She stayed silent for a moment, as if collecting, weighing, the now re-established seriousness of her thoughts. "I came back - because I had to." Her eyes suddenly seemed to lose their sparkle. "I don't like to admit it, but you're right, my big brother did bring me up - struggled on his own to keep me at school, paid for everything. What he couldn't make in the pit, he made boxing, turned professional, almost killed himself, coughing up coal dust trying to keep his weight down. And then, when I was accepted at Bristol and, of-course, couldn't afford the residence fees, he took on Barry Fridge at Newcastle Arena - Barry Fridge, Middleweight Champion. You saw Les last night, Michael he looks bad, but believe me, Ruby and I, we've seen him worse."

Her companion's face flushed, more in regret than embarrassment. "Julie, if I've upset you - I'm so sorry - that's all I seem to be good at, and there was no excuse for it, I'm just an interfering...."

"Sod! Just like my brother." Her interruption caught him completely unaware, she was smiling again. "Now take the next road to the right, it'll get us home in half the time. You can make it up to me tonight with that expensive meal you promised."

The remainder of their day passed far too quickly. Julie made a quick lunch, while Michael trudged along the allotment paths, six times. Each with a bag of pigeon food hoisted over his shoulder. Then, after a shower and a change of clothes, they went to visit her brother in Sunderland Royal.

Thankfully, when they got there and Julie had negotiated the admiring glances from every male doctor, male nurse and male orderly they met, Les seemed in good spirits. Ruby had seen to that nicely, with the two bottles of brown ale now securely tucked at the back of his bedside cupboard.

Afterwards they had a wander around Sunderland town centre. Julie did some shopping while he picked up the courage to make a phone call to Rosyth. He lied again. First about Les having an accident and needing help for a few days with the pigeons. Second about promising to keep out of trouble. Finally he left his mother with one guilt-ridden truth; he was enjoying himself.

As the evening drew closer they found the City of Light Cantonese Restaurant. In Sunderland, as expensive and elegant as it got. The enjoyment of their candle-lit meal only surpassed by the exquisite pleasure of their conversation.

Then a slow drive home, his gift to Julie - a Lurcher in a frame. Her gift to him - a giggle and an appreciative kiss on the cheek. "I've got a bottle of wine in the fridge, would you like a glass?"

He wasn't keen on wine, wasn't sure if he wanted it, but if it kept Julie Fenton in his company for another few minutes. "Why not."

They sat facing each other. Michael on the couch, Julie silently on the deer skin rug. Her long legs tucked demurely against the back of her thighs, her arm resting on the coffee table, fingers nervously stroking the stem of her three quarter filled glass. Michael now knew her well enough to recognise from her manner that whatever she was thinking, it would probably surprise him. He broke the stillness with an easy smile. "Julie, you're too quiet, what's going through your devious mind?"

"Oh - nothing."

"Are all you lawyers so honest?"

"Okay - there is something, but you'll probably think I'm being too intrusive."

Michael grinned, but now didn't feel quite so comfortable. "Well I won't know that till you ask me. So, come on - out with it!"

"Well Michael, you've told me about your life in Canada, but even Molly couldn't get you to talk about before that - was it so bad?"

She watched as his hand tightened its grip around the glass.

When he spoke again his voice seemed hollow - void of energy. "No Julie, it wasn't so bad, well most of it anyway. Compared to you, I was lucky, I had parents to look after me, and they did it well, but I let them down, I'm pretty good at letting people down."

"Was it something to do with your bother? Les said he met him years ago, said he was a handy football player, but in all the Christmas cards your mum sent since his stay in Fife, he hasn't been mentioned. Did the two of you get into some sort of trouble with the police? You escaped to Canada - is he in prison or something?"

Although Michael managed a sneer it held little spite. "Trust a lawyer to come to that conclusion. You think that's why I'm not happy about your sergeant Adams friend. - No, he's not in prison, well not the kind of prison you mean. He's trapped with the mind of a child - and it shouldn't take you much deliberation to realise who caused it."

"Michael, I apologise - please - if you don't want to talk about it, tell me to mind my own business."

Her eyes anxiously followed the glass as he raised it to his mouth, abandoning its contents swiftly down his throat before slamming it back down on the coffee table. "That's the problem, Julie. I do want to talk about it - I just haven't been able to. When you spoke this morning about coming back here from university - for Les - I almost told you then, just to prove how different we are. How you wouldn't dream of avoiding your responsibilities and how - how - I've got disloyalty down to a fine art."

She rose effortlessly from the rug and slipped onto the couch, close to him, close enough to place a comforting hand on his. "You're probably a lot of things Michael, but disloyal's not one of them. What you're trying to do for your father, what do you call that?"

He stared deep into her eyes. "Guilt Julie. - Guilt - nothing more!" He took a deep inhalation of her perfumed air. It seemed to help. "You're right about something though. Jamie, he was some footballer, would have turned professional - nineteen and playing part-time for Dunfermline Athletic. Me, I was seventeen, still at school, but we got on okay as brothers go.   Jamie, as well as his football, was working in the Dockyard, making good money for an apprentice. Of course, I had none, so when it came to the pigeons, he paid for their corn, I scraped the loft. I didn't mind that, I enjoyed working with the birds, it gave me the insight I needed into their characters - their potential. You know Julie, come the breeding season, I had it all worked out in my mind, which cocks to pair with which hens - a whole breeding programme - sure to succeed. The problem was, he was in charge, and he knew it. You know, I didn't have the guts to tell him my plans till two days before the birds were supposed to be paired up."

"He took it badly then?"

"Badly - I can still see him laughing in my face. Not one pair did he agree with - not one! He was going to pair them to produce nice colours, not a thought about racing potential."

"So - Michael, you fell out?"

"More than that Julie - much more. We were standing arguing, on the concrete path, just in front of the loft. My father and I, we'd laid it just a month before. Jamie, he looked so smart, new white suit, fancy shoes, ready to go out with his girlfriend. They were going to get married - a whole life in front of them. But I just couldn't keep my mouth shut."

"What happened?"

"We started shouting. I don't remember who threw the first punch - it all happened so quickly, and then all hell broke loose. I remember he was so strong, I should have gone down, but I couldn't - couldn't let him humiliate me. And then my mother must have seen us from the window. I didn't hear the door open - but Julie - I heard her screaming for us to stop! - And Jamie did stop. He put his fists down, turned his head to the door and I hit him with the hardest punch, Les had taught me - right - bang; to the side of his head. I watched him fall, like slow motion, I remember - I'll never forget. - I smiled - smiled until his head bounded twice off the concrete. Julie! He's got the brain of a six-year-old - I did that for him, and you know the rest. I made the perfect bloody life for myself in Canada."

Julie gripped his hand tighter staring open mouthed as he turned his face from her. She'd seen the tears welling up in his eyes, she knew this time he couldn't stop them. Her hand now moved again, slowly to his chin, then gently she manoeuvred his face back towards her. He looked lost - lost in grief, his lips were trembling almost beyond control. She placed her index finger over them, then upwards, stroking the wetness from his cheeks. "I'm so sorry Michael - I didn't realise how bad it was - how bad it still is. But Michael, you weren't to blame; it was an accident, a dreadful accident - no more than that - and you sharing it with me - I feel so privileged - so...."

Before her lips had the chance to say another soothing word, they'd reached his.

CHAPTER 31

His eyes opened into daylight, blinking sleep away as they strayed around the tiny room, then back to the ceiling and the tapping sound. Michael now realised what it was, rain - heavy rain, rattling almost tunefully on the metal roof.

He turned over on his side, the blue satin sheet moving with him, as it had done all night. Its gossamer lightness, cooling, securing them after the restrictions imposed by the quilt had long been discarded to the floor.

He gazed at the nakedness of her back, only inches away, touching distance - kissing distance. For a smiling moment he contented himself just to look, move his eyes slowly upwards to her shoulders, her flowing blond hair, then down again - down her spine, down the white smoothness of her perfect body, until they reached the edge of the sheet - placed, as if deliberately - teasingly over the bottom of her curving waist. His hand now followed, tracing the same unblemished route. His fingers gently stroked through her hair, then floated downwards, touching - caressing each ripple of bone. Her skin felt warm, her breathing so soft. Its quietness hardly audible, its movement impossible to see - only to feel.

He reached the sheet, lingered there for a moment, then slowly drew it down, revealing as it shifted inch by enticing inch, the exquisite shape of her bottom. He edged his body closer, his lips now brushing against her neck. The thought of gently - firmly slipping inside her made his chest rise further with each breath.

"Well, Michael - I see you're awake at last!"

He wasn't sure what took him most by surprise, her giggle or the ease she swivelled her body round towards him. They kissed - a slow, meandering, morning kiss. "Yes," he grinned.   "I'm awake, the noise woke me, it's raining."

"Good." She smiled.

His mouth curved enquiringly. "Good, I'm awake or good it's raining?"

She thought for a twinkling eyed moment then rolled herself over him pinning him flat on his back beneath her. "Good - you're awake." She kissed him again. "Good - it's raining. Now what can we do till it stops? I know!" As she spoke she manoeuvred him inside her, arching her back to feel the full pleasure of his depth.

Something in having her; seeing her body in daylight; witnessing the first beads of perspiration trickle down her breasts - the redness of her hardening nipples made the sound of the outside door crashing open feel beyond the realms of torment!

With a fraction of enough time to frantically separate, hide their panic beneath the dubious sanctuary of the sheet, Susan Fenton staggered into the room, her yellow raincoat dripping, her enthusiasm too youthful to knock. "Auntie Julie! A'm no' letting the pigeons out today. The rain's much too heavy. - Auntie Julie! Who's that under the cover?"

Michael kept himself hidden, hoping - praying his now stone-silent partner would somehow, eventually find the words to explain away the impossible.

"Em!- Goodness knows Susan - let me have a look." Julie tugged the sheet from over his head. "Oh! It's you Michael. Why don't you tell me and Susan what you're doing here?"

His eyes bulged open, his brain started stuttering. "Em - w - well - I'm afraid - afraid of rain - especially heavy rain"

Although both shared the chuckle, Julie allowed her little, sparkling eyed niece, the pleasure of reply. "No you're not, silly! You're ganin to marry Auntie Julie, so you're allowed to sleep beside each other, just like me ma an' da'. Wait till a tell them, they'll be that pleased!"

"Michael, are you going to stay in there all day? - You're quite safe, she's gone home - and I don't think we should get there too far behind her, she - em - she sometimes tends to exaggerate."

Despite having adjusted the spray to force three cold, it hadn't yet succeeded in dulling his acute embarrassment. Remaining wet, shivering and alone under a shower seemed infinitely preferable to visiting Daphne row, where the devil child's words were probably still ringing in her mother's ears.

He took a deep breath, switched if off, pulled the largest towel he could find around his waist and stumbled to the door, opening it only wide enough to make eye contact. "Tends to exaggerate. - Julie! - She's got enough on us as it is to get us hung - me castrated if Les finds out. - And you're saying she's going to make it worse!"

By the time they'd got dressed, had a quick coffee and Julie had locked the portacabin door behind them, some of her cheerful serenity had ceded to her now slightly less agitated partner. His eyes still reflecting anxiety, now allowed themselves a glimmer of resignation. *So,* he thought, *we've slept together, why should that be so bad? It hadn't felt that way last night - far from it - it was perfect. Okay, the morning hadn't gone quite to plan - but... A smile curved his mouth. Maybe there'll be other mornings, until Saturday anyway - then?"*

For much less time than their wants demanded, they shared the protection, the privacy of Julie's black umbrella, avoiding the puddles with a giggling jump, or if they were too big, an arm-in-arm manoeuvre around their edges. Too quickly, they reached the outer boundary of allotment doors, stepped on solid ground and saw the soot stained chimneys of Daphne Row loom in the distance.

As if in malevolent confirmation, the rain stopped, obliging them to part as Julie shook the umbrella before folding it compact, into a side pocket of her briefcase. Michael watched silently as her expression quickly merged with the business like way she was now brushing down her coat and examining her shoes for mud-stains.

When she turned her attention back to him he knew she'd become a lawyer again. Her voice sounded controlled - gentle but controlled. "Michael, do you remember when we woke up last night, you said something - something about...?"

He interrupted with a nervous grin. "Yes, I remember, saying something about being too tired - something about three times a night was definitely my limit, and no-way was I going to let you abuse my body again."

"No silly! - Not that time - before that, when you spoke about meeting Ron Adams and how desperate you are to put an end to all this, once and for all."

Michael narrowed his eyes as he turned them away. "Yes Julie, I remember."

"Well - I just want you to know, before we meet him, he's on your side, and I know he'll do his very best."

He slowly nodded his head. She was doing her job - and doing it well - paving the way for the possibility of failure.

She looked surprised when he turned back, reached his hand across her cheek, moved closer then kissed her. "I know Julie - I know he'll do his best - and I know you're on my side, but you've got to know - I can't let them down again."

As they walked on she clasped his hand. "Michael, whatever happens on Saturday you won't let them down - you never have, your father, if he was still alive, he'd be so proud of you."

As soon as she'd said it she realised she shouldn't have. Michael's eyes flashed towards her. "Proud of me! - Julie - you didn't know him. He was proud okay - proud of Jamie, but as for me, we'd either too much or nothing in common, and after what I did..."

"Michael! - You keep crucifying yourself over Jamie, but you know as well as I do, it was an accident."

He instantly withdrew his hand. "Call it what you like! - But I didn't tell you last night, my father, he never spoke one more word to me. Two months after what you so easily call an accident - nothing! He treated me as if I didn't exist."

"But Michael, he'd still have been in shock, I've seen cases..."

"No! Julie, he hated me, hated me as much as he loved Jamie - Jamie who'd given him all he'd expected, a cabinet full of trophies, a technician's apprenticeship, a bloody pension scheme - everything he never had, and of-course, Linda, beautiful Linda - she was the finishing touch. He thought the world of her Julie. She'd that air of dependability, just like my mother. She'd make his perfect son the perfect wife. And she did, make a perfect wife and mother, but not with Jamie, no Julie, with Detective Inspector Ian-bloody-Millar, Rosyth's equivalent to your friend who's going to do his bloody best for me."

She didn't consciously quicken her pace, but the silent sigh of relief as they turned into the back lane of Daphne Row confirmed her desire to seek out its dubious refuge. To her despair a single glance towards the kitchen window as she pushed open the yard door confirmed her worst fears. An open-mouthed Ruby, tea mug gripped tightly in her hands, sat leaning over the breakfast bar, too engrossed with the milk and

Cornflake spluttering words from her angel faced little daughter to notice the approaching visitors.

Julie forced a resigned smile. "Oh well, Michael, looks like we're too late, she'll just be at the bit where you forced yourself into my bed."

Despite the depth of his mood he couldn't help breaking into mock laughter. "So that's how you're going to play it. The innocent Geordie maiden, seduced by the evil Canadian!"

Her smile broadened. "Yes, exactly - and what with that scar on you forehead, which I personally quite like, and me being a lawyer, they're bound to believe me - what do you think?"

Before he could think, she'd opened the kitchen door, skilfully manoeuvring him inside in front of her.

Both heads turned from the breakfast bar in unison - both grinned - both then glanced knowingly to each other.

"Well - well! Looks like the rain must 'ave stopped Susan. Michael's no' 'aving to hide under the covers any more." Noticing that neither of her stone-faced guests were able or willing to respond, Ruby's grin widened. "An' you're just in time for breakfast - shift over Susan - gee Romeo and Juliet - sorry, slip o' the tongue - Michael an' Julie, some room. Now what tak's your fancy, Cornflakes? Or how about a nice warm bowl of porridge - maybe best the porridge, they say it's just the job if you've been over exerting yourselves."

"Cornflakes for me Ruby, thank you." The sharpness of Julie's reply betrayed the hollowness of her narrow smile.

Michael mumbled. "Okay, Ruby, if it'll keep you busy for a few minutes instead of winding us up - I'll have the porridge."

Ruby rose from her chair with an animated display of indignation. "Winding you up! - We wouldn't dream o' it, would we Susan? Now my little goldilocks, you can help me with Michael's porridge an' tell me your little story again. You know - the one about you and the two 'bares'. Now, how does it gan? Oh aye! Who's - been - sleeping - in my bed?"

By the time breakfast had been consumed at undigestionous speed, Susan had gleefully added to their silent discontent by announcing, to her mother's eagerly confirming nods, that she'd be visiting her father in Sunderland Royal as soon as her face and the dishes were washed. After that they'd be going shopping for new outfits. "A think you'd suit a nice big straw hat we' flowers ma. - An' me - a'll want pink - aye, a nice pink flower girl's dress!"

Until the front door closed firmly behind the chattering duo, Michael, and his now flush-cheeked partner, had avoided making eye contact. When eventually he did speak, his voice sounded as if his throat was sore. "Julie - eghm - he cleared the imaginary obstruction with a nervous cough - Julie - I might not be the brightest, but I get the distinct impression that Ruby and your little niece have got the idea that…."

She interrupted with a giggle. - "That my flower girl's going to be wearing pink? - Under no circumstances, Michael! - I've got it all worked out - white with red ribbons - virgin white, to match my dress - and you, Yes! - You'll look so handsome in your kilt. What colour's the Murdoch Tartan?"

They stared at each other for what seemed like an age. Long enough to share the absurdity of their thoughts, before erupting into laughter.

Although the sky was still dulled by low cloud the freshness of the ozone tinted air promised a dry day and the walk, through Julie's shortcuts to the town centre, would allow them to collect their thoughts - prepare their case for Saturday.

The nearer they got, the more Michael's concentration was diverted by the number of people they met who knew, and obviously shared his appreciation of his companion.

"Morning Miss Fenton - how's Bam?"

"Morning Miss Fenton - we've bought the horse. - It's running at Thirsk on Wednesday, the three-twenty, canna lose."

"Hello Julie, will we see you at the social next Saturday? A hear Ruby's put your name down for the Miss Wet T Shirt Contest - it's sure to be a sell out!"

Apart from the flash of irritation, as she firmly put that particular rumour to rest, she seemed so genial - so comfortable with everyone.

"Julie," he smiled, "Is there anyone you don't know around here?"

She thought for a moment before answering with a grudging smirk. "No, probably not, but there's some I'd prefer not to know. My sister-in-law for example. Imagine putting my name down for that perverts' spectacle!"

He shook his head in sympathetic agreement, hoping his disapproving frown would mask the perverted notions now hurtling through his brain.

The sight of the blue fluorescent police sign instantly altered his train of thought. Michael knew, as soon as they'd entered the sparse grey brick building, nothing less than total concentration would be demanded. Despite what Julie had said, her policeman friend would expect total compliance from him. He'd have to display that - or the pretence of it.

Sergeant Adams met them at the reception counter. "Julie! - An' you must be Michael. In you come to ma room. - Tea an' biscuits, Constable Bryant. An' mind what a said - after the tea - no interruptions!"

Constable Bryant dragged his gloating stare away from Julie, nodding a grudged acceptance to his smiling superior.

Michael had imagined him as an older version of Ian Miller. To his relief - he was wrong. The closest precedent he could thing of was Major Lockwood. Tall, thin-faced, cropped head, but with a stoop - a distinct shoulder wilting stoop, and such tired eyes, which seemed to match the greyness of his hair. A world-worn version of the Major, with one striking advantage - he lacked that over-bearing air of self-importance.

Apart from the tea interruption, the next hour passed in low-toned privacy. Michael noticed throughout, even when their host's yellow stained fingers were occupied in deftly rolling one of his seemingly continuous stream of scrawny cigarettes, his concentration never strayed.

He changed the subject only once, just after he'd reminded Constable Bryant, that 'no interruptions' meant just that, and not hanging about the room watching Julie nibble her digestive. "They think you're here to go over ma early retirement application. Think a don't ' ave a cat in hell's chance. But we'll show them - eh lass?" Julie smiled patiently. "Yes Ron, all going well, or not well in your case, we should hopefully, finally convince the medical panel at your next interview."

"But the bloody corset, Julie! - It's bloody well killing me. Ma back was sore enough without it, are you sure it'll help convince the bastards?"

Michael noticed her eyes blink. "Yes Ron, I'm sure - as sure as I know two weeks in Majorca with your lump sum and a tanned masseuse, will do away with the need for it."

He now realised what she'd said yesterday about being due a favour. Sergeant Adams, now contentedly lighting up another cigarette and relaxing back into his chair, was conning his way to an early retirement package; what's more, Julie Fenton - Seaham's answer to Florence Nightingale - was helping him.

He hid his thoughts - his smile, behind a sip of tea. He'd his own agenda to think about and thankfully it now seemed to be slowly getting somewhere.

"Well Michael, that's quite a story you've told me, an' to be perfectly honest, unless a already knew some o' the characters involved, a would find it hard to believe. Did Julie mention 'ave had a few run-ins we' the Vincents? Bad buggers, the pair o' them, but the interesting one's Raymond Pearce. Before you got here, a did a bit o' checking - nice an' discreet - like, he's an evil bastard, Michael; a'm just glad you didn't try to tackle him yourself. He's the one behind all this, an' you an' me have got to mak' bloody sure we nail him for it."

Michael nodded in eager agreement. "But what about Stenway? I'm positive he's involved, he must be, it's his pigeon - he'd do anything to win six nationals."

The detective's brow furrowed. "Aye bonny lad, Stenway's up to his neck in this alright, an' so is your good friend Major Lockwood. But we'll crack these two nuts in the fullness o' time; let's just worry about Saturday first."

Although he opened his mouth to gaping width, Michael didn't question the Sergeant further. He didn't have to; he'd convinced himself on Saturday night after visiting Les, that Lockwood was involved. How else could Stenway have been aware of their visit, how else could they have adapted the con to make such a bloody fool of him?

"Aye, army buddies, Michael. Pearce got himself Court Martialed out o' the R.E.M.E. before turning his talents to armed robbery. An' guess who was his Commanding Officer at Colchester - aye, none other than your bold Major."

Michael shook his head more in an expression of embarrassment than disbelief. *How could I have been so stupid?* He cursed himself silently. *All that crap from he Major about hardly knowing Pearce - about him being a bloody security expert, and the two of them probably shared a fucking Land Rover for years.*

Julie recognised his discomfort. "It all seems to tie in Michael, and you've helped prove that. You've made Ron's job so much easier - you'll sort it out together. Isn't that right Ron?"

"Aye, that we will lass, and your job's no' over yet bonny lad, far from it. We need someone to identify this champion Blue Boy o' theirs. There's no bloody way a'm ganin to try to catch every bird in their cree, a'm shit-scared o' the little buggers - you're ganin to be ma expert witness."

Although Michael nodded the sudden lack of conviction in his expression didn't go unnoticed. "You're no' happy Michael. You'll be in at the kill - is that no' enough?"

He forced the tightest of smiles. "Yes, that's enough, and I thank you for it - but..." He took a deep breath. "But who else will you be including in all this - the police in Rosyth?"

The Sergeant enjoyed a thoughtful draw from his cigarette before leaning over the desk, a tide of brown mist now flowing through his grinning, smoke-stained teeth. "Looks like we've something in common, bonny lad. For whatever reason, you don't want them interfering. An' it just so happens, a'm determined to leave this bloody job in a blaze of bloody glory. So Michael, a'll be telling them bugger-all, an' that includes ma lot, till it's all over, bar the handing out o' the medals."

Their eyes fastened in mutual understanding.

"So, where was I? - Aye, the plan. As far as anyone outside this room's concerned, it's a raid for stolen scrap. A'll pick up a warrant on Friday night," he winked towards Julie. "Catch old Justice Winthrope-Smythe when he's well sozzled. Now a'll be telling ma lads that your boyfriend's some expert in metals or something, they're that bloody gullible, they'll believe anything. Your job Michael is to work out when we should start keeping an eye-out. A need to know when the Lerwick birds are released, an' more importantly, when this Blue Boy o' yours should be dropping in at the Vincent's. So, when he does, by pure coincidence, that's when we'll be ganin in - the rest - an' mak' sure you listen to this carefully - the rest is up to me and Terry Vincent. A canna wait to see the expression on his ugly face. He's a squealer Michael; he knows if he doesn't come clean, he'll end up we' much worse than the broken nose your da' gave him. Now, if the pigeon's there, an' of course Raymond Pearce we' his timing clock, we're cooking we' gas. A'll persuade Terry he's to tak' the full wrap, he'll shop the pair o' them - his brother first, and av'e no doubt, after a cosy chat an' a cup o' tea in ma interview room, he'll grass-up both John Stenway an' the galloping bloody Major!."

Michael allowed himself a moments reflection before responding with a nod and the thinnest of smiles. Julie was right; her Sergeant friend wouldn't let him down - if he could help it. And his plan - it sounded close to perfect. He tried to prevent the smile fading - stop the glimmer of doubt now trying to take its place. *Close to perfect - would that be good enough?*

"What are you thinking Michael?" She'd waited until half-way down the street, the bookies and her upstairs office fast approaching, before she'd asked.

"Em - I'm thinking - I like your friend. He'll do his best Julie - I'm sure of it."

She gave him a lawyer's stare. "Is that all?"

His face reddened. "What else is there?"

Julie flashed her eyes in annoyance. "What else there is Michael - is his early retirement application. You remember? His back brace, his medical panel - and how I - your honest lawyer friend, am advising him how to deceive his employers."

She couldn't hear his muted sigh as he wrapped an arm gently around her shoulder. "Yes, Julie, I did think of it, but I know you well enough to appreciate that you're doing it for good reason."

"What good reason?"

"Well - let me guess, Ron Adams, he's a solid, hard working policeman, but, he's been working far too hard for far too long. He's burnt-out Julie; and probably sick of being passed over for younger, self-promoting bastards, like Ian Miller. And, what's more, if he doesn't get out soon, he'll probably smoke himself to death before he gets the chance to see a penny of his pension."

She didn't reply - she didn't have to - he'd understood completely, perhaps too completely.

She thought back to the breakfast bar - their laughter. Had she had the same success in disguising her motives from him then?

CHAPTER 32

"Good morning, and welcome to Race Release. The convoy of five thousand, six hundred and sixty three pigeons, competing in the English Homing Unions, Lerwick National, have been liberated today, Saturday 23rd July, at six-fifteen a.m., into a light westerly wind. - Best of luck to you all!"

Michael kept the now silent phone gripped to his ear, he needed time to think - think quickly.

His eyes then strained towards Julie, sitting quietly on the stairs, three steps above him, waiting patiently for his words. As he cleared the hoarseness from his throat he prayed she'd believe that the rush of red to his face was being caused by genuine anxiety, not the shame of deceit. "Eight-fifteen, Julie. L…light westerly, - I'll do the calculations - then, will you phone Ron Adams?"

She nodded sympathetically, as she stepped down towards him. She'd noticed the same look in his eyes more than once this week. It seemed to come without warning. One minute they'd be laughing, kissing, talking about the past - hinting of the future, and then suddenly it would appear, that lost, desperate look. The one recompense it offered was the satisfaction of soothing it away - seeing his easy smile again.

She loved his smile; it was so genuine, so free of uncertainty. It said he wanted her, just as much as she wanted him. Their week together had proved that, over and over, and not just in bed, every waking moment together had been so special - so perfect, apart from when that look, the look that now seemed to be overwhelming him again, got in the way.

She leant forward and kissed his forehead. "Don't worry, Michael, it'll all be sorted out today, now why don't we get back to the kitchen before Susan spills her milk over your calculator."

Ruby was standing facing the sink, wiping the draining board then the taps with a ferocity their pristine cleanliness didn't justify. She turned instantly, "Well - tell me."

Julie answered. "Eight-fifteen - light westerly."

"Susan, away from the table now, - gee Michael room, an' for God's sake, stop pressing those buttons - you'll flatten the battery."

Susan lifted her irritated blue eyes. "But, ma it's mine now, Michael gave it to me, didn't you Michael?"

He attempted a compliant smile. "Yes, I did, - I hope you don't mind Ruby, the twins said they already had calculators, I was thinking of picking them up a couple of Sunderland Football Strips, they say the ones they have are well out of date".

"Out o' date! - The crafty little buggers. One bloody season out o' date! Michael, a'll no' have you spending good money on football strips - wait till a get a hold o' the two devils - a'll out o' date them. Now no more talk o' buying things you've enough to worry about today without that. - Susan Fenton. A'll no' tell you again - SHIFT!"

She did shift, very quickly, allowing Michael full use of the now wiped clean breakfast bar. He removed his fathers note book from his inside pocket, placing it open to a blank page, before fumbling for his pen.

First he jotted down the distance. Julie had helped him find it last night, sharing the task of scanning through back-copies of her brother's pigeon weekly's. - Three hundred and twenty three miles from Lerwick to Murton. Below it he penned the release time - eight fifteen, then quickly, before guilt overtook him he pressed the first button.

Even Susan watched in silence.

"I've reckoned on the leaders doing forty-five miles an hour. It's only a light westerly, so it shouldn't hold them up or be a blow-home, - they'll not be doing faster than forty - five"

Three heads nodded their agreement, two confidently, the smallest, because the others had.

"So, based on that, Blue Boy should be arriving at the Vincent's around three-fifteen this afternoon, - Julie could you let Ron know, and tell him I think we should get there - say quarter-to-three just to make sure."

Julie smiled, then brushed her hand gently over his shoulder, as she left the room.

He watched the door close tight before turning his nervous stare from it. "Ruby - I'm sorry - I won't be able to visit Les today. Could you tell him not to worry I'll go see him when this is all over"

Ruby tried to mask her disappointment with a wry grin. "Aye Michael, any excuse to avoid him now that he's getting back on his feet an' probably found that surgeons knife he's been threatening to castrate you we'."

To their relief, before either of them had to explain the meaning of castrate to an enquiring eyed eight-year-old, Julie had returned. "Everything's okay Michael, but he wants us at the station a bit earlier, two o'clock."

Ruby's interruption diverted the glowering intention of Michael's reply. "Aye Julie, a was just reminding your boyfriend, how keen your brother is to see you again - at least Michael's paid him some visits - what's your excuse?"

Julie's cheeks beamed red. "Well - em - I've been far too busy, but Ruby, I promise I'll visit him tomorrow, - won't we Michael?"

Although he nodded, his eyes lent her little comfort.

Ruby now allowed herself the thinnest of smiles. "Too busy, oh aye Julie, a know how busy you've been. A met Marlon, in the Supermarket yesterday - remember Marlon - your secretary? She tells me she hasn't seen hide or hair o' you since you popped in on Monday to show Michael off. She's been worrying that you've been ill - confined to your bed or something a tell't her she wasn't far off the mark we' that one."

Noticing her sister-in-law was either unable or unwilling to answer, she started busying herself and her daughter into their coats.

Michael waited until they'd said their farewells. "Julie?"

"Please Michael, - no more. I will visit him - honestly I will - but he's my big brother and after what he said to you I've just been putting it off, that's all."

"No Julie, it's not that, it's what you said about "us" going to meet Ron Adams - I thought we'd agreed, you wouldn't be getting more involved."

Her eyes narrowed, "Oh is that what you thought? Well it so happens Ron thinks differently, he understands I can't just sit here. But don't worry I'm only going to the Police Station with you, he says I'll be able to listen in as things develop - I need to know Michael, feel part of it - is that so dreadful?"

She stood firmly, staring into his eyes until he replied with the weakest of smiles. "Okay, Julie - I understand. We'll take the car; I've one or two things to pick-up. Is there a sports shop in Seaham? No matter what Ruby says - I'd like to buy something for the twins - and there's something else, something personal I'd like to get you. So what if I drop you off a bit earlier, then meet you at the Police Station at two?"

The sincerity in his voice, - his eyes, gave her little option. "Okay Michael, but you know I don't want anything you haven't given me already," she couldn't stop the grin, "Except maybe a brick red Porsche - you remember, the one we passed yesterday, sitting in that showroom next to the Hosp..."

Michael's smile faded as he watched her cheeks flush. He'd lied to her, - lied so absolutely -so effortlessly, but it was Julie who was embarrassed. So it was about something else - visiting her brother. That didn't matter, she deserved better, - - better than a brick red Porsche - better than anything a disingenuous bastard, like he could provide.

He dropped her off opposite her office, at three minutes to one. It should have been earlier, much earlier, Blue Boy was due at quarter past, maybe before that if they were flying faster than 45mph. He tried to hide the panic now coursing through his brain. He'd left it late, probably too late, but any earlier, he'd convinced himself Julie would have suspected something. The certainty of it made him feel cold inside, so cold, he felt sure her lips would sense the emptiness of his kiss.

If they did, she didn't say, she just smiled, a caring, loving smile, then opened the car door. "Don't get lost now Michael - and remember it's the red one I like - the one with the soft top and the alloy wheels."

Michael forced a smile, hoping it didn't look too bleak - too hollow. He then drove away realising that nothing he was about to do at Murton would lessen the shabbiness of his lie.

By the time he'd sped past Seaham's "THANK YOU FOR DRIVING SAFELY" sign his thoughts were burdened with no more than the ticking of the dash-board clock. He cursed his stupidity; - he'd left it too tight. Even Les's shortcuts wouldn't get him there until quarter past. If Blue-Boy was doing faster than Forty Five, he'd miss seeing him drop - wouldn't know when to make his move.

He wished Les was with him. They'd talked it through together, how neither of them wanted the police involved, it had got too personal. "If you're that bloody determined Michael, a'll no' try to stop you, but for God's sake keep Julie away from here till it's over, - she'll see through me in a minute. Tell her a'm so angry about the pair o' you, a'm ganin to disinherit her. Tell her a think ma mate we' the Lurcher has much better prospects than a waster like you. Oh. An' one more thing bonny lad. When you're knocking hell out o' the Vincent's - tell them a'm asking for them."

He saw the reservoir from the main road. By any comparisons it wasn't big, more a large pond than a lake.

The green Water-Works sign now told him where the track started. As Les had said "Only one way in an' one way out - so don't bloody-well miss the green sign!"

Following his friend's instructions he slowed the Range Rover to a crawl, edging it forwards along the track until he reached the stark grey concrete dam.

"No further than the dam, bonny lad, or they'll know you're paying them a visit. Sit there, nice an' discreet - like, you'll no see into the compound, but you'll see the car-park, - see if the bastards are at home!"

The bastards were at home.

Michael switched off the engine, straining his eyes towards the corrugated iron gate and the two cars sitting silently in the car park. A blue Sierra Estate - a white Mercedes - Pearce's Mercedes. Exactly what Les had seen last Saturday. Now he was glad his friend wasn't with him. He'd see the sweat trickling from his forehead - see the hesitation - the apprehension building in his eyes.

Talking with Les about this moment had been so easy, now suddenly it felt different. He gripped the steering wheel, - he had to concentrate - go over the options again. To his dismay there weren't many, and one seemed to be nagging like a rotting tooth. *Turn the car, meet Julie at the Police Station - tell them he'd lied, the Lerwick Birds were up six-fifteen - tell them he was sorry.*

They'd forgive him; Julie would probably admire him for it. Ron Adams wouldn't care as long as they still got back here in time, caught Pearce with Blue-Boy and got his medal.

Only one person wouldn't forgive him for turning the key. The person, - the reason, he was here in the first place, waiting for a pigeon - a blue pigeon, with a single blood flight.

Michael cursed his fear, cursed his weakness, his eagerness to run again. This was his chance, the only chance he had to retrieve what the years - his youth had lost. The bond he craved with Tam Murdoch - the father he once had. - The father murdered by the three men, now only yards and a corrugated gate away.

The thought of them sitting in the sun-shaded compound, probably still enjoying the satisfaction of it slowly cleared the doubts away.

He heard the ticking of the clock again, one-twenty-five. If Blue Boy had already dropped he'd have to wait a bit longer. The Mercedes told him Pearce was still there, he'd have to be patient - wait until the gate opened, until he saw Pearce run to the car with a small wicker basket in one hand and a S.T.B. Quartz in the other, and thanks to Les Fenton, no black Alsatian snapping at his heels.

At one-forty-three his thoughts strayed to Julie, she'd be leaving her office, heading to meet him at the Police Station. She'd be pleased with herself - catching up with her paperwork, wondering what he'd bought her, knowing he was sorting things out her way - the sensible, safe way.

At two-o'clock, she'd wonder where he'd got to. Sometime too quickly after that she'd realise - realise exactly what kind of person she'd got involved with. The thought of it made him nauseous. In years to come, when she'd met someone decent - someone honest, she'd probably, occasionally remember their week together, then blink it away with the contempt its deceit deserved.

He wasn't sure what made his head turn so quickly, perhaps instinct, possibly the need to re-focus his thoughts, it didn't matter.

A team of pigeons, racing pigeons, around twenty of them, were heading towards the Range Rover from the north east. Michael stared open-mouthed as they crossed over him, less than two hundred feet up, skimming across the sky like arrows. Suddenly they veered due south, over the compound, over the railway embankment. In another second, maybe two, he'd have lost sight of them - lost seeing one having what appeared like an innocent afterthought - the flash of a single missed wing-beat. For a moment it seemed in two minds what to do, keep going with the others, following the example of their determination, their honesty, - or turn?

Michael snapped closed his mouth, clenching his teeth with the pressure. *It turned. - The blue pigeon. Turned.* Then folded its wings back and dropped, floating from the sky in three wide circles above the compound.

He waited until it disappeared behind the corrugated wall, then he leaned almost casually across the passenger seat and pressed the glove compartment button.

"Julie! Where the hell's your boyfriend got to? - That's five past, a canna wait much longer - what's he bloody well thinking o'? Wandering about the town shopping, when a've got six men an' two motors champing at the bit outside."

Julie stuttered, "Em - I don't know Ron - he's not unreliable, he said he'd be here on time, s-said he'd something pers...." The sudden shrillness of the ringing telephone interrupted her flush-faced excuse.

The detective's eyes flashed angrily across the table towards it, his large hand grabbing the receiver with a force that looked capable of snapping it in two.

"Bryant! - A said no interruptions!" Suddenly his tone changed, "Oh! - Bam Fenton? - Life or death. Well, put him through man, - and Bryant, if its no' life or death, a'll no' be the only one retiring from this bloody job out o' ill health. Julie it's your brother, he wants to speak to you, says it's...."

Julie interrupted with a puzzled smile. - "Life or death?"

The curtness of his nod, as he passed over the phone, instantly rid the remnant of humour from her eyes.

Apart from snapping a "Yes, Les, it's me!"   The short one-way conversation allowed few words to leave her trembling lips.

Ron Adams, now pacing the floor behind his chair, kept his piercing eyes fixed on her blanching face. He knew - had known before the phone rung, that something was wrong.

Julie's silent anguish, the sparseness of her parting words, merely confirmed it. "Les, - if anything's happened to him - I'm blaming you - you stupid - stupid...!" The phone dropped from her shaking hand. "Ron! It's Michael - he - he's gone to Murton alone. The pigeons were released at six-fifteen - he's there now!"

The detective's fist slammed down on the desk. "Julie! - Your boyfriend, - he's a fucking idiot!"

By the time he'd reached her, placed his arm gently around her heaving shoulder, his tone had mellowed. "Don't fret lass; he's a fool - but a canny one. Now lets get there before he tak's all the bloody credit."

Her eyes reacted with a tearful blink.

"Aye lass, you're coming with us. When the Chief hears about this bloody debacle a'll need a lawyer - no matter how bloody naïve you are."

Constable Bryant watched open mouthed as they rushed past reception, then out the Georgian glazed door and into the nearest of the now revving patrol cars. When the sound of the screeching tyres, and sirens dissolved into the distance, he narrowed his lips again.

"Aye - the old bastard's definitely losing his grip - six men - two motors- - an' a lawyer to look for stolen scrap.   The bad back's the least o' his problems, - it's his fucking head that needs looking at."

The Range Rover drove towards the gate, steadily gathering speed. As his foot pressed deeper, his eyes suddenly blinked an apology for the grey suited car leasing agent; he'd spoken to on the phone three days ago. "Of-course Mr. Murdoch, the vehicle's all yours until this time next week - shall we say an extra four hundred cash - with of-course a twenty five pounds discount when you return it unscathed?"

Michael had assured him he would. - For the next five seconds, he kept to his word.

Terry Vincent was ambling across the beer can strewn compound, whistling happily to himself, wondering if he'd take his plaster off tonight or leave it till tomorrow.   Thanks to Ray there was a big pay-off coming and a dirty nose plaster wouldn't go with the new denim jacket he'd promised himself.

Suddenly he stopped whistling, initially he wasn't sure why. Then he heard it - a low growling sound.   He turned his head towards the gate - the sound seemed louder

- deeper - more of a roar! Instinct told him to move, he tried to, but not quickly enough. The corrugated barrier seemed to explode in front of him, large sections lifting into the air, one ragged shard sliding over the Range Rovers roof screeching, - scraping backwards with the momentum.

For a split second, - just long enough to savour for a life-time, he at last came face to face with Terry Vincent. His nose re-broken, his gaping, blood - spewing mouth, sliding flat down the spattered windscreen. Before Michael could greet him with a smile, Terry rolled down the bonnet and disappeared.

He sat for a moment staring out at the chaos his entrance had caused. A cloud of blackened dust billowed around him, almost hiding the massive presence now impelling itself towards the car door. Mercifully it halted long enough for him to see what it was. - Another plaster nosed giant, stooping for a howling second over his brother, before hurtling onwards.

Michael gritted his teeth and waited. *Three steps more! - Come on! - Come on! - Now!* The door open with such force it propelled Reg Vincent backwards two yards, then bounced closed again, smashing against Michael's right shoulder. Michael grimaced with the pain but had no time to assess the extent of his injury. All he knew was his right hand was now too numb to open the door. He used his left, and then leapt from his seat, just in time to see Reg rising slowly from the dry-caked mud. He managed less than a half scream before Michael's boot reached his gapping eyed face. It crashed through his cheekbone, twisting his mouth to an involuntary grin. For an age he knelt upright, then swayed backwards then forwards again, like a great tree contemplating the angle of its fall. When he did eventually topple, Michael had to step back a pace to avoid Reg's swollen, distorted head, landing on his foot.

Moving from one crumpled heap to the other, testing each one's state of unconsciousness with a sharp kick to their ribs, gave him no pleasure. The dull ache now seeping from his shoulder had become more than an inconvenience. He tried to lift his arm but when it reached chest level, the pain forced him it down. Panic suddenly invaded the part of his brain cold calm had occupied only seconds earlier. His pupils widened like a startled cat's, straying around the compound - searching - penetrating every corner. Pearce was here, he felt him, and he'd know he was hurt - he'd be watching for just the right moment.

Michael stared towards the black creosoted pigeon loft. Its white doweled front ran from floor to ceiling, allowing a clear view inside. No obstructions - no hiding places - only a few dozen pigeons enjoying the security of their home, seemingly undisturbed by the turmoil they'd just witnessed.

The thought that Blue Boy was probably in there with them was suddenly torn from his mind - he'd heard the noise, flashed his eyes towards it. It hadn't been loud, a kind of shuffling sound, no more, - but enough - more than enough to know where Pearce was. It had come from the large felt roofed shed - inside it - inside the half-opened door.

Michael edged slowly towards it, halting outside, gripping his fists so tight the knuckles almost pushed through his skin. He gave the door a single, solid kick. It sprang inwards opening to its full width. He peered inside, delaying any further movement until his eyes, now huge with uncertainty, accustomed themselves to the shadowy darkness.

A trickle of sweat slid down his brow. He had to choose, - stay where he was, or go in.

If he did, the man skulking inside would have the advantage. Caution told him to wait; - a deeper, stronger urge told him he couldn't.

He moved forward, inching his way under the doorframe, blocking much of the daylight his glaring eyes demanded. Through the dirty gloom he now realised his predicament. This was no ordinary shed - neat shelves, gardening tools, half-empty pots of paint. It was more like a square-sided cavern, row upon row of metal racking, piled high and spilling over with junk, bits of engine, bits of body-work, bumpers, exhausts, corroded batteries. The acrid smell of acid and diesel caught the back of his throat.

Pearce could be anywhere - standing in the shadows, - crouching low in some unseen corner. Michael stood silent, spraying his eyes from side to side. Instinct was now persuading him to take a step backwards - back into the sanctuary of daylight. Then he heard it again, a soft rustling sound. He realised what it was before he saw it. To his left, less than five paces away, the outline of a wicker basket. Beside it, on the shelf, a metal-cased box. His mouth opened wide. - *Stenway's clock! - Stenway's pigeon!* Now nothing else mattered, he had to confirm the certainty of it - *Blue Boy! - Now, no one could doubt the truth.*

Between his third and fourth stride, the baseball bat crashed against his skull. His knees buckled below him, his eyes blinked away the darkness and turned with just enough time - enough misted vision to see two legs step nearer.

Michael bent lower then screamed with rage as he sprang forward, his arms gripping Pearce's rigid waist. It didn't stop the bat hitting him, but this time it bounced off his back. He'd caught him off balance, lessened the accuracy - the power of his swing.

The benefit was short-lived, his right arm had no strength in it - none capable of holding fast the overwhelming force now propelling him backwards, lifting him off his feet, throwing him against a storage rack. Michael's hand grasped backwards, pulling shelves of debris down as the metal frame crashed over him, pinning his back to the hard, diesel-fouled concrete.

As he struggled hopelessly to dislodge the weight crushing his ribs, he heard the laughter. Too soon afterwards he saw the grinning, grey-eyed face looming over him.

Their eyes met, - neither blinked, but Pearce suddenly gave an irritated, almost confused grunt. Michael prayed it held some importance. For the man holding the bat it did - he couldn't deliver a clean strike. The twisted metal work above his victim's head wouldn't allow it. Michael shaped his mouth to a mocking sneer - a last feeble gesture of defiance.   If he'd predicted the agony it would cause he wouldn't have made the effort.

Pearce gripped the bat handle with both hands, positioning it vertically like a fence post, then plunged it downwards through the narrow gap exposing Michael's mouth and chin.

He knew his jaw was shattered before he felt the pain.   As the agony intensified so did a strange feeling of tiredness.   He felt weak, nothing he could concentrate on - anger - fear - even Julie Fenton, persuaded him to stay awake.   If Pearce hadn't pressed the bat head hard against his jaw again, Julie's warm smile - her blue eyes, would have stayed drifting through his semi-consciousness.   Michael's eyes now re-opened, more in resentment than pain.

"Good, Michael, a thought you were sleeping - don't you want to see what a've done for you?"

Michael guessed by his snarling grin, that it hadn't included phoning an ambulance.

"Look! A've shifted that awful weight o' metal off you.   Isn't that better?   An' now a'm ganin to introduce you proper-like to ma friend".

Although he returned Pearce's stare, he couldn't manage the gloating smile.

"Aye, Michael - Mat the Bat - he's met your father, haven't you Mat?   Four times, an' you've only met him three - so this time it's special."

As the bat head swayed like a pendulum above his face Michael's gaping eyes rolled with it - waiting for the moment it would rise again.

"Say hello, Michael - say hello to Mat - he's so looking forward to this!"

Slowly - painfully his lips parted, his tongue moved, pushing tiny bubbles of blood through his broken teeth. "Mm…" the sound escaped in a stifled moan.

Pearce leaned closer, "What was that Michael, did you say something?   Speak up bonny lad - you're trying to say Mat, aren't you?   - Try again, Michael - he'll be that pleased!"

Pearce now turned his head to the side, positioning his ear closer to Michael's swollen lips.   He couldn't now see Michael's right hand feeling its way inch by inch across the concrete, narrowing the gap to his aching hipbone - to his jacket pocket. When it reached inside it, he moaned again - moaned so pathetically, Pearce grunted his impatience and made to lift his head.   To his astonishment he realised he couldn't - realised that Michael had his left arm gripped around his neck, pulling his ear even closer.   The last words he heard seemed strangely comical, "M… meet Stanley!"

Pearce gaped in confusion as the Stanley knife slid down towards his throat.   He tried to scream, before his larynx was severed, but nothing came, - nothing but a silent river of blood and the hollow sound of a baseball bat, rattling against the concrete floor.

Michael's open mouth filled with blood, - not his own.   He tried to cough it out, but the dead weight lying on top of him forced him to swallow.   Suddenly he felt tired again; he needed to rest - dream of Julie - dream of her smile.

At last he witnessed the vision of her, leaning over him. But this time she was crying - crying him to sleep.

CHAPTER 33

Pattiesmuir is small, much smaller than its cemetery.

It used to nestle quietly about a mile West of Rosyth. Now because of the new scheme it's less than half the distance. A single row of ten white harled cottages, a red telephone kiosk and a cemetery.

Since the residents of Rosyth started being buried in it Pattiesmuir Cemetery has grown well beyond the bounds it was once comfortable with. It now dominates the tiny hamlet; each fresh grave edging a yard closer to the nearest curtain shrouded house.

Apart, however, from the narrowing distance to some-ones back garden, it's still a good place to be buried - Michael always liked it.

When he was a boy, with his friends and Jamie, - sometimes even Ian Miller, - they used to visit it. Following the Park Burn, jumping across its banks at the most daring spots, hunting for rats, searching the hedgerows for birds' nests, until they reached its source. A lily covered pond, surrounded by silver birch and a copse of bluebells, hidden just beyond the cemetery. They called it 'Bell-Knowes' - it was beautiful, and probably still is.

Occasionally, as they wandered through the graveyards tree-lined paths, they'd come across someone, usually a woman, standing silently in front of a stone. Once they disturbed an elderly, rain coated lady talking openly to a cold granite slab. Ian Miller had sniggered as they walked past her. It annoyed Michael so much, on their way back to the Crescent; he'd pushed him into the burn. Ian never came with them after that.

Today Detective Inspector Miller was too irritated to snigger, too frustrated by the delay to allow not so fond memories to occupy his thoughts. He'd an important meeting at three-o-clock, another case to solve - and this time he'd solve it himself. "No bloody interference this time." He cursed under his breath.

All this hanging about a graveyard, trying to look sympathetic, bored him. If he hadn't been asked to hold a cord, he'd have made his excuses half an hour ago. - *And why not? - Thirty bloody minutes late - and still no sign of the interfering bastard.*

The delay was bad enough, but with the unexpected number of mourners turning up and Mary Murdoch insisting that Daniel should also hold a cord, things were bound to get awkward. People would talk. Even now some were probably whispering their suspicions. "Why's that young laddie Miller been picked? - He hardly knew him - and my goodness doesn't he look like Jamie, you could mistake the pair of them for twins."

Mary Murdoch wouldn't mistake them for twins - she knew better - had known for years, that her handsome young grandson would someday find out he was a Murdoch. She allowed herself a hidden smile - *And he'd taken the news so well,* she mused, *Jamie still doesn't know - but that's maybe for the best. At least now they'd met each other, and by the looks of it, are getting along just fine.*

Conscious that her smile was now forcing itself to the surface, she turned her head back round towards the hearse, touching her black gloved hand gently against its shining wing panel. One glance through the window to the dark oak coffin robbed her of her moment's indulgence. Tears now welled in her eyes as she whispered to him "Well Tam, things have changed - much for the worse - but some for the better. If only the better things had happened before you left us"

"Mary hen, how are you bearing up?"

As she turned towards the voice her face flushed. "Oh! - It's you, Maxwell - I'm fine -it's just been such a long wait. I thought they'd never let him rest - and still he's waiting."

"Aye Mary, but I've a feeling he's no' minding too much about this wee delay - and it'll not be long now - that lassie of Michael's reckons another ten minutes or so."

Mary stared fifteen yards or so beyond Maxwell. "She's a bonny one, isn't she Maxwell? - And so pleasant, but I just wonder what his girlfriend back in Canada's going to say?"

"Who knows Mary, but I've an inkling he'll have sorted that wee problem out himself. He's not bad at sorting things out, is your Michael."

"You knew what he was up to, didn't you Maxwell?"

His cheeks instantly reddened, "Em - well - I knew he wasn't going down South just to pick up a pair of young birds for Jamie. But Mary - please don't be too hard on him, I don't think Tam gave him many choices." He glanced past her through the hearse window. "Did you Tam? - Mary, he maybe can't answer us, but I bet he's in there smiling."

If he was, she now followed her husband's example, at the same time reaching out her hand to his old friend's bony elbow. "Yes Maxwell, I think you're probably right."

"Aye Mary, and that was a wise move of yours coming here, I can just imagine the rammy going on in your house the now. My Isobel, Ina Andrews and your sister, preparing a meal for thirty - three chiefs and no bloody Indians - I don't know which one's the worst."

A mischievous glint flashed across her eyes. "Well Maxwell, I can honestly say it's not Isobel, at least she won't be nosing through my cupboards - but I can't say that for Ina Andrews; and anyway Maxi, I'm better here, just to keep a wee eye on Jamie, in case he gets himself too upset."

Both glanced towards the small group of men standing closest to the open grave.

"Aye Mary, I understand what you're saying but I don't think you'll have to worry too much about Jamie. He's found himself in good company with that Geordie friend of Michael's, and it looks as if he's taken a liking to young Daniel Miller. - My goodness! You could mistake the pair of them for twins."

Maxwell was right; he was in good company - Les Fenton, young Daniel, The Pie and of-course his newly varnished pigeon basket. They were standing in a circle round it, probably chatting about pigeons - probably about the two sitting contentedly in their fresh carpet of wood shavings.

It had been Jamie's idea to bring them - his own, personal token of respect for his father.

He'd release them at the graveside, just after he'd helped lower the coffin "The Old Pied Cock and the Wee Mealy Hen - Dad's favourites - he'll be that pleased, knowing they're up in the sky above him, saying their cheerio's. - A fly past. - Like the Red Arrows. But much, much better!"

Mary now saw Julie return to her brother's side. She'd been watching her, more than she should have. But despite the number of people that had come to sympathise, *apart from Maxwell, - that Lass has been the most sincere.*

"Well, Julie! So much for your ten minutes, a thought he knew the bloody way here. - Wait till a get a hold o' him, he's depriving me o' valuable supping time."

Julie forced a muted scowl, then re-checked her watch. "Be patient will you Les. There could have been a hold-up with Ron Adams, you know how busy he is, trying to clear his desk. And don't think you'll be doing any drinking, I promised Ruby I'd look after you, and you're still on antibiotics, so why don't you just lean back on your crutches and soak up the sunshine." Her scowl now gave way to the sharpest of smiles. "Because that's all the soaking up you'll be doing today."

Michael did know the way - unfortunately Constable Bryant hadn't a clue, and having wrongly deciphered the directions murmured from his passenger's almost motionless lips, he'd taken the wrong turn-off for the Forth Bridge.

"Bryant - you're a bloody idiot!" To his added discomfort, Sergeant Adams had woken up shortly afterwards "Out o' the goodness o' ma heart a tak' you up to Scotland - the last bloody skive a'll get till ma retirement next month, an' you manage to get me lost. - That's bloody gratitude for you - isn't it Michael?"

If Michael could have managed a smile, he would have, however the jaw brace gave him little option but to nod his head. At least being unable to do much talking had avoided him having to take part in an earlier conversation. One his brain still needed time to fully comprehend.

"Aye, Michael! Stenway had another bloody heart attack. - But this time it was for real. The old rogue only lasted long enough to hear the news that his good friend, the bold Major had shot himself."

If the Detective Sergeant's version of events weren't embellished too much by the telling, Major Lockwood had arrived at Wing Holm on the Monday after the Lerwick Race - five minutes late. He'd then, after bestowing the office staff with his usual gruff "Good Morning" - crossed over to Miss Simpkins desk and planted her square on the mouth with the most permanent of kisses! He then checked the appointment's diary. Saw there wasn't much doing until ten-o-clock, when the President of E.H.U. was insisting on seeing him, and marched out of the office to his room.

Florence had never been totally comfortable with his Webley Revolver and the pot shots he occasionally took from the window. But the shot they heard that morning brought the most bewailing of screams from her still moistened lips.

Both she and Lorraine were too much in shock to do anything constructive, requiring Miss Berry, still resplendent in her orange tights and mini-skirt, to venture nervously up the stairway.

When she opened the door, without knocking, and saw him sprawled over his desk, the gun still clasped in his right hand and the blood spewing cavern, that once was the back of his head, she halted for a moment, her young eyes huge with horror. Then for some unknown reason she looked beyond him, up the wall to the stag's head - her stag's head - her only friend at Wing-Holm. She hadn't noticed the expression on its glass-eyed face before, - didn't notice that her own face was now also sporting the same blithesome smile.

The Pie was first to see them coming "Look Jamie! It's a fucking XR4 - fucking flying machine. - The silly buggers must have got lost."

Jamie didn't care if it was an XR four million. It didn't matter, Michael was here at last, he'd soon be able to let the pigeons go, they'd be wanting back home to see to their squeakers.

When the police car stopped, two down from the hearse, Sergeant Adams let his still travel worn eyes stray around the group of waiting mourners, before opening the back door.

"Em - Sarge! - Remember what the chief said about the cuffs?"

He answered in an exasperated whisper, "Bryant - for Christ Sake, get a grip lad. - He's no' exactly fit enough to do a runner on us, is he? And anyway, looks like the Cavalry's here. Is that your Detective Inspector friend Michael, a hear through the grapevine, he's a bit o' a tosser?"

Michael answered both questions with a solitary nod, then strained his eyes towards the hearse and his mother waiting patiently beside it.

Both his companions, after helping him out of the car and aiding his shuffling steps with their supporting arms, left him, with the politest of nods, to the white-haired lady, now choking back her tears.

Both then crossed over the freshly cut grass to have a chat with their Scottish colleague, wearing the formal dress uniform. "Pleased to meet you Ian, - better late than never, eh."

"No! - It's certainly not better late! And Sergeant Adams, you haven't retired yet, so, if you don't mind please address me properly - it's Detective Inspector Miller."

Constable Bryant closed his eyes even before he heard Ron Adams softly spoken response. When they opened again, his Sergeant was ambling away from them and Inspector Miller's face had turned as pale as he'd ever seen someone not dead. "C...constable! Did you hear what that man just said to me?"

"Aye, Detective Inspector Miller - he told you to 'fuck-off, you pompous little prick.' - But a could 'av'e been mistaken sir, he tends to muddle his words a bit nowadays".

The few minutes with his mother seemed to pass in a haze. He hardly noticed her holding his arm to keep him steady - hardly noticed her slip the small white envelope into the jacket pocket of the black suit Julie had brought him two days ago.

Mary Murdoch managed a knowing smile "Michael son, I found it in your Dad's desk drawer, under you and Jamie's old prize certificates, - it's got your name on it. Maybe when you're feeling better, you should open it."

After the effort of the burial he didn't feel up to much more than collapsing into Julie's arms. She'd stood behind him all through it, just a few paces away, in case he'd lost his balance. To her relief he hadn't, he didn't seem as if he knew what was going on, but there were no tears.

Jamie shed a few, but soon cheered up when he let the pigeons go. Everyone told him how clever he'd been, thinking of such a nice touch to end the proceedings. They all gazed, even Ian Miller and the Minister, as the pair of birds fluttered to the sky, circling three times over the grave before turning towards Rosyth - The Old Pied Cock, struggling gainfully to keep up with Tams Wee Mealy Hen.

Most of the mourners disappeared within seconds of the final salute, either late for appointments like Ian Miller, or keen to get a seat for the first sitting at Mary Murdoch's.

Michael was slowly turning towards Julie, when Ian inadvertently crossed through the gap between them. He'd intended to acknowledge their re-union with the briefest of nods, until Michael stopped him. "Ian - thanks for doing me that favour - it's really appreciated".

Ian Miller seemed visibly surprised by the almost inaudible rasp he'd just witnessed, but quickly regained his composure. "Well Michael. - Would that be the little favour about the Stanley Knife? - Yes, you're quite right, you should appreciate it. If the prosecution finds out it was McLagans blade and you took it with you deliberately, instead of finding one by pure luck at the scene of your crime, I think they'll add a good few years to the sentence you're going to get. - But don't worry Michael; despite what that Geordie Sergeant friend of yours just called me, I'll stick to my word. - But don't think I'm doing it for you Murdoch. - Linda begged me to, for the sake of your mum and Jamie."

With his parting speech enjoyed by no one but himself and having little time left to waste at Pattiesmuir, Ian left Julie and Michael to finally close the gap between themselves. They stared at each other for what seemed an age, then slowly, - nervously, merged into each other's arms.

He murmured softly through his cramped lips "Julie - I'm so sorry, - I don't deserve you - never will - and I don't want you waiting for me. Whatever happens, you've a life to lead and I'm - I'm…!"

"A devious, stupid, unmitigated disaster. - But don't worry Michael, I've a brother who's just the same and I've managed to put up with him for years - so, like it or not - I'm afraid your stuck with me."

He wanted to kiss her smiling face - wanted to grasp her body deeper to him, but the pain was too great.   They walked arm-in-arm back to the police car acknowledging the passing "Good lucks" and a "Well done bonny lad" from Les, with an embarrassed nod from him and a trembling smile from her.

She left him, with the gentlest of kisses to his forehead, allowing him the time he needed with his family. She glanced backwards only once, saw him hug both of them and then rejoin Ron Adams for the journey back.

Les waited for her to catch up. "Now lass, no tears, remember you're a Fenton. - Aye he's a canny lad, is your Michael - reminds me o' maself in so many ways".

Ron Adams could hardly contain himself "Bryant did you think a upset our little Inspector friend - hope he didn't tak' it too personal - like. Oh well - all's well that… - Michael! Did a tell you about ma retirement deal and how you made bloody sure o' it for me? - Solving a murder, outing the biggest corruption the pigeon game's ever had, - arresting you - sorry about that! An' to put the icing on it - buggering up ma back, good an' proper, trying to lift that dead bastard Pearce off your chest.   Aye bonny lad, a perfect wind-down for Majorca we' ma lump sum and a new medal to polish."

To the driver's and stone-silent passenger's relief the Sergeant soon tired of the story, he'd told them twice already, and after stubbing out his third cigarette, fell asleep.

Michael waited another full hour before finding the resolve to open the white envelope. It wasn't a long letter, typical of his father, straight to the point.

"Dear Michael,

When you read this I'll be dead, which is maybe just as well son, save us falling out again. We're too like each other Michael; I saw that when you were a boy, but couldn't accept it like I should have. You and Jamie, I was proud of you both, but after the accident and it was an accident - no more; I made up my mind to hate you for it. It seemed the only way at the time and I can't forgive myself for that. But that was a long time ago son and I've lost the bitterness I once had. Jamie, me and your mother have done the best we could since you left and I know you've done well. Your mum doesn't know, but I've read every letter from her sister, over and over. I couldn't accept your charity Michael, as I said we're too alike, but I know you'll do what's right by them, especially Jamie. Your mum can't look after him herself, no-matter how strong she is. Michael. I'm still proud of you and never really stopped loving you, I'm just so sorry I don't have the damn courage to tell you that, face to face.

Yours very sincerely

Dad."

Constable Bryant gaped into the rear view mirror. The last person he thought he'd see, with tears running down his swollen cheeks, was the big Canadian that cut Raymond Pearce's throat, and gave a severe doing to the Vincent Brothers.

Although he didn't need to, he felt he had to say something. "Mr Murdoch... Michael... a hope you're no' worrying about what the Sarge said - - the lads reckon you'll be out in less than a year. It was self-defence; even a drunken old sod like Justice Wynthrope-Smythe is bound to accept that."

Michael nodded his appreciation, but now seemed too distracted to care. He'd read a letter, a short one, but the sparseness of its words couldn't conceal their meaning.

Slowly, the pain seeping from his broken ribs felt lighter, his eyes now gleamed with a clarity they'd long forgotten. He folded the letter neatly, placed it carefully back into its white envelope and sat it on his lap.

For the rest of the way back to Durham he gazed down at it - couldn't let his eyes stray from it. He didn't have to read it again - every word that Tam Murdoch penned was now as clear as his son's conscience.

CHAPTER 34

Justice Wyndthrope-Smythe was suffering from a particularly nasty hangover, gained at a speaking engagement the previous evening. "Reginald Vango Vincent! - You have been found guilty of the venomous crime of murder. And it therefore gives me great pl-eghm - - excuse me. - It is my solemn duty to sentence you to life imprisonment, with a recommendation that you serve a minimum of fifteen years."

Reg Vincent stood solidly in the dock, his reaction to the Judge, blunted by the shock that people now knew his middle name.

"Terence Gene Vincent! - You have also been found guilty of the venomous crime of murder. However, due to your voluntary, and if I may say enthusiastic assistance with the Police investigation…"

"Grassing Bastard!" Reg's enraged lunge towards his brother was half-expected by the two burly policemen guarding them and therefore quickly subdued with a sharp elbow to his rib cage.

"Vincent - yes you! - The biggest one! Any further interruptions in my Court - no matter how justified - and I will - I will…!" Unfortunately, after giving him fifteen years, Wyndthrope-Smythe couldn't add a lot. "I will not be at all pleased. Now where was I? Yes, Terence Gene Vincent, I sentence you to ten years minimum." On that abbreviated note he hammered down his gavel and tottered from the Bench, halting only for a precarious moment to deliver his afterthought "Oh! - And both sentences will be served in Durham Prison."

Terry's eyes widened in horror. He spun his head round from the dock, to Ron Adams sitting two rows behind, filling in his Passport application "Adams! - A thought you said a wouldn't 'ave to go near Durham - a've got enemies there, people a've…."

The Sergeant interrupted with a smiling whisper "Grassed on? - Some you win - some you lose, Terrence, - isn't that right Reg?"

Reg Vincent's face beamed with delight. "Aye Sergeant Adams, that's exactly what a was just thinking - an' Sergeant, enjoy your retirement now?"

Michael Thomas Murdoch's case took longer to get to Court. It was more encumbered with precedent, legal argument and good character references, than the Vincent's.

That and more, had been ably provided by the Defence Team's unofficial background assistant. The one with the black suit, blonde hair and hour-glass figure, sitting pensively in the third row next to Sergeant Ron Adams. - The one who never seemed to have her sparkling blue eyes deflected from the accused.

When Justice Smythe almost apologetically pronounced his two year sentence, Michael allowed himself the briefest of smiles before raising his head to the Public Gallery.

Some, like his mother, were in tears. Some, like Les Fenton and Maxi Clark, returned him resolute smiles. He noticed only one stone-silent face - Ian Millers. Michael gave him an obliging nod. He'd kept his word. The ownership of the Stanley Knife hadn't been questioned - hadn't been used to add "premeditated" to his crime.

Julie got to his side just as his uniformed escort had manoeuvred him to the head of the prisoners exit steps. Noticing the imploring look in her eyes, they had the decency to delay his hand-cuffed departure long enough for a fleeting kiss and a whispered promise that she'd be first in the queue come visiting day.

Gateshead Low Security Prison wasn't too bad a place to do time in. Michael adapted to it quite comfortably, apart from the first couple of months, when he had to impatiently shuffle up and down the hospital block, recovering from the list of injuries the doctors had astonished him with. Dislocated shoulder, broken jaw - and several teeth, fractured ribs, bruised lungs and liver and a shattered hipbone. He hadn't realised it at the time, but when Raymond Pearce had kindly removed the metal racking from him, it had also included the stolen gearbox for a Sierra.

When he was fit enough to mix with the other inmates, they seldom bothered him. He was amazed how many knew, and detested the Vincent Brothers, especially Terry. As for Pearce, his name was still spoken in hushed tones. "Aye that's the big Canadian who cut Ray Pearce's throat - he seems a canny lad - but don't be geeing the bastard the len' o' a Stanley Knife."

Most of his time - and there was plenty of it, Michael spent writing and reading letters. As the months accrued so did his correspondence, some of it business but most were to and from the people he cared for - cared for him. Susan's made him laugh out loud. She wrote screeds and screeds. What her family was up to - how she hated the twins - how she was getting a new puppy - how Auntie Julie hadn't got herself another boyfriend yet.

The letters from his mother gave him a different kind of pleasure. Things were changing for the Murdochs. Michael devoured every word with the satisfaction only the occasional opening of his father's white envelope could exceed. Each one ended with three xxx's and a "Hello Michael - me and the pigeons are doing fine," from Jamie. - Each one added to the certainty that he'd done the right thing - the only thing.

Constable Bryant had also been quite right - "No more than a year." Michael hadn't found it difficult to earn his remission for good-behaviour, both the inmates and the screws in Gateshead shared the same unwritten code "Don't cause bother an' bother shouldn't come your way." Also, in recently adopted Durham slang for grassing - "An' no bastard does a Terry on their mates!"

He was released on Monday September 18th at nine-fifteen a.m. Despite the light breeze, the hint of warmth from the climbing sun offered the makings of a perfect Autumn day.

Julie, waiting impatiently in the visitors' car park attracted his attention with the throaty revving of her brick red Porsche. She knew this wasn't the time or place for dramatic gestures - tears of joy - passionate embraces. As soon as he sunk into the passenger's seat, she just smiled shyly, leaned over, kissed him gently almost teasingly on the lips, then drove him away.

Within minutes they were laughing again, then touching, caressing each other as much as decency and safety on the winding country roads demanded.

After thirty miles or so Michael felt almost confident enough to broach the subject again.

"Julie?" The delay after he'd whispered her name, the apprehension in his voice, paved the way for her widening smile - "Julie! - Have you thought about what I asked you?"

She gave him a mischievous grin. "Asked me what Michael?"

"Asked you every damn time you visited me - you remember - every fortnight for a year."

"Oh! That?" Julie's lips now spread to the faintest of grins. "Yes. It did occasionally flick through my mind - you know, during the odd time when I hadn't anything better to occupy myself with - like washing my hair, or watching paint dry. But marrying you Michael Murdoch. - Having to spend every night of my life making love to you - then having to float between Canada, Scotland and here, spending all your money - not a care in the world! That isn't a prospect a dedicated lawyer like me would ever contemplate - without getting it in writing. - So if you'd be as kind to open the glove compartment and sign the Marriage Licence Form - I can at last put a date on my invitation cards. Would next Saturday, when your mum comes home do?"

Suddenly he wanted her to stop the car, reach to her, kiss her with the passion - the wanting, a year of no more than touching hands over a visiting room table had intensified beyond mere deprivation.

Julie would have obliged if she could, but the road was now too narrow, too bending, too occupied by a heard of cows to risk it. "Be patient, Michael. I know what you ex-convicts are like - you wouldn't be able to control yourself, and the last place we're doing it is in the middle of the road, with an audience that's got bigger tits than I have!"

Their laughter filled the car, what she'd said was so spontaneous - so ridiculous, for the next few minutes each time their eyes met again they burst into fits of giggles. Slowly the scenery became more familiar. "Julie, I've got the strangest feeling we've been here before. Unless I'm mistaken, there's a turnip field just along here to the right, so we'll soon be saying goodbye to your chaperones - then...."

"Then we'll be nearly there, so hard luck. I'll have my big brother to protect me - until tonight anyway."

The exquisite promise of tonight - a lifetime of tonight's kept his mind happily occupied until they'd reached the turn-off to Molly's Farm. What was once a puddle-strewn, pot-holed track was now in better condition than the tar-macadam road they were now leaving.

Noticing his awed expression, Julie broke their brief silence with another giggle. "Impressed Michael? I made it one of Les's first priorities, couldn't have my new Porsche, scraping its exhaust pipe could I? And, by the way, your mum tells me your Jeep's been so handy, your Aunt Betty and her have been touring all round Alberta with it."

Michael's mouth opened wider. "They're using my Jeep!"

"Yes - but don't worry, Jake's driving it. Mabel and him have been so kind to them; your mum phoned me last night, they're having a ball. Seemingly they had a lovely evening at the Cascade on Saturday night; Jake treated them to a steak dinner. But he says the place has gone way upmarket since you owned it - and lost half its customers. Even the chef - Stan - is threatening to leave and start up his own business - Jake says he might back him, if he can improve his recipe for...."

"Fruit pudding!"

"Yes, Michael, how did you know that?"

Michael grinned, "It's his only recipe, Julie!"

"Oh! And he introduced her to your ex-girlfriend -what's her name?"

"Tammy."

"Yes, Tammy - she still sings in the place, but only when she feels like it - Jake says she treats John, the new owner like a slave."

"What did my mum think of her?"

Julie attempted but failed to conceal her smile. "She couldn't stand her, thinks she's a manipulating besom, whatever that means. - But to be perfectly honest I didn't take much interest."

They'd now reached the brow of the hill, where Michael had to swallow hard before finding his voice again. "I saw it like this Julie; - when we came to pick up Les's Pigeon corn - I knew it could be done, but my God! Julie, it's just perfect."

To add to his delight, as they drove into the newly concreted yard, Susan Fenton was pushing a Jack Russell, in a doll's pram, across it.

"Hi, Michael, a see you're out at last! - Like ma new puppy?"

He did, and said so. "So, Susan what have you called him - Jock?"

"No silly - he's a she, an' she's ca'd Tammy. Ma Auntie Julie said we should ca' her Tammy 'cos sometimes she's a proper little bitch. - Didn't you Auntie J....!" Julie heard her niece's question but was too busy making her chuckling escape into the house to answer it.

Michael would have probably caught up with her if Ruby Fenton hadn't blocked the doorway with her massive grin. "An' where do you think your ganin bonny lad? Trying to chase ma sister in law up the stairs already. Well, a'll no' have any o' that nonsense in ma house-unless it's we' me."

If anything, Ruby had put on slightly more weight, but it suited her, she looked so healthy, and her cheeks, they offered such a contented, wholesome glow.

"N...no Ruby, I was just so keen to see you and Les, congratulate you both on what you've done here, I can hardly believe it. - Is he about?"

"Oh aye, Michael, he's about. - About half a mile up the top field, measuring the size of his sprouts or something, but don't worry - hunger'll soon have him back down here again. An' anyway he's desperate to see you. - See what you think o' his plans to expand, build another shed, sell all sorts of animal feeds - no' just pigeon corn and vegetables."

Michael now realised, by the enthusiasm in Ruby's voice, that it wasn't only Les Fenton who'd benefited from the decision to give up the allotment and turn his skills to farming. He acknowledged the fact with a smiling shake of his head. "Ruby, I'll tell you the same as I've told Les, it's his business - his decisions - I'm just here for a healthy cut of the profits."

Ruby's eyes seemed to take on a sharper radiance. "So it's no' just to be chasing Julie through ma house then? - Wait till a tell her, she'll be that disappointed. Now Michael. You've some one else to see before you come in. Susan! - Tak' that silly hat off that poor dog an' show Michael the way to your Da's Cree."

"Michael, now that you're out o' jail an' getting wed to ma Auntie Julie, when will you be getting her pregnant?"

The casualness of the enquiry, as he accompanied her and the pram along the neat crazy paved pathway, added to its unexpectedness. "Oh! - Well - em - we haven't talked about that yet Susan - but why do you ask?"

"A want a little cousin that's why, an' a've spoke to Jamie, he wants to be an uncle - Uncle Jamie! He'll tell you that himself when you ask him."

Michael instantly told himself to avoid speaking to Jamie about anything except pigeons.

To his relief, half way across the large neatly trimmed drying green, the pup suddenly leapt from the pram, alerting its smiling mistress to the sound of the tractor now returning from the top field. "He's in the cree, Michael - a've got to see ma da' about something. Come on Tammy. - Now that a'm getting a cousin - lets see what da' say's about a little sister as well."

He'd no difficulty finding the pigeon loft. It was too large, too impressive to be missed.

Despite its size, Michael was taken by how it seemed to blend in with its surroundings.

Built expertly in horizontal ship-lapped pine, with a red-tiled roof and varnished to a glossy shine, the neighbouring, freshly painted farm buildings appeared comfortable with its company.

He suddenly remembered seeing lofts like it, but they had large aviaries instead of sliding louvered doors - and they'd been in Kent, Foxhole Kent, The Stenway Stud - once the home of Champions. He'd heard it was now a Chalet Park, - not a pigeon in sight, every last one having been sold at auction.

One of the more recent residents at Gateshead, serving six months for deception, said he'd been to it, bought six birds for £5 each. "Aye bonny lad, a fiver each, that was the going rate - serves the cheating bastard right eh!"

If it hadn't been for the direction of the soft whistling, Michael wouldn't have known which of the three sets of louvered doors to slide open.

As soon as he had, Jamie's beaming face turned to welcome him. "Guess what Michael - I'm on my holidays - Mum's in Canada - and I'm Bam's partner when I'm staying here. - Just like you and me were Michael - just like you and me."

He sat beside him on the bench. "Yes Jamie, Murdoch Brothers, we were some team, the two of us."

"Aye Michael, some team, but I've got a new partner at home now, - young Daniel Miller. He's a good one Michael - a good one, and handy with a football too. - The Pie says we're like twins."

Michael quickly averted his now moistening eyes from his brother's gaze, allowing them to stray almost languidly around the spacious stock compartment. Six large plastic fronted next boxes, twelve pigeons, six cocks - six hens. Eight checkers, two reds, a mealy and a blue…. Suddenly his mouth gaped open; his eyes froze wide with the shock. "Jamie! - That Pigeon...?"

Jamie laughed - laughed as loud, as freely as his brother had every heard him. "Aye, Michael - we wondered how long you'd take to know it was him - my watch says, thirty five seconds exact. - Wait till I tell Bam, he said you were such a silly bugger, you'd never notice my Champion Blue Boy!"

"B…but Jamie, - how?"

"Julie got him for me - a Policeman she knows got him out of jail. So Bam and me are keeping him now. And guess what Michael - he's moulted out his Blood-Flight, just like dad said he would. Isn't he perfect Michael?"

His younger brother stared at the pigeon's bold blue head; its silky blue feathers its sparkling, sagacious eyes -

"Yes Jamie, he's perfect - - bloody perfect!"

----oOo----

THE END